"You've made me stand in six inches of snow while you've checked out my résumé and I've had enough. Merry Christmas. Bah humbug."

And she turned and stalked off.

Or she would have stalked off if she'd had sensible shoes with some sort of grip, but the canvas trainers she was wearing had no grip at all. The cobbles were icy under the thin layer of freshly fallen snow. She slipped and floundered, and then she started falling backwards.

She flailed—and Angus caught her before she hit the ground.

One minute she was stomping off in righteous indignation. The next she was being held in arms that were unbelievably strong, gazing up into a face that was…that was…

Like every fairytale she'd ever read.

CHRISTMAS AT THE CASTLE

BY
MARION LENNOX

First published in Great Britain 2013
by Mills & Boon, an imprint of Harlequin (UK) Limited,
Eton House, 18-24 Paradise Road, Richmond, Surrey TW9 1SR

© Marion Lennox 2013

ISBN: 978 0 263 90166 5

23-1213

Harlequin (UK) policy is to use papers that are natural, renewable and recyclable products and made from wood grown in sustainable forests. The logging and manufacturing processes conform to the legal environmental regulations of the country of origin.

Printed and bound in Spain
by Blackprint CPI, Barcelona

Marion Lennox is a country girl, born on an Australian dairy farm. She moved on—mostly because the cows just weren't interested in her stories! Married to a "very special doctor", Marion writes for Mills & Boon® Medical Romance™ and Mills & Boon® Cherish™. (She used a different name for each category for a while—readers looking for her past romance titles should search for author Trisha David as well.) She's now had more than seventy-five romance novels accepted for publication.

In her non-writing life Marion cares for kids, cats, dogs, chooks and goldfish. She travels, she fights her rampant garden (she's losing) and her house dust (she's lost). Having spun in circles for the first part of her life, she's now stepped back from her "other" career, which was teaching statistics at her local university. Finally she's reprioritised her life, figured what's important and discovered the joys of deep baths, romance and chocolate. Preferably all at the same time!

For Di and for Kevin
With thanks for the dancing and friendship.

CHAPTER ONE

'PLEASE, MY LORD, we *really* want to come to Castle Craigie for Christmas. It's where we were born. We want to see it again before it's sold. There's lots of room. We won't be a nuisance. Please, My Lord.'

My Lord. It was a powerful title, one Angus wasn't accustomed to, nor likely to become accustomed to. He'd intended to be Lord of Castle Craigie for as short a time as possible and then be out of here.

But these were his half-brother and -sisters, children of his father's second disastrous marriage, and he knew the hand they'd been dealt. He'd escaped to Manhattan, and his mother had independent money. These kids had never escaped the poverty and neglect that went with association with the old Earl.

'Our mum's not well,' the boy said, eagerly now as he hadn't been met with a blank refusal. 'She can't bring us back just for a visit. But when you wrote and said it was being sold and was there anything she wants… She doesn't, but we do. Our father sent us away without warning. Mary—she's thirteen—she used to spend hours up on the hills with the badgers and all the wild things. I know it sounds dumb, but she loved them and she still cries when she thinks about them. There's nothing like that in London. She wants a chance to say goodbye. Polly's ten and she wants to make cubby huts in the cellars again, and take pictures to show her friends that she really did live in a castle. And me... My friends are at Craigenstone. I was in a band. Just to have a chance to jam with them again, and at Christmas... Mum's so ill. It's so awful here. This'd be just...just...'

The boy broke off, but then somehow forced himself to go on. 'Please, it's our history. We'll look after ourselves. Just once, this last time so we can say goodbye properly. Please, My Lord...'

Angus Stuart was a hard-headed financier from Manhattan. He hired and fired at the highest level. He ran one of Manhattan's most prestigious investment companies. Surely he was impervious to begging.

But a sixteen-year-old boy, pleading for his siblings...

So we can say goodbye properly... What circumstances had pushed them away so fast three years ago? He didn't know, but he did know his father's appalling reputation and he could guess.

But if he was to agree... Bringing a group of needy children here, with their ailing mother? Keeping the castle open for longer than he intended? Being *My Lord* for Christmas. Angus stood in the vast, draughty castle hall and thought of all the reasons why he should refuse.

But Angus had been through the castle finances now, and he'd seen the desperate letters written to the old Earl by the children's mother. The letters outlined just how sick she was; how much the children needed support. According to the books, none had been forthcoming. This family must have been through hell.

'If I can find staff to care for you,' he heard himself say.

'Mum will take care of us. Honest...'

'You just said your mum's ill. This place doesn't look like it's been cleaned since your mother left three years ago. If I can find someone to cook for us and get this place habitable, then yes, you can come. Otherwise not. But I promise I'll try.'

Angus Stuart was a man who kept his word, so he was committed now to trying. But he didn't want to. As far as Christmas was concerned, it was for families, and Lord Angus McTavish Stuart, Eighth Earl of Craigenstone, did not do families. He'd tried once. He'd failed.

As well as that, Castle Craigie was no one's idea of a family home, and he didn't intend to make it one. But for one pleading boy… For one needy family…

Maybe once. Just for Christmas.

Cook/Housekeeper required for three weeks over the Christmas period. Immediate start. Apply in person at Castle Craigie.

The advertisement was propped in the window of the tiny general store that serviced the village of Craigenstone. It looked incongruous, typed on parchment paper with Lord Craigenstone's coat of arms imprinted above. The rest of the displayed advertisements looked scrappy in comparison. Snow could be shovelled, ironing could be taken in, but there was no coat of arms on any advertisement except this one.

Cook/Housekeeper… Maybe…

'I could do that,' Holly said thoughtfully, but her grandmother shook her head so vigorously her beanie fell off.

'At the castle? You'd be working for the Earl. No!'

'Why not? Is he an ogre?'

'Nearly. He's the Earl. Earl, ogre, it's the same thing.'

'I thought you said you didn't know the current Earl.'

'The acorn doesn't fall far from the tree,' her grandmother said darkly, retrieving her beanie from the snow and jamming it down again over her grey curls. 'His father's been a miserly tyrant for seventy years. His father was the same before him, and so was his father before him. This one's been in America for thirty-five years but I can't see how that can have improved him.'

'How old is he?'

'Thirty-six.'

'Then he's been in America since he was one?' Holly said, startled.

'His mother, Helen, was an American heiress.' Maggie was still using her darkling tone—Grandmother warning Grandchild of Dragons. 'They say that's why the Earl married her, because of her money. Money was his God. Heaven knows how he persuaded such a lovely girl to come to live in his mausoleum of a castle. But rumour has it His Lordship courted her in London—he could be devastatingly charming when he wanted to be—then married her and brought her to live in this dump. What a shock she must have had.'

Holly's grandmother glared back along the slush- and sleet-covered main street, through the down-at-heel village and beyond, across the snow-covered moors to where the great grey shape of Castle Craigie dominated the skyline.

'She stuck it out for almost two years,' she continued. 'She had gumption and they say she loved him. But love can't change what's instilled deep down. Her husband was mean and cold and finally she faced it. She disappeared just after Christmas thirty-five years ago, taking the baby with her.'

'Didn't the Earl object?'

'As far as anyone could tell, he didn't seem to notice,' Maggie told her. 'He had his heir and it probably suited him that he didn't need to do a thing to raise him. Or spend any money. He never talked about her or his son. He lived on his own for years, then finally got his housekeeper pregnant. Delia. She was always a bit of a doormat.'

'She was a local?'

'She was a Londoner,' Maggie said. 'A poor dab of a thing. He brought her here as a maid at the time of his first marriage. She was one of the few servants who stayed on after Lady Helen left. Finally, to everyone's astonishment, he married her. Rumour was it stopped him having to pay her housekeeper's wages, but she did well by the old man. She worked like a slave and presented him with three children. But he didn't seem interested in them, either—they lived in a separate section of the castle. Finally the old man's behaviour got too outrageous, even for Delia. She had shocking arthritis and the old man's demands were crippling her even more. She left for London three years ago, taking the children with her, and no family has been back since.'

'Until now,' Holly ventured.

'That's right. The old Earl died three months ago and two weeks ago the current Earl turned up.'

'So what do you know about him, other than he's an American?' Holly's feet were freezing. Actually, all of her was freezing but she and Maggie had determined to walk, and walk they would. And if this really was a job… It had her almost forgetting about her feet. 'Tell me about him.'

'I know a bit,' Maggie said, even more darkly. 'His American family is moneyed, as in really moneyed. There was an exposé in some magazine fifteen years or more back when his fiancée was killed that told us a bit more.'

'Fifteen years ago?'

'I think it was then. Someone in the village saw it in an American magazine and spread it round. According to gossip, he's been brought up with lots of money but not much else. His mother seems to have become a bit of a recluse— they say he was sent to boarding school at six, for heaven's sake. He's now some sort of financial whizz. You see him in the papers from time to time, in the financial section. But back then… Gossip said he started moving with the wrong crowd at college. His fiancée was called Louise—I can't remember her last name but I think she was some sort of society princess. Anyway, she died in Aspen on Christmas Eve. There was a fuss; that's why we saw it, a hint of drugs and scandal. Apparently she was there with Someone Else. The headlines said: Heir to Billions Betrayed, that sort of thing. He was twenty-one, she was twenty-three, but that's almost all I know. Then he went back to making money and we haven't heard much since. I have no idea why he's here, advertising for staff. I thought the castle was for sale; that he was here finalising the estate.' Maggie was starting to sound waspish, but maybe that was because she was cold, too. 'You'd best leave it alone.'

'But it's a paying job,' Holly said wistfully. 'Imagine… A nice scuttle full of coal for Christmas… Mmmm. I could just enquire.'

'You're here for a holiday.'

'So I am,' Holly said, and sighed and then chuckled and tucked her arm into her grandmother's. 'We're a right pair. You're playing the perfect Christmas hostess and I'm playing the perfect Christmas guest. Or not. We've been idiots, but if we're not to be eating Spam for Christmas, this might be a way out.'

'You're not serious?'

'What do I have to lose?'

'You'll be worked to death. No Earl in memory has ever been anything but a skinflint.' Maggie turned back to stare at the advertisement again. 'Cook/Housekeeper indeed. Castle Craigie has twenty bedrooms.'

'Surely this man wouldn't be thinking of filling the bedrooms,' Holly said uneasily.

'He's the Earl of Craigenstone. There's no telling what he's thinking. No Earl has done anything good by this district for generations.'

'But it's a job, Gran,' Holly said gently. 'You and I both know I need a job. I *have* to get one.'

There was a loaded silence. Holly knew what her grandmother was thinking—it was what they both knew. They had the princely sum of fifty pounds between them to last until Gran's next pension day. Talk about disaster...

And finally Maggie sighed. 'Very well,' she conceded. 'We do need coal and it's a miserly Christmas I'll be giving you without it. But if you're planning on applying, Holly, love, I'm coming with you.'

'Gran!'

'Why not? You've cooked in some of the best restaurants in Australia, and I've been a fine housekeeper in my time. Together...'

'I'm not asking you to work—and it's only one position they're advertising.'

'But I might even enjoy working,' Maggie said stoutly. 'I know it's twenty years since I've kept house for a living and I've never kept a castle. But there's a time for everything, and surely even the Earl can't serve Spam for Christmas dinner, which is all I can afford to give you.' She grinned, her indomitable sense of humour surfacing. 'I can see us in the castle kitchen, gnawing on the turkey carcass on Christmas Day. It might be grim but it'll be better than Spam.'

'So you're proposing we play Cinderella and Fairy Godmother in the servants' quarters, mopping up the leftovers?'

'Anything that gets spilt is legally ours,' her grandmother said sternly. 'that's servants' rules, and at Christmas time servants can be very, very clumsy.' She took a deep breath and braced herself. 'Very well. Let's try for it, Holly, lass. This Earl can't be any worse than his father, surely. What do we have to lose?'

'Nothing,' Holly agreed and that was what she thought.

How could she lose anything when she had nothing left to lose? She and her grandmother both.

'Okay, let's go home and write a couple of résumés that'll blow him out of the water,' Holly said. 'And he needn't think he's paying us peanuts. He's not getting monkeys; he's getting the best.'

'Excellent,' Maggie agreed, and Holly thought they probably had a snowball's chance in a bushfire of getting this job, especially as they were insisting it was two jobs. But writing the résumés might keep Maggie happy for the afternoon, and right now that was all that mattered.

Because, right now, Holly wasn't thinking past this afternoon. She was even avoiding thinking past the next hour.

If no one applied as Cook/Housekeeper over the next couple of days, Lord Angus McTavish Stuart, Eighth Earl of Craigenstone, could fly back home for Christmas.

Home was Manhattan. He had a sleek apartment overlooking Central Park and Christmas plans were set in stone. Since Louise had died he'd had a standard booking with friends for Christmas dinner at possibly the most talked about restaurant on the island. He'd make his normal quiet drive the next day to visit his mother, who'd be surrounded by her servants at her home in Martha's Vineyard. She loathed Christmas Day itself but reluctantly celebrated the day after with him. Then the whole fuss of Christmas would die down.

'If no one applies by tomorrow, I'm calling it quits,' he told the small black scrap of canine misery by his side. He'd found the dog the first day he'd been here, cringing in the stables.

'It's a stray—let me take it to the dog shelter, My Lord,' his estate manager had said when he'd picked it up and brought it inside, but the scruffy creature had looked at him with huge brown eyes and Angus had thought it wouldn't hurt to give the dog a few days of being Dog of the Castle.

Angus was playing Lord of the Castle. Reality would return all too soon.

The little dog looked up at him now and he thought that when he left the dog would have to go, too. No more pretending. Meanwhile…

'Have another dog biscuit,' Angus told him, tossing yet another log onto the blazing fire. The weather outside was appalling and the old Earl had certainly never considered central heating. 'This place is on the market so we're both on borrowed time, but we might as well be comfortable while we wait.'

The little dog opened one eye, cautiously accepted his dog biscuit, nibbled it with delicacy and then settled back down to sleep in a way that told Angus this room had once been this dog's domain. But his father had never kept dogs.

Had his father ever used this room? It seemed to Angus that his father had done nothing but lie in bed and give orders.

Who knew which orders had been obeyed? Stanley, the Estate Manager, seemed to be doing exactly what he liked. Honesty didn't seem to be his strong suit. Angus's short but astute time with the estate books had hinted that Stanley had been milking the castle finances for years.

But he couldn't sack him—not now. He was the only servant left, the only one who knew the land, who could show prospective purchasers over the estate, who could sound even vaguely knowledgeable about the place.

Angus had decided he'd do a final reckoning after the castle was sold and not before. His plan had been to get rid of the castle and all it represented and leave as fast as he could. This place had nothing to do with him. He'd been taken away before his first birthday and he'd never been back.

But first he had to get through one Christmas—or not. If he could find a cook he'd stay and do his duty by the kids. Otherwise, Manhattan beckoned. The temptation not to find a cook was huge, but he'd promised.

A knock on the great castle doors reverberated through the hall, reaching through the thick doors of the snug. The little dog lifted his head and barked, and then resettled, duty done. If this castle was to be sold, then there was serious sleeping to be got through first.

Stanley's humourless face appeared around the door. 'I'll see to it, My Lord,' he said. 'It'll be one of the villagers wanting something. They're always wanting something. His Lordship taught me early how to see them off.'

He gave what he obviously thought was a conspiratorial nod and closed the door again. His footsteps retreated across the hall towards the great door leading outside.

Angus opened the snug door and listened.

'Yes?' Stanley's voice was as dry and unwelcoming as the man himself. As apparently the old Earl had encouraged him to be.

'I'm here about the advertisement for help over Christmas.' Surprisingly, it was a woman's voice, young, cheerful and lilting, and Angus leaned on the door jamb and wondered how long it had been since he'd heard a woman's voice. Only two weeks, he conceded, but it seemed as if he'd been locked in this great grey fortress for ever.

He could see why his mother had fled. The wonder of it was that she'd stayed for two years.

'You look very young to be a cook,' Stanley was saying dourly, to whoever it was outside the door. Stanley's disapproval was instant and obvious, even at a distance. 'Do you have any qualifications?'

'I'm not a cook; I'm a chef,' the woman said. 'I'm twenty-eight and I've been working with food since I was fifteen. I've worked in some of the best restaurants in Australia so I'm overqualified for this job, but I have a few weeks to spare. If you're interested…'

'Can you make beds?' Stanley asked, even more dourly.

'No.' The woman sounded less confident now she wasn't talking of cooking. 'Or at least I can pull up a mean duvet but not much more. My grandmother, on the other hand, used to be the housekeeper at Gorse Hall, and she's interested in a job, too. She can make really excellent beds.'

'This is one job,' Stanley snapped. 'His Lordship wants someone who can cook *and* make his bed.'

'So is it just His Lordship I'm cooking for? Can't His Lordship make his own bed?'

'Don't be impertinent,' Stanley retorted. 'You're obviously not suitable.' And, with that, Angus heard the great doors starting to creak closed.

That should be the end of it, he told himself with a certain amount of relief. He'd agreed to advertise for a cook. He'd put the advertisement in the window of the general store and no one had replied until now. So be it. Once Stanley had got rid of her he could ring his half-brother and say regretfully, *Sorry, Ben, I couldn't find someone suitable and I can't put you up for Christmas without staff. I'll arrange to fly you and your family up to do a tour before the castle is sold, but that's all I can do.*

Easy. All he had to do was keep quiet now.

But… *Can't His Lordship make his own bed?* What was it about that blunt question that had him stepping out of the snug, striding over the vast flagstones of the Great Hall, intercepting Stanley and stopping the vast doors from closing.

Seeing for himself who Stanley was talking to.

The girl on the far side of the doors looked cold. That was his first impression.

His second impression was that she was cute.

Very cute.

She was five feet three or five four at most. She wasn't plump, but she wasn't thin—just nicely curved, although she was doing a decent job of disguising those curves. She was wearing faded jeans, trainers, a thick grey sweater and a vast old army greatcoat without buttons. She wore a red beanie with a hole in it. A few strands of burnt-copper curls were sneaking through. Her lack of make-up, her clear green eyes and her wide, generous mouth which, at the moment, was making a fairly childlike grimace at Stanley, made him think she couldn't possibly be twenty-eight.

Maybe Stanley was right to reject her out of hand. What sort of person applied for a job wearing what looked like charity rejects?

'Are you backup?' she queried bitterly as he swung the door wider. Whatever else she was, this woman wasn't shy, and Stanley's flat rejection had seemingly made her angry. 'Are you here to help Lurch here tell me to get off the property fast? I've walked all the way from the village on your horrible pot-holed road. Of all the cold welcomes… You could at least look at my résumé.'

Lurch? The word caught him. Angus glanced at Stanley and thought the woman had a point—there were definite similarities between his father's estate manager and the butler from the Addams Family.

'It *is* only the one job,' he said, and found himself sounding apologetic.

'Chef and Housekeeper for this whole place?' She stood back and gestured to the sweep of the vast castle. The original keep had been built at the start of the thirteenth century, but a mishmash of battlements, turrets and towers had been added ad hoc over the last eight hundred years. From where she was standing, she couldn't possibly take it all in—the great grey edifice was practically a crag all by itself. 'This place'd take me a week to dust,' she said and then stood back a bit further. 'Probably two. And I'm not all that skilled at dusting.'

'I don't want anything dusted,' Angus told her.

'I'm not serving my food on dust.'

'Forgive me.' He was starting to feel bemused. This woman looked a waif but she was a waif with attitude. 'And forgive our cavalier treatment of you. But you don't look like a cook to us.'

'That's because I'm a chef,' she retorted. Her cheeks were flushed crimson and he thought it wasn't just the cold. Stanley's rejection was smarting.

'Can you prove it?'

'Of course.' She hauled a couple of typed sheets from the pocket of her greatcoat, handed them over and waited while he unfolded and skimmed them.

He felt his brows hike as he read. This was impressive. Really impressive. But...

'You're asking us to believe you're a chef from Australia—yet your résumé is typed on letterhead paper from the Craigenstone Library.'

'That's because Doris, the librarian, is a friend of my grandmother,' she said patiently. 'I'm here on holiday, visiting my Gran, and Gran doesn't have a printer. For some weird reason, I failed to bring copies of my résumé with me.'

'So why are you applying for a job?'

'It seems I'm not,' she said. 'Lurch here has told me you're not interested, so that's it. Meanwhile, I'm freezing. You've made me stand in six inches of snow while you've checked out my résumé and I've had enough. Merry Christmas. Gran was right all along. Bah, humbug to you both.'

And she turned and stalked off.

Or she would have stalked off if she had sensible shoes with some sort of grip, but the canvas trainers she was wearing had no grip at all. The cobbles were icy under the thin layer of freshly fallen snow. She slipped and floundered, and she started falling backward.

She flailed—and Angus caught her before she hit the ground.

* * *

One minute she was stomping off in righteous indignation. The next she was being held in arms that were unbelievably strong, gazing up into a face that was…that was…

Like every fairy tale she'd ever read. This was the Lord of Castle Craigie. She could see why the old Earl had been able to coerce women to marry him, she thought, dazed. If Gran was right, if the acorn hadn't fallen far from the tree, if this guy was like all the Earls before him…

Tall, dark and dangerous seemed an understatement. This guy was your quintessential brooding hero, over six feet tall, with lean, sculpted features, hard, chiselled bone structure, deep grey eyes, strong mouth and jet-black hair.

He was wearing a gorgeous soft tweed jacket. What was more, he was wearing a kilt! Oh, my…

But Gran had told her the current Earl was American. What was an American doing wearing a kilt?

According to Gran, he'd been an indulged but lonely child. Apart from some scandal with a dead fiancée, he seemed only interested in making money. He'd sounded aloof, alone, like his father before him.

She'd been prepared to dislike him on sight, but sight wasn't being very helpful right now. None of his background stood out on his face. None of those things seemed important.

Oh, that kilt…

'Are…are you really the Earl?' He was cradling her as if she were a child, and for some reason it was the only thing she could think of to say. *Are you really the Earl?* How stupid was that?

'Yes,' he said and the edges of his wide mouth quirked into what was almost a smile. 'But only for a few weeks.'

'You're American.'

'Yes.'

'So why are you wearing a kilt?'

What was she doing? She should be saying, *Thank you for stopping me falling but you can put me down now*. She should say any number of things regarding the way he was holding her, but he'd scooped her up, he was holding her against his barrel-strong chest and, for a moment, for just a moment, Holly was letting herself disappear into fantasy.

She'd tell this to Maggie. *He swept me up into his arms, Gran, and oh, he was gorgeous...*

Maggie would toss a bucket of cold water over her.

Reality hit as hard as her grandmother's imaginary water, and she wriggled with intent. Reluctantly, it seemed, he set her onto her feet again, but he didn't let her go. The ground was still slippery and his hands stayed firmly on her shoulders.

'American or not, for now I'm Laird of the Castle,' he told her, smiling down at her. It was a killer smile. It made her insides...

Well, enough. She had enough to tell Maggie without letting her imagination take her further.

And Maggie would remind her sharply—as she'd told her last night, 'He's not our Laird. Most owners of estates in Scotland are referred to as Lairds or Himself, because they care for the land, and for the people they employ. Not him. We've never had a Lord who came close to being Himself. Don't you trust him an inch, lass. Not one inch.'

'We've been showing buyers over the estate,' he was saying, cutting over her thoughts. 'International buyers. For some reason, the realtor thinks it's important for me to look Scottish. My father has a room full of family tartan, kilts for all sizes, so I've been striding along beside would-be buyers, grunting, trying not to sound American, while Stanley here has been answering questions in his broadest Scottish brogue. Which is why I'm looking like the Lord of All He Surveys, off to round up my trusty men for a spot of pillaging of the surrounding villages. Pure fantasy.' He grinned. 'Right. I've told you mine, now it's your turn. Holly McIntosh, if you're a skilled chef, why are you standing on my doorstep asking for a job wearing sodden canvas trainers and a greatcoat that looks like it was worn during World War One?'

'Because I'm indulging in *my* fantasy of not freezing for Christmas,' she said, so flustered she let honesty hold sway. *Don't trust,* Gran had told her. She should have added, *Keep twenty feet away.* 'Can you let me go? I need to get home before my feet drop off from frostbite.'

'Come in,' he said, gently now, almost seductively, and she shivered.

'I need…'

'To get warm. You came to apply for a job. Let's think about both. I have a blazing fire inside, hot tea or whisky if you prefer, cake—bought fruit cake admittedly, but at least it's cake—and Stanley will drive you back to the village when we're finished.'

'Finished what?' she demanded, maybe stupidly, but, to her astonishment, his smile broadened. The twinkle in those dark eyes seemed pure mischief. Dangerous mischief.

'When I've had my wicked way with you. Of course, being Lord of Castle Craigie, I've had my wicked way with every maiden in the village.' And then he chuckled, a lovely deep chuckle that matched his smile exactly. 'Sorry,' he said as he saw her expression. 'there's my fantasies running away with me again. That's the man in the kilt speaking, not me.'

'You're…' She could barely get her voice to work. 'You're not usually into wicked ways?'

'Nope. That's my kilt-wearing dark side. The normal me wears chinos, and I swear I'm not into pillaging at all.' He held up his hands as if to say, *Look, I'm unarmed and innocent*—which he didn't look at all. 'But I'm leaving my dark side out in the snow for now. I'll change back into Angus

Stuart, Corporate Financier from Manhattan, if it reassures you. It's what I've been up to now and I'll be again soon. But please, Miss McIntosh, come in and get warm and let me reread your résumé.'

Whoa. She took a deep breath, trying to recover from the way his arms had felt—were feeling. From the way that beguiling smile made her feel. From the sheer size and presence of the man. And the way that kilt…

Aagh. Stick to your guns, she told herself, desperately. *Don't trust.* You're here to apply for a job—two jobs— and you're useless unless you stick to what you intended.

Useless.

The adjective swirled, bringing her back to reality with a sickening thud. *Useless* was the word that had been hanging over her for months. That and *stupid*.

Stick to what you need.

'It's two jobs or nothing,' she managed.

'Sorry?' Angus said, confused.

'I said, this is two jobs. I'm only interested in one, and I'm only interested if you accept us both. I won't clean. I'll cook all you like but nothing else. Gran's attending a funeral or she'd be here with me but she's applying as well. I have her résumé with me, too.'

'It's just the one job!' All this time Stanley had been standing to the side, glaring at this intrusion to his territory, but now he'd decided it was time to intercede. 'We advertised one position, My Lord. I'm sure we can find some other woman to take the role.'

'Not before Christmas, we can't,' Angus said. 'No one's applied since we've had the advertisement up.'

'It's still the one job,' Stanley said flatly.

'Right,' Holly said, reality slamming back. Oh, her feet were cold. 'That's that then. Thank you for your offer of whisky and fruit cake—and even taking your kilt off!—

but we're wasting each other's time. Merry Christmas to you both and goodbye.'

And with that she hauled away from Angus's hold, turned and stomped—gingerly—away.

'If you'd really wanted a cook you should have used the newspapers,' Stanley said dourly as they watched her go.

He should have, he conceded. If he'd really wanted a cook.

He didn't want a cook. If he found a cook he'd be obliged to have his half-siblings here for Christmas. He'd be obliged to turn this castle into a home, even if it was only for three weeks.

He didn't want to.

Why?

Because, kilt or not, this place wasn't fantasy as much as tragedy. Black tragedy. His mother had pleaded with him not to come, and she'd be devastated if he extended his stay.

And he did not want a family Christmas. He didn't do Christmas. Had Louise's death and his mother's tragedy taught him nothing?

He was watching Holly stomp back across what had once been the site of a drawbridge but was now a snow-covered cobbled path and something inside him was twisting. He watched the determined set of her shoulders and he thought how she'd walked all the way from the village in canvas trainers to apply for a job he didn't want to give.

He should have said no to Ben.

He shouldn't even have come himself. He'd been stunned by his mother's reaction, her emotion as raw as if the tragedy had happened last week rather than over thirty years ago.

'Don't go near that place. Sell it fast, to the highest bidder. You don't need it. Give the money to charity—I don't care—just get rid of it, Angus.'

But he'd wanted to see.

He was the new Earl of Craigenstone. He had no intention of taking up the title, but still he wanted to see what he was letting go—as his half-brother and -sisters wanted to revisit what they were letting go. They'd lived in this place until three years ago. Their father had barricaded the place against them when their mother left, but they'd have memories and they wanted to see.

Please... The plea had been heartrending.

This wasn't about him, he thought savagely. The old Earl had had four children. Why was it just him making the decisions?

So... He'd just been offered staff. Why refuse? Personal selfishness? *Just like his father?*

He was watching Holly McIntosh march away from the castle with as much dignity as she could muster and he was thinking of his father's reputation. Mean. Selfish.

He was not like his father. Surely.

This was only for three weeks and then it'd be done. Surely his mother could cope if he explained. Surely it was time they both rid themselves of demons.

Decide now, he told himself, and he did.

'Holly...' His voice rang out over the crisp white snow, and she heard even though she was two hundred yards away.

She turned and glared, her hands on her hips. This was no normal employee, he thought. If he hired her, he'd be hiring spirit.

Christmas spirit? Holly. The thought had him bemused.

'It can be two jobs,' he conceded, but her hands stayed on her hips and her belligerence was obvious.

'Wages?' she called, not moving.

'What's the standard wage around here for a cook?' he demanded of Stanley and Stanley glared at him as if he was proposing spending Stanley's money instead of the estate's. The figure he threw at him sounded ridiculously low.

And...*I'm a chef.*

Holly's words had been an indignant claim to excellence and pride had shown through.

If he employed her he'd have a chef for Christmas. And a housekeeper. Christmas. He thought of his father's reputation and he looked at Stanley's dour face and he thought that some things had to change, right now.

'I'll pay you three times basic cook's wages and I'll hire you and your grandmother as a team,' he called. And then, as Holly's expression didn't change, he added, 'I'll pay the same rate to you both.'

'My Lord!' Stanley gasped, but he was ignored. Holly's expression was changing. She was trying not to look incredulous, he realised, but she was failing. 'Each?'

'Yes.' He grinned, seeing her inner war. 'Eight-hour days and half days off on Sunday. It's three weeks of hard work, but the money will be worth it. I can't say fairer than that.'

She took a deep breath. He could see she was searching for the indignant, assertive Holly he'd seen up until now, but his offer seemed to have sucked all indignation out of her.

'Are...are meals and accommodation included?' she ventured, sounding cautious. Very cautious. As if he might bite.

'I guess. But why do you need accommodation?'

'We don't have a car,' Holly told him. 'And, in case you haven't noticed, it's snowing and your driveway is a disgrace. It took me half an hour to trudge up here and Gran's not as young as she used to be.' She tilted her chin and met his gaze head on. 'And our accommodation has to be heated.'

'Heated!' Stanley gasped, as though the word was an abomination, and Angus thought of the freezing, musty bedrooms throughout the castle, and the great draughty staircases and how much effort and expense it would take to get this place warm by Christmas. The snug had the only fireplace that didn't seem to be blocked.

But Holly was glaring a challenge and all of a sudden he was thinking of his half-brother and -sisters, who'd lived for years under these conditions, with the old man's temper as well, and he thought...maybe he could put the effort in. Maybe he could make the place less of a nightmare for them to remember. *He was not his father.*

'Done,' he said. 'With one proviso.'

'Which is?'

'That you come in now, dry out and tell me why you're wearing those stupid sodden shoes.'

'I need to get back to Gran.'

'We'll drive you back in a few minutes,' he said, goaded. 'But I'll dry you out first. I believe I just hired you. You're therefore my employee. You can sue me if you're injured on the way to and from work, so I'm looking after my investment. Come into my castle, Miss McIntosh, and we'll talk terms.'

'And have some of that fruit cake?' For heaven's sake, he thought, stunned. She sounded hungry!

'I believe that can be arranged.'

'Then your offer is gratefully accepted,' she said and trudged back towards them. She reached the front steps and Angus walked down to meet her. He held out his hand to steady her as she climbed the icy stone steps. She stared at his hand for a long moment and then she shook her head.

'I'll do this on my own terms, if you don't mind,' she said briskly. 'I need your job. I'd also quite like your fruit cake, but I don't need anything else.'

'Nothing?'

'Nothing.' She peeped a smile at him and he saw the return of a mischief that he suspected was a latent part of this woman. 'So any thought that you might be having your wicked way with the hired help, put out of your mind right now, Lord Craigenstone. Just leave that dark side you're talking about outside. I might be coming to live in your castle, but I know my rights. Also, I've just been burned. Ravishment isn't in any employment contract I intend to sign, now or ever.'

CHAPTER TWO

INSIDE, ENSCONCED IN one of the huge fireside chairs in the snug, her hands cradling a mug of hot chocolate, Holly seemed even younger than first impressions. And even more cute. Once she'd ditched the army greatcoat, he could see even more of her. Her cropped copper curls rioted as soon as she took off her beanie. They matched her cheeks which, in the warmth of the snug, grew even more flushed than they'd been when she was losing her temper out in the snow.

She concentrated on her hot chocolate and fruit cake. She ate three slices while Angus reread her résumé and then read her grandmother's.

This might work. According to the résumés, Holly could definitely cook and her Gran could definitely clean. They might even have the skills to provide him with a decent Christmas.

But her appearance didn't fit. He glanced again at her résumé. She was a cook—no, a chef—but she was looking like something the cat had dragged in. The little dog had sidled across to her when she sat down. He'd leaped up on her knee and she was fondling him while still cradling the last of the warmth from the hot chocolate.

They looked waifs and strays both.

'If you're who you say you are,' he said slowly, 'you must be one of the best paid chefs in Australia.'

'I am,' she said and then corrected herself. 'I was.'

'Can I verify this?'

She glanced at her watch. 'Yes,' she said decisively. 'I'd like you to. It's midday here. That makes it nine at night in Sydney. I have contact numbers for the head chefs for all of the last three but one of the restaurants where I've worked. On a Monday night at this time of year, most chefs will be in their kitchens. Phone them. I'll wait.'

'But I can't phone the last?' he asked, homing in on detail.

'The last place I owned myself,' she said bluntly. 'With my partner. It didn't work out.' She hesitated and then decided on honesty. 'He was my fiancé and business partner. He robbed me.'

'I'm sorry.'

'Don't be. Ring the others.'

He glanced at her and saw her face set in a mulish expression. She wanted him to ring, he thought, and with a sudden flash of insight he knew why. She was looking like a waif and she knew it. Putting herself on a professional footing would be important for her pride.

So he rang as she ate yet more fruit cake, and he received an unequivocal response from all three chefs. Three variations of a common theme.

'If you have Holly McIntosh you have a godsend. I'd hire her back in a minute. We've heard her place here has gone belly-up. Tell her the minute she gets back to Australia there's a job waiting.'

He disconnected from the last call. She was watching him gravely, and he could see she'd settled. She was on a more solid footing now.

'You want to explain the trainers?' he asked. She'd kicked off her sodden shoes and the socks beneath. She'd done it surreptitiously, kicking them under the chair and then tucking her feet up under her, but it hadn't been surreptitious enough. Her feet would be freezing, he thought. She'd been standing in sodden canvas on ice. 'Why the soaking footwear?'

'I arrived here two days ago,' she said. 'But my baggage is still cavorting somewhere around the world. The airline says they'll find it—eventually. None of Gran's clothes fit so I'm stuck.'

'You don't think you should buy yourself some decent footwear while you wait?'

'I don't have any money,' she said flatly. 'That's why I need the job.'

'Not even enough for a pair of wellingtons?'

She took a deep breath, stared into the remains of her hot chocolate and then laid her mug down on the side table with a decided thunk. Those clear green eyes met his with an honesty he was starting to expect.

'I'm a chef,' she said. 'A good one. I and my…my ex-partner decided to set up on our own. We bought a restaurant, a great little place overlooking Sydney Harbour. We did the finances and were sure we could do it. We put everything we owned into it, or rather I did because it turned out Geoff didn't have the money he said he did. He was my fiancé. I trusted him, but I was a fool. I thought we had double the capital we had but he lied. Anyway, a month ago the creditors moved in and Geoff moved out. Fast. I don't know where he is now, but my credit cards are maxed out, I'm in debt to my ears and I'm suffering from a bad case of shattered pride. Not to mention a broken heart, although it's a bit hard to think I loved someone who turned out to be a toe-rag.'

'So you came to Scotland?' he asked incredulously. 'How does that make sense?'

'See, here's the thing,' she said slowly. 'I'm only Scottish through my Scottish dad—the rest of me's pure Australian—but I have Scottish pride and so does my very

Scottish Gran. My parents died in a car crash when I was twelve. My mother's mother took me in, but she died last year. Now Maggie's the only relative I have left and when I rang her last month and sort of implied I was in trouble and due to have a dreary Christmas I didn't need to tell her exactly *how* broke I was. She guessed. So, Maggie being Maggie, she went out and bought me a plane ticket to visit.'

'She sounds great.'

'She is great,' she said warmly, and then managed a grin. 'And she's an awesome housekeeper.'

'Yet another reference,' Angus said and smiled back and thought, *That smile*...

Whoa...

'Unfortunately,' Holly went on, seemingly oblivious to the crackling electricity generated by that smile, 'what I didn't know is that Maggie's only renting her cottage. I've always thought she owned it, but no. She's not exactly known for saving, my Gran—as in the extraordinary gesture of my plane ticket. Anyway, it only took me five minutes after I'd landed to find out her landlord has put her house up for sale. She's desperately scraping enough money together to pay for a deposit to rent somewhere else, and she's as broke as I am. She thought if I flew over we could share Christmas expenses, but how do you share nothing? So that's that. We had a problem but you've solved it. You see me here in sodden trainers, but they'll dry out. You've promised us heating and we'll have a very nice Christmas because of you. Now, if you could tell me when you want me to start...'

'Do you have your airline ticket with you?' he demanded and she looked confused.

'What? Why?'

'Is it still in your purse?' he added, gesturing to her capacious handbag. 'You haven't thrown it out?'

'No, but...'

'Can I see it?'

'You want to prove that, too?' She was still confused.

'Indulge me,' he said, and she frowned and shifted the little dog, but not very far. She fumbled in her bag and found a crumpled booking sheet and airline ticket.

'Keep those toes warm while I do some more phoning,' he said, and she listened and hugged the dog some more while he phoned.

He was ringing the airline.

When she'd tried, she'd been put on hold for hours, but the Earl of Craigenstone was not put on hold. It seemed he was a member of some sort of platinum club and within seconds he was talking to…a person! Holly's jaw just about dropped to her ankles. How did you ring an airline and get a person? Oh, to be an Earl.

What was more, the person on the end of the line seemed inclined—even eager—to assist. Angus sent a few incisive questions down the line, then handed the phone over to her.

'All sorted,' he said. 'Listen.'

So Holly listened, stunned.

'We're so sorry, miss,' the man on the other end of the line said. 'This should have been explained to you. Seeing your baggage has been missing for over twenty-four hours, you can spend what you need right away and you'll be reimbursed within four working days. It also seems your grandmother has paid an extra ten pounds insurance for baggage cover so there's no loss at all—you'll get full reimbursement if the baggage isn't found, plus a small amount extra for inconvenience. I apologise that this wasn't explained to you two days ago.'

'I…thank you,' she managed and Angus took the phone from her grasp, added a few contact details and disconnected.

'So now you can buy wellingtons,' he said.

'I…' She fought for something to say and couldn't. She stared at her feet. 'Um…'

'Just how broke are you?' he asked gently and she flushed, but there seemed no point denying things now.

'Um…really, really broke,' she whispered. 'Geoff maxed out my credit cards. I owe money to everyone and Gran used her grocery money to buy my plane ticket. I…thank you but I still can't buy wellingtons because no shop will take an airline's promise that the money's coming. But I can wait four days.'

'You can't. Here's a loan to tide you over.' He hauled out his wallet, counted out a wad of notes and held them out.

'No.' What was she thinking? For some reason, her Gran's warning came slamming back and she stood up and backed to the door. 'You've given me a job. I can't take any more.'

'This isn't a gift,' he said mildly. 'When the airline pays you, you can pay me.'

'You don't know me. How can you trust me?'

'You're my employee.'

'Yes, and Geoff was my partner and look what he did,' she snapped. 'I could walk out the door and spend this on riotous living and you'd never see me again.'

'In Craigenstone?' He grinned. 'In case you hadn't noticed, there's not a lot of riotous living to be done in this place.'

He was looking at her oddly. She caught herself—she needed to make an effort to recover.

Wicked ways. Kilts and brawny arms and a wicked smile. Her imagination and the reputation of the Earl of Craigenstone were doing stupid things to her senses. Pull yourself together, she told herself and somehow she did.

'I had…I had noticed,' she said and managed to smile. She looked down at the proffered notes. Warm feet…

'This is…wonderful. I could buy myself some wellingtons and a woolly jumper and some coal.'

'You have no heating?'

'Um…no.'

'I'll run you back to the village and we'll collect some coal on the way.'

'You're kidding. You're an Earl!'

'I didn't think Australians held with the aristocracy,' he said, bemused. 'Americans certainly don't.'

'Yet you are one.'

'Only until this place is sold,' he said, humour fading. 'I intend the title to disappear with it.'

'So Gran's ogre disappears?'

'I'm an ogre?'

'That's why I'm not letting you buy coal or drive me home,' she said. 'It's very nice of you, as is lending me this money, and I appreciate it very much, but if Gran opened the door and an Earl was standing on her doorstep, loaded with coal, she'd have a palsy stroke. Whatever that is.'

'A palsy stroke?' he said dubiously.

'I hear that's what they had in the olden days,' she explained. 'When Earls knew their place and servants knew theirs. Swooning and palsy strokes were everywhere and I don't have my smelling salts with me. So no. I know my place. Gran and I will keep to the servants' quarters and cook and dust while you're all elsewhere and I'll keep to my kitchen, and you'll hand over menus of twenty courses to be cooked in two hours, and Gran will creep in at dawn and light your fires…'

'You've been reading too many romance novels if you think I want servants creeping in at dawn…'

'That's as it may be,' she said with asperity. 'But Gran has a very clear idea of what's right and wrong and we'll do this her way or not at all. So thank you but we'll buy our own coal. When would you like us to start?'

'Tomorrow?'

'Tomorrow!'

'It's two weeks until Christmas,' he said and looked rue-fully round the room. 'This room and my bedroom seem the only places that are habitable. The castle's been under dust-sheets since my stepmother left. Any cooking's been done by Stanley on a portable gas ring—heaven knows if the range still works.'

'I need a stove!'

'That's why I want you tomorrow—we may need to order one fast. Meanwhile, I need to get the place warm...'

'That'll take a year!'

'I'll do my part,' he said. 'Can you do yours, Miss Mc-Intosh?'

'Holly,' she said, 'My Lord.'

'Angus,' he said back.'

'It's Holly and My Lord,' she said primly. 'Gran won't stand for anything else. The British Empire was built by those who knew their place and didn't step out of it.'

'So you intend to be subservient.'

'That's the one,' she said cheerfully. 'As long as you do what I tell you, I'll be as subservient as you like.'

'As long as *I* do what *you* tell me...'

'If I have a cooking range that hasn't been used for years I'll be telling you right, left and centre,' she said and rose and shoved her feet determinedly back into her soggy train-ers. 'Thank you very much, My Lord. Gran and I will see you at nine tomorrow, and Christmas will begin then.' She reached out and shook his hand, then reached down and patted the little dog. 'Goodbye until then,' she said. 'Twenty courses or not, suddenly we're going to have a very yummy Christmas.'

Angus stood in the doorway and watched her go. She'd re-fused his offer to drive her; she'd refused his offer to send

Stanley and she was trudging down the road towards the village looking like a bereft orphan thrown out into the snow.

A bereft orphan with spirit.

'You've made a mistake, My Lord,' Stanley said gloomily. He'd appeared—gloomily—behind him. 'She'll cost you a fortune.'

'Tell me, Stanley,' Angus said, in a voice any of his colleagues would have recognised and snapped to wary attention. 'How much do we have in the petty cash account?'

'I…'

'We have the rent roll from the cottages for the last month, I assume,' Angus said. 'That should cover our costs nicely. I suspect it's far too late to get central heating installed into this place by Christmas but I want every chimney swept, I want coal in every fireplace and I want oil heaters in every room. After Christmas I may need to reforest a small nation to nullify any environmental impact, but this castle *will be warm by Christmas*. Can I leave that to you, Stanley?'

His voice was silky-smooth. He was watching Stanley's face and he knew exactly what the man was thinking.

The rent rolls for this place were colossal. They were supposed to come into a cash account at the start of the month, then roll over at the end of the month into one of his father's income-bearing accounts. What he suspected Stanley was doing and seemed to have been doing for years was siphoning the rent roll into his own account for the thirty days. Angus's father must never have noticed, but Angus thought of the interest Stanley must have earned over the years he'd been employed…

However…Stanley had put up with his father, and somehow he'd held the estate together. And he couldn't sack him now—he needed him. But then he thought of Holly in her soggy trainers and he thought of the misery caused by dishonesty everywhere.

Stanley would need to scramble to get that money back into the account, he thought, hit by a wave of sudden anger. The reputation of the miserliness of the Earl of Craigenstone stopped right now. Dishonesty stopped now, too. Up until now he'd tolerated a bit of petty theft, he'd tolerated Stanley's surliness because to change things in the short time he had here had seemed pointless. But now… Now things did need to change. Suddenly Castle Craigie was aiming for a Very Merry Christmas.

'He's nice… He's lovely and he's hired us both. At such a salary! Each!'

Holly practically bounced into the kitchen, where Maggie had been disconsolately staring at a packet of pasta and an unbranded can of tomatoes. Now she stared as if her granddaughter had lost her mind.

'What?'

Holly told her the salary and then repeated it for good measure. 'And we start tomorrow. We get to stay in the castle and we get to stay warm.'

She grabbed her grandmother and hugged her and then, because she was excited, she did a little jig, dragging Maggie round the kitchen with her.

But Maggie had to be dragged. There was no matching excitement in her, and finally Holly stopped and let her go.

'What?'

'There's a catch,' Maggie said flatly. 'There's always a catch.'

'There's not. He's getting a chef and an awesome housekeeper and he's prepared to pay. I was getting those sort of wages in Sydney before…'

'Before you trusted Geoff,' Maggie retorted. 'Have you learned nothing? Men!'

'Gran, he rang the airline and got a real person. And look.' She dug her hand into her greatcoat and hauled out the banknotes. 'This is an advance on what the airline is paying me. It seems you bought me insurance. Gran, this is…'

'Give it back!'

'Are you out of your mind?'

'He's the Earl of Craigenstone. You never, ever trust such a man. We'll be indebted. He'll be demanding… You know what he'll be demanding?'

'Droit de seigneur? Any village maiden he wants?' Holly stared down at the notes in her hand and couldn't suppress a giggle. 'Gran, this is not the Dark Ages. This means dry shoes. And you know, for dry shoes I might even agree to a bit of…'

'Holly!'

'Okay, sorry,' she said, settling again. 'You needn't worry; after Geoff, I am not the least bit interested in unswerving servitude, or even interest, but we do have a job and we can walk away at any time.'

'And this money?'

'Will be repaid as soon as the airline pays me. We're not walking into the lion's den. Come on, Gran, it'll be awesome.'

'How many people are we catering for?'

That stopped Holly in her tracks. She stared at Maggie, who stared straight back.

If they were in front of a mirror they would have seen a weird reflection, Holly thought. Maggie looked like Holly with fifty years added. They looked like two curly-haired Scotswomen, the only difference being the colour of their hair—copper versus grey—a few wrinkles and an Aussie accent versus a broad Scottish burr.

'I don't know,' Holly admitted, hauling her attention back to catering. 'The butler said…'

'Who?'

'The man who opened the door. Dour, lean and mean. He looks like Lurch from the Addams Family.'

'Stanley,' Maggie snapped. 'Estate manager. Reminds me of a ferret. Lurch used to make me laugh. Stanley doesn't.'

'Well, he implied we'll only be cooking and making beds for His Lordship.'

'If he's paying these sort of wages, he'll have invited half of New York.'

'We can cope,' Holly said belligerently and then went back to thinking about the man she'd just left. 'Gran, he's gorgeous.'

'There's no gorgeous about it,' Maggie snapped. 'The man's the Earl, and he's had deceit and tyranny bred into him for generations. I'm glad I'm coming with you, lass, or heaven knows what trouble you'd get into.'

'So you will do it?'

'We don't have much choice,' Maggie said grimly. 'It's follow His Lordship's orders or starve. Nothing's changed in this village for five hundred years, and it seems it's not changing now.'

He made three phone calls. The first was to his mother, who was as upset as he'd thought she might be.

'I'm staying here until after Christmas,' he told her. 'I know how you feel about the place, Mom, but I've told you about these kids. This place is important to them. It's the least I can do. I'll give them Christmas here and then it's done.'

'You won't turn into an Earl?' She'd tried to say it as a joke but it didn't work. He heard her fear. 'That place traps you.'

'My father trapped you, not the castle,' he told her. 'I will come home after Christmas.' He hesitated. 'Mom, why not come over, too? We could lay a few ghosts. We have an awesome cook and housekeeper. If you don't mind meeting Delia…'

'I don't mind meeting Delia. Contrary to first wife, second wife mores, I don't hate her. She was my only friend in the castle. I understand why she married him and I feel sorry for her, but I still won't come. That place holds nothing but bad memories.'

'Hey, I was born here. Isn't meeting me a good memory?' He was trying to lighten things but she wouldn't be lightened and he hung up with a sigh.

Then he rang his friends and got the opposite reaction.

'You're spending Christmas as an Earl? In a Scottish castle? Awesome! How about making it a party?'

'I'll be looking after kids.'

'But a party!'

He disconnected fast before he found himself with a castle full of American financiers for Christmas, and then finally he rang the kids. Expecting joy.

But, instead of joy, he was met with silence.

'I almost hoped you wouldn't ring,' Ben said flatly.

To say he was surprised would be an understatement. After the pleading the kid had made on behalf of his family…

'Don't you want to come any more?'

'Yes, but now we can't,' the boy said. 'There's something wrong with Mum's back. The doctor says something's hitting a nerve and she has to go into hospital on Friday for an urgent operation. Gran says Mum can't look after herself afterwards, so we all have to go to Gran's apartment 'cos Gran won't move, and it's even smaller than this one. And I have to sleep with my sisters and there's no one there we know and it'll be the pits. I asked Mum could we go to the castle by ourselves and she said no, not if you're even remotely like our dad, and we looked you up on the Internet and you do look like him and it's hopeless.'

There was a long silence. Angus stared down at the ancient flagstones in the hall and the ragged little dog wound himself round his ankles and looked up at him. Expectantly?

I'm not my father. He didn't say it out loud but he thought it really, really loudly.

'Let me talk to your mum,' he said at last and, moments later, he was talking to Delia. He could hear her wariness—and her weakness and her pain.

'I have a cook and a housekeeper,' he told her. 'If the kids really want to come…'

'I can't let them,' she said and took a deep breath. 'I'm sorry but I don't know a thing about you. I only know you're the Earl and that's hardly a recommendation.'

'But the kids…'

'They'll cope without this reunion Ben's set his heart on. Kids are resilient.'

Yes, Angus thought. This lot had needed to be. And then he thought he'd hired Holly and Maggie for nothing.

'It'd be different if you were married,' Delia was saying. 'If… If I could meet your wife… I just want someone there I can trust. And I hate Stanley. You're not married?'

'No.'

'There you are, then.'

'I'm employing…'

'I don't care who you're employing. No.'

'But I am engaged. My fiancée will be here and she's lovely. Your kids will like her and you can trust her even if you can't trust me.'

What had he just said? The words seemed to have come from nowhere. He didn't think them through; they were just…there. But then he had this vision…

Holly, going down to see this woman. Holly, pleading the kids' cause.

Delia was right, he thought grimly. He looked too much

like his father to engender trust, but Holly could talk the leg off an iron pot. Anyone would trust Holly.

If she agreed…

But he'd already said it. What had he done?

'What's her name?' Delia asked, sounding suspicious.

'Holly McIntosh.' What was he doing?

'How do I know what she's like?'

'She's great,' he said warmly. 'Well, I would say that, wouldn't I? I'll need to ask if she'll come down to London to meet you.' He needed to at least concede that. 'But if she's happy to do it, I'll pop her on the train to London the day after tomorrow. If you like her, as I'm sure you will, she could bring the kids back with her. Then you could concentrate on your health. If you're better in time to travel, maybe you and your mother could still join us for Christmas Day.'

There was a sharp intake of breath from the other end of the line. Angus understood it. He was doing sharp intakes of breath all over the place himself.

He'd just landed himself with a fiancée! What had he done?

He'd lied.

But Ben's voice was still echoing. He hadn't been able to deny him.

But what hourly rate would Holly demand for this? He thought of facing her with this new job description, and suddenly he found himself grinning. He might even enjoy the bargaining.

'I never wanted to come back to the castle,' Delia said. 'I only said I would when Ben begged.'

'I can understand that,' Angus said gently. 'But, with Holly here, I think you'll find it a very different place. Holly will make it different.'

'You sound like you love her.' Delia sounded astounded and Angus thought: join the club. *You sound like you love her*? Astounded was too small a word for it.

'And Ben looked you up on the Internet,' Delia was saying. 'You're not engaged. Or…it says you were, years ago, but your fiancée was killed in a ski accident.'

Delia was sounding suspicious again, and Angus decided, lies or not, engaged or not, it was time to turn back into the aloof financier he was.

'My private life is private,' he said curtly. 'Thankfully, not everything's on the Internet. But, if you agree, I'll have Holly with you the day after tomorrow. No pressure. If you don't like her and trust her then we'll leave it but I think you will.'

'Really?'

'I promise. As long as Holly agrees to come to London.'

And as long as Holly agreed with all the rest.

Holly and Maggie had steak for tea. With chips. With apple pie afterwards. They also had a bottle of wine and then started on another. They'd stoked the fire up, courtesy of Angus's loan, they sat back by the fire after dinner and they grinned at each other like Cheshire Cats. Two well fed, warm Cheshire Cats.

'He'll probably work us into the ground,' Maggie said, trying to sound pessimistic and failing.

'We're both used to hard work and if he works us too hard we walk out and leave him to it,' Holly retorted and then she thought of the man she'd just left and added, 'but he won't.'

'He's the Earl.'

'He's a nice man.'

'I thought you said there was no such thing as a nice man.'

'Well, a nice person,' Holly conceded.

'But you think he's gorgeous. Every generation there's scandal in that castle because some silly girl thinks the Earl is gorgeous.'

'He's just nice,' Holly said stubbornly, but *gorgeous* did pop into her mind and waft around for a bit.

'We'll see,' Maggie said darkly and poured another glass of wine for them both. Then she giggled. 'I see you and me in the servants' hall for Christmas and I don't see us gnawing on the turkey carcass. I see us carving the best bits for us.'

'Gran!'

'We might even have fun,' Maggie conceded. 'If we can avoid the Earl.' And then she paused.

She needed to pause. The knock on the cottage's thick wooden door reverberated around the living room, imperative, urgent. Maggie frowned. 'It's nine at night. Who... One of the neighbours?'

She half rose but Holly was before her. 'Let me.'

'Take the poker, Holly, love,' Maggie said but Holly, sated with apple pie, wine and heat, was in no mood for axe-murderers. Without the aid of a poker, she opened the door. A blast of snow rushed in, but not as much as she might expect.

The snow was blocked.

On the doorstep stood Maggie's greatest fear. Their new employer. The Earl of Craigenstone himself.

'I'm sorry to disturb you so late at night,' he said, while Holly stared at him stupidly and thought...*What?* 'But I have an additional position to fill and I wondered if you'd add it to your position as cook...as chef.'

'What?' Holly said, thoroughly confused.

'I'm in a bit of trouble,' the Earl said. 'I've made a promise I intend to keep but, to do so...Holly, I need a fiancée. Just for Christmas. I need you, temporarily, to agree to marry me.'

CHAPTER THREE

'I KNEW IT.' The first reaction—of course—didn't come from Holly. It came from Maggie, hissing behind her. 'Didn't I tell you? Talk about a fairy tale. Slam the door in his face, Holly. He's not having his wicked way with you.'

Holly turned and looked at Maggie and then looked at the wine glass in her grandmother's hand. She gently removed it and set it on the hall table.

'Wicked way?'

'He's an Earl.' Maggie glowered.

Holly turned back and looked at Angus in astonishment. He looked embarrassed, she thought. And more. 'He looks cold,' she told her gran.

'Slam the door, Holly,' Maggie demanded again.

'I can't do that. Even if he is crazy, he looks freezing.'

'Holly…'

'He gave me hot chocolate,' Holly said reasonably. 'And enough money to buy us coal. He might be out of his mind but I'm not turfing him out into the night.' She tried to peer through the snow and failed. 'Unless your car's here.'

'I walked,' Angus said. 'It's snowing too hard to trust the road and I needed to walk. I needed to think.'

'So you've given us no choice but to invite you in and warm you up,' Holly said. 'Which we'll do as long as you don't make any more ridiculous propositions. Gran and I have had a bottle and a half of very nice wine and maybe you have, too.'

'I'm sensible,' he said stubbornly and Holly gazed up at him and thought he looked anything but sensible.

Gorgeous was the adjective Maggie had used. *Every generation there's scandal in that castle because some silly girl thinks the Earl is gorgeous.*

But still…

He was wearing the most fabulous man's coat she'd ever seen—thick grey cashmere, tailored to fit. A gorgeous black scarf. Long black boots, moulded to calves that… Okay, don't go there. His after-five shadow was dark, his hair was darker still, and his eyes… They gleamed with what she thought suddenly looked like dangerous mischief and she thought… *Maybe Maggie's right. Maybe I should slam the door.*

But this man had been good to her. This man was saving her Christmas. Maybe a small bit of eccentricity was allowable.

So she ushered him into the living room and she left Maggie in charge in case he needed a straitjacket and she made them all hot chocolate—no more alcohol for anyone tonight!—while Maggie glowered in the background and Angus filled her tiny living room with his presence.

And with his personality. He was trying to charm Maggie, trying to make her smile while Holly made the chocolate. She watched them through the kitchen door. He wasn't succeeding. Maggie was growing more and more suspicious.

Enough. She took the chocolate in, settled on the edge of a fireside stool—she decided it might be wise not to make herself comfortable—and fixed him with a look that said: *Don't mess with me.*

'Okay, shoot,' she said. 'What are you saying? I'm a chef. Gran's a housekeeper. I thought we had our contract sorted. There was no mention of marriage in anything we spoke about this morning.'

'This is another contract on top of the first,' he said and then added hopefully, 'I'll pay extra.'

'I don't give,' she said carefully, 'extra.'

'No.' He raked long fingers through his jet black hair and Holly realised he looked worried. Really worried. To her astonishment, she found herself softening. 'Of course you don't,' he said, 'but…'

'Tell me the problem,' she said and, to her further astonishment, he did just that, without taking off his coat, cradling his chocolate as she'd cradled hers this morning, seeming suddenly, weirdly vulnerable. He told it all in his lovely growly rumble—the story of three kids who were desperate to come to the castle one last time; three kids whose mother didn't trust him to care for them.

'Is that why you've hired us?' Holly asked in astonishment. 'So we can look after them?'

'I…yes. Or not look after them—their mother was supposed to be coming, too—but I need you to do the cooking and housekeeping so we'll be comfortable. But now Delia's ill and can't come with them. And she doesn't trust me to care for them.' He glanced at Maggie, who was still glowering, and he spread his hands. 'You know my father's reputation,' he told her. 'I can't blame her.'

Maggie was trying to keep stern but this man's charm was seeping through her armour. She was visibly weakening.

'So…you want me to talk to Delia and tell her I'll be responsible for the kids?' Holly asked, trying to sort it in her mind.

'Yes,' he said.

'I can do that, but there's no need for false engagements.'

'There is because I lied. Look….' There went that gesture again, the hair raking. 'I messed this up. I should have spent longer, told her all about you and your gran, tried to reassure her without lies, but she sounded frightened.'

'That's your father's reputation,' Maggie retorted. 'And his father and his father before that. And lying's what they all did.' But still her glower was wavering.

'I know, and that's what I'm up against.' Angus turned to Maggie, sensing the elderly lady's softening. 'I can't fight it but I hoped Holly could. It was a spur of the moment lie but it was made with the best intentions. I thought…if Holly goes to London to see her she can just be…Holly. There'd be no need for deception, except the big one about us being engaged. Holly's a chef from Australia with a gran who lives in the village—Delia knows you, Mrs McIntosh, and once she meets Holly there'll be more reassurance. Holly can be her own bouncy self, but with more control over me and what goes on in my castle than if she was just my chef. Don't you think it might work? Don't you think between us we can give these kids Christmas?'

'Those kids certainly have had a hard time,' Maggie said and, to Holly's astonishment, she was now definitely wavering. 'The old Earl got Delia pregnant and then offered to marry her,' she told Holly. 'I swear it was to avoid paying maintenance. I don't know what Delia was thinking to accept marriage but she did, and she's lived to regret it these last sixteen years. If His Lordship's serious…' She turned to Holly. 'If you can keep your head and be engaged to him…'

'I don't want to be engaged,' Holly gasped. 'I have no intention of being engaged to anyone.'

'It's only for Christmas,' Maggie said, as if she was a bit soft.

'No! You want me to lie?'

'You've been engaged for the last two years.' Maggie seized Holly's hand and held it up so they could see the band of white on her ring finger. 'As far as I know, you haven't even seen the ghastly Geoff since he absconded, so you haven't thrown the ring at him. You can still be officially engaged. Does it matter who to? With luck, you won't even have to lie.'

'You're asking me to put Geoff's engagement ring on again?' Holly was practically speechless.

'No,' Angus said and dug his hand deep into his coat pocket. He pulled out a crimson box and handed it over. 'You'd need this. It's the Craigenstone diamond. My father gave it to my mother and then took it back as soon as they were married—he locked it in the family vault. When my mother left she raided the vault and took it, along with everything else that was legally hers. This has been on every portrait of Craigenstone brides—except Delia—since Time Immemorial. Delia will recognise it. You have no idea of the number of letters my mother has had demanding its return and the satisfaction she had in saying she must have mislaid it. She hates it, though, so there's no harm in giving it away.'

'You're asking Holly to wear the Craigenstone ring?' Maggie gasped as Holly stared down at the extravagant diamond, surrounded by tiny clusters of rubies. Or not so tiny. The size of the diamond made the rubies look small but any one of these rubies would make a ring on its own. The thing was truly over the top.

'I'm not wearing that all Christmas,' Holly gasped. 'As well as all the other objections, what if it ends up in the turkey stuffing?'

'Just while you see Delia.'

'And then you'll lock it back in the vault.'

'That's the one.'

'I'm not taking the train wearing that.' She was looking at it as if it were a scorpion.

'I don't care if it's lost.' He hesitated. 'Holly, that ring's brought trouble to whoever's worn it. Neither my mother or I have fond memories of it. Here's a deal. If you keep this pretence up, if we pull this thing off and give these kids a Christmas to remember, it's yours. My mother and I don't value it and we don't need its worth. It would be our pleasure to give it to you. If it means these kids can have a good Christmas then it'll have gone to a good home.'

'Well, I don't want it,' Holly said with asperity. 'I'd be mugged the minute I went out in public. What use am I to anyone if I'm mugged?'

'Everyone will assume it's paste,' Maggie said soothingly. 'With you looking like you do.'

'That's supposed to make me feel better?'

'That's the other thing,' Angus said. 'We need to get you some clothes.'

'I have clothes and I'm not keeping this ring!'

'We'll discuss keeping the ring later,' he said soothingly. 'If you really don't want it, then we'll work something out but for now it's yours, so if you lose it you don't need to feel guilty.'

'You mean if I'm mugged.'

'Granted,' he said and grinned. 'You can go down feeling virtuous. But you will wear it now, and the clothes question has to be fixed as well. Maggie, where's the most expensive dress shop in town?'

'There isn't one,' Maggie said shortly. 'And you're not sending my granddaughter to London by train with the weather like it is—and not wearing that ring! If you want this done then you do it properly. You take Holly yourself. Can't you...I don't know...hire a helicopter? Isn't that what rich Americans do?'

'Choppers in this weather are more dangerous than cars,' Angus told her. 'At least the trains are still running.'

'But for how long? Trains get stuck in snowdrifts all the time.'

'Maggie...'

'You take her yourself if you want her to go,' Maggie

snapped. 'That fancy four-wheel drive you have looks like it'll get through anything; even that pot-holed driveway of yours. And the main road to London will always be clear. There's a great dress shop I've read about in Edinburgh; even royalty goes there. You can stop there on the way. Buy Holly a few expensive dresses. Then you can drive down, flash the ring, persuade Delia to let the kids come and then drive everybody back. Do it properly.'

'Gran!' Holly gasped.

'Properly or not at all,' Maggie said. She folded her arms and glared at Holly and then turned and glared at Angus.

'You're both mad,' Holly said.

'Yes, but I'm rich and mad,' Angus said apologetically, smiling at Maggie. 'And I pay for what I need and I need you. Maybe Maggie's right—it'd be better if I took you to London.'

'I'm hired to cook.'

'With this ring you're hired to be at my beck and call, acting as my fiancée with a bit of cooking on the side. Sharing everything. Except my bed,' he said hastily as he saw her face.

'You'll be a nice old-fashioned couple,' Maggie approved. Then she grinned. 'What a novelty. Do they exist any more?'

'Gran, this is crazy,' Holly gasped. 'It's impossible. The kids will know.'

'Will the kids care enough to think about it?' Maggie demanded, and then added a clincher. 'And think what you could do with the sort of money we're being offered, my girl. Even without the ring… What *we* could do with it…'

That stopped her. Holly's head was whirling but she made herself pause and think. Even without the ring— which she had no intention of keeping—some things were too ridiculous for words. But keeping this job…

They'd earn the rental deposit Gran had no hope of saving for.

That Maggie would be thrown out of her cottage at her age had appalled Holly. Her situation—she had never saved to live anywhere else when she was only renting—was entirely Maggie's fault, Holly conceded, but that didn't make it easier to accept. She'd assumed she'd live in this cottage for ever.

More worldly than her grandmother, Holly had asked the hard question: 'How could you have expected a landlord to let you live in a house for ever?' Maggie had simply burst into tears. There was no answer.

Nor was there a rental deposit.

So, she told herself firmly, start now. This was an engagement of convenience with a salary to make her eyes water. Ridiculous or not, to throw away such an offer would be nuts. Even if it involved wearing a rock. Even if it meant letting this man buy her clothes and drive her to London.

'Fine,' she said weakly. She sounded desperate and she knew it. She took a deep breath though and hauled herself together. 'But…but there are conditions.'

'Conditions?' Angus sounded wary.

'Yes,' she said, thinking of that appalling cold castle and the dust sheets and the horrible Stanley and three kids who sounded as if they needed a decent Christmas even more than she and her Gran did. 'I'll telephone Delia tomorrow morning and talk to her. If she agrees, then we'll go to London on Thursday—you and I together. But tomorrow and Wednesday…

'We'll start at seven tomorrow, won't we, Gran, and we need an open purse. If Gran can find someone else from the village to help us for two days, then I want permission to hire them, too. I want that castle spring-cleaned from stem to stern. I want the whole place warm and I want Christmas decorations everywhere. I want an excellent cooker, hired or bought, I don't mind which, but I do need quality appliances, and I want enough food in stock to make your tummy bulge. It'll cost you a fortune, Lord Craigenstone, almost as much as this ring you're tossing about, but take it or leave it.'

What a nerve, she thought. What an absolute nerve. She'd been tossed a financial lifeline and here she was, putting it at risk. But maybe that risk was necessary. If she was to organise Christmas it'd be a Christmas to remember. The thought of pretending an engagement to a lord in a gloomy, cold ancestral pile made something inside her cringe.

Life had been too appalling. These last months had been hell for her and hell for Maggie. And also maybe for these three kids?

This man before her was their ticket to time out. He was throwing money and rings around with gay abandon. So... One fantastic Christmas before the world closed in again?

'I want a Christmas to remember or no Christmas at all,' she said and met his dark eyes and held them. 'If you're serious about giving these kids a Christmas...I assume the way you're tossing cash about that money is no object.'

He met her gaze calmly, consideringly. 'I pay for value.'

'But if you're anything like your father, you'll hold onto what you pay for,' Maggie interjected. 'You're not keeping my Holly.'

'I'm paying Holly from now until New Year,' he said, still watching Holly. 'I have no intention of staying engaged for one moment longer than I must. This arrangement came out of my mistake—I told a lie on the spur of the moment and I'll pay for it. I'll pay and then I'll move on. I am not like my father. I do not hold.'

'And I have no intention of being held,' Holly said, just as evenly. 'So you can stop worrying, Gran, and start making lists. So, My Lord, do you agree to our terms?'

'Angus,' he snapped.

'My Lord,' she said serenely, 'this Christmas is going to be a fantasy Christmas for all of us. Christmas in Castle Craigie with all the trimmings. I think you should wear your kilt.'

'You want that in the contract, too?'

'Yes,' she said calmly. 'But you're getting off lightly. I could be asking you to dress up as Santa.'

'Not even for you.'

'This isn't for me,' she said without missing a beat. 'This is for three kids and for Gran. That's who I'm doing it for.'

'So you will take my ring?' He held it out again, the outrageous extravagance of it looking incongruous in the extreme in the tiny crofter's cottage.

Holly stared down at it for a long moment. A ring. An engagement ring. She'd sworn…

But this wasn't about engagement. It wasn't even about trust—or not very much. It was about giving three kids a Christmas to remember and giving Gran security. She could do this.

She thought suddenly of what else was demanded—that he drive her to London. It'd mean spending two days in the car with him and a night in London.

'I *could* go by train,' she said dubiously, still looking at the ring.

'No, you can't,' Maggie snapped. 'If you think I want to be stranded alone in that castle with His Lordship while you're stuck in a snowdrift somewhere south of the border you have another think coming. Car or nothing.'

'Is this about you or me?' Holly demanded and, amazingly, her gran chuckled. It was the first time her grandmother had laughed since Holly arrived. Holly knew that laugh; she'd loved it. Every time Gran had visited Australia, which she'd done every year since Holly was born, which possibly explained just why she was so broke now, that chuckle had filled Holly's life. Gran's broad Scottish burr, her laugh, her warmth, her adoration of her son and his wife and their little girl…

It was with her now, all around her, and she knew there was no way she could not do this.

Do it now, she told herself, before you think of any more consequences, and with that she reached forward and took the ring and slipped it on her ring finger.

'Yes,' she said at last. 'Yes, I will.'

'Excellent,' Angus said and smiled. Holly thought: *Don't do that. Don't smile. I can be engaged to you all you like as long as you don't turn on that smile.*

And, as if on cue, his smile faded, as if he, too, sensed danger.

'No strings,' she said, seemingly making no sense at all, but apparently he knew what she was saying. What she was thinking.

'No strings,' he agreed.

'Then that's all right,' she said and turned away before he could smile again, before she could feel that strong and dangerous tug…

'It has to be all right,' he told them both. Holly knew he was watching her, but she was looking—fiercely—at the ring.

'Excellent,' she managed and, with that, Holly Margaret McIntosh was formally betrothed to Lord Angus McTavish Stuart. For better or for worse.

For Christmas.

CHAPTER FOUR

AT SEVEN THE next morning Stanley arrived to take them to the castle. He barely spoke to them. He was the estate manager escorting the new hired help to his employer. He tossed their belongings into the back of the estate wagon without saying a word.

'As estate manager, he's practically above stairs,' Maggie whispered to Holly as they were transported to their new employment. 'It's a wonder he talks to us at all. As cook and housekeeper, we're definitely beneath his notice.'

But Holly had spent a restless night with a heavy ring on her finger, her unease had been building and this man's covert antagonism had her thinking: upstairs, downstairs—some things had to stop now.

All or nothing.

'We're not the hired help any more,' she whispered, flashing her ring. 'We just got elevated.'

Then she took a deep breath and moved into her newly acquired role.

'How many guests are we expecting for Christmas dinner, Stanley?' she asked from the back seat, where she was wedged with Maggie and Maggie's three large knitting baskets. Holly might only own a handbag and a plastic bag full of charity shop clothing, but Maggie made up for it in the luggage department. Everything she owned she seemed intent on taking, 'in case we need it'.

'How can we possibly need four feather dusters?' Holly had demanded as she'd watched her gran stuff cleaning supplies into Grandpa's old golf bag.

'If you think I'm using what's been lying round the castle for years you have another think coming,' Maggie had said darkly. 'If I were you, I'd be packing a rolling pin.'

'I'll make him buy me a new one if there's not a good one,' Holly had said and Maggie had chuckled again—her chuckle was seeming almost normal now.

'That's the spirit,' she said. 'Ooh, Holly, I think we might be about to have fun.'

But now, as Holly waited for Stanley's answer, she wasn't so sure and Maggie was looking nervous, too.

'You'll have to ask His Lordship,' Stanley said in a voice that said even thinking of asking would be an impertinence.

'I'm asking you,' Holly said evenly and fingered her ring with resolution.

'It's not my place to tell you,' Stanley snapped.

'As His Lordship's fiancée, I believe I can ask you everything I need to know,' Holly retorted. 'And I believe His Lordship will back up my belief that it's your place to tell me.'

Maggie gasped. There was a deathly silence in the car while Holly rethought what she'd decided last night. That it wasn't enough to tell Delia she was engaged—the engagement would have to be played out the entire time she was at the castle. Otherwise, one phone call would have the kids telling Delia they'd both lied and where would that get them?

She'd expected Angus to have told Stanley the truth. Obviously he hadn't—therefore it was up to Holly to position herself where she needed to be.

'What nonsense is this?' Stanley growled and Holly held up her ring finger so he could see it in the rear-view mirror.

'Love at first sight,' she said sweetly. 'Ask His Lordship. Meanwhile, how many for Christmas dinner?'

There was another silence while Stanley stared at the ring and Holly worried about staying on the road.

'Just His Lordship and the children,' Stanley said at last, sounding so shocked he didn't know what he was saying.

'No friends? No family retainers?'

'No!'

'Well, that makes it easy,' Holly said cheerfully. 'Thank you, Stanley.' Maggie nearly choked but Holly recalled that was just the first barrier. This next three weeks was her gran's future, she thought, and if the fiancée deception was exposed at the first hurdle the whole thing could end in disaster. Therefore, she'd do this properly or not at all.

Bring it on.

And then they rounded the last bend before the castle and His Lordship was standing at the vast doors, waiting, and she thought: *What am I thinking? Bring it on?*

What have I done?

Lord of Castle Craigie. That was what Angus looked like, even though he'd ditched the kilt. He was wearing casual clothes—cream chinos, an open-necked shirt and a lovely blue, V-necked sweater, rolled up to the sleeves.

He stood at the entrance to his castle home, he looked every inch a Lord, and it was all Holly could do not to jump out of the car and turn tail and run.

She needed to pretend to be engaged to this man?

She must.

The estate wagon pulled to a halt and Angus strode forward to open the doors for them. Nice, Holly thought appreciatively, and she liked it even more that he greeted Gran first.

'Welcome, Mrs McIntosh,' he told her, his dark eyes twinkling. 'I hope you'll be very happy in your new employment.'

'Nice,' Maggie said approvingly, echoing Holly's thoughts. 'Call me Maggie.'

'Maggie,' he said and smiled in a way that made Holly's insides do a back flip. 'And Miss…' he caught himself '…Holly.'

'Hello, darling,' Holly said and wound her arms around his neck and kissed him.

She'd thought this through last night. All or nothing, she'd thought. Either she was his fiancée or she wasn't.

It had all seemed sensible—last night.

This morning, as she kissed him and felt him freeze with shock, she thought: *Uh-oh, what do impertinent cooks get for kissing their Lord and master?*

Dismissed? Or picked up and carted to His Lordship's chambers forthwith?

There was a minefield in between.

But she kissed him properly, soundly, as a solid, assured fiancée would surely kiss her beloved. His mouth felt strong and warm. His hands fell instinctively to her waist and held and, for a moment, for just a moment, she let her body believe this was real, this was true.

Nice? Her body was thinking of better descriptors.

But it was play-acting. Her body had better get itself in control and tug back. He released her. Was she imagining it or was there the faintest hint of reluctance?

Imagination. *Know your place,* she told herself fiercely. She was a below-stairs employee, paid to act above-stairs.

'Hello…sweetheart,' the Lord of the Castle managed and she managed a grin in return.

'Very good. We can do this. You might need to do some explaining to Stanley; he's a bit shell-shocked. Okay, show us to our quarters and get this Christmas under way.'

'It's still cold,' Angus warned. 'We won't have heating until I get some tradesmen in.'

'We won't be cold, will we, Gran?' Holly said. 'We have

far too much to do. Actually, let's leave Stanley to deal with our bags. If you start with a tour of the castle, we can figure out exactly what needs to be done.'

'Twas like a great man's kitchen without a fire in it.

Where had she heard that analogy? It fitted, Holly thought as Angus led the way through the vast halls and corridors and parlours. But maybe this was worse.

Like a great man's house without a heart in it.

It wasn't just that it was cold—though it was definitely cold. It was that the place was a great stone monument with no attempt made to make it liveable.

'I think I'd rather live in a cave,' she whispered to Maggie as they followed Angus. Their footsteps echoed on the stone floor—three sets of footsteps: Angus's brisk tread, the soft hush of Holly's dried out trainers and the brisk click of Maggie's sensible low heels. Maggie had appeared all in black this morning, looking very much like a housekeeper in a very reputable establishment. Angus looked the part, too, Holly conceded, casual but still aristocratic. A Lord on his day off.

Holly, on the other hand, felt as if she'd wandered into a movie set and any minute she'd be ejected. She had to put personal feelings aside, she told herself, staring despairingly into yet another dust-sheeted something-room. Even Maggie's shoulders were sagging.

'Show us where the children's bedrooms would have been when they were living here,' she said.

Angus looked doubtful. 'I think I can find it.'

'You think…'

'Stanley showed me through once but I still have trouble figuring out where I am,' he admitted. 'I'm almost up to laying trails of salt behind me so I can retrace my steps.'

But he did find the rooms where Delia and her children had lived and Maggie and Holly stared at them in horror.

They were three bleak rooms off the kitchen. They looked as if they'd been left exactly as they were when they'd moved out. One bedroom with three hard single beds lined up in a row. A smaller bedroom with a single bed—Delia, it seemed, had left the marital bed. A tiny sitting room, four chairs, a table, a threadbare rug.

'You don't need to say it,' Angus said heavily. 'My father was a tyrant.'

'Interested only in money,' Maggie said darkly and then threw a dark look at the current Earl. 'So how come you're prepared to pay us so much?'

'Because I want these kids to have a decent Christmas,' Angus said savagely. 'Like I… Like we never had.'

'You never had decent Christmases in America?' Maggie asked and Holly saw his expression become shuttered.

'We need to make this place more comfortable,' he said tightly and Holly took a deep breath and thought that if she was going to do this—why not do it? She glanced down at the ring on her finger and thought that Angus had just bestowed on her the title of future Lady of the Castle.

Maybe she should do, then, what it seemed previous Ladies of the Castle hadn't been able to do.

This man was an Earl. Rumour was that he was absurdly wealthy. What was a future Lady of the Castle—albeit a temporary one—for, if not to spend His Lordship's money?

'They're not sleeping here,' she said flatly, and Angus and Maggie both looked at her in surprise.

'They're coming for nostalgic reasons,' Angus said. 'They might want their old bedroom.'

'Then we put clean sheets on their beds and leave this room exactly as it is,' Holly said. 'So if they want to use it they can. But they're teenagers, or almost teenagers. Let's give them the teenage fantasy. There must be some vast stately rooms in this place. Why don't we move heaven and earth and give this place—these kids—the send-off they deserve?'

'If they're coming on Friday we can hardly do much,' Angus said, but Holly shook her head in disgust.

'I thought you were an Earl. Can't Earls order stuff?'

'Yes, but…'

'Gran, you know places we can order from?'

'The village won't have…'

'Of course the village won't have,' Holly said. 'Not the stuff we want.'

And then she hesitated. Her heart was warming to the fantasy here. In truth, Holly hadn't had a decent Christmas since her parents had died. Her Australian grandmother had been into austerity, and once Holly started working in restaurants, because she didn't have a family, it always seemed reasonable that she had been rostered on.

Maggie, too… Since Grandpa had died, they'd always phoned each other on Christmas morning. 'Here's another one to get through, Holly, love,' Gran had said every time. 'If I can do it, so can you.'

Another one to get through… Holly thought of those austere beds, of kids in this appalling excuse for a home, and thought: *Why not have a real Christmas? Why not have a Christmas to make up for all the Christmases she'd… they'd missed out on?*

'If you really can afford it,' she said, talking to Angus but almost talking to herself as well, 'I'm talking opulence. Thick carpets by the quarter acre, feather mattresses, pillows by the score. I want light bulbs in all those dusty chandeliers. I want heat and light. Is there somewhere we can hire paintings?' She glanced at the empty walls and then out to the vast corridors behind her. 'We need ancestors.'

'Ancestors,' Angus said faintly.

'Any ancestors will do,' she said blithely. 'And suits of armour and stags' heads, plastic if necessary. I know what a good castle should look like and this isn't one. Maggie, I think we need a bit of help in the dusting department. We'll need electricians and plumbers. Do you know any locals who might…?'

'I know locals who'd love,' Maggie said, staring around her in awe. 'If His Lordship's happy to pay…'

'Um…wait just a minute,' Angus said faintly and Holly put her hands on her hips and fixed him with a stare.

'We're engaged to be married, are we not…dear?' she demanded.

'For three weeks.'

'Then for three weeks I'm the Lady of the Castle,' she retorted, 'and my reputation is at stake. You can just thank heaven you're not leg-shackled for life—imagine what I'd cost you then—but it's all or nothing, My Lord. Make up your mind now.'

'Plastic stags' heads,' he said, even more faintly, and Maggie coughed.

'I think I can find real ones,' she said. 'The Craigenstone Historical Society has about ten stored in their back shed. They might be a bit moth-eaten…'

'We can buy a bit of artificial fur and patch 'em up,' Holly said. 'Excellent.' She hauled a notebook from her pocket and a pencil, and wrote 'Stags' on top. 'Now,' she said happily, 'let's make lists.'

He'd set a whirlwind in motion.

This was no subservient miss. He'd employed a maker of lists.

She drew a map as she went. Every room they went in, she wrote things down.

Two-thirds of the rooms they entered, dust-sheeted seemingly for generations, Holly simply noted as DND on her list.

'Do Not Disturb,' she explained. 'If we take those dust-covers off we might disturb ecosystems that'll have David Attenborough and the Discovery Channel here by lunchtime, and we have enough to do before Christmas, thank you very much. And the kids will love exploring them for themselves.'

But in the rooms she thought they might use—the grandest of the grand—her pen went into overdrive. He stood in the background as she wrote things down and Maggie borrowed his cell phone and started calling.

'My cousin's grandson's an electrician,' Maggie told him while Holly wrote more things on her list. 'He'll be here by lunchtime, and his two sisters are at home for the holidays and would kill for a chance to check out the castle. They're great girls—we'll have this place shiny in no time. As for plumbers, Mrs McConkey's nephew will come and he has a team. Did you know three of your bathrooms are blocked? Were you planning on using one bathroom for all of you?'

Yes, he was. Stanley had already told him—dourly—there was no hope of getting tradesmen by Christmas, and here were Maggie and Holly promising tradesmen by lunchtime.

'Maggie's owed favours everywhere, and with your pay rate it's easy,' Holly said cheerfully. 'We need to move fast, though, if we're to get this done.'

Fast? They were a whirlwind, sweeping through the castle as if it were a two-up, two-down council house. He should leave them to it but it was strangely magnetic. And… Holly was wearing his mother's ring.

What was it about the ring that had him staying around, even interjecting occasionally? He had a mass of work he should be doing—the world's financial markets were still operating and he wasn't here on holiday. He was here to settle his father's affairs, but he'd brought his work with him.

He should…

'Is there anything else you need to be doing?' Holly asked sweetly, and he blinked.

'Pardon?'

'It's just…you're a bit unsettling, hovering.'

'Holly!' Maggie gasped reprovingly, but Holly grinned.

'Well, he is. Don't tell me you don't find him unsettling, too. My Lord, you're our boss. We'll be more productive if you leave us to get on in peace.'

'I thought I was your fiancé,' he growled and she grinned.

'So you are. Well, then, sweetheart, off you go and play some golf or do some other manly thing because we girls want some time together.'

Sweetheart.

'I hate golf,' he said.

'Fish, then,' she said and, to his astonishment, she reached up, took his shoulders, turned him and steered him towards the door. 'Bye, dear.'

And the door was closed behind him.

Leaving him gobsmacked.

He had a fine housekeeper in New York, an invisible being who did for him while he was at work. He left pay and a bonus at Christmas, but, as far as he was concerned, housework was a mystery.

So why was he feeling as if he wanted to be involved now?

Because one feisty Australian chef was bossing him around?

Because one feisty Australian chef had kissed him?

He could still feel it. The action had jolted him as Angus McTavish Stuart was not known for being jolted. For Angus McTavish Stuart was known for being in control. Hadn't he had control drummed into him from childhood by a bitter, wounded mother?

But then, what man ever listens to his mother? He'd gone

his own path—of course he had—and his path had led him to Louise. He'd met her in college, and she'd known about his family money. Who didn't? But he didn't see the dollar signs in her eyes and he was smitten.

Blond, beautiful, sophisticated, two years older than him, she'd twisted his heart around her beckoning finger, but in the end she was as mercenary as the old Earl had been. She was 'going home for Christmas' she'd told him two months before they were to be married. But home apparently wasn't her parents and her siblings. Home for Louise had been the ski slopes of Aspen, an equally blond ski instructor and the tree that claimed her life when she was drunk after three nights of partying.

The call had come on Christmas Eve. The kid that was Angus had grown up that night. At twenty-one years old he'd stood by Louise's graveside and he'd sworn to follow his mother's mantra for the rest of his life.

Head, not heart. For some reason, that mantra was drumming through his head now.

After one kiss?

This was a pretend engagement for sensible reasons. That was all this was, he told himself harshly as he headed off to find Stanley. Stanley was about to have an apoplexy when he learned what he was proposing spending. Stanley could also blow his story of an engagement out of the water.

For a moment—for just a moment—he toyed with the idea of telling Stanley the engagement was for real, that it was love at first sight, that he'd seen Holly in the snow with her freezing feet and he'd felt an overriding, irrational urge to sweep her up, marry her and live happily ever after.

With moth-eaten stags and lists.

He grinned. Not sensible. Not sensible at all. This mock engagement was a farce.

But…it might be fun, he conceded.

He wanted to join them.

Um…no. He was the Lord of the Castle, he told himself with wry humour. Mingling with the servants was beneath his touch.

But mingling with his fiancée?

Don't go there. Suddenly humour faded.

Head, not heart, he thought savagely in the stillness and then realized he'd only known the woman for a day. Heart? He had to be kidding.

He'd go and talk to Stanley, he told himself. That'd be enough to take the heart right out of him.

Maggie and Holly kept right on taking notes. Their last stop was the most important.

The kitchen.

Angus had briefly opened the door on his initial tour. Now they opened the door wide and Holly stared around her in dismay. Here she'd have to perform a miracle. Christmas cooking. With what?

The kitchen was geared to feed an army—maybe three hundred years ago. The fireplace was vast, open, blackened with age, full of ancient soot and dust, with great black hooks embedded in the stone at either side, where surely a spit had hung, or rods to hold hanging cauldrons.

There was a huge wooden table covered with mouse droppings. The stone floor was filthy, pitted and moulded with age.

There was one cleanish corner holding an old electric stove and a battered cheap microwave oven.

There was a little black dog huddled under the table, about as far under as he could get.

'Hey,' Holly said and bent down and inspected. The little dog backed further. But surely this was the little dog she'd last seen in Angus's study. What was it doing looking so scared?

She headed to the fridge. Obviously His Lordship had

been feeding himself. Here were foodstuffs guys thought were important. Eggs, bacon, beer. Not a lot else.

She hauled out a packet of bacon and proffered a bit to the little dog. He inched out, took it gingerly and then backed away again.

She offered more. The little dog inched forward again and finally Holly had him on her lap.

'This guy was in His Lordship's study yesterday,' she told Maggie, frowning. 'He looked fine. Ragged but fine. Now…' She fingered a bruise on his leg that had bled sluggishly. The dog was looking as if he was expecting to be kicked, hard.

'He looks like McAllister's dog,' Maggie said.

'McAllister?'

'He was the gamekeeper here for fifty years. He always had a wee terrier. The last I heard, McAllister was ill and needing to go into some sort of care. We assumed the dog went with him.' Maggie knelt and fingered the little dog's collar. 'It's McAllister's tartan,' she said. 'He must have stayed on with Stanley.' She looked doubtfully at the miserable scrap of canine misery. 'He doesn't look well cared for, though.'

'He doesn't, does he,' Holly said carefully and rose, the little dog in her arms. 'But he was well cared for yesterday. It seems our boss has mood swings. I'll be back, Gran. You make lists on my behalf.' Then she paused and stared at the great fireplace. 'I need a good stove but I need a few other things as well. If we're to work for this guy, we get a contract in writing right now, and this little guy's Christmas is included.'

Angus was having dour words with Stanley. Very dour. The man was driving him nuts, but no one else knew the estate. He had to keep him on, but the sourness of his expression made him want to eject him out of the nearest window.

'You will cooperate with everything Holly and Maggie need,' he said, silky-smooth, in a voice his employees in Manhattan would have quivered to hear. 'Understand me, Stanley, this is non-negotiable.'

'So is this.' And suddenly Holly was standing in the doorway, holding the dog he'd last seen the night before. Blazing indignation. Blazing fury. 'If you kicked this dog, then we're leaving now,' she told Angus in a voice that dripped with contempt. 'Or if you shoved him out in the snow and something else kicked him... Either way, we should walk but I'm giving you two minutes to explain. So explain how the cosy domestic little mutt I cuddled yesterday is now a shivering wreck in your apology for a kitchen.'

'He must have got in the back door,' Stanley muttered, staring at him in distaste. 'He keeps coming back.'

'You lock him out?' Holly was almost speechless. 'Your gamekeeper's dog?'

'He's a stray,' Angus said, crossing swiftly to check the dog for himself. 'According to Stanley, he comes and goes. I only found him a couple of days ago. I need to take him to a shelter.'

'He doesn't come and go,' Holly snapped. 'He comes. Maggie's sure he's McAllister's dog. McAllister worked for the castle for fifty years and you can't even keep his dog?'

'I don't know any McAllister.' Angus took the dog from her arms. The little dog came willingly, as he'd come when he'd found him on the back porch two days ago. 'Where have you been? I went out last night and came back to no dog.' He glanced at the flaming Holly. 'Okay, I know this looks bad but this is a big castle. He seems to know his way round.'

'He's been kicked.'

'I'll take better care of him.'

'How did he get kicked?'

'Holly, this is a stray,' he said gently. 'Yes, I've been

feeding him but that's no reason to glare at me like I'm a puppy-murderer. I'm not.'

'Someone is. He's your employee's dog.'

'I'll sort it.'

'You'd better,' she snapped. 'The dog's in the contract. Three weeks' board and keep for him as well. But after this…every single thing we've discussed I want in writing—signed, witnessed, sealed, the lot.'

'Even our engagement?'

She cast a look at Stanley, who was looking—surprise, surprise, dour. 'He knows?'

'That our engagement is temporary, yes.'

'It might be temporary but it's real,' she snapped. 'I'm wearing the ring of the Lady of the Castle and while I'm in charge no puppy will get kicked. He stays with me.'

'In the kitchens?' Stanley asked a trifle too eagerly, and she nodded.

'Yes,' she said. 'And don't even think about notifying the health department. Private residence, my rules apply. And I won't just be in the kitchen; I'll be all over the place, making sure this is a home for Christmas. So get used to it, guys.' She squared her shoulders and met Angus's gaze full-on.

'Sack me now or employ me on my terms,' she said and she lifted the dog back into her arms. 'Decide.'

What was he getting himself into? He was the employer here. Why did it feel the other way around?

And why did she look so cute?

'I'll write the contract,' he said weakly and she gave a brisk nod and headed for the door.

'Fine,' she said. 'Dinner's at seven.'

'I…thank you.'

'For you both?' She glanced disdainfully at Stanley but Angus realised her disdain extended to them both.

Stanley nodded, and she retreated—with dog—leaving him with Stanley.

'She doesn't know her place,' Stanley growled and Angus turned to him and surveyed him from head to toe.

'It seems she doesn't,' he said in that same silky voice. 'But I'm not sure of your place, either. Stanley, tell me all about the dog.'

CHAPTER FIVE

THEY LEFT FOR London late on Thursday morning. The stove had arrived and Holly wasn't leaving until she knew it was installed and working.

There were many things installed and working. All he seemed to have done for the last two days was sign cheques.

To say the castle was a work in progress seemed an understatement. What had seemed an empty, cold mausoleum two days ago was now, to put it mildly, a mess. But it was a warm mess, and it was buzzing with life. They were leaving Maggie in charge and she was in her element.

'You bring those kiddies back tomorrow night and I'll have the place looking more welcoming than my cottage,' she'd assured him, so they left, he and Holly—and dog.

'Because he's not staying behind,' Holly had declared. 'I don't trust Stanley.'

He didn't either but there wasn't much he could do about it. To sack the only person who knew anything about the running of the estate while he was trying to negotiate its sale was unthinkable. Having buyers arrive to see over the estate with the owner unsure even of the boundaries was impossible.

Distrust, therefore, had to be tolerated, even though he was sure Stanley had kicked the dog. He'd be rid of the man soon enough. And he thought that was what Holly had pretty much decided about her boss. She didn't trust him but she was tolerating him.

That should be fine, but it wasn't completely. The dog had soured her view of him and suddenly it seemed important he get that straight.

'I didn't kick him,' he said now as they headed along the road into Craigenstone and turned south, heading for London.

'Either you or Stanley did,' she said. 'But it's okay. He's our dog now. Gran and I will keep him. We're calling him Scruffy for now, because scruffy's what he is. But Gran's going to contact McAllister's nursing home to find out what his real name is.'

'You don't think it'd be a good idea to leave him with Maggie now?'

'She's busy. It'll also do this little guy good to have two days of cuddles. He hasn't had enough.'

'It'll be harder to get a hotel with a dog.'

'I guess you'll need to pay more,' she said bluntly and he winced.

'You don't like me much, do you?'

'I don't know you.' She cuddled the dog some more and wriggled down into the luxurious leather of his four-wheel drive. 'I thought you were nice when I first met you—I even kissed you. But that was when all I knew was that you were giving your half-brother and -sisters Christmas. The dog's reminded me that you don't always get what you see. I'm being careful.'

It was so much an echo of his mother's words—of what Louise had taught him—that it felt weird. Head, not heart? Her mantra, too.

'I would never kick a dog,' he said and she glanced at him and seemed to soften a little.

'Okay,' she said at last. 'Accepted.'

Silence. It felt better, he thought. *Accepted*. This was a woman who said what she meant.

Why was it so important to him that his word was 'accepted'?

'First stop clothes,' he said and she looked dubiously down at her faded, ill-fitting jeans. She hadn't had time to do any more than buy a pair of wellingtons and some knickers at the general store.

'My money hasn't come through.'

'This isn't from your money,' he told her. 'You're presenting yourself as my fiancée. You'll therefore be kitted out as such and it's on me.'

'You must really be rich,' she said, awed, and he cast her a sideways grin.

'Very rich.'

'As in having enough to let us do what we like at the castle and not even blink?'

'That's right.'

'Then why are you selling it?'

'Because I don't want it.'

'Can I ask why not?'

'It made my mother unhappy.'

'Do you want to tell me the story?' she asked, wriggling further down.

She's tired, he thought suddenly. She'd been working flat-out since he'd given her the job and she'd looked exhausted beforehand. She'd been under stress, worried sick, for how long?

Now she was warm, snuggled in his luxurious car, decisions taken out of her hands and he could almost see the strain shift from her shoulders.

He didn't do personal. He didn't tell people his life story, yet here, in this car, in this space, it seemed okay. It seemed part of the warmth. The intimacy?

'My mother was the only child of very rich parents,' he

told her. 'She was spoiled, indulged, stubborn and wilful, and she and my grandmother dreamed of her with a British title. My grandfather inherited his money from his very intelligent industrialist father, but he didn't inherit his brains. My grandmother was…socially eager to put it mildly. So the three of them came to London when my mother was nineteen. They met my father, a real live Earl, and they were beside themselves. He wanted her money, of course, so he wooed her with every ounce of charm he possessed. He married her with all pomp and ceremony and then he took her to Castle Craigie. That was when reality set in.'

'Why didn't she take one look and run?'

'Did I tell you she was stubborn? For some crazy reason, the title was still important. She fought and fought with my father, but then she became pregnant. It seemed my father softened a bit towards her then, indulging her a little. But just after I was born Mom's father was diagnosed with cancer. Mom was desperate to go back to the States, but my father turned into the despot that he was. He locked up access to her money, cut communications, hid her passport. I think he must have been a bit mad. Of course she managed it in the end, but the delay meant she didn't get home before her father died. He died at Christmas and she didn't reach her mother until New Year. She's never forgiven my father, or herself for being so stupid.'

'Has she remarried?'

'Are you joking? She does good works.'

'Oh,' Holly said in a small voice. 'Is she…is she happy?'

'I don't think she thinks she deserves happy.'

There was a moment's silence. Then, 'How long ago did this happen?' Holly demanded, sounding shocked.

He gave a rueful smile. 'You know how old I am.'

'Well…' Holly ruminated for a bit, patting the dog. '…that's dumb. Even if she'd fed your father arsenic she might be out of prison by now.'

'You can't force someone to forgive themselves,' he said, trying to sound light, but knowing he was failing. The thought that he'd returned to the castle was bringing sadness flooding back to his mother, and he was feeling guilty because of it.

He'd extended that guilt by inviting three stray kids for Christmas.

'It's ridiculous,' Holly said. 'Totally, weirdly ridiculous. Your mom should have married some other gorgeous hunk—preferably a kind one this time—and got over it.'

'What about you?' Angus asked mildly. 'You've been put through the mill. Are you on the lookout for a gorgeous hunk?'

She cast a fast, suspicious glance at him.

'No! Don't get any ideas.'

'I'm not a gorgeous hunk!'

'In a kilt you are. Whew! But your mother's talking more than thirty years. I'm talking months. I need time to get over my broken heart.'

'And bruised pride.'

'That, too.' She grimaced. 'That makes you safe.'

'Otherwise you'd be launching yourself across the gearstick?'

'Don't kid yourself—My Lord,' she said. 'I've heard your mother's story. I know a moral tale when I hear one and I'm good at learning.'

'So under no circumstances...'

'Under no circumstances. I'm your employee.'

'So you are,' he said and went back to concentrating on driving.

First stop was in Edinburgh, where the smooth-talking lady on the car's navigation gizmo directed them seamlessly to an elegant designer dress store in what Holly guessed was possibly the most discreetly expensive part of the city.

There was a parking spot straight out front. Angus c̶u̶
the engine and turned to her.

'You want to take my credit card and do this alone?'

'I'm not,' she said, suddenly breathless, 'doing this.
know I can't wear your ring with my ill-fitting jeans an
appalling footwear, but don't you guys have chain stores
Big, anonymous shops where I can dive in, buy clean jean
and run. And Angus, honestly, I prefer to do this on my ai
line insurance. Your card is only necessary until it come
through and I suspect there's not a lot of stuff in this sho
I could afford.'

'Let's go see, then, shall we?' He looked almost cheer
ful, and Holly glowered.

'You fancy playing Sugar Daddy?'

'I never have before,' he said. 'You want to indulge me?

'No!'

'Then indulge the kids,' he said, smile slipping. 'Thei
mother doesn't trust me and why would she? If I introduc
you and you look like you've bought the cheapest dres
you can find…'

'She'll think you're just like your father.'

'That's it,' he said, smiling again. 'So this needs to b
part of your role. Prove I'm not my father. Buy expensive
Holly, and let me pay.'

'Just how rich are you?' she demanded and he sighed an
sat down in his car again and retrieved his tablet compute
from under the seat. He hit the web and a minute later sh
was looking at an article on the Internet.

Angus Stuart. There was no mention of aristocracy here
There was a brief mention of his grandparents—he obvi
ously came from a lot of money, but that was a mere back
drop.

He'd topped the most prestigious business school in th
US. He'd been head-hunted by some of the biggest finan
cial institutions in the world. Under his financial aegis, he'

made small companies big, big companies enormous, and he was now running one of the biggest.

There was a guess at his net worth—once again, nothing to do with his inheritance in Scotland—that made Holly gasp.

'That's obscene,' she said, staring at the figure. 'It can't be right.'

'I think they forgot a zero,' he agreed cheerfully. 'But, even if they did and even if that worked against me, there's still plenty for the odd dress. Come on, Holly, we're already laying the ghost of one very miserly Earl. Let's lay it a bit more. You want me to help or you want to do this alone?'

'Maybe they'd throw me out if I was alone,' Holly said, staring from the screen to the exquisite window dressing of the shop and back again. 'This is real Cinderella territory, only I get a longer ball.' She took a deep breath and finally opened the car door. Instantly a doorman was beside her and Holly realised the vacant parking place was specifically designated for customers.

'Would Sir like me to valet park the car?' the man purred to Angus and Holly thought of her grandmother sending them here—Maggie was going to get an earful—and then she looked at Angus and he was grinning again.

This was a game to him. Maybe it could be a game to her?

The last few months had been horrific. She still had debts; she still didn't know their full extent. This was three weeks of time out before horrific took over again.

And this guy was gorgeous. This guy was rich and he wanted to indulge her. This guy was smiling a challenge and she met his gaze and tilted her chin and made herself smile back.

Maybe that was a mistake because smiling at this man… it made her feel…it made her feel…

Nothing. She was allowed to feel nothing, she told herself fiercely. She was acting out a fairy tale and that was all this was—acting.

So get on with it.

'Thank you,' she told the doorman with all the panache a woman in baggy faded jeans could muster as she alighted from the Earl of Craigenstone's car.

Angus sat on a weird Queen Anne chair, which was possibly the most uncomfortable chair he'd ever sat on, while Holly tried on clothes.

From the moment they'd walked into the shop, the manager and shop assistants assumed it was Angus who held the purse strings. Of course they did. He was wearing tailored chinos, a soft cashmere sweater and a butter-soft leather jacket. Admittedly the dog he was holding looked a bit scruffy, but Angus was dressed to fit in.

Holly was pretty much as he'd first seen her.

Despite his pressure on Holly, he'd had his doubts when they'd pulled up here. But though she still looked like a welfare case, she wasn't abashed.

Australians weren't as class conscious, he thought. She was gazing around appraisingly, as if she had every right to be here.

He introduced himself and explained his fiancée's loss of luggage—his future Ladyship's luggage, he amended, deciding to lay it on thick. They needed everything. The manager beamed and staff appeared from everywhere. He was provided with his chair. Scruffy was provided with a water bowl and a cushion. Holly disappeared into the changing room and came out looking…different.

She was wearing a pair of cream tailored trousers and a classic pastel-blue twinset in yarn so soft you could sense its softness ten feet away. Someone must have produced a comb and settled her unruly mop of copper curls into compliance. They'd powdered her nose and faded her freckles.

She looked elegant, she looked expensive—she looked exactly what the fiancée of the Earl of Craigenstone should look like.

Wasn't that what he wanted? Of course it was, he told himself, and nodded his approval. The manager beamed. 'I think we have one outfit then, My Lord.' He nodded to the assistant who'd helped Holly dress.

But Holly took one look in the full-length mirror and, to everyone's astonishment, she giggled.

'This just needs pearls,' she managed when she stopped chuckling.

Yes, it did, Angus conceded.

'We can arrange that,' the manager said and beckoned for the nearest minion. 'Mary-Anne, slip next door and ask Henry if we can try…'

But, 'I didn't say I wanted pearls,' Holly told him, her smile fading. 'This outfit might need pearls but I don't need this outfit.' She turned to Angus and whirled, showing the full effect of demure and expensive. 'Do you really think this is me?'

'Are we dressing you?' he asked. 'Or dressing a role?'

'I'm not an actor, Angus.'

'What's that supposed to mean?'

'I mean every time I look in the mirror I'll feel like an imposter. If you want to be engaged to me, no matter for how long, you need to be engaged to *me*. Me. Not what you or Gran or anyone else expects your future wife to look like. Even if I'm acting, I need to put my own stamp on the role.'

The manager looked confused, as well he might. Angus felt confused. Even Scruffy looked a bit confounded.

'You need clothes, Holly. These fit the bill.' These clothes were what he knew. These he understood. They were the clothes of a woman of…quality?

'So you're suggesting two or three more pairs of these trousers, linen shirts like this that I can pop the collar up—

Sloane Ranger style—a couple of demure twinsets, a string of pearls, tailored jackets, a little black dress or two, designer flats, court shoes—is that what we're after?'

'Yes,' Angus said definitely, and the manager beamed again.

'We can do that.'

'But I can't,' Holly said and gazed around the shop, and the more she gazed the more depressed she looked. 'I don't see anything red. I like red.'

'We have a sweet little jacket in a very tasteful burgundy,' the manager said. 'It'd look lovely over those trousers.'

'Red,' Holly said with the beginning of belligerence. 'Bright pillar box red. A red that clashes with my hair. Or turquoise green. Or a lovely canary yellow. And I'm sorry but I hate these trousers. I know they're lovely quality but they make me feel like I'm some sort of ageless display item.' She glanced out of the window, across the street. The mannequin in the opposite shop window was wearing a woollen dress, soft purple with diagonal hot pink stripes. 'That's more me.'

'Is that the sort of thing you usually wear?' Angus said faintly, while the manager started to look as if he'd swallowed a lemon.

'No, but it's what I'd like to wear,' she retorted. 'I've spent the last five years saving every cent to buy my restaurant. I wear jeans and T-shirts and my chef's uniform. I work nights so I don't socialise. I have two wedding-and-funeral outfits, one for summer, one for winter, and they're beige because people don't remember beige so you can change a scarf and wear them over and over again. But if you're serious about spending…' She flicked over a price tag and gasped. 'If you're serious about spending *this* sort of money, or, if you're serious about letting me be a fian-

ée, then I reckon I ought to be *my* sort of fiancée. Does
that make sense?'

'Yes,' he said cautiously. 'I think so.'

'But you like this?'

'It's suitable.'

'You haven't exactly chosen a suitable fiancée,' she reminded him.

'I haven't exactly chosen...' But then he looked at the
manager's dour face and he decided enough was enough.
He wasn't about to discuss temporary engagements in public.

'My mother will probably be coming over...for the wedding,' he told the man consolingly. 'She's American but
this style of clothing is exactly what she'd love. That's why
I brought Holly here. If I can leave my car here now, I'll
bring my mother—and her friends—in for a pre-wedding
shop as soon as they get here.'

'Certainly, My Lord,' the man said heavily, casting a
look of dislike at His Lord's intended. 'So your mother
has taste?'

'Yes, she does,' Angus said and Holly smiled her sympathy at the poor man.

'That's put me in my place properly,' she said and she
reached out and took the manager's hand and shook it with
such warmth that the man's disapproval gave way to something that could almost be a smile.

'I'm sorry, but I'm not promising to be a very suitable
wife of an Earl,' she told him. 'Right now, I'm a very un-
suitable Earl's fiancée. I'm sorry for your trouble. I'd like
to say I'll do better, but for now I think you'd better put all
your trust in Angus's mom.'

Which explained why an hour later they were back on the
London road, with Holly wearing black leggings, blue
leather boots that reached above her knees, a gorgeous over-

sized scarlet turtleneck sweater and a cute scarlet bere
that should have screamed at her copper curls but didn't
She had a suitcase of similar clothing in the boot and sh
looked like a cat who'd finally got herself her canary. Pos
sibly even two canaries.

She'd even managed to find a cute coat for Scruffy an
a brand new lead.

He drove and she hugged herself and looked…happy.

How could clothes make you happy? They didn't, h
thought. They were a necessity of life, yet Holly kept look
ing down at her boots and turning her ankles so she coul
admire them from all sides. Beaming and surreptitiousl
wiping away imaginary fingerprints.

'My boots are awesome,' she said some fifty miles dow
the road. 'Thank you.'

'My pleasure.'

'The airline cheque will never cover this.'

'The airline cheque was never meant to. This is you
uniform.'

'My uniform would have been the twinset and pearls.'

'It would have made you look more distinguished.'

'I don't think I can do distinguished.'

'You could try.'

'I will try,' she said and polished her boots some mor
and he thought she looked very, very cute.

The huge ring looked over the top on her finger. It wa
so big it looked…good.

Suitable for the wife of an Earl?

What was he thinking? He wasn't an Earl, or at leas
he was but he was already making tentative queries to se
if the title could be repealed. He had no wish for any so
of his, or grandson or great-grandson, to give himself air
because of outdated British aristocracy. The castle woul
be sold and he'd be done with it.

The thought gave his mother comfort, relief. Did it do the same for him?

Yes, because he had no wish to be the Earl of Craigenstone.

Even if this girl beside him was to be Lady Craigenstone?

Whoa. What was he thinking? Yes, Holly was cute, bouncy, sweet, but since when had he ever done cute, bouncy, sweet? He liked his women sophisticated, controlled, cool.

'You're being incredibly nice for a dragon Earl,' Holly said, and her words brought him up sharp.

'Dragon Earl?'

'That's what your title's always been. You have a reputation to live up to and so far you're failing. I haven't seen one thing not to like.' And then she blushed, a very cute blush that tinged her whole face pink. 'That is…I didn't mean…'

'It's not exactly a come-on,' he said gravely, 'to tell me I'm not the sort of Earl who bops the villagers with his blunderbuss and throws them in the pond.'

'It wasn't meant to be a come-on.'

'No,' he said gravely. 'Of course not.'

'And you have booked separate rooms for us for tonight?'

'Stanley booked us rooms.'

'Stanley,' she said and he heard disapproval. She snuggled the little dog close and he thought she was still having qualms about what they were doing. 'He doesn't like me, you know. Suppose he tells the kids that we're not really engaged?'

'He won't,' Angus said. He forbore to go further but he could have added that he'd told Stanley he knew about a certain bank account and if he didn't want criminal proceedings then it'd pay him to do what Angus wanted—and be nice to Holly and Maggie.

'Or you'll bop him with your blunderbuss?' Holly enquired.

'You'd better believe it.'

'Ooh, there's the dragon Earl speaking,' Holly said and chuckled again and Angus glanced across at her and it was all he could do not to pull the car to the side of the road, take her in his arms and kiss her.

Huh?

Huh was right. Was he out of his mind? She was his temporary Christmas chef. His pretend fiancée. She was his employee.

He suddenly, urgently, wished she wasn't.

'Do you mind if I use the sound system?' he asked and she blinked.

'Of course not. It's your car. If we try we might find Christmas carols.'

'I downloaded the latest stock market reports that came in overnight,' Angus said repressively. 'I'm concerned about them.'

'Of course you are,' Holly said, changing tack immediately. 'Me, too. And so's Scruffy. You go right ahead and listen and we'll tell you whether you're right to be concerned. I'm no expert, but Scruffy's great at independent analysis. The stock market reports. Let's at them. I imagine the whole world must be worried.'

CHAPTER SIX

ANGUS'S PLAN WAS to drop Holly at Delia's dreary little two-up, two-down and pick her up in half an hour or so. 'Because I look like my father. She'll hate me on sight. It's all my mother can do not to hate me. My presence won't help; it's you who needs to persuade her to let the kids come with us.'

But, 'She needs to trust both of us,' Holly decreed, and in her bright clothes, with her shiny blue boots, she exuded confidence and authority. 'All of us. You and me and Scruffy. We're a team.'

Which might possibly have worked better if the moment the door opened a skinny black cat hadn't taken one look at Scruffy, screeched and headed for the stairs. Holly hadn't been holding the dog tightly enough. He was down and after it, and it took five minutes pacifying to get Scruffy downstairs and the cat down from the curtain rod in the kids' bedroom.

Then they were left with a white-faced, obviously ill woman and dubious kids, the youngest of which—a girl of about ten—was clutching her cat and glaring at Scruffy with disgust.

'Melly doesn't like dogs,' she announced by way of introduction. It was not a good start, Angus thought, but better than the chaos of two minutes ago.

'He's McAllister's dog,' Holly said. She looked at Delia,

a woman in her fifties but who looked much older. 'And you're Delia. My grandmother knows you—my Gran is Maggie McIntosh from the village. She says I'm to give you a hug from her but after scaring your cat I'll only hug if you say so.'

It was exactly the right thing to say. The woman's face had been closed, defensive, but both of Holly's pieces of information obviously pierced the armour.

'McAllister,' she said. 'Where is he?'

'He's in a nursing home,' Angus said and Delia glared at him.

'That'd be right. I bet you put him there.'

'I never met the man,' Angus said and Holly subtly moved in front of him.

'Angus might look like your ex-husband,' she said softly. 'But Delia, he's not him. He's been raised in America and he's only just seen the castle for the first time.'

'McAllister wouldn't go into a nursing home unless he was forced. And why does his dog look so skinny?'

'We don't know,' Holly said. 'But we'll find out.'

The woman turned her attention to Holly. By her side, the children were silent. Waiting for a verdict? They'd pleaded to come to the castle. In the face of their mother's dislike, would they still wish to? Ben, the oldest, a skinny, pale kid who looked almost malnourished, was looking dismayed at the way this was going. Maybe he was also dismayed at how closely Angus resembled his father in person.

He'd begged to come to the castle. Was he now having doubts? Had they gone to all this trouble for nothing?

'You're Maggie McIntosh's granddaughter?' Delia was saying, incredulously.

'Yes, I am.'

'You look like her.'

'Thank you.'

The woman smiled a little, and the tension faded imperceptibly. 'Maggie was...almost my friend.'

'Maggie believes she is your friend. She says she definitely would have been if your husband had let her close. She'll be staying at the castle over Christmas as well. She's our Christmas housekeeper.'

'But how did you two ever meet?' She glared again at Angus and took a deep breath, obviously fighting against intrinsic revulsion at his appearance. 'How did you meet... the Earl...if this is the first time he's ever come to the castle?'

'I'm a chef,' Holly said promptly. 'Of international renown.' She glanced down at her bright clothes and grinned. 'I know, I don't look like it, but look at my hands.' She held them out to Delia for inspection and for the first time Angus looked, too. Really looked.

These weren't your normal society miss's hands. They were work-worn hands, hands that had spent years in washing-up water, hands that had come through a long apprenticeship of sharp knives and hot stoves. Her work was on display via her hands and Delia's face softened even further. She reached out and touched them.

'Maggie's granddaughter,' she said wonderingly. 'How...'

'He's eaten my food,' Holly said—which was true, even if it was toasted sandwiches made on the run during the last couple of crazy days. 'And of course when someone said he was the Earl of Craigenstone, how could I not introduce myself and ask if he knew my gran?' She grinned. 'Do you believe in love at first sight?'

'I don't believe in love,' Delia said sharply but she was watching Holly's hands, looking at the great Craigenstone ring, looking doubtful.

Her armour was indeed cracking. She was believing

Holly, and suddenly Angus was feeling the magnitude of what he'd asked Holly to do.

Holly was lying for him.

He hadn't asked her to. Well, maybe he had, in asking her to pretend to be engaged, and he ought to have thought that the first thing Delia would ask was how they'd met.

Holly was lying. It felt…huge.

'You're really a chef,' Delia whispered and Holly nodded and handed Scruffy over to the oldest kid.

'You're Ben?' she asked.

'Yeah,' Ben said, and Angus saw conflicting emotions. He still did want to come to the castle, he thought, but he didn't want to hurt his mum.

'And I'm Mary,' the second kid said. Mary, around thirteen, skinny as well, looking more belligerent than Ben. 'I hope you're looking after my badgers. There are so many setts on the estate. McAllister promised to look after them for me. Did you know there's a whole…'

'And I'm Polly,' the ten-year-old interrupted importantly. 'And Melly's my cat. I've only just got her and if Mac's going to chase her then you'll have to *do something*.'

'Mac?'

'I think that's Mac,' Polly said doubtfully, looking at Scruffy. 'But he used to be fatter.'

'Mac,' Mary said, frowning. Up until now, the entire focus of Scruffy had been centred on the cat, but now Mary walked forward and touched Scruffy tentatively on the nose. 'Mac!'

And suddenly the little dog was a wriggling ball of excitement, squirming in Angus's arms until he released him. Mary gathered him up and hugged him and sniffed, and then beamed.

'Mac,' she said emotionally. 'Mac!'

And the tension went out of the air, just like that. Credentials established, via the dog.

'So we have Melly, Polly and Holly for Christmas,' Holly said, grinning and watching Scruffy-Mac try to lick Mary's face. 'And Ben and Mary, plus whoever else is there. Excellent.' She turned to Delia. 'I will take care of them.'

But Delia had more questions—of course she had. 'Is he marrying you because you're a cook?' Delia asked brusquely, turning away from watching Mary and the dog. 'To save him money? Like his father saved money by marrying his housekeeper?'

'He's not saving money and I'm not a cook,' Holly declared stoutly. 'I'm a chef, and I'm *very* expensive. You have no idea how much I've already cost him and continue to cost him.' Her face softened. 'Angus says you're going into hospital tomorrow.'

'I...yes.'

'Do you have plans for tonight's dinner?'

'We're buying takeaway,' Ben said diffidently.

'But we don't like it,' Polly ventured. 'Grandma's coming so it has to be fish and chips 'cos that's all she likes and the cheap place sells soggy chips.'

'You don't like soggy chips?'

'Yuk!'

'Then let me cook dinner for you tonight,' Holly begged. 'For all of you. For all of us. Let me show you how I can cook.' She smiled at Delia—a smile Angus hadn't seen before, a smile that somehow made something twist inside him. 'Let me take care of you tonight as I swear I'll take care of the kids while they're at Castle Craigie. There's no dragon Earl now. There's just me—Holly—my cooking and Christmas, and there's Angus, who doesn't even want to be an Earl. Give us a chance, please.'

How could anyone deny an appeal like that? Angus surely couldn't, and neither could Delia. Holly had wrapped this little family round her little finger by dinner. With dinner.

There was no doubting Holly was a chef. From the get-go they all knew it. Her organisational skills left everyone breathless.

'Right. This is a feast and everyone gets to be included. You tell me your favourite foods and I'll make a list. Your grandma's not here yet but she likes fish and chips? She can't really like soggy chips, though. Anything else? Do you think she might prefer lobster?'

'You can't afford...' Delia started but Angus knew when it was time to step in, so step in he did.

'Cost is no problem,' he said grandly and Delia cast him a surprised look and Holly cast him a grateful look, and it was the grateful look that did that twisting again.

'Cream puffs,' Polly ventured.

'Tacos,' Ben said, looking defiantly at his mother.

'They don't go with fish and chips,' Delia managed but Holly waved objections aside.

'Of course they do. We'll just throw in another course. Delia, what would you like?'

'Chicken soup,' she said breathlessly, still disbelieving. 'I've been wanting home-made chicken soup since they told me I had to have the operation and if you made some... I could put some in the freezer for when I get home.'

'This is looking like a cool menu,' Holly said. 'Mary, what about you?'

'Chocolate pudding,' Mary breathed. 'The kind where the chocolate oozes out. I saw it on telly. Can you make that?'

'Only if we're fast,' Holly said. 'Ben, Angus...'

'Yes?' Angus said, bemused.

'You're on shopping duty. Make a list. Ready?'

'Ready,' Angus managed.

'Right. Write. Go!'

'He really is crazy about you.'

Holly was preparing the mix for the chocolate puddings.

Mary and Polly were spooning cream puff mixture onto trays. Delia was sitting beside Holly at the table. She was peeling potatoes—and watching Holly.

'No Earl that I know ever fell in love with his bride,' she said matter of factly. 'There's always a reason. Angus's father married his mother for money and prestige, and then me for convenience. But you… He can't keep his eyes off you.'

'Then I guess he's marrying me because I wear scarlet sweaters,' she retorted. 'Speaking of which, it's a bit hot. Do you have an apron?'

But Delia was not to be deflected. 'I didn't think Earls could fall in love.'

'My gran says the acorn never falls far from the tree, too,' Holly said. 'But I don't think that's true. I think Angus is a truly nice person.'

'And rich,' Delia said, and Holly chuckled and looked down at the ring.

'And rich. Obscenely rich.'

'I never got a ring,' Delia said and looked at her bare hand.

'Never?'

'Never.'

'Did you divorce?'

'No,' she said. 'It would have cost money.'

'Then you're still married to him,' Holly said slowly.

'He's dead.'

'But you're his widow.' She stared down at the ring and then stared at Delia's arthritic hands. Something twisted. She'd worn a ring for two years and it had meant nothing. This woman had never worn a ring, and something deep inside her told her it could have meant everything.

Behind her, Angus and Ben had arrived back with their load of groceries. How much had they heard? All of it? But

Angus was staying silent. She glanced back at her pretend fiancé and his face was impassive.

He'd given this ring to her. It was her wage for pretending to be the Craigenstone bride, and if it was her wage...

She could do whatever she wanted with it.

And what had he said? *'If it means these kids can have a good Christmas then it'll have gone to a good home.'* Right. If he'd said it, he must mean it. Put your money where your mouth is, Lord Craigenstone, she thought, and gave a fast, determined nod, as if confirming the decision she'd come to. The glance she gave Angus was almost defiant—*stop me if you will, but I know this is right.* She wiped her hands on the dish cloth, and then, before she could have second thoughts—*how much was this ring worth?*—she hauled the ring off her finger and handed it over.

'This should be yours,' she said. 'It is yours. Put it on now.'

'Are you...' Delia stared, open-mouthed. Everyone was staring at her open-mouthed, Angus included. 'Are you crazy? You can't. It's yours.'

'It's mine to give,' Holly retorted. 'It's the Craigenstone Bridal ring and, as far as I can see, you're still the Craigenstone bride. From where I'm looking, you haven't had many of the perks of the job. You should keep this one. Angus,' she said, 'I've restored the Craigenstone ring to its rightful owner. You might need to square it with your mother.'

'I can't,' Delia breathed as Angus stared at her as if she'd lost her mind.

'But I'm sure it's the right thing to do,' Holly went on. 'Isn't it, Angus?' She tilted her chin again and met his gaze. Maybe she had no right to make such a gesture, but somehow, seeing Delia, thinking about that great gloomy castle, knowing even a little about what this woman had been through, the thought of wearing this ring herself was preposterous.

'Oh, Mum, it's gorgeous,' Mary breathed.

'Is it really yours?' Ben demanded, and they were all looking at Delia, at a woman worn down by poverty and hard work, who should have been gazing at a ring and seeing how much it was worth in terms of feeding her family but instead was looking at the ring as if it were a gift without price.

'No one treated me like a Craigenstone bride,' she whispered. But then she gazed up at Angus. 'Your father gave this to your mother,' she said, and echoed Holly's thoughts. 'I have no right…'

Uh-oh, Holly thought. Uh-oh, uh-oh, uh-oh. Was she crazy to have made such a gesture? Giving away something that held such history?

Was she out of her mind?

But Angus had said it was hers, and he'd said it in front of witnesses. And now the corners of Angus's mouth were curving into a smile.

'Nice one, bride,' he said and grinned and put his load down on the table. Then he took Delia's twisted, work-worn hands in both of his and held them.

'You have every right,' he said gently. 'I didn't see it until now, but of course Holly's right. You're my father's widow. He treated you abominably. You're ill. We're giving your kids a Christmas to remember, so why not give you one, too? Take this ring, Delia, instead of the equivalent ring my father should have given you years ago.'

'But Holly…' The woman was torn. She looked from Holly to Angus and back again, distracted and distressed. 'You gave it to Holly.'

'It's the Craigenstone ring,' Angus said. 'My mother should have returned it to Craigenstone after the divorce but…'

'But I know why she didn't,' Delia retorted and the faintest of smiles started behind her eyes. 'Oh, My Lord…'

'Angus,' he said sharply. 'You, of all people, shouldn't be using titles. Unless you want me to refer to you as the Dowager Lady Craigenstone.'

'Is that what you are?' Ben and Mary breathed as one.

'Maybe,' Delia said diffidently, and fiddled with the ring. With longing. 'I was a fool to ever think it'd mean anything but I guess I'm still a fool. With this ring...' She took a deep breath, twisted the ring so it settled in its rightful place and then looked at Holly. 'Somehow, with this ring I feel like there was some value in our marriage. That it wasn't a complete sham—that I wasn't a total fool. I know that doesn't make sense, but there it is. Thank you,' she said. 'But you...now you don't have an engagement ring.'

'Then I'll need a replacement,' Holly said happily, and picked up the lid of an empty sauce bottle. 'This'll do. Ben, your next job is to punch a hole in this and round off the edges. Then let Angus check it and he can slip it formally back on my finger. Job's done. Now, doesn't everyone have more jobs to do? Let's get cooking!'

Any lingering doubts as to Holly's cooking ability were laid to rest. She served tiny tacos with guacamole as a starter, then a chicken soup to die for, followed by a seafood banquet which had everyone in the family groaning because there was too much food. But they made a recovery. The irresistible; individual puddings oozed molten chocolate when a spoon broke the crust, with lashings of cream on top. Finally Holly produced coffee and tea and tiny cream puffs that made everyone think they could eat one more thing. Or two. Or even three.

Even Delia's grumpy mother was smiling—smiling too at the ring her daughter was wearing.

'He never gave her anything. Not a thing. And yet here you are...'

'Here we shouldn't be,' Angus said, glancing at his watch. 'You're going into hospital in the morning, Delia.'

'At eight. I'm not allowed to eat after midnight,' Delia said and smiled. 'I think I might manage.'

'Do you have anyone to take you?'

'We'll get a taxi,' Delia's mum said.

'I'll organise a driver,' Angus told her. He hesitated. 'And are you happy for me to take the kids back to the castle?'

'I wasn't,' Delia said. 'But I am now.'

'I'll make sure they phone you every night,' Angus promised. 'And Holly and I will be in touch with the hospital all the time as well.' Then he hesitated. 'Holly…?'

And Holly knew what he was asking. She read it on his face, and she knew it was the right thing. Ben had said Delia would be in hospital for three days and would then be spending her convalescence with her mother. It'd be great if she wasn't worried about her kids. The kids really wanted to come to the castle, but it meant a pretty bleak Christmas for Delia and her mother.

'Of course,' Holly said softly, and Angus gave her a smile that almost made her gasp. But before she could react, he'd turned back to Delia.

'If you're well enough, could I send a car to collect you and your mum for Christmas, too?' he asked. 'We could all care for you.'

'Care,' Delia gasped. 'At Craigenstone?'

'I know, the two words don't seem to go together,' Angus said. 'But Holly's made a difference.'

'She surely has,' Delia breathed. 'Oh, My Lord…'

'Angus,' he said sharply.

'Oh, Angus then,' she breathed. 'Yes, please. And Holly… You're so lucky to have her.'

He was lucky to have her? A woman who gave away a ring that was worth a fortune? Did she know how much it was worth? Could she have guessed?

Did she care?

To say he was blown away would be an understatement. He'd handed her the ring on impulse. It had been a crazy, generous gesture guaranteed to get her cooperation over Christmas. Any woman he'd ever known would have been stunned by such a gift. That Holly, who he knew was in financial extremis, could calmly give it away…

He wasn't angry. How could he be angry—the ring had been hers to give—but to say he was overwhelmed by the gesture was still putting it mildly.

He'd never known such a woman.

They were quiet in the car on the way to the hotel. In truth, Holly didn't know what to say, where to start. She'd given away the Craigenstone ring.

What was it worth? She couldn't begin to imagine.

'Can you…I don't know…take it out of my wages?' she said at last, feeling swamped. What had possessed her to do such a thing? It hadn't been hers to give. She thought of the debt she already had in her name and she thought, wow, this would see her sink without trace. Cooking in outback mining camps was the best way to make money. That was where she'd be, she guessed, for the next hundred years.

'Do you have any idea of what it's worth?' he asked quite casually, and then, as she said nothing—there seemed nothing to say—he told her.

'We had it insured before I brought it with me,' he said. 'That's base price of the components. At auction it'd go for more.'

She couldn't speak. There were no words.

'My mother will have kittens,' he said.

Silence. More silence as he negotiated the heavy London traffic.

What was she supposed to say?

'Um…you should never have given it to me,' she said and he glanced across at her, his expression unreadable.

'I didn't think you'd value it so little.'

'That I gave it away? It was precisely because I valued it so little. You should never have used it as a bribe. I would have worked for you anyway.'

'Really?'

'You pay pretty good wages,' she managed. 'Without diamonds.' She fell silent again, thinking of the ring, thinking of the number of zeroes, thinking this whole situation was absurd. She hugged Scruffy—or Mac?—because he grounded her. He was her one real thing in this absurd situation.

'Why did you bring it to Scotland?' she asked at last.

'My mother wanted it included in the sale and paid back to the estate. She took it because she knew it'd infuriate my father. She never wanted to make money from it.'

'Well, you certainly won't make money from it now. I… that was dumb. But it was your own fault,' she said, fighting for a bit of spirit. 'Fancy you giving it to me. What on earth will your mother think?' Her voice faltered a little. 'Will…will you need to tell her?'

'Of course.' He thought about it for a bit and then added: 'Maybe she'll make no complaint. She liked Delia.'

'She liked…'

'Delia was a housemaid during my mother's time. I believe they were friends when my mother needed a friend. The decisions Delia made after my mother left…well, right or wrong, they're past and she's more than paying for them. As for the ring… It paid for itself tonight,' he said softly. 'Good one, Holly. How did you guess how much she needed it?'

'You agree?' she asked, stunned.

'Of course I do. Here I was, waving it round as a bribe and all the time it had a true home waiting. It just took a Holly to find it. Do you know what, Holly McIntosh? You're amazing.'

'I am not,' she said, astounded.

'Don't argue with your boss,' he said and turned to look at her.

They'd stopped at traffic lights, which was just as well, Holly thought numbly because somehow she met that look. And what followed was one long frisson of something so deep, so powerful, she had no hope of explaining it.

For the look went on and on, as if neither could figure how to break the moment. Finally, tentatively, he reached across and tugged her forward. She found herself leaning into him, closer, closer…

A car honked behind them, and then another. More. A cacophony, reminding them where they were and that the lights were green and they needed to move on.

Angus gave a rueful laugh and tugged away.

'Later,' he said and Holly flinched as reality hit. She backed into her seat and tried to make her racing heart settle. What had just happened? What was she doing? Was she nuts?

'No!'

'No?'

'I'm a pretend fiancée,' she retorted. She held up her weird sauce-bottle ring. 'I'm not a real one. Get over it.'

'We'll fix that in the morning,' he said, glancing at the ring with a smile.

'Oh, for heaven's sake, I'm over rings. This one's fine. This engagement's for the sake of the children and they helped make this one.'

'You don't want another diamond?'

'This is the third engagement ring I've had,' she reminded him. 'And the last!'

'For ever?'

'You'd better believe it.'

'Holly…'

'No,' she said severely. 'No kissing. No touching. I'm wearing a sauce-bottle ring to remind me that this engagement is a farce. It is a farce, My Lord, and you'd better believe it.'

CHAPTER SEVEN

THE HOTEL WAS over-the-top, breathtakingly gorgeous. Holly sat in the front of Angus's car and stared in awe.

'I've heard of this place,' she breathed. 'I never dreamed…'

'It's as excellent as its name suggests,' Angus said. 'I stay here every time I come to London.'

'Of course you do,' Holly said and then looked doubtfully down at the dog. 'Will they let Scruffy in?'

'Stanley organised it,' he said. 'There won't be a problem.'

There wasn't a problem. Or not much of a problem.

'We've put you in the top floor suite,' the manager told them; he seemed to have sidled from nowhere at their approach to the reception desk, smoothly replacing the girl on duty. 'It has access to our rooftop garden for the wee dog.' He glanced at the wee dog and his face stilled—clearly there were wee dogs and *wee dogs* and this one didn't quite fit his idea of the sort that would fit this establishment.

'Excellent,' Angus said. 'Two bedrooms?'

'One.' The manager frowned. 'Your man did say accommodation for you and your…partner.' He glanced down at Holly's finger and his face froze still more.

'But His Lordship doesn't like sharing with my dog,' Holly said. 'He…he snores. And he smells. He can't help it, but there it is.'

The man gazed at Angus and his expression took a slight turn towards sympathy. It was clear he was wondering how His Lordship had become lumbered with such a crazy duo as Holly and Scruffy. And then he turned apologetic, truly regretful at having to lumber him still more.

'I am sorry, sir,' he said. 'But we don't have room to manoeuvre. Being the last shopping week before Christmas we're fully booked. You have a one-bedroom suite on the top floor. There is a settee. If you like, we can make the settee up into a bed, but…'

'Yes, please,' Holly said and then at the man's look, she tilted her chin. 'I'm an old-fashioned bride,' she said.

'As you wish,' the man said. 'We'll make it up for you, My Lord.'

My Lord. Angus had used this hotel before, but only as Angus Stuart. Stanley had used his title, then. Angus felt his mouth tighten. He'd given orders: make the booking, a suite with two bedrooms, dog-friendly and don't use my title.

Stanley did what he wanted. Stanley had been doing what he wanted for years, he thought. This room was probably his payback for the blast he'd given him for the dog. Still, he was stuck with the man until the castle sold. He was stuck with his dishonesty and his prejudices and his innate dislike of Holly.

But not here he wasn't. Here he had a one-bedroom suite with the woman who was wearing his engagement ring, albeit a very odd engagement ring.

Holly. She looked wonderful. She was wonderful. She was a colourful, warm, vibrant woman who'd just charmed his siblings and his suspicious stepmother.

She was also instinctively retreating.

'Don't even think it,' she muttered as they headed for the lifts.

'What?' He tried to sound innocent but he knew he'd

failed. She glanced at him as if she could read him in neon letters and it was all he could do not to flinch.

'You know very well, so don't even think about thinking about it,' she retorted. 'One errant thought from you and I'm ringing Gran.'

'A worse fate could befall no man.'

'Are you sure you didn't set this up as a one-bedroom?'

'If I'd had nefarious plans I wouldn't have ordered a suite,' he retorted. 'No settee. Though, come to think of it, I always order a suite.'

'Of course you do.'

'There's nothing wrong with being rich.'

'No?' She swivelled to stare at him. 'I wouldn't know.'

'And it's not my fault you're poor.'

She bit her lip at that. They'd reached the bank of lifts. She stood, hugging Scruffy, waiting for the next lift to arrive. Biting her lip some more.

'No,' she said at last. 'It might even be fun to be rich sometimes.'

'Yet you gave the ring away.' He reached out and touched Scruffy, rubbing the little dog behind his ears. He really wanted to reach out and touch Holly but he knew, he just knew, that there was no joy down that road. 'You could have bought a small restaurant with that ring.'

'Wow,' she said, and then the lift arrived and they entered and she leaned against the back and hugged Scruffy and stared straight in front of her.

'Wow,' she said again, more slowly. And then, 'I'm glad I gave it to her, then. Delia should have it.'

'She should,' he agreed gravely. 'But it was a very generous gesture.'

'It should have been made by you,' she said. 'Years ago.'

'I didn't think about it. I didn't know Delia and I didn't understand the situation. But if my mother had given it to Delia years ago, my father would have taken it back.'

'I guess.'

'So you've righted a wrong,' he said. 'Well done, you. But you've done yourself out of a restaurant. Maybe I could help…'

'If you're about to say: let's not use the settee and I'll buy you a restaurant, Scruffy and I are hightailing it out of here right now.'

'Hey,' he said. 'I know you're not that sort of girl.'

'Are you that sort of…Lord?'

'Buying myself village maidens? I don't think I've had enough training,' he retorted and grinned. She looked so cute and so defensive and so…Holly.

But then the lift stopped. The doors swung open and they were in their suite and Holly fell silent. Very silent.

It might only be a one-bedroom suite, but what a suite! Angus had stayed here before, but not like this. Stanley had obviously laid on the title, and maybe also stressed that money was no object, for it seemed they were in the penthouse. The living room was vast. The dining table could seat a dozen, and the windows circling them showed a three-sixty view all over London.

'Oh, my…' Holly popped Scruffy on the floor and did a slow tour, taking everything in. Everything.

For some reason, Angus stayed by the door, watching the girl, watching her reaction.

He was accustomed to luxury—he'd never needed to stay in anything less than a five-star hotel in his life—but Holly…

'This is fantasy stuff,' she breathed. She'd completed her tour and came back to him. 'You have a dressing room that's bigger than my apartment back in Sydney. You have a spa the size of a small swimming pool.'

'We,' he said faintly.

'You,' she snapped. 'Scruffy—and yeah, I know, I should call him Mac but he still feels like Scruffy and he's my security—Scruffy and I are going to haul one of these settees into a corner. Which one makes up into a bed, do you think? We'll then pretend we're peasants. Which, in fact, we are. Angus, your bed…it could take a dozen village maidens.' She grinned suddenly, awe giving way to humour. 'You can have 'em if you like,' she said generously. 'I'll cook 'em breakfast. There's a full kitchen!'

'But I forgot to pack them,' he said mournfully. 'My village maidens.' He gestured to his small valise. 'Socks and jocks is all.'

'And you wouldn't even let the staff carry those up for you,' she said reprovingly. 'Have you no sense of dignity?' She gazed round again and smiled back at him. 'Very nice. Scruffy and I approve. Okay, we're set. You have a bedroom bigger than a football field. Off you go and wallow, village maidens or not, and let Scruffy and I go to sleep.'

'Your bed's not made up yet.'

'The manager said it will be. I'll just…I don't know… I'll try and decide which window to look out of while I wait.'

'You don't want a spa?'

'No!'

'Scared?'

'Yes,' she said repressively. 'And so's Scruffy.'

'There's no need to be,' he said and then he hesitated.

It was not much after nine. He knew she had a gorgeous dress—two gorgeous dresses—in her baggage. He'd watched as she'd chosen them. He could suggest they go downstairs, have a drink, listen to the band, maybe dance…

He knew instinctively she'd refuse.

'Scruffy could do with a walk,' he said, but in answer she unflicked the lock to the nearest door and stepped outside. Here was a rooftop garden, complete with miniature lawn!

'Problem solved.'

'I didn't mean a bathroom walk,' he retorted. 'I meant

a proper walk. Besides, it's freezing out there. Anything he managed would freeze mid-stream. I suggest we put on our big coats and go down to street level. The buildings block the wind. London's full of Christmas. We could do the tourist rubber-necking thing—walk round with our mouths open.'

'I could,' she said and she suddenly sounded a trifle wistful. 'I've never been to London.'

'Then it's compulsory,' he said. 'And now you even have some decent shoes. Coat. Scarf. Hat. Come.'

She hesitated. She really didn't trust him, he thought, and maybe he didn't blame her. He wouldn't trust a lord with his name, and Holly had been hurt before.

He wanted to make that hurt better.

The thought was so sudden and so powerful that it took him by surprise. He watched her hesitation and he thought…

He didn't know what he thought. Only that he was feeling something he'd never felt before. Something he'd never known he could feel.

The urge to reach out and touch her was so huge it was almost overwhelming, yet somehow he held himself back.

Head or heart? Since Louise, head was his mantra, yet here he was, forgetting.

What was he thinking? It was way too soon, too sudden, too inappropriate.

As stupid as falling for Louise?

And thankfully Holly was no longer looking at him. The door had swung open and the bellboy was there with her luggage—courtesy of their shopping, her bags contained a whole lot more than his.

'I bought a cashmere scarf,' she said as the bellboy left, pouncing on it and hauling it from a shopping bag. Suddenly she sounded happy again. This was how Holly was meant to sound, he thought. Happy and laughing and carefree. 'Or, rather, you bought it for me,' she corrected herself. 'I love it. Red and purple and bright, bright yellow. This is just the night to christen it. In honour of your scarf, Lord Angus, let's go for a walk.'

The night was indeed cold. Scruffy wore his brand new tartan coat and his brand new lead. There'd been no snow here, or rain, so the pavements weren't icy. Scruffy was certainly not objecting. He was a gamekeeper's dog, he'd been cooped up all day and he practically pranced along before them.

They weren't the only ones who were out. This was one of London's most popular tourist precincts. Many of the restaurants and shops along the riverfront were still open and there were lots like them, rubber-neckers, tourists taking in the Christmas feel of this great city.

'It's awesome,' Holly whispered as she recognised her first landmark. A drunken party of revellers lurched towards them. Angus steered Holly aside and held her until they passed. They started walking again, but somehow Holly's gloved hand stayed in his. He kept holding and she didn't pull away.

Surely it was an unconscious gesture for both of them, meant to keep them close in the crowds. She'd be a bit nervous, in unfamiliar territory. With the crowds around them, with Christmas lights, buskers, flashing window displays, he'd moved into protective mode and she'd simply accepted what surely must have come naturally.

Surely no big deal, he thought, but the strange feeling around his heart was growing stranger. This was uncharted territory.

This was a gesture of trust…

'Say hello to the lion,' Angus said and Holly stared at an incongruous lion standing sentry to Westminster Bridge. This was a magnificent lion, but…

'Don't look,' Angus told Scruffy. 'You needn't think this is a London fashion. Victorian times called for Victorian measures. This is the Coade Lion and every man in London feels the tragedy that Victorian prudishness has made him sing falsetto.'

Holly choked with laughter and he felt her relax still more. And the feeling around his heart grew…stranger.

They were walking across the bridge now and Holly was silent, taking in the sights and sounds of night-time London. A double-decker bus swept by, one of the many carrying tourists around London. Maybe she'd like a ride.

But then he thought…Christmas. The first time he'd ever come to London he'd walked in on evensong at Westminster Abbey and been blown away by its history and its beauty.

He glanced at his watch. Eleven. There'd be no chance of getting into the Abbey at this hour.

But still he veered towards it because the Abbey itself was enough to take a man's breath away without even going in. As they got closer, as he steered woman and dog towards the entrance, he heard music wafting outwards. It was music to make a man hesitate.

He glanced along the side wall and saw a uniformed security guard.

'Any chance of going in?' he asked and the man shook his head.

'Choir practice, mate,' he said amiably. 'Not open to the public. Unless you're associated with the choir.'

'I'm about to make a donation to the choir,' Angus said. 'A sizeable one. You might mention it to the choir master if you would. And, of course, a tip to you because of Christmas.'

Something slipped between the two men's hands. The security guard glanced down and his eyes widened.

'If you say no, then no it is, but I hope you won't,' Angus

continued. 'After all, it's Christmas, the time of giving. I just need you to give me the opportunity to be generous.'

Which explained why, two minutes later, Holly was perched in an ancient pew, leaning against a vast stone pillar in the place where generations of Kings and Queens had been married and buried, where Londoners had worshipped for hundreds of years, and where now a choir of some of what must surely be the finest voices in England were practising Christmas hymns she'd learned as a child. The hymns were so familiar to her that suddenly, here, now, it was Christmas, it was Westminster Abbey and nothing else mattered in the world.

The choir master had beamed them a beatific smile as they'd entered—*what had Angus written on that cheque?*—but now, apart from the choristers, they were alone.

Holly had been running on adrenalin ever since she'd discovered Geoff's betrayal. She'd been trying to figure how to settle debts, to pay overdue wages—to survive in the mess her creep of a fiancé had left her. She'd been gutted by Geoff's dishonesty. Her parents' death had taught her not to trust the world, but she'd trusted again and Geoff had thrown that trust in her face.

Then, when she'd arrived in Craigenstone, she'd discovered her grandmother facing eviction and the sense of desolation and loss had just got worse.

She'd spent the last days working like a Trojan. Today had been just as crazy, but now the world seemed to have stopped to take a breath.

She was seated in a pew whose background made her tremble. Who else had sat here? Angus was right beside her—*right beside her*—in his gorgeous cashmere coat with the slightly suspicious bulge under his arm. That was why he was sitting so close, she told herself. He needed to disguise the bulge that was Scruffy. But the man who'd bustled forth when they'd first entered had been silenced by whatever Angus had put in his hand, the choir master was happy with the cheque Angus has produced, and no one was asking questions.

And the music was all around her, piercing places she'd thought were thoroughly armoured. The choir was singing a layered, magnificent version of *Silent Night*. Her mother had sung this carol to her, and she wouldn't mind betting Maggie had sung it to her father. *Silent Night* was a song for the whole world, and yet here, in this place, it was her song, intensely personal—it was as if they were singing it just for her.

Or maybe they were singing for Angus as well, for his hand was still holding hers. Apart from a little cheque writing, even as they'd smuggled the little dog in, even as he'd held him close under his coat, he hadn't relinquished his grip and she hadn't tugged away.

Why not?

She didn't want to pull away. It was as simple as that. She shivered, but it wasn't from cold or from fear.

It was a shiver of pure sensation. Here in this night the ghosts were out: Christmas Past and Christmas Present.

It was a shiver caused by their linked hands, and by something deeper, something she didn't understand.

Trust? Could she learn to trust yet again?

What sort of question was that? A crazy question, that was what.

But, lack of trust aside, when Angus dropped their linked hands and put his arm around her waist she didn't object. She couldn't object to anything on this night. Magic was all around them, and for this one amazing time she could forget debts, landlords, thieving fiancés, distrust, a world where fate was precarious, and she could just *be*. She was a woman side by side with a man who took her breath away, in one of the most beautiful places in the world.

They listened and listened and the feeling between them seemed to grow and grow. Within the silence and the music something was forming that she'd never felt before, that she had no hope of understanding. She didn't trust it but she didn't care because, right now, trust wasn't important.

She felt as if she were floating, weirdly, out of her body but wonderfully, wonderfully, wonderfully.

And then the choir started on the *Hallelujah Chorus*. This was hardly a rehearsal. This was the triumph of the night. The voices soared and the Abbey seemed almost to melt with beauty and power and, before she could soar through the great vaulted ceiling, which was what she felt she was about to do, she made one last desperate attempt to pull herself together.

'We need to leave,' she whispered, not caring if he could hear her desperation. 'One minute more and I'll be on my feet singing with them.' Or something more drastic. Something she had no idea about.

'This I have to see.'

'This you don't have to see,' she whispered fiercely, forcing herself to sound matter-of-fact. As if this was no special night. No special place. No special man. 'I have the singing voice of a tomcat. It's scary. Angus, let's go.'

'Really?'

'The way I'm feeling, I'm about to melt in sheer awe,' she whispered back. 'I'll ooze down into these flagstones and merge into all these graves, which wouldn't be fitting. This is the place for Kings and Queens and the likes of Charles Darwin. I'm just an Aussie cook.'

'Chef,' he said and she gave a wavering smile but she did manage to pull away, to head out through the vestry—trying not to run, she felt so panicked—leaving Angus to follow if he would.

He did. The security guard nodded to both of them, beaming a goodnight. *How much had Angus given to him?*

Angus fell into place by her side, popped Scruffy back down on the pavement and made to take her hand again.

But this time she kept her hand firmly to herself. What had she been thinking? Something had happened in there. Her world had shifted, and she was trying desperately to find even ground again. To make her head work and make sense.

She'd been thinking she could wipe the slate and start again.

Back there, seduced by the place, the music—and the sensation of this man so close to her—she'd been thinking it felt right to be held by the Lord of Castle Craigie. Was she mad?

She'd been thinking the world could right itself—that somehow she could learn to trust. She knew she couldn't, but one more moment of listening to those voices in that place with this man holding her and she wouldn't have been responsible for what happened. A girl had to be sensible.

'Head, not heart,' Angus said and she flashed him a suspicious glance from all of three feet away.

'What?' The comment had come from left field and she veered from determined to confused.

'It's what I've been telling myself for years,' he told her. 'Don't let sentiment hold sway.'

She stopped and stared. It was so much what she had been feeling…so much what she had been telling herself…

'So you were feeling it back there, too.'

'I'm still feeling it,' he said. 'Sensible or not.' He offered his hand again but she looked at it as if it might be a scorpion.

'You're saying head, not heart, but you're also giving in. Ignoring your own advice?'

'I'm suggesting we could take a risk,' he said, and the way he said it…it was as if he was making an effort to keep his voice light. 'The way I'm feeling…maybe the risk is worth it.'

The way I'm feeling… There was enough in that to take a girl's breath away, but a girl had to keep breathing—and had to keep thinking sense.

'I'm over risks,' she managed. 'You gamble when you have enough to lose without catastrophe. I don't have that luxury. I've gambled before, and I've lost my life savings and more besides. If you think I'm going down that road again…'

'Ah, but we're not talking about gambling,' he said, humour resurfacing. 'Unless I'm mistaken, you don't have any life savings to lose. You just gave away your ring, so how can you gamble without a stake? There's nothing being put on the table here except the way we're both feeling.' He hesitated. 'You are feeling it, aren't you?'

'It was the music.'

'Just the music?'

'Okay, I don't know,' she said honestly, still three feet from him. 'But it's scary to think that it can be anything else.'

'Scary for me, too,' he said. 'I've never fallen for a girl in blue boots before.'

'You can't fall,' she said a little bit desperately. 'I'm your employee and things have changed since peasants followed their lords. Yours is a position of power, and current politics says propositioning me is against the rules.'

'So if I wasn't Lord of Castle Craigie…'

'You are.'

'But if I wasn't,' he said stubbornly, 'you might consider…I don't know…hand-holding a bit longer?'

'See, there's the problem,' she said, deciding to be honest. They were back on Westminster Bridge. The night was still now, and icy-cold. There were still sightseers veering around them but suddenly they faded—the noise, the

Christmas glitz, night-time tourist London. There was simply a man and a woman cocooned by some sort of connection she didn't understand—a connection that isolated them, linked them, held.

She shivered, a racking shiver that had nothing to do with the cold, and he reached out instinctively and touched her face.

She didn't flinch.

'I won't hurt you,' he said gently. 'I'm not Geoff.'

'No,' she said, linked to his gaze. Things were shifting, changing and she felt herself shudder again. She'd been too badly hurt. Too badly betrayed. Her head was screaming at her to step away, that her heart couldn't be trusted, but every instinct was to move forward. To let this man hold her.

'It's too soon,' she managed feebly and he nodded but, instead of withdrawing, he took her hand in his again.

'Of course it is,' he said, gravity fading. 'Much too soon for commitment. If we want to take this further we need a couple of years of careful consideration, lawyers going through the ramifications in triplicate, lots and lots of careful, nit-picking investigation. So let's not.'

'You're holding my hand.'

'Friends can hold hands,' he said. 'They can hold hands while interim ramifications are sorted. Call this preliminary negotiations.'

'O…Okay,' she said cautiously.

'This is friendship by the book,' he said. 'Head, not heart. I have fallen before,' he said gently. 'It ended in disaster. You're not the only one with a broken engagement to your name, but mine ended in death as well as betrayal. So it's hand-holding only.'

'Fine by me,' she said. But was it? She was feeling the warmth of the link between them, the strength—the wonder? But behind the warmth of the link was the shock of his words. She heard the pain behind them, the lesson learned. She didn't need to ask more.

'In a day or two I might stroke your hair,' he was saying lightly, as if to get this back on a normal footing. Slight flirtation, nothing more. 'Just lightly and the agreement is that I provide a comb to fix it afterwards. And I'll let you adjust my tie on Christmas Day.'

'Gee…'

'I know,' he said nobly. 'It sounds too familiar for words but I think we can handle it. It's one small step at a time for the likes of us. Now, let's go home.'

'Back to the hotel,' she said, flustered, because suddenly it seemed important to differentiate between 'home'—personal—and 'hotel'—part of impersonal negotiations within a relationship she didn't understand in the least.

'Hotel,' he agreed cheerfully and swung her arm with their linked hands. 'You're right. Home is something other people do together. Not us.'

CHAPTER EIGHT

ONLY OF COURSE, even though it sounded impersonal, it wasn't. They should have booked two rooms on different sides of the hotel. They were far too close, and Angus was far too large and male and gorgeous, and Holly was warm and full of the sounds of the choir and the wonders of the night and the way Angus had organised things and just…Angus.

The hotel provided hot Christmas punch—the waiter arrived with it steaming, moments after they returned. Without being asked, he flicked on the gas-flamed fire and departed. Fake logs crackled in the fake hearth, and there was some sort of expensive fragrance of pine wafting through the warmth.

It was all too much. Holly was fighting desperately to keep up defences she was starting to doubt she even wanted.

This night… This man…. This moment…

Angus poured the punch and it would have been surly to refuse, but the moment the warmth hit her stomach she knew she was in trouble.

The glow started from the inside out. Her clothes were too hot for this room. She should strip off her sweater but she wasn't brave enough. She was hardly brave enough to move.

Scruffy had collapsed in a tired heap in the luxurious dog basket the hotel had provided. She needed him, she thought, as the punch warmed places she hadn't known had been cold. She needed to hug him for defence. She needed…any defence she could find.

She was looking out of the great plate glass windows at night-time London sprawling below, and Angus was behind her, watching the sights as well, or maybe watching her; she didn't know and she wasn't about to turn and find out.

'Holly,' he said and the sound of his voice did something to her. Something deep and magical and irresistible.

Head before heart? Whatever their backgrounds, it wasn't working. He was too gorgeous. He was too male. He was too…here.

'Mmm…mmm?'

'Legal considerations seem to be speeding up faster than expected,' he said softly, and she did turn then and look at him and what she saw…

He was as unsure as she was, she thought. Earl of Craigenstone? No. He was just…Angus. Looking at her gravely. Asking a question with his eyes.

Could she trust?

And more. Something in his expression told her that this was as big a leap for him as it was for her.

Could *he* trust? Could *he* step forward?

Nonsense, she told herself, head trying desperately to get a word in over heart. He's just a guy with a woman in his apartment trying to do what guys the world over would do in this situation.

But… His words came back. *Mine ended in death*… This man was more wounded than she was. This man.

Angus.

'Angus, I'm scared,' she whispered before she could help herself. 'The way I'm feeling…I've just been sky-rocketed from a relationship that almost ruined me—a relationship where I trusted far more than I should. I don't think… I can't…'

'You can't kiss me?'

'I want to kiss you,' she said, and her voice held all the longing in the world. 'But you're way out of my league. You're a billionaire American and Lord of Castle Craigie to boot. It scares me.'

'I can understand that.' He took her glass from her hand and laid it on a side table. 'Holly, I'm as unsure as you are. I don't fall for bright chefs in blue boots either, and yes, the way I'm feeling…scared might be a good word for it. But I'm feeling that I need to kiss you. Would that be mutual?'

'No!'

But she was lying. They both knew she was lying. There was that between them… It was intangible but real, as if there was a bubble wrapped around them, not constricting, just gently, wondrously closing in, propelling them closer and closer together.

The fear was receding. The uncertainties. The barriers. One by one they were slipping away into the night.

'Holly…' he said and it was too much—the night, the warmth, the fragrance of Christmas. Or maybe it was more than that. Maybe it was the months of betrayal, where nothing had been what it seemed, where the ground had slipped from under her feet, where foundations had become shifting sand.

And for this man it had been the same.

Angus's hands were held out and the shifting sand was still there, but here, before her, was a link she could take and hold. But she shouldn't. She mustn't. But here he was and the warmth was all around them, and all she did was want.

She wanted so much.

And stupidly, idiotically, irresistibly, she lifted her hands and let him take hers in his. She felt him tug her forward and she felt herself be tugged until her breasts were touching his chest, until she could feel the strength of him enfolding her, the soft brush of his sweater, the heat and strength of his chest underneath.

His breath was on her hair. His hands were tugging her waist, pulling her closer, closer.

She was melting. Fears, reservations, caution, were all disappearing in the magic of this night, this place, this man.

She wrapped her arms around him and she held as well, allowing her body to simply rest on his, his head on her hair, his arms holding her close—her heart transferring to his?

No! That was fantastical nonsense, the stuff of romance novels. This was merely a moment in time, a pre-Christmas weirdness, like kissing your boss in front of the water cooler.

Or not. He didn't feel like her boss. He felt like…Angus. *He was her boss.*

So what? her body was screaming at her. Are you going to reject this moment because of your crazy scruples? Are you going to push away this magic?

It would have taken a stronger woman than she'd ever be, because Angus was putting her a little away from him, gazing down at her with those deep, gorgeous, questioning eyes, smiling, just faintly, a smile that said he was as unsure as she was but oh, he wanted…

She knew nothing about this man. Earl of Craigenstone…

She looked at him now and something inside her saw not the Earl of Craigenstone but the remnants of a scarred childhood—rejection from his father, bitterness from his mother, an engagement she knew nothing of except it had ended in disaster, fear of emotional attachment that meant that even now he was looking at her with desire but still she could see the reflection of her own uncertainty.

More. There'd been happy relationships in Holly's past— her parents had loved her to bits, and so had her grandparents. This man, though…

He was flying blind, she thought. He cupped her face in his hands, he gazed down at her and she thought this should be the scenario where the wicked Lord had his way. But this was no wicked Lord. There was only Angus and he wanted to kiss her and all she had to do was allow those gorgeous, wondrous hands to tilt her chin…

And of course she did. How could she not? He was here, he was now, he was her gorgeous Liege Lord, but he was her man besides. Her knees seemed to be giving way beneath her, as did her principles, as did her fears.

There was only Angus. There was only this moment.

She lifted her hand and traced the contours of his face, as if she had to know him, she had to feel every inch of him, and with every fragment of touch the feeling went further.

He was gazing gravely down, waiting, waiting and she knew there'd be no compulsion. No would mean no. But yes…

Yes was out there, filling the room, making her heels suddenly lift from the floor so she was on her toes. So he could draw her in and enfold her to him, so she could finally, wondrously allow his mouth to meet hers…

So he could kiss her as she ached to be kissed.

She could finally be where she needed to be.

Oh, the kiss…

She knew kisses. Of course she knew kisses. She was a woman who'd been engaged, who knew her way around in the world, who knew men.

She didn't know this man. She didn't know this kiss.

It was a fusing of two opposing charges. It was heat and power and promise. It was a surge of something that rocked her almost from her feet, that made her tilt those heels higher, that made her melt, sink into him, take as he was taking.

That made her want…

She wanted this man as she'd never wanted anything

more in her life. But maybe that wasn't true. *Want* was too
small a word.

It was as if her mouth had located her true north and
was holding. This was her true course. This was her man.

Her body was hard against his, her breasts crushed
against his chest and she could feel his racing heart. Hers
was racing in response. The world was shifting, lighting
colours appearing that she'd never known before, shards
of sensation rushing through that she'd never felt, never
thought she could feel.

But now wasn't the time to question anything; now was
simply for letting this power take over her body, opening
her mouth, allowing her man to deepen the kiss, demanding
that she too could take the taste of him, the feel of him…

Her man. Her Lord? Her Angus.

They were by the great plate glass windows, the lights of
London were all around them and, if London cared to gaze
upward, two star-crossed lovers were silhouetted against
the penthouse windows of one of the finest hotels in the city
and it looked like magic. For Christmas magic happened…

But then…how old had Holly been when she'd realised
Santa was a fairy tale? How had she felt when reality finally broke in, as break in it must?

As break in it did, now.

She'd been tugging him close but she wanted him closer.
She shifted to hold him tighter, to mould her breasts against
his chest…and her makeshift ring caught in the wool of
his sweater.

Such a tiny thing, and a different woman might have
tugged and torn and not cared, but his sweater was gorgeous cashmere and she'd been hugged against it and she
loved it and the thought of ripping it felt like hurting him.

So she froze so she didn't hurt it further—and the kiss
broke. He loosed her a little to see what was wrong.

'I'm stuck to your sweater,' she managed. Her voice

didn't work properly. Nothing was working properly. 'My ring…'

'Leave it.'

'Let me unhook it.'

'It can stay hooked,' he growled, gathering her tight again. 'It's an engagement ring. Isn't that for bonding two people together? Isn't that where we're headed right now?'

She stilled. She let the words echo in her head, and with that echo she felt cold, hard sense shove its way in.

Bonding two people together…

What was she thinking? How long was it since she'd ripped off Geoff's ring? How long was it since she'd thought she was…bonded?

'No!' The word broke from her lips before she even knew she was going to say it. 'No!'

No? Of course no.

He heard her panic and he replayed his words, and in that fraction of a moment he knew they'd been the stupidest words he could have used. Here he was with a woman he hardly knew and he was talking of tying her to him. When he knew her background… When he knew her fears…

Was he out of his mind?

'Let me…let me unhook it,' she was saying, or she was trying to say it but her voice had changed. She'd changed.

There was nothing for it but to relax his hold and then, as she was still stuck, he hauled his sweater over his head and moved away still further.

Her ring and her finger were still inside his sweater. He was no longer attached.

He felt…empty.

'Tug the ring off so we can fix it,' he told her, but she shook her head, her expression shuttered. Something inside had recoiled and it was staying that way.

'I'm keeping the ring on,' she told him. 'I made a deal.

I've given Delia your ring and I'll wear this one for three weeks but it doesn't bond me to anything.'

'Of course not. But love…'

'*I am not your love.*' She practically yelled it, then turned away, twisting the sweater inside out, as if it was desperately important to unhook herself even from his sweater. 'Of all the crazy set-ups… What were we thinking?'

'I know what I was thinking.'

'No! Angus, I'm on the rebound. I'm not ready. And I don't think you really want…'

'I do really want,' he said, trying to gather his wits. Knowing he needed to step back but it was almost killing him to do so. 'But I can wait. Holly, how long does it take to unhook a ring?'

'You'll need to wait longer than that,' she said savagely. 'Lord or not.'

'Can you cut it out with the title?' And suddenly more than Holly's past was in the room between them. His ghosts were all around them. His words were an explosion, his anger coming from nowhere. 'Holly, I'll wait for as long as you need to wait,' he told her. 'But this will only work if you think about me and not my ancestry. *I am not my father.*'

And that was another dumb thing to say. He raked his hair in disbelief that this had suddenly changed so appallingly. He met her gaze and he saw fear. He'd shouted. Of all the idiots, he'd shouted.

Appalling was too mild a word for it.

Where had the ghost of his father come from? He felt ill.

'Holly, I'm sorry,' he said, trying to get a handle on what had suddenly become a situation she looked as if she wanted to run from. He had to wipe the fear from her face. Concentrate only on that, he told himself. Nothing more.

Step back. Step right back.

'What I just said was dumb,' he said at last. 'No, I'm not my father, but you already know that. What I am is your boss.' Deep breath. 'Holly, I've employed you for three weeks. After that, I won't be anything to do with any inherited title and you won't be my employee. It'll also be that much further from Geoff's treatment of you. My father's my ghost and Geoff's yours but we can be free. Holly, believe me, I'm not holding you to me now, and I won't hold you to me then, but I can wait and see what happens—when we're both free.'

She didn't answer. She didn't even look at him. Stupidly she was still trying to untangle the sweater.

He should help her but he daren't approach. He could still sense her fear.

Three weeks. Such a short time to lay ghosts…

But, until the New Year, she'd be living in his castle. The thought was good.

'We both should step away,' he managed. 'Tonight's been great but we're both obviously tired. Right now, I'm not making sense even to myself. So let's both go to bed—with a door closed between us.'

She nodded, still clutching the sweater. 'Yes.'

'Holly…'

'Doors. Boundaries. We need them,' she said dully. 'Goodnight… My Lord.'

'Please don't call me that.'

'It's what you are.'

'Until I sell,' he conceded. 'But after that I'll be living in the US and I am not My Lord there. This fantasy will be over.'

'Good, then. Excellent.' Her face was set, expressionless, as if she was carefully hiding her emotions. 'Tonight's been part of that fantasy,' she said. 'And fantasy knows its place, so let's move past it. It's more than time we went to our separate beds.'

'Holly…'

'Forget the personal,' she managed and finally handed

him his untangled sweater. 'You're my employer so forge
the kiss. Think of me as hired help, a sauce bottle ring
paid for in cash fiancée.' She held out her finally freed
beringed finger. 'I need to bash out a few rough edges bu
that's what I am. Angus…'

'Yes?'

'Go to bed,' she said gently. 'Because I really, really
want to kiss you again but it's just as well my ring saved
the day. This is an impossible situation and we both need
to keep our heads. If you're the least bit interested in kiss
ing me when I'm done being your servant and your fian
cée then you can think about propositioning me again, bu
by then hopefully I'll have my head together. We've both
been stupid. Kissing's done. Go to bed.'

He went to bed but he didn't sleep. He lay and stared at the
ceiling and watched the flickering lights from the city play
over the plaster. Eventually he rose and stared out over the
river. He poured himself a whisky and then tossed it down

There was a tentative scratch on the door, low down
Dog. He opened it a fraction. Holly was through there and
he wouldn't wake her. Scruffy padded through, jumped
on his bed and looked at him as if he was expecting night
time confidences.

With the door safely closed, it was safe enough to talk
to the dog.

'I want her,' he said simply and Scruffy kept on gazing
at him as if more was expected, more was to come.

It was hard to resist a dog with his head cocked to one
side, especially when the words were already in his head

'I'm not pushing her,' he said into the silence. 'I don'
take and hold. I'm not like my father.'

For some reason he was remembering his eighth birth
day. His grandmother had given him a piggy bank, a weird
looking pig that grunted when a coin was dropped on its

ongue before it proceeded to 'devour' the coin. He'd loved
t. He'd also loved the bright coins his grandmother had
given him to go with it.

'You could use your money to buy ice skates,' his mother
had told him but he'd shaken his head and proceeded solemnly to feed his money to his pig.

Maybe he'd thought he could get it out later. Maybe he
hadn't even wanted ice skates. No matter, the next thing
he'd known, his mother was sobbing.

'He'll be just like his father,' she'd told his grandmother.
'I know it.'

And then, when he'd decided to study finance...

'How can you be interested in money? You are just like
him.'

And finally, when he'd fallen for Louise...

'How do you know you love her? You just want her,
isn't that right?' And appallingly, as grief and humiliation
had given way to insight, he was left wondering whether
she was right.

Just like his father... His mother seemed to have softened over the years, she let him be, but the old accusations
were always there to haunt him.

Enough. It was more than time to be over the past, he
told himself. Right now, Scruffy was eying him sideways,
as if there was something deep he didn't understand. It was
as if the little dog was saying: *The most gorgeous woman
you've ever met is right through that door and you're on
this side thinking about past history. Are you mad?*

This dog had brains.

Maybe he was mad. Maybe they both were. If they could
shake off the past, Holly would be lying in his arms right
now, skin against skin, her lovely body moulded to his, her
warmth, her breath against his lips, her hands...

'Cold shower,' he told Scruffy and Scruffy looked at
him again as if he were crazy.

'I might well be,' he told him. 'But sometimes a cold shower is sensible. Believe it or not.'

Scruffy didn't believe him. He knew it.

He didn't believe it himself, or part of him did but the other part was telling him his feet were heading for the bathroom when they should be heading for the door to the sitting room.

'Sense prevails,' he muttered savagely. 'How do I know the difference between wanting and loving? I can't, and I will not take advantage of an employee.'

'So sack her,' he demanded of himself.

'Yeah, right. That's what your father would do. Go take a shower.'

She'd heard the door open, just slightly, and she'd held her breath.

She'd heard Scruffy wuffle through, she'd heard Angus's soft greeting and she'd heard the door close again.

She heard Angus head to the shower.

She lay and listened to the muffled sound of running water and she tried, really hard, not to imagine the Lord of Castle Craigie as he was now. Naked under running water. Rivulets of water running over a body she just knew would turn a girl's knees to water. That jet-black hair dripping, water running over his face, his shoulders, his chest, down…

'You're a sad case,' she told herself and hauled her bed-clothes over her head to block out as much sound as she could, and tried and failed to block out the images being conjured.

Why was he taking a shower now, an hour after they'd gone to bed?

A cold shower?

That brought more images and a girl could almost groan

f she didn't think that maybe the walls were too thin and
a girl shouldn't do anything of the kind.

She'd sort of like a cold shower herself. Or a good brisk
walk in the snow, but it was the wee hours in a strange city
and a girl had some sense.

But sense was in short supply. If her ring hadn't caught…
If Angus hadn't made that crack about bonding…

That kiss had melted sense entirely. If Angus had wanted
her tonight she would have…

Yeah, well, let's not go there, she told herself. Sense had
prevailed and it was just as well.

And sense would stay prevailing. She knew that now,
somehow, things had been put on the right footing. For the
next three weeks she was chef and pretend fiancée and that
was it. Then she'd take her money and run.

Fast.

CHAPTER NINE

THINGS WERE STRAINED between them the next morning, but okay. They could do this. They had to do this because the kids were waiting.

They found the kids packed and excited, but torn about leaving their mum. A limousine was ready to take Delia and her mother to hospital as soon as they left. Delia was tearful but determined to let the children go.

'I never would have let them if I hadn't met you,' she told Holly. 'I can't believe His Lordship is marrying someone so lovely.' She gazed down at the Craigenstone ring, still blazing on her finger. 'I'll get Mum to wear this while I'm in hospital and it'll give her pleasure as well. I can't believe you've been so generous.'

'It's Angus who's generous,' Holly told her. 'If he hadn't agreed I never could have done it.'

Delia eyed Angus dubiously. He was busy stowing baggage and cat-carrier into the back of the car, and explaining to Scruffy why the cat was out of bounds. They had space to talk, and suddenly it seemed as if Delia had the courage to probe.

'So...you love him?' Delia asked.

Holly hesitated, twisting the weird little tin ring on her finger. She was supposed to be this man's fiancée. Her lie had to continue. 'I guess I must,' she said. She watched

Angus some more and thought…maybe I'm not lying. Heaven help me, maybe I'm not.

'If you're not sure…you be careful,' Delia said urgently. 'It's not my place to say, but oh, my dear, the Craigenstone men can be charming when they want something. Charming and ruthless.'

But if he'd been ruthless he could have had her last night, Holly thought, as finally they waved goodbye to Delia and set off northwards. He hadn't pushed. He'd respected her suddenly imposed boundaries. So far, she hadn't seen a hint of ruthlessness.

Though she had seen more than a hint of charming.

She was about to see more. They'd barely crossed the Scottish border when Angus turned off the motorway.

'Quick deviation,' he told them. The kids were being amazingly quiet, amazingly subdued in the back seat. They'd been told by their mother to stay subdued, Holly thought. They must have been for this wasn't normal. They'd stopped an hour back for lunch, there'd been little conversation then and there was no protest now.

Agree to everything—was that what Delia had told them? Was that the way she'd tried to deal with the old Lord?

She eyed Angus and tried to figure just how ruthless this man could be. He was rich in his own right. You didn't get rich by being a doormat.

He wasn't a doormat, but ruthless? The word stayed with her, a question. She'd accepted Geoff without nearly enough questions. She was asking questions now.

Why? He had no intention of coming near her for three weeks. After that, he'd be back in the States and she'd be in Australia. There was no need for questions.

But the way she was feeling…

He glanced across and met her gaze and smiled and

something inside her melted, as it had melted before. Oh help, this was nuts. This was teenage crush territory.

Was this why the Earls of Craigenstone had been deemed dangerous for generation after generation? All they had to do was smile.

'I thought we'd pay a visit to my father's old keeper, McAllister,' he said. 'Maggie found out where he is—in a nursing home not far from here. I thought he might like a visit from Scruffy.'

And she melted again, just like that. Ruthless? Ha!

She glanced down at her crazy ring and she thought that if it had been a bit less rough she might have spent the next three weeks *really* pretending to be a fiancée.

And where would that have left her? She was in an emotional mess already. Would she break her heart over Angus as well as Geoff?

She hadn't actually broken her heart over Geoff. He'd smashed her pride, he'd humiliated her to her socks, but had she felt for him what she was feeling for Angus?

No! No, because she wasn't feeling anything for Angus except sheer, unadulterated lust. It must be lust. The man was exuding more testosterone than any man had a right to and it was doing things to her insides…

'Do you have a comb?' he asked and it was as much as she could do to get her voice to work.

'Wh…why?'

'Scruffy's going to meet his master,' he said. 'He might like to look his best.'

If she'd felt emotional before, what happened next almost wiped her.

The kids stayed outside. They knew McAllister but they reached the foyer, smelled the unmistakable smell of hospital-type institutions and backed away like alarmed colts.

'Don't you like McAllister?' Angus asked and Ben nodded.

'He was…great. But he won't be now, will he?'

'So you're sending us in as forward reconnaissance?' Angus asked, grinning, and Holly's heart did that crazy twist again.

'He won't want to see me,' Holly ventured. 'I'm not part of this. It's you who's Earl of Craigenstone.'

'Yes, but you're my fiancée and it's your job to support me.'

'Angus…'

'Yes…dear?'

'Fine,' she said and girded internal loins and tucked a gleaming Scruffy—or as gleaming as Scruffy was ever likely to get—under her arm and headed inside with Angus.

The nurse at reception eyed Scruffy askance but she wasn't given a chance to object.

'We've brought Mr McAllister's dog to pay him a Christmas visit,' Angus said and smiled at her and the girl was no more impervious to that smile than Holly was. Of course she nodded, of course she smiled back and she led them down to a lounge area where a dozen very old persons were desultorily watching television.

She gestured to a *very* old man in the corner. 'There he is. Dougal, you have a visitor.'

The old man was slumped in something that looked a cross between a wheelchair and a bed. He was wearing an ancient tartan sweater, grubby trousers and a tweed cap that looked as if it was welded to his head. It'd have to be stuck there because the old man's head hung so low his chin reached his chest. He didn't look up when his name was called. He didn't move.

Oh, help. No wonder Scruffy—or Mac?—had been left behind, Holly thought. This man looked as if he'd been old for ever. Was it even worth trying to get through to him?

Unconsciously, her arms tightened around Scruffy, as if to protect him from seeing his master in such a state, but Angus was made from sterner stuff than she was. He took Scruffy from her, strode across the room and squatted before the old man in the wheelchair.

'Dougal,' he said, and then more firmly, 'Dougal!'

The man's head lifted fractionally but it was definitely a lift and it was enough for Angus to gently insinuate one little dog onto the man's knees, under that bowed head.

He lifted one of McAllister's hands and laid it on Scruffy's head. 'This is your visitor,' he said firmly, loudly enough to be heard across the blaring television. 'We've brought him all the way from Castle Craigie to see you, so you might as well say hello. The kids say his name is Mac. Is that right?'

There was a moment's stillness, from dog and from man. The focus of the room was no longer on the television. One of the residents leaned forward and hit the remote and the sound of the soap they were watching died.

Scruffy was perched where he'd been put, on McAllister's knees. The little dog stared upward and McAllister's hand moved, as if involuntarily, to hold…

But he couldn't hold for suddenly the strange smells and sounds and place faded to nothing as a light bulb switched on in the little dog's head. From where Holly stood she could see the second he realised… This man who was holding him…

McAllister! McAllister! His total, obvious joy exploded, upward and outward.

But it was as if he knew the old man was fragile. He was going nuts, but gently nuts. He was writhing upward, his entire body trembling with shock and excitement, pressing closer, licking the old man's chin, practically turning inside out with delirious joy but gently, gently, not one scratch…

And now the old man had done his own recognising.

His hands were holding, hugging, and his age-lined face was practically collapsing in on itself. He hugged the little dog close—or as close as a wriggling, whimpering, licking bundle of canine ecstasy could be hugged—and tears started tracking down the wrinkled cheeks.

'Mac,' he said brokenly in a voice that sounded like rasping gravel. 'Mac, boy, you've found me.'

The whole room was watching them now. There were sniffs from all while they watched the greeting, a long, lovely ode to devotion past. There was no hurry. They were taking their time, these two, two old mates back to being one.

'That's…that's the first word I've heard him say for six months,' the nurse behind Holly said, and Holly turned and handed her a tissue. She'd just fished a handful of them out of her bag. She wasn't sharing many, though—she needed them herself.

'How long has Mr McAllister been here?' Angus asked and there was an edge of steel in his voice that Holly was starting to recognise.

'Eighteen months,' the nurse said. 'I'd just started working here when he came in. Apparently he had a stroke at work. He was in hospital for weeks and this was the only place that had a long-term vacancy. He came by ambulance; he's never had a visitor but about a week after he arrived a guy who said he was the manager of the place he worked dumped a whole lot of his stuff here.'

'A man called Stanley?'

'I'd have to check.'

'He has no other visitors?'

'No.'

'Can he keep his dog here?'

'No.' But the girl had lost her efficiency and was sounding human—and apologetic. 'I'm so sorry but he can't. The owner doesn't allow any pets, even visiting. I'm breaking rules letting you in here.' She smiled an apology. 'But I'll let you keep breaking them for a while. Some things are worth it.'

'Can we take him out into the garden?' Angus asked and two minutes later they were wheeling a wrapped-up Dougal and dog outside.

The kids were there. They stared at Dougal with horror—this stroke-affected old man was obviously a very different Dougal to the one they remembered—and then Ben finally found the courage to talk.

'D...Dougal. Do you remember us? I'm Ben.'

'O...of course,' the old voice whispered. 'Ben, lad. Eh, where've you been?'

'London,' Ben said and it was like removing a cork from a bottle; the voices were freed and suddenly all three kids were talking at once, clustered round the chair-cum-bed, and Angus and Holly were on the outside, watching.

'We can't stay long,' Holly whispered, still clutching her tissues. 'Not if we're to get back to the castle before dinner. Oh, but Angus...'

'Are you any good at nursing?' he demanded and she looked at him as if he'd lost his mind.

'What?'

'Nursing? If not, is Maggie? Either one of you?'

'As a nurse I make a very good chef,' she said, suddenly seeing where his thoughts were taking him. 'Angus, I can't. I'd love to but I'm your chef and your fiancée for Christmas. I can't be anything else.'

'If we all helped...'

'He's so frail.'

'But if we could have him for Christmas. I don't know anything about nursing either, but Holly...'

'Just how many people,' she said carefully, 'are you thinking of inviting?'

'It's a very big castle, and I have employed someone who's said to be an excellent chef.'

'I'll feed him but that's all I'm capable of. And Angus, wouldn't it be cruel? To take him and then bring him back here?'

'He's not coming back here,' Angus said, grimly determined. 'I'll find him somewhere better. Somewhere he can keep Scru…Mac.'

'Oh, Angus.'

'But first, Christmas.' He turned and walked back to the entrance with Holly, leaving Dougal in the garden with the kids. The nurse who'd greeted them was standing in the doorway.

'Problem,' he said. 'We want to take Dougal home for Christmas but we need a nurse.'

'A private nurse,' she said cautiously. 'I don't know…'

'For the right person, I'll pay twice the going rate,' he said. 'Plus accommodation, in Castle Craigie. Plus all the Christmas trimmings.'

'Really?'

'Really.'

'That'd be fantastic,' the girl said, and suddenly she sounded wistful. 'And Dougal's a sweetie.' There was a couple of moments silence while they saw her doing internal calculations.

'I've got my holidays,' she said at last. 'But my mum's alone and we have Christmas together.' Her face was suddenly kind of hopeful. 'My…my dad died last year. It's going to be a bleak Christmas. But Mum used to be a nurse, too. Dougal's very frail. He could do with two nurses.'

'Expanda job,' Angus said. 'Why didn't I see that coming?'

'Sorry?'

'No. The more, the merrier,' he said, and suddenly he was grinning. Holly looked at him, startled. He had the attitude of a man about to toss pound notes to the masses. 'When do your holidays start?'

'Next F-Friday.'

'Then what if I send a car—or do I need to hire some sort of ambulance? Can you organise that? Yes? And of course I'm paying your mum, too. Now, let's go make sure Dougal wants to come, and see if he has any aunts or mothers or cats or wolfhounds that he'd like to put on my payroll as well.'

He was a very nice man.

He was her employer.

He was gorgeous.

Tucked back in the car, cuddling Scruffy-cum-Mac, Holly felt herself near to tears. Of all the impulsive, crazy gestures... Dougal had wept when Angus outlined his plans, and Holly had felt the need to steer Angus out of there before any other solitary geriatric had crossed his path.

'Our castle's filling up,' she said.

'I'm going to wear my kilt.' He sounded deeply contented and she cast an amazed gaze at him.

'You sound smug.'

'As soon as I saw that wardrobe full of kilts I knew I wanted one Christmas as Liege Lord.'

'What's Liege Lord?'

'I'm not sure but it sounds important. I bet it involves sitting at the head of that vast dining room table with an epergne with tiger heads in the middle, and slicing the Christmas turkey with a ceremonial sword.'

'Maybe two turkeys,' she said.

'We Lords can handle two turkeys.'

'Why don't you want to be a full-time Lord?' she asked curiously. 'Why the rush to sell?' The tensions of the night before were still with them, she could feel them, but somehow what had just happened had made her relax a little.

'I belong in the US.'

'If your home is your castle, then you belong here.'

'Ask my mother whether that holds true,' he said, humour fading. 'She's appalled I'm here now.'

'Why don't you invite her as well?'

'What, my mother?'

'Everyone else is coming,' she said. She was feeling… how to describe the way she was feeling? She was heading back to a castle with her boss, with a car full of kids and dog, with the kids' mother and grandmother, aged retainer and nurse and a nurse's mother following. Punch-drunk might describe it.

Kissed might describe it as well.

'As…as long as you made sure she knows the engagement is pretend,' she added, feeling even more disoriented, but more and more thinking that if the castle was to be full, why not make it really full?

For some reason, what had happened with Delia and with Dougal was shifting perspective past the personal. She and Maggie had been heading for a bleak and solitary Christmas. It would be anything but solitary now, and somewhere this man's mother was living with ghosts and it seemed as if they were making her solitary as well.

Her relationship with this man was causing tension, but she could get over that. Hopefully. And more people, more to do, would help.

'She'd have a pretty good idea as soon as she saw that ring,' Angus said, guy-like, focusing on practicalities. 'I need to do something about it.'

'Tell everyone you're waiting for the after-Christmas sales before you buy one,' she told him. 'As the Earl of Craigenstone, that's entirely believable.'

'It is, isn't it?' he said and suddenly his voice was savage and the tension was back. The kids were dozing in the back seat, listening to their music on a sound system that could thankfully be muffled in the front. It had been a long drive. There was now less than an hour to go, and it seemed as if they were cocooned in the front of the car, with nobody to hear them, with a weird sense of connection that might have everything to do with the kiss of the night before. 'Holly, you don't want my mother here and she's already said she won't come. She loathed the place.'

'Did she loathe the place or loathe your father?'

'Same…'

'It's not the same,' she said stubbornly. 'Gran and I will make this Christmas stupendous. We're intending to lay ghosts all over the place.'

'Let's have Hogmanay,' a sleepy voice said from the back seat. 'Then it's not just Christmas. We can have Christmas and then at New Year we can have a party for everyone and say goodbye to the castle and everyone in the whole village.'

'What's Hogmanay?' Angus and Holly said as one.

'New Year!' Ben's voice was incredulous. 'Don't you guys know anything? In Scotland Hogmanay's bigger than Christmas. It's a goodbye to the old year, in with the new. Other big landholders hold parties for everyone on the estate. I told our father that once and he just snarled, but it'd be so cool to do it. With a bonfire and everything.'

'Hey, fun,' Holly said.

'Hey, wait for my snarl,' Angus retorted, but he was grinning. 'So you want most of the world to come for Christmas and everyone left over to come for Hogmanay?'

'Yes,' Holly and Ben said in unison.

'If this road wasn't icy I'd throw my hands up in the air,' Angus retorted. 'I thought I was Liege Lord, in charge of all I survey.'

'The peasants are revolting,' Holly said smugly and Angus glanced over at her, seeing her smile, the cheery wink she was giving Ben, the flush in her cheeks and the gleam of excitement at the challenge ahead and he thought...he thought...

He thought the peasants weren't revolting at all. And one peasant was so far removed from revolting that every piece of personal armour he'd ever loaded himself with was in danger of disintegrating into dust.

But he wouldn't invite his mother again. The thought of her, in her Christmas black, with her Christmas grief and her accusations... No. That was the real world. This was a pretend Christmas, nothing to do with reality.

Maggie had had two days and two girls from the village to help, and Maggie and two girls—plus her tame electrician and plumber—were a force to be reckoned with. As they rounded the sweeping driveway and the long grey fortress-type castle came into view—it was covered with fairy lights.

Covered with fairy lights.

It was just dusk. There was a collective intake of breath. Angus even stopped the car.

'What...?' he breathed.

'You...you did say to do whatever was needed to make these kids welcome,' Holly managed, looking at the fairy lights, looking at the castle and thinking how much it had cost her to string one row of fairy lights across her apartment entrance last year.

'Wow,' Mary breathed from the back seat. 'It's a fairy castle.'

'It's your home for Christmas,' Angus said, managing to recover. 'Welcome back to Castle Craigie.'

And the shocks didn't stop there. They walked into the hall and the first impression was warmth. The second was sheer, over the top Christmas.

There was a Christmas tree standing in the vast baronial hall, and it wasn't just a Christmas tree, it was practically a full-grown pine. It was decorated with what must be every conceivable ornament Maggie had been able to drum up—no tasteful colour coordination here—and it glittered on a scale that took every single one of their breaths away.

Except Scruffy-cum-Mac. Holly put him down, he headed straight for the base of the tree—and Holly had to race across and grab him before he could raise his leg.

'Welcome home, My Lord.' Maggie was at the head of the stairs, dressed in severe housekeeping black, and Holly had to bite back a giggle. Maggie was part Gran, part housekeeper, part actress and she was filling her role to perfection. 'And these are the children of the castle. Welcome back, Misses and Sir. Can I show you to your bedrooms?'

Maggie turned and trod stately upward, the actress in her in full swing. The kids stared after her in awe, they followed tentatively—and then, from where they stood, Holly and Angus heard gasps of wonder, awe, incredulity. It seemed that Maggie had decorated a bedroom for each of them in the main part of the castle, and in the style that each of them had never dreamed of.

'I've got two suits of armour in my room,' Ben yelled out to his sisters. 'Wow! Wait until I tell my mates on Facebook.'

Holly giggled and then glanced up at the man beside her and her giggle died.

He was looking…grim.

Grim? Why?

'What's with the face?' she asked, and she saw him physically brace and shift and his smile came back on.

'Face?'

'Like Scrooge seeing Tiny Tim's tiny corpse because he didn't share his turkey.'

'I'm sharing.'

'For this Christmas only?' she asked curiously. 'Do you usually share?'

'I don't usually need to share.'

'Need? Or want?'

'There's no need to get personal.'

'No, but there's want,' she said, suddenly, impertinently, wishing to dig a little deeper into the past of this enigmatic Lord. She glanced at her weird ring. 'As a fiancée, I need to understand my true love.'

'Your pretend true love.'

'Oi,' she said. 'You want me to shout to the top of the Christmas tree that this engagement's fake? These kids will go home. Maggie and I will head off in a huff. You'll be left with McAllister and Stanley. If we're engaged, then I get to pry a little. Why does the sight of a Christmas tree and whooping kids make you look like you've just swallowed lemons?'

'Lemons!'

'Lemons,' she said definitely. 'Give.'

What was it with this woman? No one in his extended circle of friends and acquaintances would push past his personal boundaries like this.

'I don't do Christmas,' he said at last, and she stared at him as if he were out of his mind.

'Um…it's a bit late to tell us that now,' she managed. 'You've opened the castle, you've invited the hordes, and I have two turkeys, two puddings and the ingredients for every conceivable Christmas goodie in the pantry. Plus Gran already has Christmas plans afoot, and the kids are already planning Hogmanay.'

'I know.'

'So why…?'

'My fiancée died on Christmas Eve.'

'I accept that,' she said thoughtfully. 'I can see that must have been devastating. But wasn't that a long time ago?'

'Yes,' he admitted. 'But then we hadn't been into Christmas when I was a child either. My grandfather died at Christmas.'

'That's right,' she said thoughtfully. 'Was he old?'

'Seventy-two.'

'Okay, then,' she said. 'Got it.'

'You don't "got it".'

'No,' she admitted. 'I don't got it. Tell me.'

Tell her? Why? And how? It was dumb, how such a long ago tragedy still affected his life. He'd never talked about it, but every Christmas there it was—his mother deep in mourning while the rest of the world seemed to burst with flashing lights and colour.

His mother still wore black on Christmas Day. Actually, she wore black every day.

'You can't stop grief,' he said but the explanation sounded weak even to him.

'No, but you can keep it to yourself. Your mother…'

'Holly, she's over it. I'm over it. It's just background.'

'But it still makes you purse your lips at Christmas decorations.'

'I do not purse.'

'You do so purse.' She sighed and put her hands on her hips. 'Okay, you're over it. Prove it. As Christmas host, it's your duty to enjoy Christmas, starting now. Come into the kitchen and help me make mince pies.'

'I can't cook!'

'Of course you can. If you can handle the stock market you can handle a recipe, and what else are you going to do? The kids will be exploring old haunts, and with all these people I've invited I could use a kitchen hand.'

'I'm not,' he said cautiously, 'a kitchen hand.'

'No. You're a fiancé with a big black hole where Christmas should be,' she said blithely. 'I intend to fill it. I have Christmas carols on my phone and I have a beaut little travel amplifier that can boom them through the kitchen. I intend to sing along. How can you resist that, Lord Angus?'

He couldn't. He knew he couldn't.

He didn't.

Holly McIntosh was a sucker for heroes. Any hero. Give her a good romantic movie and she'd fall every time. The only time a movie got her really upset was when a perfectly good hero ended badly. Ooh, the end of *Butch Cassidy and the Sundance Kid,* where two perfectly good heroes went down together, still had her smarting at the waste.

She carried her heroes in her heart for months after seeing an excellent movie, and she didn't let anything mess with her images.

The Lord of Castle Craigie was a hero. She'd decided it the moment she'd met him. Those dark, shadowed eyes, the sculpted face, the fact that the first time she'd met him he was in a kilt, with his castle, his haunted background... Yep, she was in meltdown and *that kiss* had just compounded things. If her ring hadn't snagged at just the wrong moment she knew she'd have gone to bed with him and made love to her very own romantic hero.

And yet...and yet...

Suddenly tonight the hero image had slipped a bit. The image wasn't tarnished, it was just that she was seeing the human bits underneath more clearly. The Lord of Castle Craigie as a solitary child, spending Christmas with a grieving mother who never let her son escape a past which, in truth, was nothing to do with him. And then some kind of no-good fiancée dying on Christmas Eve. Okay, she knew nothing about the long-dead Louise, but right now she was prepared to put her in the same category as Geoff. Low life.

Because she'd hurt her hero?

She was kneading one lot of biscuit pastry while Angus—under her supervision—was crumbing butter into flour ready for the next batch. Her fingers were required for kneading but what her fingers really wanted to do was curl into frustrated fists. His mother… His fiancée… They were both in her sights.

What a way to treat a child, she thought, glancing at his still set face, but then, what a way for the old Earl to treat his wife. She might judge the unknown Louise, but maybe she needed to cut Angus's mother some slack. To be locked in this castle while her dad was dying, for no better reason than a crazy sense of control, would probably have damaged anyone.

'Angus, why not push your mother to come?' she urged again. This was none of her business. She had no right to urge, but to have ghosts perpetually in the shadows… 'How can she let ghosts ruin her Christmas for ever? If she's miserable, I can tell that you won't enjoy yourself. Her ghosts are your ghosts. Bring her here and let us blast them out of the water with mince pies and mistletoe. If she'll come, let's show her that life can go on.'

'She wears black,' Angus said inconsequentially.

'Black's elegant—it'll look stunning among all our glitz. She'll match Maggie. Honestly, Angus, if you don't invite her you'll regret it. I can see by your face that you'll be thinking of her all Christmas.'

'What could I possibly say that'd make her come?'

'Tell her you really are engaged,' she said. 'Tell her you've given me the heirloom ring but I seem to have lost it already. Tell her I'm adorable and cute and dumb and you've fallen hard and you're thinking of getting married on Hogmanay. You've invited all the villagers to attend and you're besotted. Make me sound like a gold-digger. I suspect there's not a mother in the known world who won't get on a plane with that impetus.'

'You're joking.'

'You can't pull it off?'

He thought of his mother's reaction if he really did say those things. And then…he thought of his mother's Christmas.

It wasn't that she was deliberately playing Miss Havisham, he thought. It was just that she'd got herself into a roller coaster where Christmas every year was the bottom of her ride.

Even the top wasn't very high, he thought, and he looked at Holly in her crimson apron with Father Christmas emblazoned on the front, and her bright blue boots—she'd hardly taken them off—and he thought this Christmas Holly would cheer anyone up.

Maybe he could lay a few ghosts, he thought. If he could get his mother here… Underneath the layers of sadness, maybe there was a grandma in the making.

Grandma. Um…he was moving ahead here. Grandchildren.

Children.

He'd never thought of having children, except as some vague, nebulous concept he might or might not expect in his future. But suddenly his future was here, now, standing before him, elbows deep in pastry, eying him with a distinct challenge.

'Christmas is for family,' she said. 'I was desperate this year so I headed to Gran. You guys sound like you've been desperate every year, so why not head here? We'll have fun.'

Fun at Christmas. The concept was alien.

Holly. She was almost alien as well, as far from his world as it was possible to be.

Christmas. Hogmanay. Castle Craigie.

'That mixture's crumbed enough,' Holly said, hauling him back to the here and now. 'Give it to me and start another.'

'How many mince pies are we making?' he demanded, startled, and she grinned.

'How many mince pies does your mother eat? I've just added another batch to my list. But think about it, Angus— Christmas, holiday, Hogmanay, family—wow this is a year to celebrate.'

'I thought you just lost your real fiancé—plus all your money?'

'So I did,' she said serenely. 'Deep down, I'm a bucketload of misery, but misery likes mince pies just as much as anyone else.'

Misery had got herself thoroughly, totally distracted. Misery had almost forgotten to be miserable.

Every now and then a wash of remembrance would flood back—of her cute little apartment in Sydney, now in the hands of the receivers, the staff she'd had to let go, her humiliation at the hands of a man she'd thought she could trust with her life. But mostly she was just too busy to care. She had the Christmas to end all Christmases to prepare for, and then Hogmanay.

'Hogmanay is huge on most of the big Scottish estates,' Maggie told her. 'It's always been a source of sadness that the old Lord wouldn't do it. Now you've talked this Lord round your little finger...'

'I have not!'

'You have, even if you won't go there,' Maggie said serenely. 'And this year marks the end of the estate as we know it. Somehow, we seem to have gained permission to put on the feast to end all feasts, so let's get this celebration planned.'

And in the slivers of time not spent cooking and planning, when Holly could lie in bed and stare at the ceiling and think of Geoff and his betrayal, another face intruded.

The Lord of Castle Craigie. A man who, astonishingly, was throwing his heart into the festivities to come and was trying his utmost to show three needy kids a very good time.

This afternoon they'd headed off on the estate tractor to find a yule log. 'I'll order one if you really need one,' Stanley had said sourly, but Angus and the kids had ignored him and headed for the woods.

'Come with us, Holly,' the kids had pleaded. 'Don't you want her with us, Angus? She can't spend all her time in the kitchen.'

Angus had looked at her with a quizzical smile and she could have gone—she could—only sense was still there, yelling in her ears, saying: *get to know this man better first.*

And then they'd brought back the yule log, a great lump of green timber that would no sooner light than fly, and Maggie had decreed another was needed, and Maggie would personally select the log, so off they'd set again and once more Holly had stayed behind.

Fingering her odd little ring and feeling an ache in her heart grow deeper.

Why had he employed her to cook when he wanted to be with her? He and his assorted tribe headed off into the snow for the second time, with Maggie giving instructions as to where the rotten wood would be, the kids whooping behind or cadging an occasional lift on the running boards and Scruffy-Mac perched on his knee and he thought—the only thing needed to make this perfect was Holly.

He'd seen the longing on her face as they'd set off. She wanted to be with him.

No. Um…she wanted to be with *them.* There was a difference.

But…but…

How long did it take a man to know his own heart?

No time at all, he thought as they rounded the bend in

the drive and the castle was out of sight. She'd return to her kitchen, they'd get back in an hour or so and the whole castle would be filled with the results of her cooking.

And she'd smile as they walked in. As he walked in.

A man could come home to that smile for the rest of his life.

How would she fit in Manhattan?

She didn't have parents. As far as he knew, she had no unbreakable ties to Australia, and Maggie had to leave her cottage. If he asked Maggie to join them...

'Left!' Maggie was perched behind him on the tractor. 'That's the third time I said it. Any further and we'll be in the loch.'

'Sorry,' he said and veered left towards the woodlands. 'Maggie, have you ever been to New York?'

'No.'

'Would you like to go?'

'Why would I want to go to New York? No one would understand my accent.'

'Everyone would love your accent.'

'What exactly are you proposing?' she demanded.

'Nothing yet,' he admitted. 'It's just...if I ever thought... of proposing...for real...'

'Give her time,' Maggie said sharply. 'She's still raw.'

'I know that.' He hesitated. 'How much time?'

'How would I know?' Maggie demanded. 'My Rory wrote to his mother the day he met me, saying he'd met his bride. While he was doing that, I took my best friend Jean to look at wedding dresses in the most expensive bridal boutique in Glasgow. But I've heard tell that other people take their time to make up their minds, and I do think Holly needs time. It's just I have no idea how long. And she needs to be sure. After all, you're the Lord of Castle Craigie and, knowing that, a girl would need to be very sure indeed.'

* * *

My Rory wrote to his mother the day he met me, saying he'd met his bride.

Maggie's words stayed in his head as he played with the kids, joining in a snow fight, losing more of his dignity all the time. He'd become Angus. He was becoming almost a friend to his half-brother and -sisters and, to his astonishment, he found he was enjoying himself—a lot. Family. He'd hardly had one and now it was a strangely sweet sensation. Making the kids happy. Making them smile, and having them make him smile back.

But family… Was that why Maggie's words stayed with him?

My Rory wrote to his mother the day he met me, saying he'd met his bride.

Her words mixed with the crazy conversation he'd had with Holly over the mince pies—and finally that night he cracked and phoned his mother.

'I think you should come for Christmas,' he told her on the long distance call. 'There's someone I need you to meet.'

'Who?' He heard his mother's sharp intake of breath, followed by unmistakable fear. She'd be frantic the castle was having its own effect on him.

'A girl called Holly,' he told her. 'She's…extraordinary.'

'Angus! You've been there for less than a month.'

'And I've known Holly for less than a week. Time's immaterial. Mom, I've given her your ring.'

'You've what? After a week? Are you out of your mind?'

He was following Holly's instructions to the letter and it was working. He could feel his mother's fear; the same thing that had happened to her was happening to him. It'd work. She'd be over here so fast, to rescue her son from some harpy's clutches…

But suddenly that didn't seem such a good idea. *Make*

me sound like a gold-digger. That was Holly's order and if he did it, yes it'd work, but at what cost?

He did not want his mother to think his Holly was a gold-digger.

His Holly? He stood staring out into the snow-filled night and he felt his world shifting. One slip of a girl, one mince pie maker, one changer of worlds.

Family.

'She gave it away,' he heard himself say and listened to his mother's incredulous silence. He used a bit of that silence to form a few more words, to form a few more thoughts, to form a new resolution.

'She's adorable,' he told her. 'Yes, I gave her your ring, and yes, I'd love it if it was on her finger now, but she gave it to Delia because she thinks Delia needs it and wants it more. She's right; Delia should have it. Mom, Holly's adorable. I've never met anyone like her. She's currently wearing a sauce bottle top as a ring as a sort of joke, but come the New Year I want to buy her something permanent. To be honest, I don't know if she'll have me yet but the more I know her the more I know I'll push with everything I can. I would love you to meet her. I'd love it if you could come to Castle Craigie and share my Christmas, meet my Holly and say farewell to this place which treated you so badly but has maybe changed my life for good.'

'You really want me to come?'

'Yes.'

'And you've fallen in love?'

'I think I have.'

'Then don't talk about pushing,' she said, suddenly urgent. 'Don't you dare. She really gave the ring to Delia?'

'She thought it was rightfully hers.'

'It is, too,' his mother said thoughtfully. 'I never thought of it, but…your father really was a frightful man. He had charm by the bucketload but he was emotionally empty.'

'I know that.'

'So this Holly…'

'She's not emotionally empty.'

'And you?' his mother demanded. 'I've often thought…'

'That I'm emotionally empty?' Angus demanded, remembering all those accusations that had hurt so much. But then he thought that maybe he had been. If so, it was from years of practice, though, and years of training. Head, not heart.

But now wasn't the time to recall the past. Now was simply the time for saying it like it was.

'When Holly's around all I seem to feel is emotion,' he said simply. 'Mom, the ring thing…we did it to persuade Delia to let her kids come here for Christmas. Holly's my pretend fiancée, but I'm hoping…well, you know what I'm hoping. Come and meet her and see why.'

'I'm coming,' his mother said. 'I'm on my way!'

CHAPTER TEN

HOLLY AND HER grandmother had planned a Christmas that would live in the memory of those present for ever.

It started at dawn. The great bell attached to the castle chapel pealed all over the valley. The chapel hadn't been used—who knew?—maybe for centuries. Stunned, Angus grabbed a robe and headed out there—and found Holly swinging from a bell rope.

He'd been in this chapel just once on his first tour of inspection. The windows had been boarded up, the place was full of cobwebs and he'd taken one look and backed out.

But now someone had taken the boards from the windows, someone had stripped the cobwebs, someone had dusted and polished.

The tiny chapel was exquisite. The first weak rays of morning sun were shimmering through ancient stained glass. The pews were polished, the flagstones scrubbed and a massive bouquet of wild foliage stood on the altar.

And, above the nave, a girl in crimson pyjamas was pulling the bell rope for all she was worth. It was so high she almost lost her footing as the bell swung to its extremities. She was swinging with it, flushed, beaming—a ridiculous, red-headed urchin with her eyes full of mischief.

'Merry Christmas,' she gasped as she saw him. 'I thought this was the best way to get you up. There's egg nog and pancakes, and porridge for Dougal, and even pavlova because Mary said that's Delia's favourite food and I want her to eat something for breakfast. A week out of hospital and she's still as weak as a kitten. I'm so glad we have two nurses. But Angus, it's going to be a huge day and if I don't get breakfast into you all soon it'll be time for Christmas dinner and think of the waste! So up an' at 'em, Castle Craigie.'

She hauled the rope again and the force of the great brass bell almost lifted her off her feet.

She was irresistible. He wanted to walk forward and take her into his arms. Instead he walked forward, caught the rope and took over the pulling. 'You'll wake the entire valley!' he said but he kept pulling. The great booming chimes were echoing all around them. Christmas, here, now, they said—and something else. The pealing in of a new chapter of his life?

Including Holly?

'Excellent,' she said and plumped down on the nearest pew, giving weight to his new realisation that bell-pulling was harder than it looked. 'Santa believers will be up anyway and if you don't believe in Santa, you should.'

'Why did you clean the chapel?'

'We wanted to. Your mother and I did it yesterday when you took the kids out sledding. She remembered it. She says she used to come here and sit when she was at her loneliest. We snuggled Delia up in cushions and rugs and she supervised.'

'My mother and Delia…'

'Apparently Delia was a scared housemaid when your Mom was here. Now they seem the best of friends. Your Mom even approves of me giving her the ring.'

She did. What was happening here was truly astonishing. Helen had arrived ready to be appalled, but no one could be appalled for long in the Holly-and-Maggie Christmas Castle. They'd transformed it and those who arrived were sucked right in. The Castle was almost full. Dougal was here with his nurses—and with Scruffy-Mac permanently glued to his knee. Delia was here with her astounded mother. The kids and Melly the cat were here, whooping, whooping, whooping, filling the Castle with their life and laughter. Teasing Angus. Being bossed by Holly. Making this place a family home.

As his mother had walked into the Castle, Holly had swooped on her with joy. 'You must be Helen. We are so, so happy that you've decided to come. I need to tell you before you come an inch further in that I've given away your ring, but please don't hate me.'

Any reservations Helen might have held had died right then. She'd been given the old Earl's room but Holly and Maggie had redecorated in a fashion that took her breath away. She'd come down to dinner that night in her customary elegant black but Polly and Mary had looked at her in astonishment.

'Why are you wearing a black dress?' Polly had demanded, ten years old and obviously not one to keep her feelings to herself. 'Everyone's pretty except you. Okay, Maggie wears black but only when she's being boss of the world as Castle Housekeeper. She wears pretty at night.'

Maggie had choked on her champagne and there'd been general laughter. His mother had smiled it off too, but, to Angus's astonishment, she'd made him take her into Edinburgh the next day. She also rejected the twinset and pearl place. She'd come back with colours.

His mother had been wearing colours for six days now, not quite as vibrant as Holly's but almost, and Angus, who couldn't remember his mother wearing colour ever in his life, was astounded every time he looked at her.

It was down to Holly. His miracle-maker.

He tugged the bell while she got her breath back, the

great bell rose and fell, rose and fell; he looked down at the girl at his feet…

'I didn't buy you a diamond for Christmas,' he said before he could stop himself, before he could even think that this was hardly the place, hardly the time. 'But I wanted to. I still want to. Holly, I'm laying ghosts all over the place and, employer or not, I can't wait. As soon as the shops open after Christmas, can I take you in and make it official? Holly, I know I hired you as my temporary fiancée, but the position's now been declared permanent.'

She didn't reply. Maybe she couldn't because the bell was still ringing out and it seemed vitally important that it keep ringing. Maybe he was afraid that if he stopped there'd be silence, and into that silence would come refusal.

'You're pretty amazing,' she said at last between peals and he paused and there was a hiccup in the ringing but she shook her head. 'No. Not everyone's up yet. Keep pulling.'

'I believe,' he said between pulls, 'that I've just proposed. I think I need to go down on bended knee.'

'Don't do that.'

'Holly…'

'Yeah, I know you want to,' she said, almost thoughtful. 'It's dumb. This feeling between us…it's like a spell. Neither of us thinks it's sensible…'

'Why isn't it sensible?'

'Well, I'm broken-hearted for one,' she said, and he had to strain to hear above the peals. 'Practically jilted at the altar and robbed of all my worldly goods as well as my pride. If I said yes now it'd be on the rebound.'

'Would it?'

'I think so,' she said cautiously, and it was too much; he released the bell rope and the great bell slowly swayed to silence. He sat down on the pew beside her and she turned to face him. She looked…puzzled. Was puzzled how a woman was supposed to look after a proposal of marriage?

'I'm scared,' she said but she didn't look scared at all.

'Why?'

'Because I don't trust myself? Because this feels like a Cinderella story? Because I've made one ghastly mistake already—and I knew Geoff for years before I agreed to marry him, so how can I fall for you in two weeks? My parents died and I felt…empty. When Geoff left I copped that emptiness all over again and how can I expose myself to that sort of hurt again?'

'I wouldn't…'

'I don't know you wouldn't,' she said inexorably. 'What do I know about you other than you had a fiancée once you hate to talk about and you're scared you might be like your father?'

Those qualms were reasonable. He could answer them—except the last.

The last made him feel ill.

'I was engaged to Louise when I was twenty-one,' he said. 'She was after a rich husband. I was young and dumb. I was humiliated to the core, which is why I don't talk about it, but Holly, a love affair at twenty-one might just possibly be classified as irrelevant now. But for the rest… If you think I might possibly, remotely be like my father then you should run a mile. But it's irrelevant, too. I'm not the Lord of this castle. It's not who I am. I'm selling and running.'

'It's not just the Lord thing.'

'I think it is,' he said roughly. 'Every one of the long line of title-holders has lived in this place and lorded it over their minions. I'm going back to New York, Holly. I'm renouncing the title and all it entails. I'm going back to who I was before my father died, and I want, very, very badly, to take you with me.'

'You can't go back to who you were before your father died,' she said, still looking puzzled. 'You're different. Like me… I'm a whole different woman to the woman Geoff dumped. I doubt myself now.'

'Don't doubt me,' he said, strongly now, taking her hands in his and holding. 'Holly, I don't have doubts. I know it's fast, but you're wonderful. More than wonderful. Marry me and come and live in Manhattan. Bring Maggie if you like. I'll set you up in a restaurant. You'd be amazing—Manhattan would love you.'

'Have you been into my egg nog?' she demanded. 'I know I have. I had to get up and make it so of course I've tried it while I was stuffing the turkey. So now I'm sitting in an ancient chapel in red pyjamas and I've had two lovely swigs of egg nog and you're here making too-much-egg-noggy statements. Angus, this is crazy.'

'This is true.'

'No. It's nuts. And I'm cold,' she said inconsequentially and she shivered to prove it.

He started to haul off his robe but she stood and backed away.

'Cold feet,' she said, but he looked down and saw her gorgeous thick furry boots, courtesy of her finally located luggage.

'Figuratively,' she said. 'Inside, I'm all a wobble.'

'Does that mean you're turning me down?'

'Not…' Still that puzzle remained on her face. 'Not yet. Not today. But I'm not saying yes, either.'

'Holly, I am not my father,' he said steadily. 'I swear. We will leave this castle behind.'

'What your father was about was never about the castle.'

'I think it was. My mother's here making a pretence at keeping cheerful but I see her staring at these walls and I see her shudder. The ghosts here could never let us be happy. Besides,' he said, smiling, 'Manhattan's warmer. Anywhere's warmer than Scotland in winter.'

'So it is, but Scotland in winter's where we are and where

you're proposing,' she said. 'And it's where I need to make up my mind. But if I'm not to serve breakfast in red pyjamas then I need to run. You've employed me as a chef as well as a fiancée, Lord Angus, so now I need to put my chef hat on and let Christmas run its course.'

He'd never had such a Christmas. Even the surly Stanley was seen to smile. Holly and Maggie had woven Christmas magic, and if the new owner of the estate turned out to be someone who'd raze the castle and turn it into a golf resort then so be it, the castle was going out in style.

There was so much food—magnificent food. Everyone was groaning by mid-morning but still fronting up for Christmas dinner and then still staggering to the tea table.

Angus felt weird but fantastic, Lord of all he surveyed, head of a sort-of-family that he'd never known existed. At Holly's insistence, he stood at the head of the table feeling almost out of body, carving a turkey that looked as if it had been on steroids. How had Holly managed this? For a start, how had she managed to find such a turkey, because she swore—to the always-enquiring Mary—that it was both free range and organically farmed.

Not that Mary would have suffered if she hadn't been able to eat turkey. The vast table was almost groaning, and Angus looked around at his strange mix of assorted guests and tried to figure how Holly could have them all mixing, laughing and happy.

Because that was what they were, right down to Scruffy-cum-Mac and Melly the cat.

There was Christmas music all around them. Ben was apparently a techno whizz and Holly had put his talents to use, even if as a self-respecting adolescent Ben thought woofers and sub woofers and associated coolness were wasted on *Jingle Bells*. His pay-off was that every fourth song was one of the ones he'd been recording with his mates.

There were games inside and out, and there were gifts for everyone.

Angus hadn't thought of gifts—or he had but Holly had just groaned when he'd mentioned it on Christmas Eve and chuckled and said, 'Thank heaven the world doesn't depend on men to keep it running.' The gifts were small but awesome—dumb games, movies of old comic-book characters. And cup cakes, individually designed, each an exquisite work of art personally designed for the recipient. Even Stanley got a kick out of his, a cup cake with a clever construct of Stanley with his ancient tweed cap and his great hook nose somehow softened to make him look fun.

Holly…

Holly.

When had he fallen in love with her? he wondered as the day wore on and he watched the life and laughter surrounding her. When had she bewitched him? For bewitched he was. She might still have reservations, but he had none. If she'd accept him, he wanted this woman with him for the rest of his life.

He thought of his life in Manhattan, as it had been and as it could be. This joy and laughter for ever. Was it greedy to want it to start now?

Maybe he shouldn't have asked her this morning. Maybe he'd rushed it.

No matter. He'd just keep asking. She'd lose her scruples the moment he got her out of this castle, with all its memories. This place was nothing to do with him. His father's history was nothing to do with him. Without this castle, she could fall in love…

Patience. Time.

'Oi. We're going outside to make snow angels and then we're taking plastic bags up the hill and riding down. You want to come or you want to stand daydreaming into the fire all day?'

It was Holly—of course it was Holly—bundled up like a snow bunny, her cheeks already glowing in anticipation of the cold.

Merry Christmas, Holly, he said silently to himself as he shrugged on his coat and prepared to follow Holly and the whooping kids. 'Every Christmas will be merry now that I've found you.'

Take your time, she told herself. Don't let yourself believe you've fallen in love. He's rushing you. He wants to marry you before he even knows you.

But... There were two Holly voices in this conversation, each as strong as the other. *But he's heart-stoppingly gorgeous. He'd kind, he's gentle, he's rich...*

Since when was rich important?

If all other things are equal, rich is very handy, thank you very much. It'd be soooo nice to be out of debt.

You'd let him pay your debts?

I might.

That's immoral.

So I have an immoral streak. Get over it.

This internal conversation was doing her head in. She should be concentrating on steering her plastic bag but, try as she might, the plastic bag took her exactly where it wanted. Soft snow was mounded at the bottom of the run; she knew she'd end up buried so she might as well chat as she went.

You've fallen in love; you know you have.

And that's why it's so important to keep your head. Otherwise you'll end up as a kept woman in some Manhattan apartment and you'll be in as big a mess as his mother was.

He says Maggie can come too. That's hardly the action of a man intent on isolating his lover.

Yes, but that's a con. Take Maggie away from her be-loved Scotland? He knows she'd never leave.

So what will she do?

What will you do?

Whumff! She hit the snow bank head-on, and in she went, buried to her ears in soft snow. The kids, who'd learned quickly the skill of hauling back on their bags to avoid the ignominy of burial, hooted with laughter, but a gorgeous man in a kilt strode across, reached out his hands and hauled her out.

She came up too fast. She was too close.

She was breathing far too hard.

'You're a very bad driver, Ms McIntosh,' he told her, smiling down at her with that smile that made her toes curl.

'I'm bad at lots of things,' she managed, now totally breathless.

'You'll fit in fine in Manhattan. Wait and see.'

'No, you wait and see,' she retorted. 'Angus…'

'Yes?'

'Just wait and see. Please.'

She couldn't sleep. It had been the most wonderful Christmas of her life. She'd worked harder than she ever had, she'd played harder, she'd put more thought into gifts, she'd worried more about who was enjoying themselves, she'd set herself a target of sending everyone to bed happy and she thought she'd succeeded. Old Dougal had gripped her hands before his Christmas-sated nurse had helped him to bed and said, 'I don't even mind going back to that place now. I'll remember this forever.'

Forever might not be for very long, she thought, remembering the old man's frail handshake, but right now he was in bed happy, probably asleep, and so should she be. She was happily exhausted. But…

But what?

But nothing. She pushed back her covers and padded across to the long slit window through the two-foot thick stone walls. The moonlight was playing on the snow. In the distance she could see the twinkling lights of the village—did everyone have a Santa Claus on their chimney?

'God's in his heaven, all's right with the world,' she murmured, and it was, but sleep was far away.

She'd loved Angus today. He'd thrown himself into Christmas heart and soul. He'd played dumb games with the kids, he'd seemingly made everyone happy, he was a host whose kindness spread to each and every one of his guests.

Christmas had been wonderful because of Angus.

Angus...

She'd go and check the ovens, she told herself, feeling desperate that sleep wouldn't come and her dreams only had one direction. A Liege Lord in a kilt to die for...

No! Ovens, she told herself fiercely. She'd discovered the huge cleaned-up range was fantastic for bread-making but it needed to be stoked and damped down for the night and she hadn't quite got the hang of it. She could just go see...

She shoved her feet into her furry boots and headed downstairs, pleased to have purpose behind her insomnia—and her errant thoughts. But then...

Angus was in the hall. He had his back to the great hearth, where the yule log smouldered and where lesser logs burned with dancing flames.

He looked up as she came downstairs, but he didn't smile. It was almost as if he was expecting her.

'I'm...I'm going to check the ovens,' she said, struggling to make her voice work.

'Maggie and I already checked them. Maggie says they'll be perfect for your bread.'

'I...thank you. I'll go back to bed, then.'

'Holly...' And all of a sudden he was right there, right at the foot of the stairs and a girl should turn and run but there was no way in the world this girl was turning and running. Not now. Not on this magic night. Not when this man was standing before her, looking like…

Like he loved her?

Every sense was screaming be sensible at her, but there was something below, something so deep, so primeval that sense didn't stand a chance. Angus was right here, right now, and yes, a sensible woman should back away because she'd made a lot of very sensible resolutions and so had he, but suddenly there didn't seem to be an ounce of sensible left in either of them.

'Angus,' she said stupidly and he smiled and took her hands and drew her to him.

'Holly,' he said and it was as if wedding vows were spoken with that word. Love, honour, commitment—somehow she heard them all. Maybe it was wishful thinking, maybe it was pure fancy, but her head was no longer responding to instructions. This was pure heart. This was pure, instinctive need.

For this was her man and he was holding her, needing her and she wanted him as she'd wanted nothing else in her life.

'Come to my bed,' he said as he kissed her hair and drew her closer, closer and her body melted, just like that. She had nothing left to fight with and who wanted to fight anyway? This was her lord, her love, her gorgeous, gorgeous Angus, and he wanted her and she ached for him and nothing else mattered.

'You're already wearing my ring,' he told her. 'I love that you're wearing it, but it involves a promise. You're not my paid fiancée, Holly McIntosh, you're the woman I want more than anything else in the world. I'd give you my castle, my kingdom, my heart. I do give them to you. Holly, I love you and I want you in my bed. I want you for the rest of my life. I'll take a no if I must but if you could possibly see that scrap around your finger for the gold it should be...'

'I think I do,' she managed, somehow getting her voice to work. 'I'm sure I do.' And she wound her hands around his body, tilting her face to meet his, feeling his arms enfold her, lift her and finally carry her in triumph up the sweeping staircase to the vast lordly bedroom beyond.

'I do,' she whispered as he pushed the door open with his foot, as he carried her across the bedroom, as he laid her with all reverence on the huge four-poster bed and then sank down beside her to gather her in to him. 'Oh, Angus, I do, I do, I do.'

CHAPTER ELEVEN

THE TIME BETWEEN Christmas and Hogmanay was magic. Time out of this world. A fairy tale. For those within the castle walls, the rest of the world might not have existed.

And the way Holly looked at Angus, the way Angus looked at Holly, was just perfect.

'They're such a wonderful couple,' Delia said, over and over again to anyone who'd listen. 'I never thought I'd see a Lord of Castle Craigie who knew what it was to love.'

'He's my son,' Helen said fondly, seemingly finally reassured. 'He's nothing like his father.'

But, strangely, Maggie wasn't so certain. She watched her granddaughter with eyes that held reservations, but by the end of the week even she was being drawn into the fairy tale. Or Angus and Holly were trying to draw her in.

'You'll come to Manhattan with us,' Holly said and she'd managed to laugh.

'I won't, but we'll worry about that in the New Year. This is like the Cinderella story, with midnight being the day after Hogmanay. For now, let's soak up the ball.'

'It won't end,' Holly said stoutly. 'Gran, he's wonderful. He's not the least like his father. You must be able to see it.'

But, *I don't see him giving much,* Maggie thought. *Yes, he's being generous but Helen says he can afford to be. In the end he's talking about taking my girl back to his cas-*

tle, to his Manhattan. You show me a Lord that gives and I might believe it.

She didn't say it, though. Holly was in a bubble of love and laughter, and for this time, for this magic season, she wouldn't burst that bubble. She could only hope that the bubble was an old woman's worried fancy, and Holly's happy ever after was solid, loving fact.

'Angus is so much fun,' ten-year-old Polly exclaimed as she swooped past, freshly baked muffin in her hand, on her way from one Very Exciting Adventure to another. Angus had organised ice skates and they were off to try their skills on the shallow pond behind the chapel. 'But Holly's awesome, too, and Angus has wrapped Mum up in blankets and she's there waiting to watch me skate. This place is like magic. Even Mum says it's magic.'

And she was gone, enthralled with her fairy tale, leaving Maggie with her faint doubts and her desperate hope that she was wrong.

'I hope it's me being paranoid,' she muttered, but then she knew…what Holly didn't know. She hadn't explained it to her before the job came up, and afterwards… Would Holly have taken the job if she'd known? Probably not.

'But it shouldn't make a difference,' she told herself. 'He has every right to do what he's doing.'

But maybe it did make a difference. The more she saw of Angus's wealth, the more she thought it.

When she'd pushed Holly to go to London with him she hadn't thought through the ramifications. Almost as soon as they'd left, those worries had surfaced and they were on the surface still.

So tell Holly?

She'd figure it out. In time.

Would she mind?

Oh, Holly… Maggie thought, deciding that Holly might mind very much.

'I'll tell her after Hogmanay,' she told herself. 'After her Cinderella midnight.'

* * *

Hogmanay. Holly and Maggie had put more effort into this than they had Christmas, and they had the entire Castle population behind them. Even the children had worked. This was the party to end parties, the farewell of the Castle to the village. Everyone was seeing it as the landmark it was.

'It's the end of a long line of appalling landowners,' Angus said in grim satisfaction. 'I've had an offer from an Arabian oil tycoon. I'm heading to Glasgow on Wednesday to sign. He'll turn the place into a magnificent hunting and golf resort and the old Lords of Castle Craigie will be nothing but a dim memory.'

On the surface it seemed perfect.

But…

Maggie watched the preparations and knew she wasn't the only one feeling desolate, but it wasn't her way to show self-pity, not on such a day. They had the old place gleaming. They'd been cooking for days. The kids had built a bonfire to end all bonfires. They'd organised games for all ages. Holly had even attempted to make enough haggis to feed all.

Maggie watched the villagers come, she watched their awe at the transformation, and she thought: what if…? What if…?

What if nothing. Angus was selling and moving on, as was his right. He'd take Holly with him as was his wish.

The Lord of Castle Craigie had the last word.

It wasn't until the bonfire was lit, until the first leaping flames had died down a little and Holly stood among a group of weary, food-and-fun sated villagers that she realised there was sadness.

She'd been watching the flames. She turned and the two women closest to her were hugging each other, and one was weeping.

Who knew why? Maggie knew these people but she didn't. It wasn't her business to enquire.

But she'd spent the past couple of weeks making people happy. These tears seemed wrong.

'Can I help?' she enquired gently of the two women. 'Would you like me to take you into the Castle, show you to somewhere private?'

'I…no, thanks, miss.' The dry-eyed one was suddenly moist as well. 'It's just…it's going to be so hard. We got the final notices yesterday.'

'Notices?'

'Vacating requirements,' the woman said. 'Two months. Mr Stanley says that's more than generous but it's still heart-breaking. We've been here all our lives. It's fine for them who can afford to buy, but so few of us can. With the latest financial crisis, even those of us with good paying jobs can't get credit to buy. Craigenstone's finished. Your Gran… Us… This day marks the end. It's the first time in living memory the Lord has celebrated Hogmanay, that he's acted like a Laird instead of a Lord, but isn't it fitting that he's celebrating being shot of the lot of us?'

And Holly's mind turned to stone, just like that.

The sale of the Castle. *Craigenstone's finished.*

Oh, my…

Her head was whirling, trying to grasp facts, and the facts she saw looming up out of the abyss were appalling. And it was as if the abyss had been there all along, but she hadn't looked. She hadn't seen it. She hadn't even glimpsed it.

How could she have been so blind?

Gran hadn't told her.

But she had. Her head was sending her back three weeks ago, to the day she'd arrived.

'The landlord's selling after all these years. I should have saved, but Holly, somehow I never dreamed… What a stupid old woman.'

She'd heard Maggie say it and she'd felt ill, but she'd imagined one landlord, one cottage. Not an entire village.

'What…what do you mean, acting like a Laird and not a Lord?' she managed and one of the women gave a short, humourless laugh.

'A Laird is Himself,' she said. 'He's the keeper of the estate, the one who cares. We've never had one here and now we never will. We've always had a Lord, but what good is that to us? Nothing at all, and now less than ever.'

They turned away, distressed, and Holly was left on her own. She found her feet wandering aimlessly to the back of the bonfire, away from the crowds. She needed space.

She needed sense.

She was Australian. She hadn't seen the picture, but now…she'd read enough historical novels to get what was happening.

The estate wasn't just the castle; it was the whole of Craigenstone, and an oil tycoon buying an estate to form a hunting/golf resort would want as many of the picturesque stone cottages as he could get. It sounded as if Angus had offered to let the villagers buy theirs if they wanted—if they could afford it—but the remainder would go in the sale.

She saw Stanley standing a little apart, with the same grim stance as he'd always had. She didn't like the man. She knew Angus was only putting up with him because there was no one else who knew the place, but still, he gave her the creeps.

Now she forced herself to go forward and talk to him.

'How many cottages are being sold to their tenants?' she asked him directly and he didn't even bother turning towards her to answer.

'Ten.'

'Out of?'

'Sixty. The buyer would have taken them as a job lot but His Lordship insisted tenants be given the option.'

'Nice of him,' she snapped and something inside her snapped too.

When she thought of what this Christmas had cost there hadn't been a quibble. She'd looked Angus up on the Internet; he'd even shown her. He was part-owner of one of the biggest financial institutions in the world.

Christmas here would be a drop in the ocean of his wealth. What he'd get for this village would be nothing in his vast financial ocean.

But he wanted to be shot of it. While he owned the Castle he was compared to his father; he was Lord of Castle Craigie and he didn't like it.

So why not sell it?

He was selfish, just like Geoff, she thought, feeling sick to the heart. How could she have been so blind *twice*?

Her feet were still acting of their own accord, finding their way seemingly all on their own to the back of the crowd, where he stood, a tall, solitary lord surveying the scene he'd created.

She'd thought she loved this man. She'd given him her body. And her heart?

No! Head, not heart. Had she learned nothing?

'Angus…'

He turned and saw her and he knew at once that something was wrong. His brows snapped down in a frown. 'Love?'

'I'm not,' she said carefully, 'your love.'

'That's not what you said this morning.'

'This morning,' she said carefully, 'I didn't know you were evicting an entire village.'

'I'm not,' he said, startled.

'You're selling the estate. The entire district of Craigenstone.'

'I am, but…'

'But what?'

'But it's time it stopped being feudal,' he said gently. 'This Hogmanay might well be in keeping with centuries of tradition, but a Lord has no place in these people's lives. You know that. All I'm doing is moving into the twenty-first century.'

'All you're doing is going home to Manhattan.'

'That's unfair.' His dark brows had snapped down. 'Holly, these people don't want me. They didn't want my father or my grandfather before him.'

'Maybe they did, but they didn't get them.'

'I don't know what you mean.'

'I mean this village is gorgeous,' Holly said. 'It's ringed by mountains, it's freezing in winter, it's probably invaded by midges in summer, yes there are downsides, but even I can see that this is a community, not a collection of individual cottages. And a community needs a leader. Yet you're going to make a fortune and walk away, leaving these people with what? Golf?'

'With their own homes.'

'Not with their own homes. Ten out of sixty are buying. The rest are leaving.'

'That's their choice.'

'How can it be their choice? How dare you say that?' She was practically yelling. 'With the global financial crisis in full swing, how do you expect someone like Gran to get a loan? Her parents, her parents' parents and parents' parents' parents lived in this village, right next door to the cottage she lives in now, and as a bride she moved next door, to where her husband's people had done the same. They've never been offered the choice to buy, so they've never thought of it. And now, pow, eviction, and off they'll go to some welfare housing in the city. If they're lucky.'

'Would you keep your voice down?' he said and, to her fury, he sounded amused. The bonfire was still crackling. The bagpipes, which someone had been playing in the back-

ground, had died while everyone watched the flames so
Holly's fury could be heard. 'Holly, it's not that bad. If anyone really wants to stay, they can.'

'How?'

'I've organised finance. I have it available. If your Gran
or anyone like her wishes to stay in their cottage then they
can. The rent they're paying now will cover the interest.
It's an interest-only loan, not repayable until they move out,
or in the case of direct descendants, until the next generation moves out. Then the cottage will be sold and the loan
called in at point of sale. Villagers can elect to sell any time
they want—no pressure.'

'That's not what Gran told me.'

'It's what I'm telling you.'

'Even if it's true, it's still splitting the village; you're still
killing a community.'

'That's nothing to do with me,' he said, but as she looked
at him she saw a faint trace of unease. This night—or,
more, this gathering in the Castle over Christmas—must
surely have shown him how important community could
be. 'Holly, the feudal system is dead. I can't be expected to
stay here as Liege Lord, the same as my father.'

'So you're acting as ruthlessly as your father would have:
abandoning them, heading off to Manhattan to make more
money...'

'That's not fair.'

'Why does Gran have to sell her house?'

'She doesn't.'

'She does. She doesn't have a choice. And why is Edna
Black crying? Why is Essie McLeod sobbing along with
her? Why is this whole community disintegrating while
you make money?'

'Holly...'

'Head, not heart,' she said, and the anger had suddenly
gone. 'The acorn never falls far from the tree. Dumb Holly,

that's me. And blind. Geoff robbed just me but you're robbing a whole community. I can't believe I've been so stupid. You are like your father.'

'How can you say that?'

'So why are you going back to Manhattan? Your father would have done exactly what suited him. Isn't that what you're doing? I don't know the ins and outs of finance, but I know Gran is destitute—that's why I was forced to work for you. Right. I've worked for you. I've been your chef and your fiancée for Christmas and beyond, but Hogmanay is now over. My official contract finishes tomorrow, just as soon as I've done the washing-up, stripped the beds and put back the dust covers.'

She wrenched—with some difficulty—the crazy metal ring from her engagement finger and handed it back. He took it without a word.

'Sense prevails,' she said dully, stepping back. 'I've made one stupid, stupid mistake, I walked straight into another and I'm done.'

'Holly, I love you.'

'Well, I don't love you,' she said and gave the lie to her words with a sob. 'I can't. Angus, I want heart and that's all I want. I know this is dumb, but somehow I want the whole fairy tale. I want a man who truly knows how to be a Lord. A Laird even.'

Holly disappeared—to the kitchen? To start the washing-up? To cry her heart out? He desperately wanted to follow, but first he had to get some facts.

Half an hour talking to villagers gave him an outline. Yes, he should have talked individually to his tenants before, but he'd been here such a short time, enough to see his father's neglect, the contempt in which his father was held. He'd thought he'd pack up and leave as soon as he could. Only Ben's phone call—and then Holly bursting onto the scene like a Christmas angel—had interfered with his plans.

So as far as the sale went, he'd left the communication with the villagers to Stanley. Stanley was in charge of the rent roll. He knew each of the villagers individually, so Angus had worked out his terms and left it to Stanley to talk to them.

But now it seemed Stanley hadn't talked to them—he'd written. One of the villagers who lived closest heard Angus's tight-lipped questions and nipped home fast. He came back with two letters.

Angus read, and a cold fury started burning deep within. Was that an oxymoron? Cold and burning? But that was what this felt like. He felt ill.

Holly's accusations were just.

He'd left this to Stanley. He knew Stanley was guilty of petty dishonesty, he didn't like the man, but it had been so much easier to leave it with him.

Why had he done what he'd done? He paced, and paced some more, and then he made a couple of calls. To the agent in London who specialised in large estates, who'd been handling this sale, who was earning so much from it that he didn't mind taking a call at this hour. And then to the Middle East, to the accountant of an oil tycoon.

Then he went and found Dougal. The old man was still awake. He'd been out in his wheelchair, watching the bonfire. Now he and his little dog were propped up in bed watching the dying embers through the window, watching the villagers drift home, watching the end of the estate.

He was astonished to receive his late night visitor, but in half an hour Angus realised the man's mind was still razor-sharp and coldly vindictive. Towards Stanley and towards Angus's father, who'd employed him.

'He told me Mac'd been given a home by Rob at the pub,' he said as a parting shot. 'Lying hound. He just booted Mac out. I don't know how he's survived. As far as Stanley was concerned, we were both better off dead.'

It was a fitting epitaph to the accusations whirling in his head. His father. Stanley. Himself. Some of those accusations were aimed squarely at him.

Then he sat down in silence in the Castle library and stared bleakly into the night.

You're killing a community.

It was a cold thought and it was absolutely true.

What to do? How to repair such damage?

Not sell? The contract wasn't irreversible. But if he didn't sell... He'd seen the cottages, the roads, the infrastructure. He'd seen the grinding poverty. The place needed a massive injection of...something.

Love?

Holly?

That was crazy thinking. He had to think like a financier here. A financier was what he was.

He was also Lord of Castle Craigie. It was a role he didn't want, he'd never wanted, but that was what he was.

A Laird as well as a Lord? Somewhere, in the night's conversations, that distinction had been made crystal-clear.

Finally at dawn he rose and walked to the gilt mirror over the fireplace. A bleak figure looked back at him, unshaven, tired, grim. He was still wearing the kilt of his forebears. He was dressed in the Highland battledress of ages.

So... He was the Lord of Castle Craigie ready to face barbarians from without, but it seemed the barbarians were within. This battle was nothing to do with the oil tycoon who'd offered to buy this place. It was a little to do with Stanley. Soon, when he had his facts fully together, he'd go and face the man.

But it had everything to do with himself.

He wasn't like his father.

He wasn't, he thought grimly, and he knew, he just knew,

that given this current set of facts the old man would have walked away without a backward glance. What the oil tycoon was offering was truly staggering.

But Holly would expect…

Holly did expect, and so did he. He cast one last look at the letters, at the figures, and something within him settled into a rock-hard resolve.

He needed to talk to Stanley, he thought. Now.

And then he needed to talk to Holly. If she'd listen.

CHAPTER TWELVE

HOLLY HAD CRIED herself to sleep. This was dumb. It was the behaviour of an angsty, lovesick teenager. Even when Geoff had done his worst she'd felt anger and disgust and distress but she'd never sobbed into her pillow over him. Over humiliation, yes, and over desperation at her financial position, but never over Geoff the man.

But last night—or in the wee hours when she'd finally cleaned up the kitchen—she'd crept upstairs and hauled her blankets over her head and given way to despair—a despair only matched by the loss of her parents. Her grief seemed to go that deep. Bone-deep.

She'd been so tired and so distressed she hadn't so much as combed her hair. She knew she had ash on her face, she knew her eyes were swollen from crying, she knew she was a sodden mess and when the knock came at the door she dived under the covers and yelled, 'Go away.'

Then she peered out from under the covers again and checked her bedside clock. Seven. She'd crawled into bed at four. Three hours' sleep.

But her contract said she still had to work today—her last day. Did the hordes want a cooked breakfast?

She would do this, she thought determinedly. She would fulfil her contract and take the money promised her. Then at least Maggie would have enough for a rental bond.

Something good had to come from this mess.

'Breakfast in half an hour,' she yelled to the knocker. 'Go away.'

Instead the handle turned and the door opened inward. Angus.

She should have locked the door.

The door didn't have a lock.

She should have wedged the chair against it. She did not want this man in her room.

Angus.

He hadn't slept. She could see that at a glance. He was exactly as he'd been last night, in full Highland regalia, smoke-stained, five o'clock shadow and then some, tired, strained, grim as death.

'We need to talk,' he said, but she shook her head and sat up, hauling her bedclothes to her neck.

'There's no need. What's done's done. I'm finishing up at lunch time. Everyone's leaving. You and Stanley can do your worst.'

'You think I'm an ogre, don't you.'

She took a deep breath, trying to see sense, trying for a bit of justice here. This man hadn't asked to inherit. He didn't want this place. He'd come, he'd sold, and he was moving on.

Oh, but the pain he was causing…

'Stanley's been taking a cut,' he said, slicing across her thoughts. Jumping right in where her thoughts were centred. He hadn't come into the room—he was standing at the door as if he had no right to come further.

'Stanley,' she said cautiously, trying to fight back judgement for a moment. Let the accused speak…

'I can't lay it all on Stanley.' His words were as bleak and hard as his face. He stood against the door-jamb as if he were in the dock admitting murder. 'But it is my fault. Back in Manhattan I'd never have let an unknown employee have such responsibility, especially one I already suspected of dishonesty, but here it seemed I had no choice. I came over to settle the estate, sell it and get back to Manhattan. Stanley was the only retainer left who knew the place. I gave instructions but they weren't followed. That's up to me. I suspected the man was dishonest; I just hadn't dreamed how much.'

'What's…so what's he done?' She could barely get her voice to work. She wasn't inviting him in. She wasn't lowering her bedclothes from around her neck. Bedclothes and distance were fragile armour but they were all she had.

'He took a kick-back from the buyer's financial men,' he said. 'He gets ten per cent of the value of any cottage included in the purchase. Stanley knew he had to communicate my offer to let each cottager buy, but he failed to mention the financial help I'd organised. So therefore every cottager was faced with a two-month eviction notice unless they could find finance on commercial terms. In this climate…'

'Financial help? You were offering…what?'

He told her. He stood and watched as she listened. He watched as he saw her thinking of the offer, how much it would have meant to Maggie, how much it would have meant to every cottager struggling to come to terms with leaving.

But she still didn't lower her bedclothes.

'It's better,' she said at last. 'I mean, it's good. So, now you know, you'll fix it?'

'I'll fix it. Stanley's sacked and already gone. I hope to never see the man again, but my lawyers will be following him. No contract's set in stone yet. Every cottager who wants to stay will be able to.'

'Great,' she said. 'That's that then.'

'Yes.'

Fantastic, she thought. Justice had been served. Maggie

could stay. The village of Craigenstone would go on being Craigenstone. She should be whooping.

She wasn't.

'So you'll reorganise the cottage sales and go back to Manhattan?' she asked dully.

'See, there's the thing,' he said, gently now, as if he'd only just figured it out for himself but was afraid to say it aloud. Afraid to make it real. 'I don't think I can.'

'Leave?'

'No.'

'Wh...why not?'

'Because this estate needs a Laird.' And then he smiled, a tired, rueful smile, and he glanced down at his smoke-stained kilt, his sporran, all the trappings of his title. 'Maybe it needs a man the villagers can refer to as Him-self. Someone who cares. This estate's been run down for generations. I spent a lot of last night talking to McAllister. It's amazing how awake he can be when his passion's firing and, at the first talk of estate restoration, fire it did. His body's failing but his mind is razor-sharp. One hint from me and orders came thick and fast.'

'Orders?' Her bedclothes had slipped now, just a little, not so much as you'd notice, and she wasn't noticing. She was too busy listening.

'This valley has no industry at all. There was a wool-len mill on the estate until thirty years ago, but it fell into disrepair during my father's time. It needed massive up-keep but my father closed it rather than spending money, and its loss caused untold poverty for the crofters. Appar-ently our sheep produce the finest fleeces in all of Scot-land. The reputation for our product remains to this day, but the land's been let go to ruin, the crofters forced off the land by poverty, the market ignored. If I was to put in some decent infrastructure...restore the crofts...build more cottages rather than sell...put money back into restoring our flocks for fine wool…McAllister says there's enough of our sheep left to pull the flocks back together. He also says there's enough of the skills remaining in the old folk to get the mill restarted. Craigenstone Woollens. We might just make it work.'

'But Angus, you're talking years,' she said, trying to get her head around what he was saying. 'You're talking… passion.'

'Yes. And I'm talking staying here,' he said. 'I'm talking about not being like my forebears. I'm talking about bringing this valley back to life.' And then he paused. 'I'm talking life, my Holly. Here. With you. With the kids if they want to stay, and it seems right that they do. With McAllister behind me for as long as he's able. I'm talking about forever.'

'You've decided this in one night?' She was so breathless she could scarcely get her words out. 'How can you have decided so fast?'

Still he didn't come near. Maybe he didn't think he had the right. Maybe he thought she'd scream the roof down. 'Because it's been a long night? No,' he corrected himself. 'It's been a long three weeks. Three weeks to change a life?'

'I don't know what you mean.'

'Can I come in?'

'Yes, if you don't touch me,' she managed.

'Are you scared of pillaging?' He threw her a weary smile, and that smile…it made her world turn inside out.

'Angus, I'm scared of me, not you,' she admitted. 'Up until yesterday, my hormones were going nuts for you and yes, they still are, and you're still wearing that kilt and your legs are doing my head in, but I made my decision last night and I'll stick to it.'

'Even if my parameters have changed? Even if your accusation that I'm just like my father shoved something home that should have been shoved home years ago, and has been the catalyst for massive change. Holly, your accusations are just. Maybe my mother's fears have been just. I live for myself—I always have. I don't try to do harm. I put my head down and work and I make a lot of money, but I've never thought of the bigger picture. Or maybe I should make that the smaller picture. The financial corporation I run gives a lot to charity. I give when I'm asked, but I don't give because I see need. That's obviously because I don't look.'

'But you did look when Ben asked to come here,' she admitted. 'You did ask Dougal to come. You've filled the Castle.'

'Yes, but that was because you were here,' he said bluntly. 'When I advertised for you I didn't even want you. If I hadn't found you I would have had an excuse not to have the kids here. I didn't give myself.'

'So…so now what?' she managed, and finally he walked forward, he moved to her bedside but he didn't touch her. He was still keeping his distance. Employer speaking to employee who'd thrown accusations at him and quit.

'I've fallen in love with you, Holly McIntosh,' he said softly into the stillness of the morning. 'More. I've fallen in love with what you are, and it's what I want to be. I want to be able to give like you do. I want to be able to live like you.'

'What, fall in love with rubbish men?' she demanded, and he smiled.

'You've fallen in love with one and a half rubbish men. The final half has redeemed himself. Or intends to redeem himself. Holly, think about what we could do with this Castle. Think! We could turn this place around. Craigenstone would come to life again. I have the capital to inject. I'd love to do it; I will do it. Holly, if I need to, I'll do it alone, but I don't want that. I've fallen in love with my wonderful Christmas gift, my Holly, my girl who's turned my life around.'

'You…you don't want to go back to Manhattan?'

'I'll need to go back and forth from time to time,' he conceded. 'The company's running smoothly but I'll still need to maintain my interest to fund what we need to do here. But…you've never been to Manhattan.'

'No.'

'Would you like to go?' And then, before she could speak, he put his hand up. 'Don't answer. Not yet. I'm not asking for a Manhattan bride. I'm asking for a bride for Castle Craigie. I'm asking for a Lady for a Lord, a Herself to match Himself, a woman who'll help make this Castle, this whole estate, truly grand. And who'll occasionally accompany her husband on his business travels—when he really needs to be away and when he can't bear to be parted from her.'

'Angus…'

'Because I can't bear to be parted from you, Holly,' he said softly, putting his fingers on her lips, and then he stooped and took her hands gently into his. 'I love you, Holly McIntosh and I'll do whatever it takes to make you love me. If that means every time I go to Manhattan I need to take along three kids, their mum, your gran, a dog, a cat, Dougal, his nurse, this whole amazing entourage, then so be it, but my days of being a loner are over. I don't want to be Lord of Castle Craigie alone, my love. It's quite a title and it needs to fit us all. I think Lord should be another word for family. Lord of Castle Craigie. Us.'

And then, as she failed to speak—for how could she speak when her eyes were wet with tears?—he tugged her forward and she felt the last of her armour slip away. He tugged her into his arms and he held her, as if she were the most precious thing in the world, and Holly McIntosh's world changed right there, right then.

Her Lord had found his Lady. Cinderella had found her prince.

Holly had found her Angus.

'Will you marry me?' he said, the words muffled in her hair and somehow she managed to nod. It was a pretty weird nod, though, when she was so close, so close…

'Yes,' she managed.

'And will you love me?'

'Of course I'll love you,' she said through tears. 'I love you forever, forever and forever. I wanted to. I thought I did the first time I saw you, especially in that kilt, but Angus, I didn't trust…'

'You had reason not to trust. But can you now?'

'Maybe,' she said between kisses. 'Maybe, my love, as long as you keep wearing that kilt, maybe I know I can.'

It was a great day in the history of the tiny village of Craigenstone when Lord Angus McTavish Stuart took one Holly Margaret McIntosh to be his bride.

They were married in the chapel of Castle Craigie—of course they were—but the chapel was tiny and there wasn't a soul in the district who didn't want to be part of this joyous day. Marquees had been set up with sound and vision so this wedding could be shared by all.

'She's our girl,' the villagers declared, conveniently forgetting Holly's father had gone to Australia and married an Australian and Holly spoke with a broad Aussie twang. For this day she was Our Maggie's granddaughter, a local, their girl taming the Lord of Castle Craigie.

For Angus was still the Earl of Craigenstone. No one wanted him to renounce the title. The villagers saw Angus taking on the title as a beginning of a new and bright future, not a continuance of the same.

He was moving mountains, this new Lord of theirs. Their Laird. Already an army of workers was repairing roads, restoring long neglected cottages, preparing crofts for the sheep that Angus planned would return to bring prosperity back to the valley. The old ways had been superseded by the new but there were many who craved quality and craftsmanship, and Angus's business acumen saw a niche that wasn't small.

The mill was being rebuilt. The old folk of the village were being turned to for advice, for teaching. The village hummed and there was already talk of young ones, drifted away for generations, returning to take part in this new resurgence.

And it all hung on this couple, this darkly handsome Lord, who looked just like his father but who wasn't the least like him, and his astonishing half Scottish, half Antipodean bride.

And now the day had come. Angus stood before the altar in his wedding finery—the Stuart tartan, the dress sword, tassels, sporran, every piece of Scottish gorgeousness Holly could convince him to wear. Dougal was in his wheelchair by his side, looking almost as fine, waiting with his Lord for the woman who'd made this happen.

Holly.

And here she was, rounding the great Castle walls in a dray. Maggie was by her side, dressed to the nines as well—someone had to use that Very Expensive Dress Shop in Edinburgh—and she was giving the bride away, for there was no way in the world she was letting another do it.

The dray came to a halt. Holly jumped down almost before it stopped, not waiting for the dozen men who'd surged forward to help. Mary and Polly collected her train—vintage lace because this was Maggie's gown recycled, but there was nothing recycled about this bride.

She looked exquisite, She was exquisite. Angus thought, as he watched his bride make her way towards him. The deep cream gown fitted her to perfection and her copper curls glowed and glinted in the afternoon light.

She'd always glow, he thought, and somewhere in his heart he felt room to be sorry for the unknown Geoff, who'd treated her so badly and in doing so had given Angus, given this valley, these people, so much.

'I've got your ring safe,' Ben whispered as Holly grew nearer but Angus didn't hear. He had eyes only for his bride.

From this day forth…

They'd fill the Castle, he thought, with their family, their friends, their animals. They'd make this place a home as it truly should be a home. It might be a great grey fortress on the outside but on the inside… Holly had brought her heart to this Castle and it was transformed.

More, she'd brought her heart to his, and that was transformed as well.

'My love,' he said softly as she reached him and he took her hand and drew her to stand by his side. 'You look beautiful.'

'You don't scrub up too badly yourself,' she said and grinned and he chuckled, a lovely deep chuckle that had every lady in the congregation sighing and knowing exactly why it was that Holly was marrying this man.

But Holly knew more. She wasn't marrying him for his smile or his laugh. Nor for his Castle, his title or his money.

She was marrying him because he was her Angus; it was as simple as that.

She smiled up at her husband-to-be, a lovely heart-warming smile that was as much of a match for his chuckle as it was possible to make.

'No laughing. This is serious,' she said softly. 'You've promised me a gold ring and that's what I'm here for.'

'You won't give this one away?' he asked and her smile died.

'I won't,' she said, and her eyes met his and he knew what she spoke now was absolute truth. 'This one's for ever.'

* * * * *

"Oh, Damien. I really am sorry I dragged you out of bed, but I've been working up the nerve to approach you concerning a certain, um, issue, for weeks now."

One look at Lucy Cordell's fresh face had Damien wishing he'd put something on under his robe. Still, he was very fond of Lucy. He led her into his suite as she blushed and said, "Thank you, Dami. You're always so kind to me." All at once her big eyes brimmed with moisture.

"Luce?" He jumped up, went around to her and knelt by her chair, taking care as he did it that the damn robe didn't gape and embarrass them both. "What is this? Tears? Now dry your eyes and tell me what's been troubling you."

Lucy hesitated. "Oh, Dami. I've been out of the mainstream for so long. But not anymore. I'm well and I'm strong and I'm living my dream. And I really need to get started on doing the things that healthy women do—"

Dami made another stab at finding out where all this was going. "So you came to me for advice then?" He reached for his coffee cup.

And Lucy said, "No. Not advice. Sex."

He set the cup down sharply. "Say again?"

"Dami, it's so simple. I want you to be my first."

The Bravo Royales: When it comes to love, Bravos rule!

HOLIDAY ROYALE

BY
CHRISTINE RIMMER

First published in Great Britain 2013
by Mills & Boon, an imprint of Harlequin (UK) Limited,
Eton House, 18-24 Paradise Road, Richmond, Surrey TW9 1SR

© Christine Rimmer 2013

ISBN: 978 0 263 90166 5

23-1213

Harlequin (UK) policy is to use papers that are natural, renewable and recyclable products and made from wood grown in sustainable forests. The logging and manufacturing processes conform to the legal environmental regulations of the country of origin.

Printed and bound in Spain
by Blackprint CPI, Barcelona

Christine Rimmer came to her profession the long way around. Before settling down to write about the magic of romance, she'd been everything from an actress to a salesclerk to a waitress. Now that she's finally found work that suits her perfectly, she insists she never had a problem keeping a job—she was merely gaining "life experience" for her future as a novelist. Christine is grateful not only for the joy she finds in writing, but for what waits when the day's work is through: a man she loves who loves her right back, and the privilege of watching their children grow and change day to day. She lives with her family in Oregon. Visit Christine at www.christinerimmer.com.

For my sons,
Matt and Jess.
Happy holidays
and all my love.

Chapter One

At eight-thirty on Thanksgiving morning, Damien Bravo-Calabretti, Prince of Montedoro, heard a knock on the outer door of his palace apartment.

Damien had given his man, Edgar, the holiday off. That left the prince to ignore his uninvited, way-too-early visitor—or get out of bed and answer the door himself.

He was quite comfortable in his bed, thank you. Paying no attention to the continued tapping seemed the most attractive option.

But the knocking continued.

And then he thought, *Vesuvia?*

And that had him glaring at the coffered ceiling far above his bed. *Not V. Please.* It was much too early to have to deal with V.

Besides, it was over between them. She knew that as well as he did.

Not to mention she was supposed to be in Italy, wasn't she? And there were guards at every entrance. She couldn't just stroll in uninvited. How could she have gained access to his rooms, anyway?

Who knew? A man never did when it came to V.

And if it *was* V, he could forget drifting back to sleep. She would keep right on knocking until he gave in and answered. The woman was nothing short of relentless.

Muttering a few choice expletives under his breath, Dami shoved back the covers and grabbed his robe. He shrugged it on and belted it as he strode down the hall.

By the time he reached the door that led out into the palace corridor, he was angrier than he should have allowed himself to be. He yanked the door wide with a scowl on his face, prepared to tell the impossible woman on the other side exactly what he thought of her.

But it wasn't Vesuvia after all. It was sweet little Lucy Cordell, whose brother, Noah, would be marrying Damien's sister Alice in the spring.

At the sight of his less-than-welcoming expression, Lucy's pink cheeks flushed red and she jumped back with a soft cry. "Oh! It's too early, isn't it? You weren't even up…." She gave him a dazed once-over, from his bare feet to the section of naked chest displayed where the robe gaped a bit, and upward. She took in the dark stubble on his jaw and his uncombed hair.

Dami instantly felt nothing short of sheepish. He straightened the robe and raked a hand back through his hair. "Luce. Hullo."

"Go ahead, say it. Too early, I knew it."

"No. Really. It's fine. Not too early at all." If he'd known it was Lucy, he'd have put something on under the robe. Dami was very fond of Lucy. She was so fresh scrubbed and sincere—charming, too. And she did look fetching this morning, all big brown eyes and short tousled hair, and a smart and imaginative ensemble she had no doubt created herself. He could almost forgive her for dragging him from his bed.

She was not soothed by his assurances, but instead winced and scrunched up her pretty face. "Yikes! I get it. You've got company, right?" And then she was off and chattering. "Oh, Dami. I'm sorry, truly. I don't want to interrupt anything, but I've been working up the nerve to approach you concerning a certain, er, issue, for weeks now."

"Working up the nerve?" He gazed at her, bemused. "What issue?"

"Ugh. I hate myself."

He gestured her into the suite. "Come in. We'll talk."

"But you're *busy*...."

"No, I'm not. And I promise you, I am completely alone."

"Really?"

"Truly. Now come in."

But she only sighed and covered her eyes with her hands and then spread her fingers enough to peek out at him. "This is so awkward and weird, isn't it? But I just, well, this morning, I finally couldn't stand it anymore."

He stepped to the side and waved her in again. "Whatever it is, let's not discuss it out here in the hallway. You must come in. We'll have coffee."

She didn't budge, except to drop her hands away from her face and wrap her arms around her. "I just *had* to see you. And so I decided to go for it, before I lost my nerve, you know? But of course, I see I should've at least waited until nine or...later or whenever you... Oh, my Lord." She let her head fall back and groaned at the carved painted ceiling overhead. "You would think

I had no manners at all." She looked at him again, her gamine face crumpled in misery. "Oh, Dami. Sorry, sorry. This is awful, isn't it?"

"Luce, what *are* you on about?"

She blinked at him again, her mouth trembling. "You know what? I'll just come back later and maybe then we can…"

The flood of words stopped when he caught her hand. She stared up at him, her mouth slightly agape in a confused expression that he found simultaneously humorous and captivating. "Come inside now." He gave her fingers a tug.

"Oh, I just don't…"

"Luce." He snared her darting gaze and held it.

"Oh, God." Her plump cheeks puffed out with a hard breath. "What?"

"Come in. Please."

That did it. Finally. She gave him a sad little nod. And then, slim shoulders drooping, she let him draw her over the threshold.

Pausing only to shut and lock the door, he led her down the hallway, past the sitting room and his bedroom, the dining room and his small study. At the back of the apartment, he had a narrow galley kitchen for those times when he preferred to dine in private. He led Lucy to the small table by the one window at the end and pulled out a chair. "Have a seat."

She dropped to the chair cushion, folded her hands neatly in her lap and didn't utter a word as he got to work grinding the coffee beans, filling the French press and setting it on the cooker to brew. He would have preferred, while they waited for the coffee, to run back down the hall and throw on something more appropriate than his black silk robe.

But he was afraid if he left her alone, she just might bolt. He couldn't allow that. Clearly, she did have something to say to him. It was all very intriguing. He wasn't letting her go until she revealed what had brought her to his door.

He said, "I'm surprised to see you at the palace at this hour."

"But I'm a guest here. I have a beautiful little room on the third floor with a bathroom right down the hall."

"I thought you would be staying at the villa with Alice and Noah."

"Well, the truth is I asked Alice if she could get me in as a guest here at the palace instead—for the life experience, you know?" Something evasive in her expression tipped him off that "life experience" wasn't all of it.

"And because of Noah?"

She shrugged. "He's promised to stop hovering over me and to let me lead my own life, but he still thinks he knows what's best for me. Here at the palace, I'm on my own. I take care of myself without my big brother keeping tabs on where I go and when I come in at night." She loosed a gusty sigh. "Honestly, Dami. Sometimes he acts like I'm twelve instead of twenty-three."

"He loves you and wants to be certain you're safe and well."

For that she shot him an I-don't-want-to-hear-it look. He let the subject drop.

The coffee didn't take long. He poured her a cup, got out the cream and sugar and even found a couple of pastries in the bread box. He put the pastries on a serving plate, set them each a place, along with napkin, fork and spoon, and then took his own cup and settled into the chair opposite her. "There. Drink your coffee."

Obediently, she spooned in a little sugar, poured in a drizzle of cream, stirred and sipped. "It's good."

"Life is too short for bad coffee."

A sudden smile tugged at the corners of her mouth.

He shook his head. "Something amuses you?"

"It's too weird, that's all. Being served coffee and sweet rolls by a prince...."

He waved a hand. "Under everyday circumstances, my man, Edgar, would prepare the coffee. But Edgar is elsewhere this morning."

She blushed again, the color flowing upward over her sweet, velvety cheeks. "Thank you, Dami. You're always so kind to me." All at once her big eyes brimmed with moisture.

"Luce?" He jumped up, went around to her and knelt by her chair, taking care as he did it that the damn robe didn't gape and embarrass them both. "What is this? Tears?"

She sniffled. "Oh, Dami..." Her scent drifted to him: cherries and soap. So very Luce. It made him want to smile.

But he didn't. He kept a solemn face as he took the silk handkerchief from the breast pocket of his robe. "Here, now. Dry your eyes."

With a sad little sigh, she dabbed at her cheeks. "I'm being ridiculous."

"You are not, nor have you ever been, ridiculous." He rose—and then hesitated, not wanting to leave her side if she was going to keep crying.

She waved his handkerchief at him. "Go on. Sit back down. Your coffee will get cold."

So he returned to his chair and took his seat. "Eat a pastry, why don't you? Your choice, raspberry or almond."

Obediently, she transferred the raspberry brioche to her plate and took a bite. The red filling clung to her lower lip and he watched as the tip of her pink tongue emerged to lick it clean. "Yum."

He prompted, "Now. What is this 'issue' that you've come to me about?"

She sucked in a long breath. "First of all…"

"Yes?"

"Oh, Dami. First I really, really need to thank you."

"But why?"

"Oh, please. You know why. For coming to my rescue when I was running out of options and had no idea what I was going to do."

He gave her a one-shouldered shrug. "You've already thanked me. Repeatedly."

"But I can never thank you enough. You came and you helped me with Noah when I couldn't get through to him and I didn't see how I ever would." Her brother had been reluctant to let her go away to fashion school in Manhattan. "I live in New York City now because of you. I live in the greatest old building with the nicest neighbors because of you." She laid her hand against her upper chest, where the tip of a pale scar was just visible above the neckline of her striped top, which she wore with great panache, along with a short, tight, floral-print skirt, a wide black belt and ankle boots. "Thank you."

"You are completely welcome. I'm glad I could help—and you were the driving force in your own liberation. You have to know that. *You* made it happen."

"But I couldn't have done it without you being willing to fly to California to save me." Her brother, Noah, owned a large estate in Carpinteria, near Santa Barbara. "You stood up for me with Noah, and you took me away." She plunked a scrap of paper on the table and pushed it toward him. "This should pay you back, at least a little."

He saw that it was a check for a large sum of money and shook his head. "Don't be absurd. Noah paid for it all." Her brother had finally seen the light and given her his blessing to follow her dream—along with the all-important backing of his enormous bank account.

"Dami, you flew me to the East Coast in your own private jet. You leased me my beautiful apartment in your amazing building without asking for a deposit or anything. And I may be way naive, but even I know that my rent is impossibly low."

"Put your money away."

She drew herself up. "No. I will not. I have my trust fund now and I'm doing fine. I owe you this money, at least." She'd grown quite stern suddenly.

And he realized that to continue refusing her in this would only be ungracious. "Fair enough. Consider me repaid in full."

A glowing smile bloomed. "Excellent."

He transferred the almond brioche to his plate and cast a second dismissive glance at her check. "So, then, was that it—the 'issue' that's been troubling you?" How disappointing, to think her blushes and nervous chatter and unwilling tears came down to a nonexistent debt she felt driven to repay.

But then she pressed her soft lips together and shook her head.

Anticipation rose in him again. "So there's more?"

She nodded. And then dipped her head and spoke to her half-eaten brioche. "You and your girlfriend, Vesuvia…?"

V? She wanted to talk about V? Whatever for? *He* certainly didn't. But she'd stalled out again. And she was still staring at her plate as though she didn't have a clue how to go on. Warily, he prompted, "What about Vesuvia?"

Her brown head shot up and she met his eyes. A tiny gasp escaped her. "I mean, she's so impossibly beautiful and glamorous and…it seems like she's always on the cover of my favorite magazines…*Vogue* and *Bazaar* and *Glamour* and *Elle.*"

He arched a brow at her and asked in a tone he took care to make lighthearted, "Do you want me to introduce you to V for some reason?" God. He hoped not. But perhaps she had some idea that V might be willing to wear her designs.

"Introduce me to her? Oh, no. I don't. Not at all."

Relief had him settling more comfortably into his chair. "So, then?"

"Well, are you, um, still together with her?" The question came out in a breathy rush.

He was tempted to remind her that his relationship with V was really none of her business. But he couldn't quite bring himself to do that. He liked Lucy too much and she was far too flustered already. So he said, "No, we're not seeing each other any longer. I'm afraid it didn't work out."

Lucy stared at him rather piercingly now and he had the oddest sensation of being under interrogation. "So you're broken up, you and Vesuvia? And you're not in a relationship with anyone else?"

He couldn't help chuckling. "Yes, we are, and no, I'm not—and, Luce, my darling, don't you think it's time you told me about this so-urgent issue of yours?"

She sagged back in the chair with a groan. "Oh, Dami. It's just… Well, there's a man. A special man I met."

"A man?" He was totally lost now. From V to a *special* man?

"Yes. He's just way hot. He's an actor. He lives in my building in NoHo— Well, I mean *your* building. Brandon? Brandon Delaney?" She seemed to be prompting him.

He shook his head. "No idea."

She kept trying. "Blond hair, the most amazing butterscotch eyes…"

Dami had a property manager and a superintendent for the building and only a vague idea of who lived there. Some of the apartments were co-op, others leased. And *butterscotch* eyes? Was this a man or a dessert? "I'm afraid I don't recall this Brandon."

"Oh, Dami. He thinks I'm a *child,* you know? And I'm not a child— Well, yes, okay, I *am* inexperienced, not to mention naive. I get that. But I'm not stupid. I've simply been sick for most of my life and kind of out of the mainstream of things. But not anymore. I'm well and I'm strong and I'm living my dream. And I really, really need to get started on doing the things that normal, healthy women do—now that, at last, I *am* a normal, healthy woman. Dami, I need to, you know, hook up."

He tried not to look as befuddled as he felt. "Hook up."

"You know…have sex?"

"Er, yes. Of course I know."

"But see, I feel so awkward and strange about it." She lifted both hands and pressed them to the sides of her head, as though trying to keep what was inside from escaping. "I mean, I've met a few guys in Manhattan this past month and a half." She let go of her head and waved her slim arms about in her excitement over something of which he still had no clue. "I've met a few guys and I've tried to picture myself with one of them, but the idea of doing it with any of them just doesn't feel right—except for with Brandon. I find Brandon extremely attractive and I definitely could get something going with him. But he's very much about his acting and he's big on life experience and he won't hook up with me because he doesn't have sex with boring, innocent women."

Damien's head was truly spinning. "You…asked this Brandon fellow to…?"

"Oh, no!" More blushing. "Not straight out, I mean. I don't know him well enough to ask him straight out."

"Oh, of course. I see." He didn't, actually. Not in the least.

"But I did try to kiss him…."

"And?"

"He caught my arms and kind of held me, really gently, away from him."

"You mean you didn't kiss him after all?"

"No. He stopped it before it happened. And he looked in my eyes and told me that it could never work, that I'm so young and inexperienced and I wear my emotions on my sleeve. He said he would never want to hurt me, but of course he *would* hurt me because I would be in over my head with him. He said he doesn't, you know, sleep with virgins and that he's got no time for anything serious right now anyway, because acting is his life."

What a fatheaded ass. "You are adorable, Luce, and thoroughly charming. Don't let anyone ever tell you otherwise."

She put one of those flying hands to her heart. "Oh, Dami. See? That's how you are. Not only have you treated me like someone who matters from the first time I met you. Not only did you come to my rescue and fly me to Manhattan when I'd almost given up on ever getting there. Somehow you just instantly, always, say the exact thing that I need to hear."

He made another stab at finding out where all this was going. "So you came to me for advice, then?" He reached for his coffee cup.

And Lucy said, "No. Not advice. Sex."

He set the cup down sharply. "Say again?"

"Dami, it's so simple. I want you to have sex with me. I want you to be my first."

Chapter Two

Damien found himself experiencing the strangest sensation of complete unreality. "Dearest Luce. Did you just ask me to be your lover?"

She nodded, her shining brown head bouncing up and down as though on a spring. "Oh, yes. Please. I *like* you, Dami. I truly do. And when I think of having sex with you, it doesn't seem like it would be too awful—and you *are* so experienced. I really do need someone who can help me be more sophisticated and you just happen to be about the most sophisticated person I know. And as for having sex with you, well, you seem like you would know what you were doing and I…" The words ran out.

He started to speak but fell silent when she moaned.

And then she let out a cry and put her hands to her cheeks as though in an effort to cool her fierce blush.

"Oh, God. You should see your face. This is not going well, is it?"

"Luce, I—"

Before he could say more, she shoved back her chair and leaped to her feet. "Seriously. I don't know what I was thinking. This is a bad idea. A really stupid, utterly inane idea. And now you're going to think I'm such a complete child, a total dork…"

He got up. "No, I do not think you're a child. Truly, it's all right. It's…"

But she didn't stay to hear the rest. She whirled and bolted for the door.

"Luce!" Dami went after her and managed to catch up with her halfway down the hall to his private foyer. He grabbed her hand. "Wait."

She moaned again and tried to pull away. "Let me go."

He held on. "Please. Don't become so worked up. I promise you, you're neither a child nor a dork. And I'm quite flattered."

There was yet another moan. "Oh, no, you're not."

He lifted the hand he'd captured and kissed it lightly. Then he wrapped his other hand around their joined ones. "Listen to me."

A little whine escaped her.

"Tell me you're listening," he coaxed.

"What?" She sagged against the hallway wall, between two handsome nature prints he'd bought at one of his sister Rhia's charity art auctions. "All right. Yes, I'm listening."

"I *am* flattered." He tried a hint of a smile and watched her soft lips quiver in reluctant response. "Really, Luce, you are so unpredictable. You know, I find I never know what you might do or say next. But at the same time, at heart you are so wonderfully direct, so honest."

"Direct and honest," she grumbled, but at least she'd stopped trying to make him let go of her hand. "Ugh. So I'm a good person, but I'm not especially exciting—that's what you're saying."

"No, that is not what I'm saying."

"Yes, it is."

He moved in a fraction closer, keeping their joined hands between them, connecting them. The scent of soap and cherries was a little stronger now, sweet and tart and so very…clean. "Don't forget. I said you are unpredictable, too. That makes you exciting."

"No…."

"Yes. It does, I promise you. And may I add that you are also like a breath of fresh air, both bracing and sweet." He watched her flushed face and thought how very much he liked her, how he'd liked her from the first time he met her, at her brother's Carpinteria estate when she'd dragged him to her sewing room and showed him several of her creations, after which she'd plunked her portfolio down on the cutting table and started flipping through the pages, chattering nonstop about her ambitions as a fashion designer.

Now she gazed at him through big eyes full of hope and trust. "Oh, you do know how to dish out the compliments."

"It's easy when I'm only telling the absolute truth."

"Oh, right. Sure you are."

He turned his mouth down at the corners in a mimic of sadness. "Luce. You wound me."

She started to giggle—and then she blinked. "Wait a minute."

"Yes?"

"Are you telling me that, um, you *will?*"

Ouch. Leave it to Lucy to cut right to the heart of the matter.

The thing was, he wanted to tell her yes, that he would be her lover. He truly did. But he was no more a seducer of virgins than Brandon of the butterscotch eyes. He absolutely did find her attractive, but in the way one finds a child attractive, because she was pure and honest, innocent and sweet yet also funny and surprising and perceptive, too. Not to mention splendidly talented. However, he couldn't quite make himself think of her as a grown woman, as an eligible female he might take to his bed.

She was watching him suspiciously. "Long silence. I'm taking that for a no."

Above all, he did not want to hurt her. "You truly are lovely, Luce. Your shining seal-brown hair, those enormous eyes that tip up so playfully at the corners. That one dimple in your left cheek that's deeper than the one on the right when you smile…."

"You're an absolute genius at making me feel good-looking."

"Because you *are* good-looking."

"But you still haven't answered my question," she accused. "I'm thinking that's not a good sign."

The solution came to him. "Tell you what."

For that he got an eye roll. "Stalling. That's what you're doing, right?"

"Well, yes. I suppose that I am."

"Oh, I knew it." She wrinkled her cute nose at him. But at least she no longer seemed on the verge of shedding more tears.

He qualified, "However, I am stalling in a good way."

"Ha." She made another attempt to free her hand from his hold.

He didn't let go. "Listen. Please."

"Fine, fine." She tipped her head from side to side, her words a singsong. "Go ahead."

"We'll take things a bit slower."

That brought a frown to crease her smooth brow. "Slower than what?"

"You're here for the holiday weekend."

"I am, yes."

"We'll spend the time—or much of it, anyway—in each other's company."

"You mean like we're dating?"

"Yes. As though we were dating."

"Oh, Dami. I may be naive, but I'm so on to you. I know what you're doing. You're trying to let me down easy."

She had it right, but he had no intention of admitting that. "Come to the kitchen." He tugged on her hand again. "We can finish our coffee…." He expected her to require more coaxing and encouragements before she'd agree to sit at the table again and discuss the situation frankly.

But as she so often did, she surprised him. She said, "Yes. All right." And she followed him back the way they had come.

In the kitchen, Lucy reclaimed her seat at the table and Dami refreshed their coffee cups before settling opposite her again.

Lucy watched him. He really was so nice to look at, in his sexy black robe and all, with that slice of sculpted chest on view, with his thick dark hair and his eyes that sometimes seemed the darkest brown and then, in certain lights, a green so deep it was almost black. So different from Brandon, who was clean-cut and outdoorsy with a handsome, open sort of face. Dami exuded power and ease, a hint of danger and strangely, humor and tenderness, too. They called him the Player Prince. Everyone said he'd been with more women than her big brother, Noah. Which was seriously saying something.

Noah used to be quite the lady-killer. But in the past year or so, he'd changed. He'd stopped seeing women at all for a while. And then he'd found Dami's sister Alice. Lucy did adore Alice. Alice was perfect for Noah. Lucy felt real satisfaction knowing that she could strike out on her own and her big brother had someone to love him the way he'd never let himself be loved before. Someone to keep him honest and stand up to him when he got too full of himself.

"Luce." Dami was frowning at her. "What *are* you thinking?"

She sipped her coffee. "That my brother's happy with your sister, and I'm really glad about that." Well, she *had* been thinking about Noah and Alice—*after* she'd admired the man across from her in his sexy robe.

"They *are* good together," he agreed.

She laughed, feeling lighthearted suddenly. Okay, she got the message that Dami wasn't up for teaching her the ways of love and sex. But at least he hadn't acted as if he couldn't wait to get rid of her, the way Brandon had when she'd tried to put a move on him. Dami would still be her friend always—somehow she just knew that—no matter what gauche, immature thing she did or said.

"What is so humorous?" he demanded.

"I don't know. I was really scared to ask you. And

now I've done it, and…it's okay. The sky didn't fall. You didn't toss me out the door on my butt."

"I would never toss you out the door—on your butt or otherwise."

"Exactly. I love that about you."

He ate a little more of his pastry and then he said thoughtfully, "I do realize I have something of a reputation with women. But even someone like me doesn't instantly fall into bed with any female who wanders by, no matter how fetching and well dressed she might be." A wry smile twisted his mouth. "Or at least, I haven't for the past few years."

This was getting interesting. "You're saying you had a lot of indiscriminate sex when you were younger?"

"I suppose I did, yes."

"You suppose? Oh, come on, Dami. You did or you didn't."

He chuckled. "I like you, Luce."

She beamed. "It's totally mutual."

"And I think that spending time together over this long weekend is a way to find out if there could ever be more than friendship between us."

Yeah, okay. She fully got that he was only being nice to her. And his suggestion of the two of them together for the weekend, just having fun, wasn't what she'd come for.

But so what?

It would be wonderful to spend a whole weekend at his side. And maybe a little of his smoothness and elegance would rub off on her. That certainly couldn't hurt. She might not get the whole sex-for-the-first-time thing over with, but at least she could acquire a little sophistication—if that was possible in a few short days.

She sipped her coffee and he sipped his. When she

set her cup down, she said, "So, then. Sunday I'm fly-ing back to New York. And you're saying it will be you and me, together in a dating kind of way, today, tomor-row and Saturday."

He inclined his dark head. "Starting this morning with the Prince Consort's Thanksgiving Bazaar on the rue St.-Georges."

Dami leaned close to her. "Ignore them," he whis-pered. "Simply pretend they're not there."

They stood side by side on the cobbled street, in front of a booth that sold handmade Christmas orna-ments. By then it was nearing eleven in the morning. Lucy couldn't resist a quick glance over her shoulder.

The street was packed with milling holiday shoppers and the air smelled of savory meats, fried potatoes and baked goods from the numerous food booths and carts that jostled for space with the stalls offering jewelry and handmade soaps, pottery and paintings and all kinds of bright, beautiful textiles. People chatted and laughed, bargained and shouted. And there were children every-where, some in strollers or baby carriers, some clutch-ing the hands of their mothers or fathers. And some running free, zipping in and out among the shoppers, cause for fond amusement and the occasional cry of, "Watch out, now," or, "Slow down a tad, young man."

Even in the holiday crowd, though, it was easy to pick out the photographers lurking nearby. Each had a camera in front of his face, the wide lens trained on the Player Prince.

Dami elbowed her lightly in the side. "I said ignore them."

"But they're everywhere."

"Yes, my darling. But they know the rules within the

principality. Here they are careful to keep their distance. Believe me, it's much better than in France or England or America, where they come at you without mercy, up close and very personal, firing questions as they click away." His voice was low and teasing and almost flirtatious. Or maybe she was just reading into it after their discussion of earlier that morning. Most likely, Dami wasn't flirting at all but only being kind to her.

And she was going to completely take advantage of his kindness and love every minute of it. "What happens if they approach you?"

"Someone from the palace guard or my brother Alex's Covert Command Unit will appear from the milling throng and escort them directly to the border."

"Just like that?"

"Yes," he assured her. "Just like that."

Dami had three brothers and five sisters. Lucy had yet to meet them all. "Alex is your twin, right?"

"Yes, he is. We're identical, though no one ever has any trouble telling us apart. Alex has always been the serious one. And you know me." He gave a supremely elegant shrug. "I make it my mission in life to take *nothing* seriously."

"What is a Covert Command Unit?"

"A small, specially chosen and trained corps of Montedoran soldiers who are always at the ready to take action in a critical situation." He said this in his usual lighthearted tone.

"Seriously?"

He nodded at a passing couple and they nodded back. And then he told her, "All the family's bodyguards are from the CCU. And my sister Rhia's husband, Marcus, is one of them—and, Luce," he said indulgently, "will you please forget about the men with the cameras? To keep slipping them sideways glances only encourages them."

She laughed and caught his arm and grinned up at him. "I can't help it. Dami, you know how I am. Home-schooled. Most of my life, I hardly ever left the house—except when I had to be rushed to the hospital. I have a lot of life to catch up on. Everything fascinates me, even pushy men with cameras."

The merchant in the booth, a large woman with a wide, lined face, held up a pair of snowflake earrings, delicate and silvery, accented with tiny rhinestones that caught the late-November sunlight and twinkled festively. "Highness. For the lady...?"

Dami nodded. "Very pretty. Yes, she'll have them." He handed over the money without even a glance at Lucy for approval.

Lucy almost protested, but the woman in the booth looked so pleased and the earrings were pretty and not that expensive. Also, it did seem good practice for becoming sophisticated to pretend to be the sort of woman who casually received trinkets from a handsome prince.

The merchant put the earrings in a small cloth pouch and passed them to Dami, who gave them to Lucy. She thanked him and they moved on to the next booth, where she spotted a bright scarf she wanted and whipped out her wallet. The vendor glanced at Dami, as though expecting Dami to buy it for her.

Lucy did speak up then. "Please. Here you go...."

The vendor scowled and kept looking at Dami, who put on an expression both grim and resigned. The merchant took her money with a disapproving shake of his head. And Dami bought a child-size leather belt studded with bits of silver.

She almost turned to him then and asked why the

merchant had wanted him to pay for her scarf and what was with the child-size belt. But then, what did it matter, really? She knew already that he was generous to a fault. And maybe the belt was for one of his nephews.

As they moved on, he bought more gifts for children, boys and girls alike. He bought toy trucks and cars and any number of little dolls and stuffed animals. He bought a tea set and three plastic water pistols, Ping-Pong paddles and balls, packets of crayons, colored pencils and a stack of coloring books.

She finally asked him, "Who are all these toys for?"

He only smiled and advised mysteriously, "Wait. You'll see."

She might have quizzed him some more, but she was having far too much fun finding treasures of her own. Just about every booth seemed to have at least one small perfect thing she wanted. The bazaar was giving her so many ideas for new designs featuring the colors and textures all around her. A kind of glee suffused her. It was like a dream, *her* dream, from all those lonely shut-in years of growing up. That she would someday be well and strong and travel to exciting places and be inspired to make beautiful things that women all over the world would reach out and touch, saying, *Yes. This. This is what I want to wear.*

But wouldn't you know that Dami got quicker at detecting her choices? And the merchants all seemed to expect Dami to pay. They ignored the bills in her hand and grabbed for the ones in his.

She finally had to lean in close to him and whisper, "Okay. Enough. I mean it, Dami. If I want something, I am perfectly capable of buying it myself."

They stood, each weighed down with bags and packages, beside a flower stall where glorious bouquets of every imaginable sort of bloom stood in rows of cone-shaped containers. He bought a big bouquet of bright flowers, then took her arm and guided her to the side, out of the way of the pressing crowd. "Do you realize that this bazaar was established over thirty years ago in honor of my father, in the year that my oldest brother, Max, was born?"

"How nice. And what does that have to do with why you keep buying things for me when I have plenty of money of my own?"

"It has everything to do with it."

"I don't see how."

"My dearest Luce," he said with equal parts affection and reproach, "Thanksgiving is, after all, an American holiday. Yet Montedorans embrace it and celebrate it. They do this for my father's sake. And this bazaar was named for him because he gave my mother happiness—and a son, very quickly."

"How virile of him. And why do you sound like you're lecturing me?"

He actually shook a finger at her, though his eyes glittered playfully as he did it. "My darling, I *am* lecturing you. We celebrate Thanksgiving in Montedoro for the sake of my father, and this bazaar exists in respect for my father. And when a Bravo-Calabretti prince attends the bazaar, he tries to buy from each and every vendor, in *thanksgiving* for the gift the Montedoran people have bestowed on us, to trust us with the stewardship of this glorious land."

"Well, all right. Wonderful. You bought a bunch of things. And you paid for them. In thanksgiving. But no way are you expected to pay for *my* things."

"Don't you see? Each item I buy blesses the vendor. The *more* I buy, the better."

She laughed. "Good one. I'm actually helping you out when I let you buy my stuff."

Along with the usual all-around hotness, he was looking very pleased with himself. "That's right. And the vendor, as well. Surely you cannot deny us these blessings."

She stared at him. He looked at her so levelly under those straight dark brows. His mouth held a solemn curve. But the usual mischief danced in his eyes. She accused, "You're making this up."

"Why ever would I?" Lightly. Teasingly.

She still wasn't sure she believed him. But he had a point, she supposed. Why would he make up a story like that? And the vendors really had seemed to want him specifically to be the one to pay.

She tried to explain, "It's just that you always look like you're teasing me, Dami. Even when you're serious."

"Because I *am* teasing you—even when I'm serious."

She shifted the mountain of bags in her arms in order not to drop any. "You're confusing me. You know that, right?"

He bent a fraction closer and she caught a hint of his aftershave, which she'd always really liked. It was citrusy, spicy and earthy, too. It made her think of an enchanted forest. And true manliness. And a long black limousine. "Try to enjoy it," he said.

"Being confused?"

"Everything. Life. All these people out for the holiday. Sunshine. This moment that will never come again." Suddenly, she wanted to hug him close. There was something so…magical about him. As though he knew really good secrets and just might be willing to share them with her. He added, "And won't you please believe me? The Thanksgiving Bazaar is in my father's honor and the more I personally buy here, the happier the merchants will be."

She groaned, but in a good-natured way. "I think I give up. Buy me whatever you want to buy me."

He inclined his dark head in a so-gracious manner that made her feel as if she'd just done him a whopping favor. "Thank you, Luce. I shall."

By then they'd strolled the length of one side of the rue St.-Georges and bought goods from about half of the booths. Dami set down the bouquet of flowers and a few bags of toys and got out his phone. He made a quick call. A few minutes later two men appeared dressed in the livery of the palace guard.

The guards carried their packages for them, falling back to follow behind as they worked their way up the other side of the street, buying at least one item from each of the vendors. The ever-present photographers followed, too, snapping away, their cameras constantly pressed to their faces, but they did keep enough distance that it wasn't all that difficult to pretend they weren't there.

Midway back up the other side of the street, they came to the food-cart area, a separate little courtyard of its own in the middle of the bazaar. The carts reminded Lucy of old-fashioned circus cars, each brightly painted in primary colors, some decorated with slogans and prices and pictures of the food they served, others plastered with stenciled-on images of everything from the Eiffel Tower to jungle cats. Dami bought food from each cart—pastries, meat pies, sausages on sticks, cones of crispy fried potatoes, flavored ices, tall cups of hot chocolate. There was no way the two of them could have made a dent in all that food. But conveniently, groups of

Montedoran children had gathered around. They were only too willing to help. Dami bought food and drinks for all, while the food sellers smiled and nodded and accepted his money. Were they grateful to be so richly "blessed"? Or just pleased to be doing a brisk business?

Lucy decided it didn't matter which. Dami had been right. She was enjoying the experience, reveling in this moment that would never come again.

When they left the food carts, the children followed, falling in behind the palace guards with their high piles of packages.

Dami spotted someone he knew across the street. He waved and called out, "Max!"

The tall, gorgeous man with the unruly hair and mesmerizing glance bore a definite resemblance to the prince at her side. He returned Dami's greeting and then went back to his negotiations with a vendor who sold scented soaps and bath salts.

Lucy asked, "Your oldest brother, right?" Dami nodded. "Will he make the rounds of every booth?"

"And buy something from each one."

"No wonder the vendors feel blessed. I mean, there are nine of you, brothers and sisters together. That's a lot of blessings."

"We don't all attend every year. But we do our best to make a showing—and come on now. We still have several booths to go."

They visited the remainder of the booths, piling more packages into the arms of the two guards. When they'd finally made a stop with every vendor in the bazaar, it was nearing two in the afternoon. Neither of them was hungry, as they'd done a lot of sampling when they'd fed the children at the food carts. Thanksgiving dinner at the palace took place in the early evening, so they didn't have to hurry back to get ready.

"What next?" Lucy asked.

Dami sent one of the guards off with Lucy's purchases and orders to have them delivered to her room. "This way," he said, and took Lucy's hand.

It felt lovely, she thought, almost as though they really were together in a romantic way, her hand in his strong, warm one, the guard with all the bags of toys behind them, and a trail of laughing kids strung out along the street, following in their wake. It wasn't far down to the harbor, and that was where Dami led them, to a little square of park along the famous Promenade, which rimmed the pier where all the fabulous yachts were docked.

"Right here," he said at last, indicating an iron bench beneath a rubber tree. They sat down together and the guard put all the packages at their feet as the children found seats on the grass around them.

And then Dami began passing out the toys and coloring books, the dolls and stuffed animals, with the guard helping out to make sure everyone got something. A ring of adults stood back out of the way, and Lucy realized they were the parents of the children. Some parents had little ones in their arms or in strollers. The guard made sure even the smallest ones received a toy.

It was all so charming and orderly, like some fantasy of sharing, the children laughing and chattering together, but in such a well-behaved way. Once or twice she heard raised voices when one child wanted what another one had. But all Dami had to do was glance in that direction and the argument would cease.

When all the bags were empty and every child had

a gift, Dami asked the gathered children, "Would you like to hear a story?"

A happy chorus of yeses went up.

And Dami launched into a story about a little boy and a magic book, a laughing dragon and a secret passage into a special kingdom where a kind princess ruled with a gentle hand. There was an evil giant who never bothered to bathe or brush his teeth. The giant captured the princess. And the little boy and the laughing dragon rescued her with the help of spells from the magic book.

When the story was over, the children and the ring of adults applauded and the children cried, "One more, Prince Dami! Only one more!"

He obliged them with a second story, this one about a brave girl who saved Montedoro from an evil wizard who'd cast a sleeping spell across the land. Applause followed that story, too, and a few called, "One more!"

But Dami only laughed and shook his head and wished them all a richly blessed Thanksgiving. The children went to find their parents and Dami took her hand again and pulled her to her feet.

"That was wonderful," she told him. "Did you make up those stories yourself?"

A so-Gallic shrug. "I'm not that clever. They are Montedoran folk tales, two of many. A century and a half ago a Montedoran named Giles deRay gathered them into a couple of volumes, *Folk Tales of Montedoro.* We all know the stories. It's something of a tradition over the holidays for the princes of Montedoro to pass out gifts they've bought at the bazaar and tell the children a few of the old tales."

"What a beautiful tradition."

He was watching her, a half smile curving those killer lips of his. "You find everything beautiful. I think, Luce, that you are the happiest person I have ever known."

His words warmed her. "I prefer happiness. It's so much more fun than the alternative."

"You sound like Lili, my brother Alex's wife— Liliana, Crown Princess of Alagonia."

"Oh, yes. I've heard of her. And Alagonia is an island country off the coast of Spain, correct?"

"Yes. We—my brothers and sisters and I—grew up with Lili. My mother and Lili's mother, Queen Evelyn, were great friends. Lili was always the nicest person in the room. Of course, she ended up with Alex, who was not nice at all. The good news is that he's much better now since he's made a life with Lili."

"Are they happy, your brother and Princess Lili?"

"They are, yes. Ecstatically so."

"I'm glad. And you've got me thinking. Can a person be both happy *and* sophisticated?"

He did the loveliest thing right then. He touched her, just the lightest caress of a touch as he traced his finger down her jaw to her chin and tipped her face up fully to him. "What? You're afraid you'll have to choose?"

Her tummy felt all fluttery and her pulse beat faster. Oh, he was very, very good at pretending they were dating. "I don't want to choose—but if I had to, I would choose happiness."

He moved a fraction closer, his finger still touching her chin. "It's good to know you have your priorities in order."

"Dami?"

"Yes?"

"Are you going to kiss me?" Somehow she had let her eyes drift to half-mast.

"Would you like that?" he whispered, his smooth, low voice playing a lovely tune all along her nerve endings.

She couldn't stifle the soft, eager sound that came from her throat. "Oh, that would be fabulous. Yes."

"Are you sure? The paparazzi are watching. A kiss would definitely make the tabloids."

She couldn't hold back a giggle. "Oh, come on." She opened her eyes a little and saw that he was smiling down at her, a tender sort of smile that made her tummy more fluttery than ever. "It's too late to back out now."

"Luce, you are so innocent—and yet so delightfully bold."

"Bold. Good. I like that a lot. As a matter of fact, I…"

There was more she'd meant to say. But at that moment, the ability to form words deserted her.

His warm, soft, wonderful mouth settled, gentle as a breath, on hers.

Chapter Three

Kissing Luce.

And not on the cheek. Not a swift brush across the mouth in passing. Not on the forehead or the tip of her cute nose.

Kissing Luce in the *real* way.

Damien hadn't actually planned to do that.

But her sweet pink lips were tipped up to him and her bright brown eyes were halfway shut and she managed to look so very inviting in her adorable clean-scrubbed, cheerfully angelic sort of way.

Plus there had been the joy of the day with her—and really, there was no other word for it. Joy. Lucy Cordell was a joy. The world through her eyes was a magical place. A good and generous place, a place of endless wonder and simple, perfect pleasures. To see the world with her, through her eyes, was a fine and satisfying experience indeed.

But he'd already known that. Every time he saw her, it was like that. The world was fresh and new again and he would do anything to hear her laugh, to watch her smile.

However, the kiss?

No. The kiss had not been in his clever plan to enjoy the weekend with her, to offer her his company and a large helping of Montedoran tradition and then send her back to New York as innocent as ever.

Kisses, *real* kisses, didn't fit in the plan.

But in the end, how could he resist?

His mouth touched hers and she let out the tiniest, most tender of sighs. Her sweetness flowed into him.

And it was…

More.

Much more than he had expected. Far beyond the boundaries of what he'd intended.

It was a light kiss, a gentle kiss. His mouth against hers, but chastely. Not in any way a soul kiss.

And yet, still, a revelation.

He breathed in the scent of cherries and he saw, all at once, what he had been able to keep from himself before. He saw that she was sweet and innocent, yes.

But she was not a child.

And now that he'd done it, now that he'd felt her lips against his, breathed in her breath, listened to her tiny sigh, he wasn't going to be able to unring that bell. The spilled milk would not flow back into the bottle. The cat was out and was prowling around now, thoroughly unwilling to go back in the bag.

Henceforth and forever, when he looked at Lucy, he would see a grown woman. A grown woman he could so easily desire.

The temptation tugged at him to reach out and gather

her closer, to deepen the kiss, to explore this new Lucy, the one he hadn't let himself see before. And why not? He'd never been a man who put much store in resisting temptation. What was the point? Better to give in. Life was too short and pleasure too...pleasurable.

But somehow and for some reason he didn't even understand, he kept his hands to himself. He lifted his head and she opened her eyes and he felt absurdly, ridiculously proud of himself.

"Oh, Dami," she whispered happily, searching his face.

He touched her neat little chin again, because he could. Her skin was poreless, creamy, fresh. "It was only a kiss," he shamelessly lied.

She corrected him with a glowing smile, "An absolutely perfect kiss."

He offered his arm. She took it. Together they turned for the car that waited to take them back to the palace.

Thanksgiving dinner at the Prince's Palace was a family affair. A very large family affair. Large enough to be held in the ornate formal dining room of the State Apartments. It was to be dressy but not formal.

Lucy wore a plum-colored lace creation of her own with little satin straps over the shoulders and a skirt that came to just above her knees. Her deep purple satin pumps had big satin bows at the heels. The dress showed enough skin that she didn't look *too* innocent, but the cut was more youthful than clingy and that made it nice for a family affair.

At first they all gathered in the Blue Room next to the dining room. Drinks were served. She didn't spot Dami right away, but she did see Noah and Alice on the far side of the room talking to another couple Lucy didn't recognize. Alice wore a gorgeous copper-colored dress and held Noah's arm and he smiled down at her with such a look of love and contentment Lucy found herself grinning in satisfaction at the sight.

But then she got worried that Noah might see her and wave at her to join them. She did love her big brother, but the last thing she needed was him hovering over her. He could be like some fussy old mother hen with her.

Objectively, she couldn't blame him for wanting to look after her. They'd lost both their parents way too soon and he had a deep-rooted fear that something awful would happen to her. She'd been ill so much growing up that his fear only intensified. Any number of times, Noah had found just the right specialist to save her at the last minute when she was at death's door. She loved him, she did. He was the best big brother in the world. And he kept promising he understood that she was ready to run her own life now. Sometimes she believed him. And sometimes she wondered if he was ever going to get off her case.

She circled away to another side of the room, putting a large gold-veined Ionic column between her and Noah. Perfect. Now she was completely out of his line of sight.

"Your dress is adorable and your shoes are very naughty." The deep, smooth voice came from directly behind her.

She turned. "Dami. There you are." He wore a beautiful dark suit and he was hands down the best-looking man in the room, which was really saying something, since all the Bravo-Calabretti princes were totally sigh-worthy, including Dami's father, Evan, the prince consort.

He handed her a crystal flute. "Champagne?"

She took it. They raised their glasses and she took a fizzy sip. "Yum."

"Happy Thanksgiving."

She watched his mouth move and a little shiver slid through her. Her lips kind of tingled. It might have been a few leftover bubbles from the champagne—or it might have been that she couldn't help remembering the kiss that afternoon.

How could a simple soft press of his mouth to hers be so very exciting? She might not be all that experienced, but everyone knew that an intimate, sexy kiss was wet and usually involved tongues. The kiss by the Promenade had been nothing like that.

And yet, somehow, *everything* like that.

She had to keep reminding herself not to get her hopes up, that Damien's kindness and generosity to her during this special weekend meant he cherished her friendship—and nothing more.

"Come." He took her bare arm, causing havoc beneath her skin, a sensation equally exquisite and disorienting. "I must introduce you to my parents, who will soon be your brother's in-laws."

She ordered her feet in their high satin heels to go where he took her.

Her Sovereign Highness Adrienne of Montedoro and her prince consort, Evan, were every bit as gracious and friendly as Dami and Alice. Adrienne, who had to be at least in her mid-fifties but looked forty at the most, said she'd heard so much about Noah's sister and was pleased to get to meet her at last. She knew of Lucy's ambition to work in fashion and she complimented Lucy's dress and got her to confess that, yes, it was her own design. Evan asked about when her first semester at the Fashion Institute of New York would begin.

"Right after New Year's," she said. Her feet hardly seemed to touch the inlaid marble floor as Dami led her into the dining room. "They're amazing, your parents."

"I'm afraid I have to agree with you."

"I can't believe they knew so much about me—let alone remembered what they'd heard."

"Luce. They're not young, but they're hardly to the age where the memory starts to fail."

"Oh, stop. You know what I mean. Your mother rules this country and has nine children and their spouses and *their* children to keep up with. And yet she still manages to recall that her future son-in-law's little sister, whom she's never met, wants to be a fashion designer."

"Yes, she's a marvel," he agreed matter-of-factly. "Everyone says so—and here we are." He pulled back a gilded chair with a blue damask seat.

She sat down and he took the chair beside her. There were place cards, creamy white, lettered in flowing black script. "It's so nice that we somehow ended up seated together."

He took the chair beside her and leaned close. "I'm on excellent terms with the staff."

She faked a disapproving glance. "You got someone to mess with the seating chart."

"I requested a slight rearrangement."

With a laugh, she leaned closer. "And I'm so glad you did."

The woman seated on his other side spoke to him and he turned to answer her. Lucy took that moment to soak up the wonders around her. The dining room was as beautiful as the Blue Room. The walls here were scrolled and sculpted in plaster, blue and white, with more of those gold-veined Ionic pillars marching down one wall, interspersed with mirrors. The floor was gold-

and-white inlaid marble in star and sun patterns, the coffered ceiling a wonder in gold and brown, turquoise and cream. Giant turquoise, gold and crystal Empire-style chandeliers cast a magical light over everything.

The long dining table with its endless snowy cloth, gold candlesticks and gold-rimmed monogrammed china seated thirty. Every seat was occupied.

Including the one five seats down across the table, where her brother, Noah, sat next to Alice.

Of course, Noah was looking right at Lucy. And frowning. When he saw that she'd noticed him, he slid a glance at Dami and then back to her, making it all too clear he didn't like her choice of a dinner companion.

Which was totally crappy and hypocritical of him. After all, he and Dami had been friends first, bonding a little more than two years ago now over their mutual interest in spectacular cars and fabulous women. Noah seemed to have some idea that Dami wasn't really her friend, that Dami was only out to make her another notch on his bedpost.

Which just made her want to laugh. Because hadn't she tried to convince Dami to do just what Noah was so afraid he would do? And hadn't Dami been a complete sweetheart about it, letting her down so easy she was still floating several inches above the inlaid floor?

The older gentleman on Lucy's other side spoke to her. "What a positively charming frock."

She put Noah firmly from her mind and turned to the old guy with a friendly smile and a soft, "Thank you."

He had thick white hair, wore a smoking jacket and sported a Colonel Sanders goatee. "Count Dietrich Von-Delft," he said. "Her Highness Adrienne is my second cousin once removed."

She gave the old fellow her name, explained her relationship to the Bravo-Calabretti family and told him how much she was enjoying her holiday weekend in Montedoro. He said she was very lovely, a breath of fresh air—at which point she started suspecting he might be putting a move on her.

On her other side, Dami chuckled. That gave her an excuse to turn to him. The gleam in his eyes told her he knew exactly what the count had been up to. She chatted with Dami about nothing in particular for a few minutes. And then the first course was served.

Through the meal, she tried not to look at her brother and not to get too involved in any conversations with "Richie," as the count insisted she call him. He actually was kind of sweet, but he leaned too close and he looked at her as though he wouldn't mind helping her out of her so-charming "frock." It was kind of flattering, if also a bit creepy. She did want to learn about lovemaking, but not from a guy old enough to be her grandfather.

After the meal, they all returned to the Blue Room, where after-dinner drinks were served and Prince Evan gave a nice speech about how wonderful it was to have his family around him on Thanksgiving night. There was music, a pianist and a singer who performed Broadway standards and holiday tunes, but not very loud, so everyone could visit. Lucy met more Bravo-Calabrettis. She managed to steer clear of her big brother, which was great. But then there was Count Richie. He seemed to constantly pop up out of nowhere, grinning flirtatiously through his goatee, every time she turned around. She treated him politely every time and then slipped away at the first opportunity.

Around eleven-thirty the party began to break up. Princess Adrienne reminded them that the annual Thanksgiving Candlelight Mass would be held at midnight in the St. Catherine of Sienna Chapel in the palace courtyard.

Dami took her hand and wrapped it around his arm and they followed along with the others, outside and down the wide stone stairs to the chapel. It was a beautiful service, though Lucy hardly understood a word of it. She enjoyed the flowing beauty of the priests' robes, the spicy smell of the incense, the glow of all the candles and the beautiful voices of the men and women in the choir.

When it was over, Dami led her back to the Blue Room, where more refreshments were served. They lingered for a while, visiting with his two youngest sisters, Genevra and Rory.

Finally, at about one-thirty, he walked her upstairs.

Damien stood with Lucy at the door to her room.

The hallway, narrower than the one outside his apartment, was lit by wall sconces turned down to a soft glow.

"I don't want you to go," Lucy said in that enchanting way she had of simply saying whatever popped into her mind.

He felt the same, reluctant to leave her, and that struck him as odd. He would see her in the morning after all. She still had her hand wrapped snugly around his arm. She let go—but then she caught his fingers. Her touch was cool and somehow wonderful. "Come in. Please. Just for a moment."

He knew what waited on the other side of the door. A single room with a bed, a chair or two, an armoire and maybe a small desk. It seemed inappropriate for him to go in there with her, and he found his reluctance absurd. Just because there was a bed didn't mean they had to use it.

He said, though he did know that he shouldn't, "Just for a minute or two—why not?"

"Yes!" She pulled him in.

It was just as he'd pictured it. Her bags and packages from the Thanksgiving Bazaar were piled atop the armoire. The maid had been in and turned down the bed.

She stood on the rug in the center of the room, her hands behind her, looking very young. "I should have something to offer you...."

He gave her a sideways look and a half smile. "How about a chair?"

Both hands appeared from behind her and waved around a bit. "Take your choice." He chose the one under the small window. She sat in the other, crossed her slim legs and smoothed her lacy skirt. "I had an amazing time tonight."

"You always have an amazing time."

She tipped her head from side to side as though reciting some rhyming verse in her head. "You're right. I do. I can't help it. Especially now, here in Montedoro, where I feel like I'm living in my own private fairy tale."

"Complete with a lecherous old aristocrat in an ancient smoking jacket."

She laughed, a happy little sound. He thought of V for some reason. Of the differences between Luce and V. V would have been brassed off to have some old man following her around trying to flirt with her. Not Lucy. Lucy had been patient with Richie. Patient and kind. "He was actually very sweet. But a little bit... relentless."

"A *little* bit?"

"Okay, a lot. But I liked him, though, and I didn't want to hurt his feelings."

"I know you didn't." His own voice surprised him. Too low. Too…intimate.

She almost smiled, her soft lips pursing just the slightest bit, so the dimple in her left cheek started to happen but then didn't quite. He stared at the white flesh of her throat and wondered what it would feel like to kiss her there, to scrape that softness lightly with his teeth.

And that was when he knew he needed to get out. Now. He stood.

A tender little "Oh!" escaped her and she jumped up, as well. "You're going already?"

"I really should." Something was the matter with him. He seemed unable to master his own voice. First too low, now too stiff.

"But I…" She hesitated.

"What?" Now he sounded ridiculously hopeful. What was this? He hardly knew himself—his voice not his own, his heart pounding away in the cage of his chest as though hoping somehow to break free. You'd think he was twelve again, surviving his first crush.

She settled back onto the heels of those naughty satin shoes. "You're right. I have to let you go." Regretful. Resigned. And then she smiled, her gamine face lighting up from within. "I mean, you've been amazing and there's always tomorrow."

His shoes were moving, carrying him with them. Suddenly he was standing an inch away from her. She gazed up at him and he saw there were gold and green striations caught in the velvet brown of her eyes. "Yes," he heard himself say, "tomorrow…"

And then he was doing what he had no intention of doing, lifting a hand, brushing a finger down the side of that white throat, bending close to her, capturing that soft, slightly parted mouth.

So good. Her breath tasted of apples, fresh. Sweet. He touched her lower lip with his tongue, testing the warmth and the wonderful softness.

She let out a throaty little sound.

And then she lifted her slim arms and wrapped them around his neck. He followed suit, sliding his hands over the dusky, soft lace in the curve of her waist, gathering her in, deepening the kiss that was not supposed to happen.

Her body fit against him, slim and warm and soft. Her breasts pressed into his chest.

So good. Too good.

He felt what he wasn't ever going to feel with her: heat. Tightness. He was starting to grow hard.

That did it. Arousal woke him from the trance that had somehow settled over him. Slowly, gently, with great care, he clasped her slender waist again, lifted his mouth from hers and pushed back from her just enough that she wouldn't feel him growing thicker and harder against her belly.

She gazed up at him, eyes dreamy, still smiling. "Um. Good night," she whispered.

"Night, Luce." Miraculously, he had regained command of his own voice. He sounded so calm, completely relaxed, in full command of himself, though he was none of those things at that moment.

He let her go and turned for the door, and he didn't stop moving until he was on the other side of it and it was firmly shut behind him.

* * *

Alone in his apartment, Damien poured himself a last brandy.

His cell phone vibrated. He took it out of his pocket and saw it was V. He didn't answer. There was no point in talking to her. She would only yammer at him as usual, saying all the things he'd heard a thousand times before. It was an endless loop with V, a train on a circular track going round and round. He refused to get back on that train. How clear could he make it? He was off the train and staying off.

But he did check his voice mail: three messages. All from V. He deleted each one before she got out more than a few annoyed, impatient words.

And then he set the phone on a side table and drank his brandy and told himself the weekend with Lucy needed to stop. He couldn't afford to spend tomorrow and the next day with her. He would have to back out of the rest of their time together.

Somehow.

It had been a giant mistake, his clever plan to turn her down without hurting her tender feelings. It had become a trap for him, a trap of his own making. It was the problem of the bell that couldn't be unrung, the cat out of the bag, the milk spilled on the ground.

She had started it, started the change in the way he thought of her. She'd done it when she'd asked him to make love to her. She'd put that impossible idea into his head and before he knew it, he was starting to see her in a whole different light. And now he couldn't stop thinking of doing exactly what she'd asked him to do.

Now all of the things he liked best about her—the easy charm, the pleasure she took in every smallest thing, the complete lack of drama, her authenticity and straightforwardness, her kindness to old Dietrich—all those things worked as a snare for him.

She enchanted him.

Thoroughly.

He hadn't missed the cold glances Noah kept giving him during dinner—and afterward. Noah did not approve of Damien spending so much time with his sweet baby sister.

Damien got that. And now that he'd started to see Lucy as a potential lover, he didn't much approve of it, either. It wasn't a good idea. If Dami and Lucy did end up in bed together, well, what then? Would a sweet, naive girl like Luce really be ready to simply enjoy the experience and then move on?

No. He couldn't see it. And that meant that he had no right to keep on with this.

Somehow, tomorrow he had to find a way to let her know that their long weekend together was over after just one day.

Something wasn't right with Damien, Lucy kept thinking after he left her room.

He'd acted so strangely. Jumping to his feet out of nowhere, telling her he had to go—and then stepping right up close and kissing her, a beautiful, sexy, romantic kiss. And then racing off as though he couldn't get away from her fast enough.

Talk about mixed signals. Just when he started acting as if maybe he could see her in a man/woman way after all, he'd yanked open the door and left her standing there with her lips all tingly from his kiss and her yearning arms empty. Something had definitely spooked him.

And come on, wasn't it obvious what?

Noah.

Had to be. Those dark looks Noah had been sending her? No doubt he'd been sending them to Dami, too. Those looks must have gotten to Dami.

It wasn't right. And Lucy was not putting up with it. She needed to fix the problem. And the more she considered the situation, the more it seemed clear that she needed to fix it tonight.

So she changed into jeans, a slouchy sweater and her favorite Chuck Taylor high-tops, and off she went, along one corridor and then another, down a couple of flights of stairs and yet another hallway to a side entrance where a uniformed guard took her name and entered it into his handheld device. Then, with a brisk bow, he opened the door for her and out she went into the middle of the Montedoran night.

It wasn't that far of a walk to Alice's villa in the adjacent ward of Monagalla. And she was moving fast, wanting to get there and get the confrontation over with. It wasn't fun having it out with Noah. He was a great guy, but he had that little problem of being so sure he knew it all—including what was good for Lucy—even when he didn't. There could be shouting.

Too bad. She'd fought long and hard for her independence and her big brother could not take it back from her now.

She found Alice's villa easily enough. Her high-tops made no noise on the cobbled street. Lucy ran up the stone steps and stood in the glow from the iron fixture above the door, ringing the bell.

Nobody answered at first. Probably because it was after two in the morning. But she knew they were in there. Where else would they be?

Finally, after five rings, the door was drawn back. Michelle Thierry, Alice's assistant and housekeeper, stood on the other side clutching her plain blue robe at the neck, her pale hair flattened on one side, looking half asleep.

Lucy almost felt guilty. Yeah, okay. She probably should have had it out with Noah earlier—like the first time he'd shot her one of those disapproving looks. Maybe she shouldn't have spent the previous evening evading him. Two-thirty in the morning wasn't exactly the best time for a family chat.

"Miss Lucy," Michelle said, her voice brisk even though her eyelids drooped sleepily. "What a complete surprise. Is there an emergency?"

Too late to back down now. Lucy drew herself up. "Sort of—I mean, there is to me. I need to talk to my brother."

Michelle blinked away the last cobwebs of sleep and stepped back. "Well, I'll just go and wake him, why don't I?"

"Thank you. That would be excellent."

Michelle ushered her into the living area, with its fat, inviting sofas, comfortable chairs and beautiful antiques. "Do make yourself at home. I'll tell him you're here."

"We already know. Thank you, Michelle," said Alice from the doorway. She also wore a robe, a gorgeous red silk one painted with flowers and vines. Her brown hair was loose, tangled on her shoulders. Noah, in sweats, his hair looking blenderized and a scowl on his face, stood directly behind her. "Go back to bed," Alice added softly to Michelle.

With a nod, the housekeeper left them.

"What the hell, Lucy?" Noah grumbled as soon as the three of them were alone.

Alice pulled him down onto the sofa beside her and asked Lucy, "Are you hungry? Thirsty?"

Lucy perched on a chair. "No. I just need to get a few things clear with my brother, that's all. Then I'll let you both go back to bed."

Noah raked his hair with both hands and grumbled, "Is there some reason this couldn't wait until morning?"

She ignored the question and demanded, "Did we or did we not have an agreement about who runs my life?"

He shook his head and muttered something unpleasant under his breath. Alice sent him a warning look, one he pretended not to catch.

Lucy let out a hard breath. "Well, since you're not going to answer me, I'll answer for you. We *do* have an agreement. I run my life and *you* don't interfere."

"Interfere? What? I didn't—"

"Don't say you didn't, Noah. You know you did. You were giving me dirty looks all night long."

He did more grumbling under his breath. Alice took his hand and twined her fingers with his, but she didn't say anything. She didn't jump in to ease the tension, didn't take his side just to please him. That Noah's fiancée didn't rush to appease him made Lucy love her all the more. Finally, he came out with it. "What's going on with you and Damien?"

"Is that in any way your business?"

"Of course it's my business. You're my sister and I love you. And you said that you and Damien were just friends. *He's* said that the two of you are just friends. But you weren't acting like just friends tonight."

She reminded herself that she had absolutely nothing to hide. "We *are* friends and we always will be and we're spending the weekend together in a, er, dating kind of way."

"A...dating kind of way?" Noah looked at her as though she'd lost her mind and stood in grave danger of never finding it again.

She hitched her chin higher. "That's right. Dami and I are dating. For the weekend. We're...finding out if we might want to, um, take it to the next level." Okay, she had nothing to hide, but still. She wasn't quite willing to admit that she'd asked Dami to be her first lover. No matter how she phrased that, she didn't think it was the kind of thing her big brother needed to know.

"Dating," he repeated in a low, angry growl. "Dating for the weekend."

"Isn't that what I just said?"

Noah yanked his hand free of Alice's and shot to his feet. "No! Uh-uh. Absolutely not."

Lucy stood, too. No way she was letting him tower above her. "You have nothing to say about it, Noah. Nothing. At. All. And that's why I'm here tonight. To remind you that you are not in any way the boss of me and you need to get that through your thick—"

"Lucy, come on. Damien? Are you insane?"

"Wonderful. Now I'm crazy. Great, Noah. Fabulous."

He speared his fingers through his hair again—and dialed it back a notch. "All right. Sorry. I meant that you're...not thinking clearly."

"Whatever you meant, it was crappy. And you're wrong."

"I'm only trying to make you see that you need to get real here. Damien's not a guy who's ever in it for the long haul. He'll hurt you, break your heart. Why do you want to do that to yourself? Where's the win for you in that?"

"I think you're wrong about Dami, too. But that's not the point."

"Of course it's the point."

"No. The point is that it's my decision what happens between me and Dami—well, mine and Dami's. You have no say in what goes on between him and me. And I want you to admit that, to keep your word and get your nose out of my life like you promised me a month and a half ago that you would."

"But you can't—"

"Noah. Yes, I can." She took the few steps that brought her right up in his furious face and then she planted her feet wide, folded her arms across her middle and said, "Stay out of it. Leave it alone. Leave Dami alone. He doesn't deserve to have you all over his case just because he's willing to show me around Montedoro and treat me like a queen."

"She's right, Noah," said Alice, surprising them both by speaking up quietly from her seat on the sofa after staying out of it so completely until then. "You've said what you wanted to say and Lucy's heard every word. Now you need to back off and remember that she's all grown up and fully in charge of her own life and affairs."

Oh, yeah, Lucy thought. Alice was so the best thing that had ever happened to Noah—not to mention a true friend to Lucy in the bargain.

At that moment, Noah thought otherwise. He whirled on Alice and opened his mouth to light into her. She stared straight back at him, her body perfectly relaxed but fire in her eyes. And he shut his mouth without speaking, turned on his heel and went to the French doors that looked out on the night.

For several fairly awful seconds, nobody said a word.

Alice caught Lucy's eye and gave her a tiny nod, one

that seemed to say it would all work out. Lucy nodded back, hoping against hope that Alice had it right.

And then, at last, Noah turned to face the room again. "I don't like it."

Lucy straightened her shoulders. "Got that. Loud and clear. Will you stay out of it?"

He shut his eyes, winced—and then he muttered wearily, "Just…try not to get your heart broken. Please."

Her eyes felt kind of misty suddenly. "I will be fine. I promise you—and *will* you stay out of it? I need you to say it. I need your word that you'll leave it alone."

He rubbed at his jaw and looked away again, toward the night beyond the glass doors.

She asked a third time. "Noah. Will you?"

And finally, he faced her once more. He let out a low sound, raised both arms to the sides—and then dropped them hard. "Yeah. Fine. I'll stay out of it."

Like pulling teeth sometimes, getting him to say what she needed to hear. But at least he *had* said it. And she actually did believe him. "Oh, Noah…." She went to him.

He opened his arms and gathered her close. She teared up all over again when he whispered, "Damn. This should be easier…."

"I love you, big brother."

He hugged her even tighter. And then, as he'd promised to, he let her go. "Stay here tonight. It's way too late to wander around Montedoro by yourself."

She shook her head. "It's not far back to the palace and I'll go straight there. Don't worry, I'll be fine."

"But you—"

"Noah." Alice got up and went to him. She took his hands and put them at her waist and lifted her arms to link them around his neck. "Darling…"

He scowled down at her. "What?"

"Lucy will be perfectly safe."

"But I don't think—"

"Her choice. Her life. Remember?"

He muttered something Lucy couldn't quite make out. Alice laughed. And Noah bent and whispered something in her ear. She laughed again. Finally, he spoke to Lucy. "Good night," he said resignedly.

She escaped quickly before he could think of more reasons why she should stay.

At the palace, she went back in through the side door she'd used when she left. The same guard was there. He ushered her inside and then punched at his handheld device again, probably checking her off as safely returned.

By then it was after three. Past bedtime and then some. She went up to her room and flopped down on the bed and pressed her fingertips to the ridge of scar tissue between her breasts and thought about how she ought to be tired.

But she wasn't. It was a miracle, really, to be so strong. To stay up half the night, to run down the hill called Cap Royale on which the Prince's Palace stood, have a big fight with her brother and then run back up again—and still have energy to spare.

She was wide-awake. In fact, she just knew she wouldn't be able to sleep yet.

Not until she'd talked to Dami.

Yes. Absolutely. She needed to talk to Dami right away.

Tonight.

Chapter Four

Damien woke when the knocking started.

He squinted at the digital clock by the bed. Three thirty-six on Friday morning. And he knew instantly who it would be.

Lucy, of course, with some issue she just *had* to settle now.

He wasn't annoyed, though he absolutely ought to have been. And it never even occurred to him not to get up and answer. He did, however, take a moment to pull on a soft pair of trousers and a black sweater.

When he reached the outer door of his apartment, he hesitated, aware of a rising sensation in his midsection, of the too-rapid beating of his heart: anticipation.

Yes.

Excitement.

Definitely.

He smiled to himself. He was being absurd. How

could he just *know* it would be Lucy? And why was he
rushing to the door when he fully intended to call an
early end to their time together?

Ridiculous. Laughable.

It was probably only some random palace guest lost
on the wrong floor, knocking on the nearest door in
hopes of being pointed in the right direction.

The knock came again. He opened the door.

And there she was just as he'd known she would be,
in a big floppy sweater and skinny little jeans and the
cutest pair of pink high-top canvas shoes.

Something disconcerting happened inside his
chest. He rigorously ignored it. "Luce. My darling."
He lounged against the door frame and tried to look
exhausted and thoroughly put out. "Did you notice?
It's past three in the morning and once again you've
dragged me from my comfortable bed."

She glowed at him. "It's really late, I know. I'm being
unbelievably rude. I hope you'll forgive me, but I have
to talk to you."

Just as he'd expected. She *had* to talk to him.

No. Absolutely not. He needed to gently but firmly
send her away. And then tomorrow at a decent hour, he
could take her aside and explain to her that he'd seen the
light as to their holiday weekend together. He hated to
back out on her, but the whole thing was off.

Yes. That was exactly what he should do.

He peeled himself off the door frame, stepped back
and pulled the door wider. "Do you want coffee?"

"No, nothing. Just to talk." She chose the first door
off the entry, which led to his sitting room. He gestured
toward the two sofas facing each other on either side of
the fireplace with its carved Louis Quinze red-marble
mantel. She took one sofa and he took the other.

He felt way too excited and also on edge. So he made a show of getting comfortable, resting one arm along the sofa back, hitching one ankle across his knee. "What brings you from bed at this time of the night?"

She leaned toward him and braced her forearms on her thighs, folding her hands in front of her knees. "Oh, I haven't been to bed yet. I went to see Noah."

The back of his neck went tight. He lifted his hand from the sofa and rubbed at it. "You dragged him from bed, too?"

"I'm afraid I did, yeah."

"And how did that go?"

"It was pretty rocky." Her expression belied her words. She was grinning, pleased with herself.

"Luce. What are you telling me?"

She sighed and sagged back against the cushions. "The weekend. That's what we've got, you and me, to maybe make something happen. I've got no time to fool around here. I realized I needed to deal with Noah right away. He was giving me dirty looks all night. And I know he was looking at you the same way."

He tried a lazy shrug—though he didn't feel the least lazy. "It's hardly a surprise that he wouldn't be happy seeing the two of us together. Your brother's my friend. But he doesn't want me paying too much attention to his sister. He sees that there's no future in that for either of us and he doesn't want you hurt."

She sat forward again. "That's pretty much what he said. But we both know he was wrong. You won't do anything to hurt me. You would never hurt me, Dami. It's not how you are."

"Luce. That's exactly how I am. Don't you know about me? I grow bored too easily. And when I do, I move on."

She raised her hands, spread them wide and then waved them in circles. "Oh, don't be silly. You know what I mean. We have an understanding. You're, er, helping me, or you *might* help me. I mean, we're being together in a dating sort of way, and then maybe, if the feeling is right, we'll get down to the part where we take off our clothes and have great sex… Well, I mean, I would hope that it would be great. But even if it isn't, that's okay, too. I mean, I've heard that it's often pretty awkward the first time and I…" She let the words trail off as color flooded upward over her sweet round cheeks. "Ugh. I seriously hope to become more smooth and sophisticated by hanging with you. So far it's not happening."

He wanted to tell her she didn't need to be sophisticated. She was far too enchanting already. But extolling her charms was not the goal here. "And did you explain to Noah that you plan to end up in my bed?"

Her slim back snapped straight. "Are you kidding me? Please. Some things are none of his business— including what's really going on between you and me."

Dami reminded himself again that he needed to tell her this had to stop. But he kept forgetting what he needed to do because of what he *wanted* to do—which was to touch her. He ached to get up and sit on the other sofa with her, and the ache made a very distracting prickly feeling beneath his skin. He said flatly, "Your brother only wants you to be happy."

"Oh, Dami, come on. What he wants is for me to be *safe*. And to him that means under his control. If he had it his way, I would be back in California sitting around in my room. He wants me to be where he can check on me at regular intervals just to make certain I don't need medical attention, stat, even though I've been well and strong for two years now. He still has issues because our parents died, because of all the times I *almost* died. He's getting better at letting me make my own decisions about things, but he's not all the way there yet."

As always, she was thoroughly out-talking him— which on the one hand, he found frustrating. On the other hand, he only wanted her to go on talking. He only wanted to get up and sit on the other sofa with her and hear her lovely, breathless voice in his ear as he brushed his hand against her cheek and breathed in the scent of her skin and pressed his lips to her hair.

He stayed where he was and soldiered on. "I'm trying to tell you that Noah's right to be annoyed with you and to be angry at me."

"No. No, he is not right. He's out of line. Which is why I went to the villa and woke him up and told him so."

"Luce, I—"

She barreled right over him. "And I know that it bothered you, him giving you those angry looks. He's your friend and he's been acting like such a jerk to you. That wasn't right. But it's okay now. Really. You don't have to worry about it anymore. It took some doing— and Alice's help—but I finally got through to Noah."

"Tonight? You're saying you worked it all out with him tonight?" It was the last thing he'd expected.

She nodded eagerly. "I did, yes. Tonight. He's promised to stop with the deadly glances. And to totally get off my case. Honestly, he won't be embarrassing either of us with any big-brother scenes, I can promise you that."

Did he believe her? "You're certain about this?"

"Yes. Of course I'm certain. We argued. Alice backed me. And at the end, I asked Noah to stay out of it and he promised that he would. Then he hugged me and he let me go. It was another big step for him. Really. Like I said, he's getting better." She was waving her arms about as usual, hands swooping and diving like soaring doves. "He's learning to accept that I'm an adult with my own life, a life that is completely independent from him."

Dami realized he did believe her. If there was any doubt that Noah had surrendered this particular field, he would have been able to see it in her adorable open face by now.

Not that it really mattered whether Noah was leaving it alone or not. Noah had never been the problem, not really. Dami's plan to show Lucy a beautiful holiday weekend in lieu of seducing her—*that* was the problem.

It wasn't working. It had been a bad plan from its very inception. Less than twenty-four hours ago he'd been so sure he could never find her physically attractive. She'd shot down that certainty in the space of an afternoon.

After that chaste kiss at the harbor, he'd known he had a problem.

And how had he dealt with that problem? Why, by kissing her again that night, at which time his body had actively responded to the taste of her mouth and the feel of her pressed against him, filling his arms. He was as bad as old Dietrich VonDelft, sniffing around after an innocent who had a right to learn about love from someone as sweet and untried as she was.

"Luce," he began severely, despising the stiff, stuffy sound of his own voice, "I have something I really must say to you."

Instantly, her face changed. Her mouth went soft

and her brown eyes went stormy. "Oh, no. What is it? What's the matter now?"

"I've been, er, reconsidering this situation, meaning this weekend, you and me, together."

She made a small unhappy sound. "Reconsidering? Why?"

"We have to be realistic."

"What? But I *am* realistic. I promise you, I am."

"I'm only saying that on second thought, it's a bad idea."

She gulped. "A bad idea...?"

"Think about it. Where can it go, really? Have you sat down and honestly considered how you'll feel if we spend a night together? Have you given any thought to what would happen next?"

She blinked. "Omigod. You're worried about the same thing Noah's afraid of. That you'll hurt me. That you'll break my heart." And then she turned her elfin face away and slid him the most endearing sideways glance. "You *are* worried about that, aren't you?"

How did she do that? Get him at a disadvantage with simple honesty and a sideways look? "I'm your friend, Luce."

"I know that. Of course you are."

"I'm your friend and I want you to have so much. I want you to have what you need. And what a lovely young woman needs is a young man as eager and hopeful and...pure at heart as she."

"Oh, no." She shook a finger at him. "Oh, Dami. Really. I told you. I'm totally behind the curve on this. I need someone to *teach* me, to bring me up to speed. I don't have time to be fumbling around with some guy who's as inexperienced as I am—and as far as your hurting me, your breaking my heart… Can't you see? I'm not like that. Not like most inexperienced girls."

"But you *are* inexperienced. And it's wrong for me to take advantage of you."

"Take advantage? No, that is not what you're doing. You would be doing me a favor. A very special kind of favor."

"No."

"Yes! You and Noah, you're both so afraid I'm going to get my heart broken. But see, my heart was broken for most of my life. Yeah, okay, it was technically a birth defect that caused a faulty valve. But it made me different, made me feel I would never have all the things everyone else takes for granted. I always tried to put a smiling face on it, but deep down my heart was broken for all the life I would never have."

"But now you're well," he reminded her, preparing to go on and explain calmly and gently how she only had to be a little patient. She would meet someone special and nature would take it from there.

But before he could say that, she went right on. "Exactly. I'm well. New techniques were developed and I had the surgery I needed, finally." She put a hand to her breast. "My heart is now *un*broken. And yeah, okay, I might be hurt by a man, by love gone wrong. I might suffer the way any woman suffers when she loses the guy who matters most. But even if that happened, so what? That's what real life is. Being hurt, getting up and going on. And maybe, if you're richly blessed, finding true happiness in time. I'm up for that. For whatever happens. Because my heart is *un*broken and now I'm strong enough to see a heartache through to the happiness on the other side."

Damien stared at her. How could he help himself?

She really was amazing. He could just sit there and listen to her chatter away, waving her pretty hands, saying things that touched him, things that made him feel glad simply to know her, to be her friend.

But he had to do the right thing by her. He had to make her see the light. "That's just it. It all becomes convoluted and complex between men and women when sex enters into it. It's rarely as simple as you might want it to be—especially when it's your first time."

"I see that, I do. That's why I chose you. Because you do love me." He must have winced, because she added quickly, "Settle down. Take a deep breath. I mean as a dear friend. You love me and I love you and you have always shown such care for me. Noah wants me to be safe. And you know what? With you, I will be. I have no doubt of that. I will be safe and treated right. And when it's over, I swear to you, I will smile at you and wish you the best of everything and let you go."

Damn it to the depths of hell. What could he possibly say to that?

Not that it mattered what he might have said, because of course Lucy was still talking. "Tell me the truth," she demanded, biting her soft lower lip.

"Er...which truth is that?"

She gave him another of those sweet sideways glances. "Remember when you kissed me in my room earlier?"

As though he could possibly forget. "What are you getting at?"

"You...liked it, didn't you?"

He opened his mouth to tell her a lie—and nothing came out.

She shook that finger at him again. "Dami, I may be inexperienced, but I saw the look on your face. I felt

your arms around me. I felt…everything. I know that
you liked kissing me. You liked it and that made you
realize that you *could* make love with me after all. That
you could do it and even enjoy it. And that wasn't what
you meant to do when you told me we could have the
weekend together. That ruined your plan—the plan I
have been totally up on right from the first—your plan
to show me a nice time and send me back to America
as ignorant of lovemaking as I was when I got here."

"Luce…"

"Just answer the question, please."

"I have absolutely no idea what the question was."

"Did you like kissing me?"

Now he was the one gulping like some green boy.
"Didn't *you* already answer that for me?"

"I did, yeah. But I would also like to have you answer it for yourself."

He wanted to get up and walk out of the room. But
more than that, he wanted what she kept insisting *she*
wanted. He wanted to take off her floppy sweater, her
skinny jeans and her pink canvas shoes. He wanted
to see her naked body. And take her in his arms. And
carry her to his bed and show her all the pleasures she
was so hungry to discover.

"Dami. Did you like kissing me?"

"Damn you," he said, low.

And then she said nothing. That shocked the hell out
of him. Lucy. Not saying a word. Not waving her hands
around. Simply sitting there with her big sweater drooping off one silky shoulder, daring him with her eyes to
open his mouth and tell her the truth.

He never could resist a dare. "Yes, Luce. I did. I liked
kissing you. I liked it very much."

A small pleased gasp escaped her. She clapped her

hands. "Then there's no problem. It's all going to work out. We'll have our weekend. We'll see how it goes." God, she was something extraordinarily fine. So eager and lovely, her eyes shining with anticipation at the possible pleasures to come.

And who did he think he was fooling? He was who he was. When confronted with temptation, he inevitably found a way to surrender to it. She was right. He knew that he wanted her now, and that changed everything.

He only prayed that when it ended, he could still be her friend.

Chapter Five

Five hours later Damien sat across from her at a small round corner table in his favorite café, a narrow window-fronted shop on a side street in the mostly residential ward of La Cacheron.

"I love it here," Lucy declared. She was looking amazing, as usual, in a short ruffled skirt, a white schoolgirl blouse, black suede boots and a bright yellow sweater. Amazing and wonderfully young, he thought, so fresh faced and glowing after staying up most of the night battling first with her brother and then with him.

"What, exactly, do you love?" he asked, so that she would continue talking and waving her hands about.

She put out both arms to the side, palms up. "I love the black-and-white linoleum floor, the dark wood counters, the waitresses in their little white aprons, those plain shirtwaist dresses and sensible shoes. They look like they've been working here all their lives."

"Most of them have." He sipped his café au lait and nodded at their server, Justine, who was tall and deep breasted with steel-gray hair. "Justine has been serving me since before I could walk. Gerta, our nanny, used to bring us here at least twice a week."

"Us?"

"My brothers, my sisters and me. Sometimes my mother or my father would bring us. They've always loved it here, too. The croissants are excellent and Justine and the others always knew to wait on us without a lot of fanfare so we would be comfortable and able to enjoy just being a family out for a treat."

She ate the last bite of her croissant. "Um. So good." A flaky bit of pastry clung to her plump lower lip.

He imagined leaning across and licking it off. "Finish your coffee," he said a little more gruffly than he meant to.

She dabbed at her lip with her napkin and then sipped her coffee slowly. "Are we in a rush?"

"We don't want to miss the Procession of Abundance."

"Ah, yes," she answered airily. "I read the guidebook. It's an age-old Montedoran tradition that always occurs on a Friday at the end of November. A parade of farmers and vintners marching the length of the principality to the Cathedral of Our Lady of Sorrows in order to have their seeds and vines blessed, thus ensuring bountiful crops in the year to come."

He nodded approval. "Very good. But don't forget the donkeys."

She pressed a hand, fingers spread, across her upper chest. "I can't believe I forgot the donkeys. The farmers and vintners all ride on donkeys."

He gave another nod. "As did our Lord on Palm Sunday and Mary on the way to Bethlehem, the donkey symbolizing loyalty and humility and the great gift of peace, which brings the possibility of abundance. Ready to go?"

She set down her white stoneware cup. "I just want to look at the pictures first." And she swept out her left arm to indicate the sketches and paintings that jostled for space on the dark wood-paneled walls. A moment later she was up and strolling the length of the shop, her gaze scanning the framed oils, watercolors and pencil drawings created by local artists over the years.

He left the money on the table and got up and went with her. She stopped opposite three drawings grouped together on the back wall. One was a street view of the café's front window, one of a slightly younger Justine, in profile, bending to set a cup on a table. The third was the front window again but seen from inside. A fat cat sat on the window ledge looking out.

Lucy said, "I do like these three. The cat reminds me of Boris." Boris was her fat orange tabby.

"Is Boris still in California?" When he'd taken her to New York, they'd had to leave Boris behind in the care of Hannah Russo, Lucy's former foster mother, who was now Noah's housekeeper.

Lucy shook her head, her gaze on the cat in the drawing. "Hannah brought him to me a few weeks ago. He likes it in Manhattan. He sits in the front window and watches all the action down on the street—very much like this cat right here." He knew she'd already checked for and found the scrawled initials, DBC, in the lower left-hand corners of each of the sketches. Lucy was always after him to dedicate more of his time to painting and drawing. She added, "These are so good, Dami. When did you do them?"

He slid his arm around her waist, allowing himself the small, sharp pleasure of touching her, of feeling the warmth of her beneath the softness of her cashmere cardigan with its prim row of white buttons down the front. "Years ago. I was studying briefly at Beaux-Arts in Paris and drawing everything in sight. I came in for coffee, had my sketchbook with me. Justine gave me a box of pastries in exchange for these."

She leaned into him a little. He caught the scents of coffee and vanilla—and peaches. Today she smelled of peaches. And she scolded, as he'd known she would, "You should spend more time drawing and painting."

It was delicious, the feel of her against his side. "Life is full of diversions and there aren't enough hours in a day."

"Still…"

He turned her toward the door. "Let's go. The Procession of Abundance won't wait."

After the parade, they strolled the Promenade in the harbor area, not far from where he'd told stories to the children the day before.

She chattered gleefully about her upcoming first semester at the Fashion Institute of New York. She'd been to the school and pestered some of her future instructors for ways she might better prepare for the classes to come. As a result, she was designing accessories and working with fabrics she hadn't used before.

And then, again, she brought up his painting. "I know you have a studio here in Montedoro. I want you to take me there."

He teased, "Never trust a man who wants to show you his etchings."

"But that's just it. You *don't* want to show me. You keep putting me off."

He took her soft, clever hand and tucked it over his arm. "I'll consider it."

She bumped her shoulder against him and flashed him a grin. "And I'll keep bugging you until you give in and let me see what you've been working on."

"But I haven't been working on any of that. I'm a businessman first. And you know that I am."

"You're an artist, Dami," she insisted. "You truly are."

"No, my darling. *You* are. Now please stop nagging me or I won't take you to the holiday gala at the National Museum tonight."

Her big eyes got wider. "Oh, that's right. I'd almost forgotten about the show at the museum. There will be an exhibit of that new car you've been working on, the Montedoro, won't there?"

"You make it sound as though I built the car personally."

She put on an expression of great superiority. "I know how to use the internet, believe it or not. I read all about the new sports car and how you helped design it."

"So, then, we're agreed."

She sent him a look. "Agreed about what?"

"You'll go with me to the gala tonight. We'll drink champagne. I will dazzle you with my knowledge of Montedoran art. And you'll stop giving me grief about how I should spend more time in my studio."

Lucy wore red to the gala that night. Her own design, the dress was strapless, of red satin, with a mermaid hem and a giant jeweled vintage pin in the shape of a butterfly at the side of her waist. She felt good in that dress—comfortable and about as close to glamorous as someone everyone considered "cute" was ever going to get.

Dami said, "Wow," when he saw it. And she had to admit, the way he looked at her, all smoldering and sexy, had her convinced that the dress was just right.

The National Museum of Montedoro filled a very old, very large rococo-style villa perched on a hillside overlooking the harbor. Dami's sister Rhiannon, who was a year older than Alice, worked there. Rhia oversaw acquisitions and restorations. She greeted the guests as they entered the museum.

Seven months pregnant, wearing royal-blue satin, Rhia had that glow that so many pregnant women get. She kissed Lucy on the cheek and said that Alice and Noah were expected any minute now. Lucy shared a glance with Dami over that. He frowned a little, probably doubting that Noah would behave himself. Lucy flashed him a confident smile. Noah would behave himself, all right. If he didn't, he'd get another middle-of-the-night visit from his little sister.

Rhia said, "Follow the Hall of Tapestries. The Montedoro Exhibit is in the South Gallery. You can't miss it."

They proceeded down a long hallway hung with beautiful tapestries, some of them very old, to a large two-story room with tall windows overlooking the harbor. The second floor was a balcony rimming the space. Guests could stand at the railing up there and gaze down on the action below.

The gallery was already milling with people in full evening dress sipping champagne. A jazz quartet played on a stage near the windows. A sleek red sports car gleamed under spotlights in the center of the room.

"It's so beautiful," she told Dami at the sight of the new car.

"It has to be," he said. "After all, it's called the Montedoro."

They made their way around the exhibit. Lucy took her time, studying the photographs and scale drawings and reading the descriptions that detailed the creation of the new car. The Montedoro would be available to exclusive individual buyers that coming May and offered for sale in upscale auto dealerships all over the world in the fall. Many of the drawings were signed DBC.

Evidently, Dami saw her checking out his initials. "See? There's more to life than painting and sketching fat cats in windows."

"Noah told me that you took a degree in mechanical engineering and design."

"I like to keep busy."

"You're way too modest."

"Oh, no, I'm not." He leaned closer and his warm breath brushed her temple. "I have a lot of interests. And I become bored very easily."

"You hide your abilities behind your jet-setter facade."

"Does anyone actually say *jet-setter* anymore?"

She drew her shoulders back. "I do. It's a perfect way of saying shallow-rich-people-who-fly-all-over-the-place-in-their-private-jets. Just IMO, of course."

He pretended to hide a yawn. "I hope this isn't the beginning of one of your lectures concerning my wasted artistic talent. I thought we had an understanding about that."

"You're right." She did her best to look contrite. "We do. And I didn't mean to insult rich people with too much time on their hands."

"As opposed to hardworking rich people, you mean?"

"Well, you have to admit, a hardworking rich person is much more admirable."

"Spoken like an American."

She scolded, "And would you please stop telling me how easily you get bored?"

He leaned even closer and whispered, "Done."

She breathed him in. He did smell wonderful. "Terrific."

He touched her hair, tracing the line of it along her temple and cheek then following the shell of her ear. A little shiver of pleasure went through her and he whispered, "Not bored now. Not with you...."

They were sharing a lovely, intimate smile when she heard the disturbance by the wide arch that opened back onto the Hall of Tapestries. Dami was facing the entrance. He could see what was happening. His tender look turned to a scowl. Lucy followed his gaze to the stunning woman surrounded by admirers and eager photographers just entering the exhibit.

It was Vesuvia.

And she looked even more magnificent than she did on the covers of all those glamorous fashion magazines, with magnetic almond-shaped eyes, cheekbones to die for and lips so full they should be X-rated. She was very tall, with shapely shoulders and long, graceful arms. Her lion's mane of tawny hair fell to the middle of her back and her perfect round breasts seemed to defy gravity. She wore a low-cut white gown that clung lovingly to every curve and was slit high on the right side to reveal a whole lot of toned golden-skinned leg and a pair of Grecian-inspired metallic sandals with the straps wrapping halfway up her otherworldly calves. She laughed and tossed her acres of hair and the photographers went into a frenzy of picture taking, calling encouragements to her and begging, "Vesuvia, this way!" and "Vesuvia, over here!"

Dami leaned close again, "Don't stare, Luce. It only encourages her."

Lucy turned back to him, feeling slightly dazed, the way you do when you stare directly into the sun. "Sorry, Dami. How can I help it? She's pretty amazing to look at, you know?" She glanced again at his ex-girlfriend just as the woman raised her golden arm to send Dami a little wave, a come-and-get-me smile on those impossibly large lips. And that had Lucy whipping her head back to catch Dami's reaction.

But his gaze was waiting for her. "You look as though you're watching a tennis match."

She didn't deny it. "Am I?"

"Not on my part. I've conceded that game."

Are you sure? she longed to ask. But no. Maybe later when they were alone, if it felt right, they might talk about his ex. Because they were friends and they trusted each other.

But to get into all that now, well, uh-uh. Time and place, it wasn't. Plus, Lucy found she felt… Well, not jealous, exactly. How could she be jealous? She and Dami didn't have that kind of thing going on.

But at a disadvantage. Yes, that was it. Like suddenly she was walking around blindfolded in an unfamiliar room, groping at the furniture, trying to find her way.

Vesuvia and her posse were headed for the scale model of the Montedoro in the center of the exhibit. A man and a woman broke from the group. The woman wore a black sheath cocktail dress and the man a dark suit. Both had on ear-to-ear smiles. They came right for Lucy and Damien.

"Watch out," Dami warned. "Ad executives." He named a major international advertising company.

"Your Highness," fawned the woman. "How *are* you?"

Dami nodded. "Wonderful to see you." He introduced Lucy. She murmured a hello.

The woman gave her a quick nod and got right to the point. "I wonder, a few pictures? You and Vesuvia and the Montedoro? Is it possible, do you think?"

"Of course," he said. "I'll be right over."

The man said, "Excellent."

The woman said, "Perfect."

And then they both turned and went back to where Vesuvia was laughing and tossing her head in front of the red car.

Dami wrapped an arm around Lucy's shoulder, drew her close to his side and spoke softly in her ear. "We want to keep the Montedoro in the news. Unfortunately, that means I have to try to say yes to any and all shameless photo ops whenever the car happens to be involved."

Lucy didn't like it. And it annoyed her that she didn't like it. She kind of did feel jealous after all. Ugh. Jealousy was not in her plan.

Dami did the loveliest thing then. He pressed his lips against her hair, just above her right ear. "Luce? Are you all right?"

Really, she had to stop crushing on him. It just wasn't fair, wasn't part of their arrangement. She put on a bright voice. "Of course. I get it." And she did. He and Vesuvia might or might not be through, but pictures of them together would fuel rumors about them and their stormy relationship. The pictures would make all the tabloids—and the Montedoro would be in all the pictures. "Go ahead with your photo op. I'm just going to look around the other exhibits a little."

He pulled her close again and pressed a kiss to her forehead. His lips were warm and soft and a thrill went through her. She felt the affection in that brushing caress. At the same time, she couldn't help thinking, *Oh, Dami. On the forehead? Way to make me feel like a child.*

Still, she met his eyes one more time and smiled like she didn't have a care in the world. And then she left him so he could go and pose with his ex.

She headed for the Hall of Tapestries, trotting as fast as her mermaid hem would allow, determined to make a quick escape from the South Gallery. But she wasn't quite quick enough. As she passed under the wide arch that got her out of there, she spotted Noah and Alice coming straight for her.

They saw her. What else could she do but deal with them? If she took off running, Noah would assume there must be something bothering her. And then when he got into the gallery and saw Dami and Vesuvia together, he would guess what that something was.

He might get mad about it in his protective big-brother way. Or he might just feel sorry for her because she'd been crushing on Dami and look where that had gotten her. Neither of those possibilities was acceptable. Okay, maybe she wasn't gorgeous and sophisticated with perfect breasts and legs for days. She had other things going for her. Among them her pride.

No way Noah was going to see her suffering over Dami—not that she *was* suffering over Dami. She wasn't.

Not much, anyway.

She waited, smiling sweetly, as they approached her.

And then she stood there for five full minutes chatting with them, telling them how impressed she was with the car Dami had helped to design and how she couldn't wait to check out more of the museum.

Then Noah said, "Where is Damien, anyway?"

She gestured back toward the gallery behind her. "Major photo op with Vesuvia."

Alice said, "That's right, Vesuvia's the spokesmodel for the Montedoro." She lowered her voice to a just-between-us level. "They signed her for the job before she and Dami got completely on the outs."

Completely on the outs. That sounded kind of good—not that it was anything Dami hadn't already told her.

About then, Rule, who was second-born of Damien's brothers, came toward them with his wife, Sydney. Alice waved them over. Lucy was able to say a quick hello to the prince and his wife and then move on. She tried to go with dignity and slow steps, her head high.

The Hall of Tapestries took her back to the grand entry in the center of the villa. Rooms and other hallways branched off the entry like the spokes of a wheel. A curving staircase soared up behind the information desk. The main directory told her there were three stories of galleries to explore.

She began with the north wing on the ground floor, in the three galleries dedicated to textiles and clothing. First off, she found a gallery full of beautiful examples of Montedoran clothing through the years. There was an excess of what she thought of as the Little Dutch Girl look—blousy homespun shirts with snug lace-up bodices worn over them and full embroidered skirts, layers of lacy petticoats beneath and frilly aprons on top.

The next room had the finery that the princely family had worn. The exhibit spanned hundreds of years,

with examples of clothing worn by many generations
of the Calabretti family. The gowns were spectacular,
some of them sewn with pearls and semiprecious stones.
The lacework, even yellowed with age, stole her breath.

The wedding gown was there, the one Princess Adrienne had worn when she'd married Dami's dad. Lucy
had been drooling over pictures of that famous dress
long before she was old enough to hold a needle and
thread. The gown held pride of place in the center of
the exhibit, in a tall glass case. Lucy stood and stared
at it for a long time.

It really lifted her spirits to see it close up, the impossibly perfect embroidery, the exquisite lace, the thou-
sands of sewn-on seed pearls. Looking at Princess
Adrienne's wedding dress reminded her of the great
adventure that lay before her as a designer. It made her
remember that her life was rich and full and good. That
she was *not* going to be jealous of Dami and his ex—
or if she was, a little, it was okay. Even the unpleasant
emotions were part of being alive and she would take
life over the alternative any day of the week.

Warm hands clasped her waist. Dami. "How did I
know I would find you here?"

She'd been so transported by the legendary wedding
dress that she hadn't seen his faint reflection in the
glass of the protective case. But she saw him now. She
turned to him and brought her palms up to rest on the
satin lapels of his jacket. "I can now say I've seen *the
dress* in person. Not to mention generations' worth of
serious Calabretti style. I've also already checked out
the various examples of traditional Montedoran dress."

He still held her waist and his eyes gleamed down at
her. "Are you saying you're ready to move on?"

She hooked her arm in his. "Where to next?"

He took her back to the main entrance and up the stairs to the Adele Canterone Exhibit. For an easy, companionable hour they admired the art of Montedoro's great Impressionist painter.

They ran into Noah and Alice again on the way out.

Alice said, "Come back to the villa with us, you two. We'll share a late supper."

Lucy instantly suspected that Noah might be up to something. She gave him a long narrow-eyed look.

Noah was all innocence. "What? Good company, something to eat. Is that going to kill you?"

Lucy couldn't help grinning. "Fine." She glanced at Dami, who nodded in agreement. "We would love to come." Then she teased her brother. "Because I can see you're on your best behavior."

Noah made a growly sound. "Do I have a choice?"

And Alice answered sweetly, "No, you do not."

So they went to the villa and shared a light supper, the four of them. Overall, it went pretty well, Lucy thought. Noah and Dami seemed fine with each other. If there was tension between them, it didn't show. They talked about Montedoro and also about some business deal they were working on together.

And the coolest thing happened just as they were leaving.

Alice took her aside. "I know you're going to be busy with school and everything. But is it possible you might be able to design my wedding dress? It's just the design I would need, by mid-February if you can manage it. Then I'll have it made."

Lucy grabbed her and spun her around and they laughed together. "Are you kidding? I can do that. And absolutely, yes. I would be totally honored—and do you have ideas about what you want?"

"A thousand of them. I'm counting on you to focus me down."

Then Noah butted in, wrapping an arm around Lucy. "When you come home for Christmas, you two can get to work on it."

Noah knew very well that she planned to stay in New York for the holiday. Still, he'd been a sweetheart all night, so she made an effort to answer patiently. "Noah, we've been over that. I'm having my first Christmas in my own place, remember?"

He opened his mouth to start telling her all the reasons she really needed to come to California.

But Alice grabbed his arm, pulled him close and kissed his cheek. "I love you. Shut up."

And miracle of miracles, Noah actually did shut up. And he did it without looking the least pissed off.

Damien had a car waiting at the curb outside the villa. They rode back to the palace in comfortable silence.

He was having a great time. Being with Lucy really worked for him. She saw beauty in everything and she wasn't afraid to let her enjoyment show.

He couldn't help comparing her to V, who'd been just next door to manic during the photo op. All flashing eyes and flying hair, hanging on him for the cameras, she'd hissed in Italian that she was furious at him for not taking her calls. She'd sworn she'd never forgive him. He'd reminded her softly that it was over. She'd given him a melting look for the photographers' sake while calling him any number of unflattering names under her breath. All he could think of was getting the hell away from her.

As it turned out, Lady Luck had his back on that

score. The ad people had said they wanted a few more shots just with V and the car. He'd slipped away. And things had improved dramatically when he found Luce in the north wing of the museum, gazing with stars in her eyes at his mother's wedding gown.

A few minutes after they left Alice's villa, they arrived at the palace. A guard let them in.

Dami said, "I'll walk you up to your room."

And she took his arm and begged so prettily, "Please. Can't we just go to your apartment and talk for a little while?"

It wasn't a good idea. He knew that. True, in the darkest hours of the morning before, he'd been weak, he'd indulged himself and imagined that becoming her lover was inevitable.

But he'd had time to see the light since then. She mattered too much to him. He couldn't bear to lose her. If he took her to bed, there would be bad feelings when it was time to move on. Someone would be bound to get hurt. Someone always did.

Therefore, he'd circled back around to his original plan. He would show her a memorable weekend, minus the part where they ended up in bed together. She understood that their making love wasn't a given. She'd said it herself: they would see how it went. He planned to see to it that it went nowhere.

"Dami." She tugged on his arm. "What *are* you thinking about?"

He studied her fabulous elfin face. "That you remind me of a princess from a Montedoran fairy tale."

She colored prettily. "Thank you." And then she commanded, "Take me to your apartment."

He opened his mouth to remind her that it had been a

long day, but somehow what came out was, "Yes, Your Highness. This way...."

In his rooms, they went straight to the kitchen. She asked for hot chocolate. He made it the way they did in Paris, chopping bars of fine-quality bittersweet chocolate and whisking the bits into the heated milk, stirring in brown sugar and a few grains of sea salt.

She admired the Limoges demitasse and sipped slowly. "Dami. Your hot chocolate is even better than your coffee."

He poured himself a cup and sat down opposite her.

And she said, "I probably shouldn't admit this. It will only prove all over again how gauche and immature I am...."

He set down his cup. "You're not. Admit what?"

She sucked her upper lip between her neat white teeth, then caught herself doing it and let it go. "When you went to pose for those pictures with Vesuvia?"

"Yes?"

"I actually got jealous."

As a rule, when any woman mentioned jealousy, he tended to get nervous, to feel hemmed in, under pressure. But with Lucy he only felt flattered at her frankness. And a little bit guilty for deserting her. "I shouldn't have left you...."

"Oh, don't you dare apologize. You didn't do anything wrong— Well, except when you kissed me on the forehead. That made me feel about five."

"It was a kiss of affection."

"I know. Still. Five."

"Fair enough, then. No more kisses on the forehead."

"Cheek, temples, ears, lips... Well, just about anywhere is great. But not smack-dab in the middle of my forehead."

Kissing her just about anywhere sounded way too appealing, and he probably shouldn't be thinking about that. "All right. Not on the forehead." He found he needed to be sure she had it clear about V. "And about V?"

She was midsip. She swallowed fast and set down the cup, big eyes getting bigger. "Yeah?"

"Nothing to be jealous of. I meant it when I told you that Vesuvia and I are over."

She turned the painted gold-rimmed cup on the delicate saucer. And then she sipped again. "You were, um, exclusive with her for quite a while."

"Yes."

"But you have such a rep as a player, as someone who never makes it exclusive with any woman...."

"I was exclusive with V."

"Why?"

He looked into his cup of chocolate and then back up at her. "You are *very* nosy."

She nodded, a sweet bobbing motion of her pretty head. "Yes. I am. I know. But only because I'm your friend and I want to understand you better."

He believed her. And so he explained, "When I met V, I was looking for the right wife. I wanted someone suited to me. At first V behaved reasonably for the most part. She's bright and beautiful. I thought we could make it work together. I was attracted to her."

"You loved her."

"Love wasn't really the issue."

"But when you get married, love is *always* the issue."

He gave her his most patient look. "No, Luce. Not always."

"So then why did you choose her?"

"I found her attractive and intelligent. I thought we

had a lot in common. She's descended from a very old Italian family. We know many of the same people. I never proposed marriage to her, but V understood that I needed to marry and she told me more than once that she wanted to be my wife, to be a princess of Montedoro."

"You *needed* to marry? Why?"

He'd assumed she knew. Apparently not. "You haven't heard of the Prince's Marriage Law?" She shook her head, so he explained, "The Prince's Marriage Law decrees that all princes of Montedoro are required to marry by the age of thirty-three or be stripped of all titles and relieved of the large fortune they each inherit by virtue of their birth."

She made a low sound in her throat. "Well, that's just wrong."

"It's a controversial law and has been abolished in the past. But then the Calabretti line almost died out. My grandfather had it reinstated."

"You'll be thirty-two in January…."

He put his hand to his heart and teased, "You remembered."

"Of course I remember. Aren't you worried you won't find the right woman?"

"But don't you see? I did worry. And I was practical. At the age of twenty-nine, with plenty of time to spare, I went looking for a bride. And you can see how well that went."

"Not well at all."

"So I'm becoming more philosophical about it. What will happen will happen."

"Dami," she scolded, "it's your inheritance…."

Now he looked at her sternly. "I'm fully aware of

that. You are not to worry about it. It's not your concern."

She was quiet. But only for a moment. "So, then, you're telling me that Vesuvia didn't love you, either. She just wanted to be a princess."

"And that was all right with me. I needed a suitable bride. She liked the idea of marrying a prince."

"Oh, Dami. You sound so cynical."

"Because I *am* cynical."

"No, you're not. Not in your heart."

He chuckled. "Go ahead. Believe wonderful things about me if you must."

"Thank you. I will." She leaned toward him, all eyes. "What changed your mind about proposing to her?"

"At first, as I said, she behaved reasonably. But she didn't *stay* reasonable, because at heart she's *not* reasonable. In the end, it's always a big drama with V. She can't just…sit at a table and talk, over cocoa." He watched her smile, only a hint of one, a slight lifting at the corner of her tender mouth. "With V there must be grand gestures, and often. She craves expensive gifts and constant attention. She loves to stage a big dramatic scene. I can't count the number of times she walked out on me in restaurants after telling me off in very colorful Italian."

"Whew. Yeah. I can see how that would get pretty old after a while."

"It's been over for months now, really. At least, as far as I'm concerned."

"Not for her, though?"

"Let me put it this way. I'm through. I've told her I'm through. She says she understands and then she starts calling again."

"So maybe she loves you after all. Maybe she *still* loves you...."

"Luce, it's not love. Believe me."

She reached across the table and put her soft hand over his. "You look so sad, Dami."

Sad? Was he? "My parents married for love."

"Oh, yeah." She squeezed his hand. Her touch felt so good. "They're, like, legendary, your parents. The American actor and the Montedoran princess, finding true love, living happily ever after...."

With his thumb, he idly stroked the back of her hand—until he realized he was doing it and released her. She gave the tiniest shrug, pulled her arm back to her side of the table and slowly ran a finger around the rim of her demitasse. He thought about kissing her—and not on the forehead.

And what were they talking about?

His parents. Right. "Growing up, we all—my brothers and sisters and I—loved what they had. We all knew we wanted to grow up and have that kind of love for ourselves. Well, except for my twin, Alex. Alex was always...separate. Alone. But in the end, he found his way to Lili. He found true love after all. That's what we do, we Bravo-Calabrettis. We marry for love. We mate for life. Of the nine of us, only my youngest sisters, Genny and Rory, haven't found the one for them yet. They have plenty of time. They're both in their early twenties—like you."

"And what about you, Dami? You haven't found the one." She regarded him solemnly. "I hope you do."

He thought how perceptive she was, really, for someone so young. Once, Alice had told him that Lucy was more grown-up than he realized. He hadn't believed her at the time. But he was beginning to see he'd been wrong.

"Dami?"

He gave a low laugh. It was a sound without much humor. "No, I haven't found 'the one.' I honestly believe now that I'm the exception who proves the family rule. I enjoy the thrill of a new romance. I can't get enough of the chase. But I don't have what it takes for a lifetime of happiness with one woman."

"Oh, come on." She cast a glance at the ceiling and gestured grandly with both hands, the way she liked to do. "So it didn't work out with Vesuvia. You know what Hannah would say?"

He put on a pained expression. "Don't tell me. Please."

Lucy only grinned. She was very fond of her former foster mother. "Hannah would say, get over yourself. Try again. Forget finding someone *suitable*—look for someone to love. And choose a nicer woman this time."

"Nice women bore me—present company excluded, of course."

She fluttered her eyelashes. "Good save."

"I *am* the Player Prince after all. It's my job to be smooth."

She drank the last of her cocoa. "That was so good it had to be sinful." Then she pushed her chair back and stood.

He gazed up the length of her, taking in the pretty curves of her bare shoulders and the brave beauty of that inch of scar tissue her gown didn't hide. "Did I tell you that you are incomparable in red?"

She dimpled at him. "It never hurts to say something like that more than once."

"You're very fine, Luce. Absolutely splendid." His

pulse had accelerated and his breath came faster. Warning signs, he knew. Temptation was calling again and the urge to surrender becoming more insistent.

He knew what to do: move, get up, break the sweet spell of this breath-held moment. Stop thinking that he wanted her more today than yesterday, more now than an hour ago, more in this minute than the minute before.

And what was he doing, anyway, keeping on with this, with her? If he wasn't going to take her to bed, he needed to stay away from her.

But he wasn't willing to do that. He wanted this time with her as much as she seemed to want it with him.

The truth skittered through him, striking off sparks: he didn't want to stop. And he wasn't going to stop.

Impossible. Sweet Lucy Cordell, of all people. He never would have imagined. Not in a hundred years.

But he imagined it now, in detail. With growing excitement. In spite of her brother's probable fury. Even if it ended up costing him her friendship.

Really, he ought to be a better man. Unfortunately, he wasn't.

She stepped away from her chair, pushed it in and came around the table toward him in a rustle of red satin, her eyes never letting go of his, all woman in that moment, the girl he had known before eclipsed, changed. When she stood above him, she reached down and put her hand on his shoulder.

Her touch burned him, made his throat clutch, tangled his breath inside his suddenly aching chest. He couldn't bear it. He caught her fingers, brought them to his mouth, pressed the tips of them against his lips. Heat seared his belly and tightened his groin. She sucked in a sharp breath. He kissed her fingers one more time and then let go.

That was when she said so sweetly, "Stand up, Dami. Please."

Chapter Six

Damien rose and stood with her and tried to think what to say. "Luce…"

She lifted on tiptoe, so her sweet mouth was so wonderfully, perfectly close. Her breath smelled of cocoa. "I haven't had a lot of kisses. I mean, real kisses. On-the-lips kisses."

He whispered her name again. "Luce." Somehow her name was the only word he had right then.

She continued on the subject of kisses. "Two from you, so far. Two from a boy I met in Cardiac ICU at a very excellent hospital in Los Angeles. His name was Ramon. He was getting better, they said. And then one night, out of nowhere, he died. He had the most beautiful crow-black hair." A single tear escaped the corner of her left eye.

He dipped his head, kissed that tear, tasted the salty wetness on his tongue.

She drew in a shaky little breath, put her hands on his shoulders as though bracing herself—and continued, "A boy named Troy kissed me in middle school. It was one of the few times I was well enough to go to school for a while. He kissed me out under the football bleachers. I promised to meet him in front of the school in the morning. But I got bad in the night and there was another surgery and I didn't go to school again for three years."

He made a low noise in his throat, a noise of encouragement, and he pressed his lips to the pretty arch of her left eyebrow.

She went on, "And then there was this boy in high school, a very pricey private school. I went there for three months in my junior year. Noah was rich by then...."

Her brother had started from nothing. Lucy's illnesses had spurred him on to greater and greater success. He'd needed a lot of money to make sure she got the very best care available.

Lucy went on. "The boy in high school? His name was Josh and he lived in our neighborhood in Beverly Hills— This was before Noah bought the estate in Carpinteria. Josh took me to the homecoming dance and I kissed him at the door when he brought me home. He never called me after that. I called him twice, left messages with his mom. And then a few weeks later, there I was in an ambulance again. I was homeschooled exclusively after that. I never saw Josh again and I never kissed anyone else until last year."

"You had a boyfriend last year?" He hadn't known.

"Uh-uh. It was at one of Noah's parties. A man named David, a business associate of Noah's. David would have done more than kiss me, but I got cold feet—and don't you dare tell Noah."

"Never." He growled the word and tried to recall if he'd ever met this David. He didn't think so, which was probably just as well.

"Promise me," she whispered.

"I swear on the blue blood of my Calabretti ancestors, on the honor of all the Bravos who came before me, that I will never tell Noah that you kissed a man named David at one of Noah's parties."

"Wow. Now, *that's* a vow."

"I'm so glad you approve."

She gave him her best Mona Lisa smile. "But you need to seal it with a kiss."

He didn't even hesitate. There was no point. He accepted that now. Unless she called a halt, he was in. All the way. He bent and captured her mouth, tasted chocolate and heat and a sweet, slow sigh.

She wrapped her arms around his neck and swayed closer. He felt the giving softness of her breasts against his chest. Not the least childish, the softness of those breasts. "Dami…"

He pulled her closer still, not even caring anymore that she might feel him unfurling against her belly. He only went on kissing her, dipping his tongue into the moist heat beyond her parted lips, sharing her breath, the world a wonderful place that smelled of peaches and chocolate and something else, something of Lucy, fresh and clean and womanly, too.

After a while, he lifted his head. He gazed down into those shining brown eyes.

She whispered, "That's three kisses from you. Give me another."

He drank in the sight of her flushed upturned face. "You're greedy."

"I need a lot of kisses. I've been deprived." And then she giggled.

That did it. That naughty little laugh of hers made him greedy, too. He swooped down and took her mouth again.

She cried softly, "Oh!" against his lips.

And then he kissed her long and slow and deep, sweeping a hand down to press the small of her back, pushing his hips against her, aching to have her, to feel her tight heat all around him.

She moaned a little, and she lifted her lower body up and into him. Eager. And so very sweet.

That time when he lifted his head, she took the lapels of his jacket and guided them over his shoulders. He allowed that, catching it as it fell, tossing it onto a far chair. She started on the buttons of his shirt.

He caught her hands, kissed them, one and then the other. "Anticipation is a fine thing."

She tipped her head to the side and considered. And then she blushed again. "I'm rushing it, huh?"

"I want you right now," he whispered. "I want to bury myself in you and hear you moan beneath me."

Deeper color flooded upward over her throat, her chin, her plump cheeks. Her scent intensified. "Oh. Well. Okay…"

He bent and scraped his teeth along the side of her throat.

She let out a small rough little sound and clutched him closer. "Dami…" She made his name into a plea.

He caught her earlobe between his teeth and worried it lightly. Then he whispered, "Will you be guided by me?"

Another sound escaped her, more tender than rough. She shifted her fingers up into his hair, pulling his head down into the warm woman-scented curve of her throat. "Yes. Please. That's what I want. For you to teach me."

He took her shoulders then and gently held her away from him—just enough that he could meet her wide, dazed eyes. "First of all…"

"Yes?" Breathless. Hopeful. Impossibly sweet.

"We don't have to hurry."

She groaned and then pressed her lips together.

He touched her hair. Like living silk. "Say it. Whatever you're thinking. Don't hold back."

She winced. "Well, it's just that, um, yeah, we kind of do have to hurry. I mean, it's already Saturday morning. I'm flying home tomorrow. We need to get this done."

He wanted to laugh at her total frankness, but he didn't. He held her gaze. "As your friend, I must warn you against men who say 'trust me.' But trust me."

She laughed then. "Oh, Dami."

"Do you trust me?"

She didn't hesitate. "I do. Absolutely."

"Good." He caught her hand. "Come with me."

Dazed, amazed, excited and very nervous, Lucy went where he led her.

To his bedroom.

It was a large room with a high, coffered ceiling from which hung a giant iron chandelier. The bed had an intricately carved headboard and finials shaped like crowns. The turned-back sheets were cobalt-blue satin, the bedding in deep blue and gold and red.

Unreality assailed her. Alone with Dami in his bedroom. Who knew?

He turned on a torchère lamp beside the bed nice and

low. The chandelier was on, too, but also low. She could see clearly enough, but everything was soft and shadowed. Which was great. The pleasant dimness eased her nerves.

At least a little.

He took her shoulders again, his long fingers warm and sure against her bare skin. Still, she shivered at the touch, scared and also excited for what was to come.

"Second thoughts?" he asked.

Her mouth went dust dry. She swallowed to try to get some moisture going. "No. Really. I want to do this, I truly do...."

His smile was way too knowing as he stepped back from her and began to undress, first dropping to a chair to remove his shoes and socks, then sweeping upright again and getting rid of everything else. Quickly, so gracefully, all his beautiful clothes were gone in what felt to her like an instant, as she just stood there staring.

At least the saliva had flooded back into her mouth.

He was a magnificent man, honed and tanned, with a broad, deep chest and shoulders and a belly you could scrub your laundry on. Her gaze trailed down over hard, narrow hips. The muscles in his long thighs were sharply defined. Even his feet were beautiful, long and perfectly shaped.

She did more absurd gulping as she let her glance stray upward again. This time, she allowed herself to look directly at the most private part of him. He definitely wanted her. His manhood curved up, thick and fully aroused, from the dark nest of hair between those powerful thighs.

That he wanted her was good. Excellent— Well, except for the definite largeness of him. She couldn't help it. She wondered what all virgins probably wondered.

"Seriously, Dami. Are you sure it's going to fit?" The words were out and hanging in the air between them before she stopped to think how ridiculous they would sound.

But he didn't laugh at her. He only brushed a finger slowly down the outside of her arm, bringing the goose bumps to bloom where he touched. And he said in a low rumble, "I promise you, Luce. We'll take all the time we need. You'll see. It will fit. That's how it is with men and women. We are made to fit."

"Well, of course I know that. But it's still, um... yikes. You know?"

He went very still, waiting—and watching her so closely, his eyes that strange deep black-green right then, dragonfly green. He asked, "Do you want to stop? Any time you want to stop, all you have to do is say the word."

"No. Uh-uh. I absolutely do *not* want to stop."

One corner of his sinful mouth quirked up. How did he do it? How did he stand there in front of her without a stitch on looking so comfortable in his own skin he almost didn't seem naked at all?

His finger started moving again, across the slim rolled-satin belt at her waist, pausing at the jeweled butterfly pin. He traced the shape of it and then he let his finger trail upward. He touched her breast just with that single finger. He found her nipple beneath the satin, inside the thin cup of her strapless bra. He rubbed his finger up and down until the nipple hardened.

Lucy gasped. She couldn't help it.

And then he used his thumb, too, rolling it a little, until she felt a certain flooding of heat down low, felt a thin, shimmering cord of desire forming, connecting her breast to her core. She drew another ragged breath as he moved to the other breast and repeated the process.

Then he leaned close. He licked her at her temple. The moisture made a cool spot, right there where her pulse beat above her ear.

He blew on that spot, increasing the coolness. And then he whispered, "Take off your belt...."

She did it, fumbling a little, removing the vintage pin and unhooking the clasp beneath. He took them from her and set them on the bedside table.

"Luce." He licked her temple again, caught a bit of her hair between his lips and tugged. Then he pressed his mouth to her hair. She felt his warm breath sift over her scalp. "Luce?"

"Yeah?" Her own voice sounded...different. Tentative. And breathless, too. She wished fervently to be more experienced, not to be so obviously out of her depth. Her wish was not granted.

And somehow Dami made that seem all right. "Please turn around."

She remembered to breathe again and the air rushed into her hungry lungs as she ordered her feet to move. Three careful steps and she was facing away from him, staring at the shadows in the corners of the room, at the waiting blue satin sheets on the wide carved bed.

He touched her shoulder, as though to steady her. And then he took down her zipper in one long, slow glide. The dress dropped around her ankles.

He wrapped one of those big hard arms around her and kissed the side of her neck. "Step out of it. Careful, now...." She lifted one satin stiletto and then the other, cautiously stepping free of the gown. "Don't move," he warned softly. He let go of her long enough to scoop the dress up and deposit it safely over his clothes on the bedside chair.

Then he wrapped both arms around her. He pulled her against him, his heat and hardness all along the back of her, his manhood pressing into her, making her moan, making her little red panties wet.

He cradled her breasts. It felt...so good. She let out a long sigh, and her head fell back to rest against the hard muscles of his chest. "Should I...take off my shoes?"

He kissed her ear. "No. Leave them on. There is nothing so fine as a beautiful woman in red satin shoes."

A beautiful woman. He meant *her,* Lucy. And she knew it was just Dami, just how he was. He had all the right words to make a woman want him, and he didn't hesitate to use them—and somehow when he used them, he made her believe him. He made her absolutely certain that she was every bit as beautiful and desirable as he kept saying she was.

He continued to caress her, first dipping his thumbs into the cups of her bra, easing the semisheer fabric out of the way so her breasts came free. She looked down at his big dark hands holding her breasts, rolling the nipples. At the narrow white gleam of her heart-surgery scar.

And it was so wonderfully unreal, so perfectly erotic. So totally thrilling in an otherworldly kind of way. Her hips were moving, rubbing back against him. And he kept on touching her.

Her bra fell away. She let out a small cry of surprise. He only growled low in his throat and scraped his teeth along the ridge of her shoulder, easing his mouth into the curve of her throat, sucking a little.

She brought her hand up and back, hungry to touch

him. Wrapping her fingers around his nape, she eased them up into his thick dark hair.

Time flew away. His hands were everywhere and she gloried in their knowing, hot glide over every inch of her. She had his strong, tall body at her back to steady her. And she was suddenly liquid and moving, rocking slow and loving it, as his hands moved lower, pressing at her belly, fingers easing under the elastic of her panties, finding the heart of her.

One finger drifted in where she was wet and hot and hungry. He worked such shimmering magic on her willing flesh. She was wild by then, completely outside herself. Her panties were gone, ruined—he had taken the narrow elastic on both sides and torn it so he could more easily remove them from between her shaking thighs.

And then she was naked except for her red shoes, naked with Dami, standing in front of him, her hips rocking back against his hardness, in the dim light by the wide bed.

He took her thighs and gently guided them wider, using his strong legs to support her as he did it so she didn't stumble in her high heels. And then he was *there* again, his brilliant fingers stroking her, doing the most amazing things to her wet, needful flesh. He eased one finger inside. And then another, stretching her in the most delightful, thrilling way.

And she was…riding. Riding his strong hands, riding his big body behind her. She was making such a racket, moaning and sighing. And she didn't even care. Didn't care about anything but his hardness at her back and his fingers within her. And the low words he whispered to her. Hot, wicked encouragements, praise for her heat and her wetness, her body's hunger, her greediness…

There was a light. A light that curled through her,

burning, somehow liquid. It grew outward in a widening coil. It filled her and flowed out the top of her head, streamed from her fingertips, poured through the soles of her red shoes.

And then it intensified. It was all heat and wet and it was centering down in the core of her, gathering tight where he stroked her, where he made her body open for him, open and burn.

She felt the moment. She knew it, the secret thing she'd never shared with a man before: her climax. It shuddered through her, over her, drowning her in waves of glory.

Dami stayed with her, those wonderful fingers seeming to know what to do, when to keep stroking her. And when to go still, to hold her, to press just the right spot as the pulsing became a shimmer again, a slow, lovely fade into something so perfectly, wonderfully easy and loose.

He had his arm around her waist again. And then he was turning her, scooping her up high against his chest.

She wrapped her arms around his neck and offered her mouth to him. He took it in a slow, thorough kiss as he laid her down on blue satin and then stretched out beside her, easing an arm under her head, gathering her into him, her cheek against his chest, her hand over his heart.

His lips touched her hair again, a kiss both tender and firm.

She closed her eyes for a time. The room was so quiet. His body was big and warm, her own personal heater.

When she looked again, he was watching her through eyes that were black now, limitless and so deep.

She lifted up on an elbow and gazed down at him.

He returned her look out of the center of some wonderful stillness. She marveled, "Dami, this is just how I pictured it, only better. I mean, what you did to me was so hot. And now I'm lying here naked with you in this big manly bed of yours."

"My bed is manly?" He seemed pleased.

"Oh, definitely. Yes. But the point is, it's okay, you know? You and me, naked, together. It's comfortable, easy. Good." By then she was waving the arm she wasn't leaning on. One wide sweeping gesture bopped him on the nose. "Oops."

He only laughed. "I'm glad you're happy. But please don't break my nose."

"Sorry. I promise, I'll be careful." It seemed only natural to let her hand drift lower. He was still hard. She traced the muscles of his belly—but hesitated to touch that most manly part of him. She couldn't help asking, "Does it hurt to be so big and hard?"

He gave her that beautiful half smile of his. "In a good way, yes."

"Do you need…?"

His smile went full-out. "Over the years, I find more and more pleasure in this particular sort of suffering. I enjoy the ache. I find that getting there really is a lot of the fun, that sometimes the longer it takes, the more satisfying the conclusion."

She really did want to touch it. "Is it all right if I…?"

"Yes." Gruff. Low. Like the purr of some big sleek wild animal, no less dangerous for being easy and loose, relaxing in his lair.

She explored at her leisure, loving the smooth, silky feel of his skin there, the flared mushroom shape of the head. He lay very still as she touched him and his breathing changed, becoming faster, shallower. When she bent to kiss him, he let out a low groan.

That made her smile as she lowered her mouth on him and took him inside. He whispered encouragements. She knew she wasn't doing that good of a job. But he never complained. He eased his fingers into her hair, curving them around the back of her neck as she took him in and then let him out nice and slow. He didn't try to take control. His hold was loose, gentle. And she liked that so much.

It made her feel powerful and sexy and womanly. Her mouth surrounding him, her hand wrapped around him, she was running that show.

Running it all the way to the finish, as it turned out. Beneath her hand, she felt him pulsing. His body stiffened. He let out a low, deep moan. "Luce, you should let me…"

No way. She was doing this and she was doing it right. She stayed with him, swallowed him down. He tasted like sea foam, musky and salty. He held her tighter against him right there at the end, and he growled out her name in a way that sent a hot thrill zipping through her, because she had done it, given him pleasure, just as he'd done for her.

She kissed her way up the muscular center of him, feeling naughty and bold.

He took her and turned her and tucked her against him. "Sleep."

"Huh? But we only just got started."

He chuckled. "Greedy." He sounded pleased about it.

"Dami, there's only so much time and I have so much to learn."

"Sleep," he said again.

So she closed her eyes—not for long, she told herself. Just for a little while....

When she woke, he was kissing her.

She looked down and his dark head was tracing the length of her scar as he feathered kisses along it. He kissed her breast, found another scar—a small horizontal one from years ago when she'd needed a temporary pacemaker after surgery.

He went lower. He kissed the little cluster of drainage-tube scars.

And lower still...

The things he could do with his mouth, with his tongue...

No doubt about it. She had made the right choice to come to him to get up to speed on making love.

He did it again, brought her all the way to the top of the world and then over the edge, with his mouth that time. And then he took her hand and pulled her up out of the bed and led her into the kitchen. He made them more of his delicious hot chocolate. They sat together at the table sipping cocoa without a stitch on. It was strangely erotic, like those dreams you sometimes have where you're naked someplace you would never go without your clothes on.

Once she'd finished her chocolate, he told her to get dressed, and when she had everything back on but the panties he'd torn, he said, "Now I want you to return to your room and get some sleep. I'll come for you at eleven."

"But, Dami, we haven't... I mean, it's been amazing. But we're not finished yet."

He bent close and whispered in her ear. "Don't wear any panties."

Her breath caught on a gasp. "You mean…?"

"For all day and into the evening. No panties. And don't cheat. Wear a dress or a skirt. No tights, either."

The place where her panties should have been was suddenly damp. "Oh, Dami. You are very bad."

"So I've been told. No knickers, and whenever you notice that you're without them, think of me."

Chapter Seven

All that Saturday, Lucy did think of him.

And not only because she was walking around without her panties.

How could she not think of him? He was the best friend she'd ever had, not to mention the hottest, smoothest guy she knew.

He sat across from her at another café, where they had coffee and a real breakfast. She ordered a mushroom omelet and toast with jam.

"Eat everything," he commanded. "You have to keep your strength up...." And he gave her a look. Intimate. Teasing. That look said he knew she had no knickers on. That look made promises concerning what he would do to her as soon as they were alone.

She couldn't wait, though he seemed quite happy to make her wait.

"Eat," he said again.

And she did. She ate every bite of her omelet. Both pieces of toast, too. Slathered in jam.

After that he took her where she really wanted to go: his studio, in a villa on one of the hills surrounding the harbor. He kept a flat on the lower floor. They didn't even go in there.

Upstairs in the studio, he'd had all but the load-bearing interior walls removed. His sketches and oil paintings were everywhere, some tacked to the remaining walls, some on easels or spread out on the rough worktables. It was a beautiful space, full of light even in the cool month of November. It was also chilly, though, and dusty. He turned on the heat and admitted he hadn't been there in months.

That gave her another opportunity to remind him that he should be making time for the things that mattered.

He only backed her up against a wall between a drawing of a small dark-haired girl in traditional Montedoran dress and another of a white goat chewing on a straw hat. "No lectures. Not today." And then he kissed her, a slow, lovely kiss during which he eased his clever hands inside her coat and caressed her breasts through her sweater. He also trailed his fingers up her thigh, taking her skirt along, too.

When he touched her where she wasn't wearing any panties, she moaned into his mouth as her body instantly responded. He went on touching her, stroking her. She went over the top right there while he kissed her, by the window that let in the pale late-autumn light, against the white wall.

As the fierce pleasure faded to a happy glow, she laughed and dared to put her hand down between them to feel how what he'd done to her had excited him, too. She was just running her fingers up and down the long tight bulge at his fly when the cell phone in his pocket started to vibrate.

He muttered, "Ignore it," and captured her mouth again.

But she turned away, grinning and more than a little bit breathless. "Go on, answer it—at least check and see if it's anything important."

"It's not." He bit the side of her neck and then stuck out his tongue and licked where he'd nipped her.

By then the phone had stopped its soft buzzing. She gave in and turned to him again with a willing sigh. His warm lips settled on hers.

And the phone started vibrating a second time.

He swore against her mouth—and then he lifted his head, took the phone from his pocket and switched it off quickly. But not before she saw that it was Vesuvia. He glanced up at her as he shoved it back in his pocket again and must have seen something he didn't like in her expression. "Don't *you* start in on me."

"What? I didn't—"

He stopped her from saying more by kissing her again, a long, thorough kiss, more artful than passionate. She accepted that kiss. Like all his kisses, it was too good to pass up. But the mood was pretty much trashed.

In the end, even a lover as skilled as Dami had trouble getting back into a sexy encounter after dual interruptions from the ex. He braced an arm against the wall above her shoulder and leaned his forehead against hers. "Sorry, Luce."

She tipped her head up and kissed him again, but quickly that time, brushing her lips across his. "Does she…call you a lot?"

He pushed away from the wall—and her. Impatiently,

he insisted, "It honestly is over with her, if that's what you're asking."

"I believe you. I was only…" She found she didn't know how to go on.

"What?" he demanded.

"Well, I mean, I just feel bad, that's all."

"For her?" His eyes flashed dark fire.

She held his gaze and shook her head. "No, Dami. For you. Because it didn't work out with her and I think that you really did want it to. And, well, yeah, maybe a little for her. Before he found Alice, Noah had a couple of girlfriends like that. They just wouldn't let it be, you know? They wanted more from him than he was willing to give them and they kept calling him and he was frustrated and angry and didn't know how to get through to them that over was over."

He braced his arms on the table behind him, leaned back on it and studied his fine Italian shoes. "Yes. Well, it *is* over."

"Got that. Truly." *Also that you want this subject dropped.* And really, it wasn't a bad thing for her, she thought. To be so sharply reminded of all that the beautiful man before her *wasn't* willing to give.

They had this brief magical time together. He was being so good to her, so thoughtful and tender and brilliantly instructive—not to mention very, very sexy. He was giving her what she hadn't even really understood she needed so much: to discover all the things she'd missed about passion and sex and to feel safe and cherished and free to be her whole self while it was happening.

She promised herself that tomorrow when it came time to say goodbye, she would definitely remember not to cling. And no matter how much she wanted to hear his voice, she wouldn't start calling him all the time.

He looked up, one dark eyebrow lifted. "Shall we move on?"

"Yes, we shall."

"Have you been to Casino d'Ambre?"

"No, and I really, really need to see that." She gave him a big smile and held out her hand. "Let's get out of here."

Half an hour later, as he took Lucy on a tour of Montedoro's world-famous casino, Damien was feeling more than a little guilty about his behavior at the villa. He'd been gruff with her when he'd had no reason to be—other than he'd been kissing her and touching her and thoroughly enjoying himself. And then the phone had gone off twice and ruined the moment.

He'd felt rotten—about V and her games. About Lucy witnessing once again what a bad choice he'd made in getting involved with V in the first place. About how his life seemed somehow rudderless lately, without direction.

Which was absurd, really. He'd always taken life as it came and had a fine time of it. He was *still* having a fine time of it, and he didn't plan to change.

Lucy took it all in stride. She didn't let his earlier bad attitude put a damper on the day. She didn't push; she didn't sulk. She was as lighthearted and full of fun as ever, wide-eyed at the beauty of the legendary casino, clapping when some tourist won a bundle at roulette.

After the Casino d'Ambre, they strolled the shops of the Triangle d'Or, the area of exclusive stores, restaurants and hotels surrounding the casino square. Workers were everywhere that day putting up the Christmas decorations around the square, ushering in the season. Holiday music filled the air.

Damien took Lucy's hand as they walked. He leaned close and teasingly reminded her to pay no attention to the ever-present paparazzi. He made an effort to be extra attentive after the uncomfortable moments at the villa.

They'd stopped to watch a couple of burly work-men hang a giant lit wreath above a shop door when she sighed and sent him one of her dewy-eyed smiles. "Christmas in Montedoro. I'll bet it's almost as beautiful as Christmas in Manhattan."

He squeezed her fingers, twined with his. "I know your brother is angling to get you to go home to California."

"He can angle all he wants. I'll be in New York City for the holiday season. Just wait and see."

He let go of her hand so he could wrap an arm around her and pull her closer. She laughed, a happy, carefree sound. And so he bent his head and kissed her, right there on the Triangle d'Or for the two workmen and the crowds of busy shoppers and everyone else to see.

When they started walking again, he kept his arm around her and she leaned her head on his shoulder. "Thank you, Dami. For giving me this beautiful, perfect Thanksgiving. It's turning out to be everything I could have hoped for."

He pressed his lips to her fragrant hair. "No thanks are needed. Ever. You know that."

She looked up at him then. Her eyes were so solemn. "You are the most generous person I know."

He wasn't, and she really ought to remember that. "Not really."

She elbowed him in the ribs. "Yeah. Really."

"If you keep making me sound so exemplary, I'll decide it wouldn't be right to seduce you this evening."

She widened her eyes in pretended terror. "Omigod, no! I take it all back. You're a horrible man, a scoundrel, a total dog."

He flattened his lips and arched an eyebrow, going for an evil leer. "Wonderful. You've convinced me. I'll be taking complete advantage of you after all."

They returned to the palace a short time later. By then it was a little after six. There was a light buffet laid out on a sideboard in the main dining room. They filled plates and sat together to eat.

After that he walked her to her room. He kissed her, a kiss he let go on a little too long. A kiss that tempted him to push the door open behind her, to carry her in there and finish what they'd started the night before.

But no. Once he had her naked in his arms, he wasn't going to want to let her go until the morning, when they would say goodbye. And tonight was the annual Prince's Thanksgiving Ball. She couldn't miss that. It was a memorable part of a Montedoran Thanksgiving.

Reluctantly, he broke the kiss and promised to return for her at nine.

In his apartment, Damien got out his phone, turned on the ringer again and checked his messages and calls. He discovered that V had called only those two times. And left one voice mail.

He sat for a while actually considering calling her, trying one more time to speak reasonably with her, to convince her that she had to leave it alone, move on. And then he went ahead and played back her message even though he never played her messages anymore, because he'd grown weary of listening to her call him bad names in Italian.

Surprisingly, her voice was calm. She spoke English, which surprised him almost as much as her even tone. V was fluent in English, but she considered it a barbaric language, unmusical and crass.

"Dami. I can guess where you are. With that skinny, plain little American nobody, the one with hardly any hair." A laugh, soft, knowing. The bitch. "You're all over the internet with her, the two of you at the bazaar on Thursday and the museum last night. Really, Dami, what am I going to do with you?" A long sigh. "I know, I know. You have to follow every cheap flirtation to its logical conclusion and I'm going to have to leave you alone to pursue this new and incomprehensible infatuation. And guess what—I believe I will do just that. Enjoy yourself. I've had enough. When you finally see what a fool you've been, you'll be sorry. But of course, there won't be anything you can do about it. Because I am finished. You hear me? It's over, *finito. Ciao.*"

Damien got up from the sofa and paced to the window. He wasn't angry, exactly, just annoyed at her spiteful remarks about Lucy, who never hurt anyone, who only brought joy.

And there was a bright side to this. Or there could be. V had sounded as though she'd finally accepted the inevitable.

He put the phone to his ear again and played the message through a second time.

Yes. Very possibly a real goodbye.

He went back to the sofa, kicked off his shoes and stretched out. A certain buoyancy had come over him. He felt distinctly optimistic.

It didn't hurt his new, improved mood that for now,

anyway, there was no need to consider calling V after all. If she'd meant what she'd said, he wouldn't be talking to her again.

And if she hadn't meant it…

Well, he'd walk that plank when he came to it.

"I work as a nanny," said Lani Vasquez, leaning closer to Lucy in order to be heard over the din in the crowded ballroom. The musicians had taken a break and now everyone seemed to be talking at once. Lani went on, "I came from Texas with Sydney when she married Rule." *Rule,* Lucy reminded herself. *Second-born after Maximilian.* "And now I take care of their kids, Trevor and Ellie. It's such a great job. I love the kids and Sydney is very hands-on, so I get a lot of time to myself. Tonight she and Rule are at their villa with the children, so here I am enjoying the Thanksgiving Ball." Lani flashed a bright smile. "I love it here in Montedoro. I never want to leave."

Prince Maximilian, the heir apparent, who'd been standing a few feet away chatting with a beefy older guy, stepped closer. He and the black-haired nanny from Texas shared a warm glance. "Lani's a writer," he said. "She's writing a series of historical novels set in Montedoro."

"Someday I intend to be a *published* writer," Lani added. "Someday *soon,* I keep hoping."

"Lani has an agent in America," said the prince. The man was clearly a booster of the pretty nanny. "She's right on the brink of that first big sale."

"The brink." Lani gave a small uncomfortable chuckle. "As I said, we can hope."

"It can't be long now." Max seemed to have no doubts about Lani's inevitable success.

"His Highness has two children, Nicholas and Constance," Lani told Lucy.

"I remember seeing them at Thanksgiving dinner." Lucy pictured them: a dark-eyed boy of seven or eight, a little blonde girl a year or two younger.

Lani went on, "Their nanny, Gerta, and I have become good friends."

Max said, "Gerta's like a second mother to them. They're very attached to her."

"Gerta. I've heard that name before— Wait, I know. Dami told me that he had a nanny named Gerta."

"That's right," Max replied. "Gerta was our nanny, too. She looked after all nine of us when we were small. Gerta's part of the family, really."

Lani said, "We all hang out together. The four children, Gerta and I. That's how Max and I have gotten to know each other a little. His Highness is the world's foremost expert on the history of Montedoro." She said it proudly, with real admiration, apparently as much a booster of the prince as he was of her. "And he's arranged it so that I have unlimited access to the amazing original materials in the palace library."

"Wow." Lucy was impressed. "Talk about an invaluable research resource...."

Lani and the prince shared another lingering glance. "Exactly," Lani said. "The library contains the correspondence of the Calabretti princes over hundreds of years. There are historical documents going back to the Middle Ages. I could never find such a treasure trove anywhere else."

Right then Dami, who'd gone off to chat up some business associate, appeared at Lucy's side. He greeted his brother and Lani. The music began to play again.

Max offered Lani his hand. She took it and they went out on the floor to dance.

Lucy watched them go. "The prince and the nanny. I'm lovin' it."

"What are you talking about?" Dami sounded surprised.

Lucy chuckled. "Oh, come on." She watched the two dancing. They had eyes only for each other. "It's obvious those two have a thing going on."

"No. Never." His tone was flat, unequivocal. She glanced at him. He was frowning. And then he said grudgingly, "Yes, all right. It's a little odd."

"Excuse me? Odd?"

"Max only dances with his sisters and our mother."

"Well, yeah. That is kind of odd."

"That's not what I meant. You don't understand." He watched Max and Lani until they danced out of sight. Then he shook his head. "Never mind."

She moved in a fraction closer to him and brushed her bare arm against the superfine wool of his sleeve, loving the heat in her belly, the shiver of anticipation for the night to come, when it would be just the two of them at last and they would finally finish what they'd started the night before. "Don't blow me off, Dami. There's something going on between the two of them. They're a mutual admiration society, I kid you not. And when they look at each other... Bam." She lifted her fisted hands and then popped all her fingers wide to illustrate.

Dami eased an arm around her waist and drew her in front of him. She felt him at her back and longed to lean into his heat and hardness. However, if she did that, she'd probably start rubbing on him next. And it wouldn't be appropriate to go all X-rated at the Prince's Thanksgiving Ball.

He said in her ear, "Max loved his wife, Sophia. He loved her and only her from the time they were children. When he lost her, we all worried that he wouldn't be able to go on."

She craned her head back to him. He dipped his closer. She said, "And that's all so romantic, I know. But hey. The guy's still alive. He has a right to a little happiness with someone who's still breathing, don't you think?"

"Luce." He spoke into her ear again and his warm breath stirred her hair. "I'm only telling you that you've got it all wrong."

She craned her head back once more. "No. Sorry. You're the one who doesn't get it. I know what I saw."

He caught her hand. Heat shimmered up her arm from the point of contact as he whirled her to face him. His dark eyes glittered, inviting her. "Dance with me."

She became sharply aware once again that she had no panties on. Her belly hollowed out and her breath caught. And she felt very naughty and wonderful and wild. "I was wondering if you were ever going to ask."

He pulled her out on the floor and took her in his arms.

Dancing with Dami. It was as easy and natural as breathing, though Lucy had never been that good of a dancer. She hadn't had a whole lot of opportunities to practice. Dami, on the other hand, was a *great* dancer. He could make any woman look good on the dance floor.

He had danced with her on the night that she'd met him. Noah had thrown one of his parties that night. There'd been a six-piece combo and dancing outside on the loggia. Prince Damien had asked her to dance and she'd felt like a princess. A very skinny, rather pale princess, it was true. At the time, she'd still been recovering from that final surgery. But that night, being too skinny with dark circles under her eyes didn't matter. She'd felt like a princess dancing with Dami, knowing already that he would be her friend.

Now he held her so lightly, guided her so effortlessly. Her gown, strapless navy-and-black organza and guipure, seemed to float around her peep-toe high heels, unhampered by boring gravity. They danced two dances.

And then Noah cut in. "Mind if I dance with my beautiful sister?"

With a graceful nod, Dami surrendered her to her brother.

She went into Noah's arms and watched Dami's broad back as he wove his way through the other dancers, moving toward the full bar set up between a pair of marble pillars in a far corner.

"Your dress is beautiful," Noah said. She thanked him. "What time's your flight tomorrow?"

She suppressed a sigh. After all, she'd told him more than once before. "Eleven-thirty."

"We haven't seen enough of you over the weekend."

"I know, it was a short visit. But I've had a wonderful time."

A hesitation, then, "With Damien."

She returned his gaze, unwavering. "Yes, Noah. With Damien."

They danced for several seconds without speaking, which was fine with her. Then he said, "Dami's a good man."

"He's the best."

"If he hurts you, I might have to kill him."

"Oh, stop it. Dami would never hurt me. And no matter what happens, you don't get to kill him. Murder is a bad thing— Plus, Alice would never forgive you if you killed her brother."

He scowled. "You've become so…stubborn and determined the past few years."

"I was always stubborn and determined, but when I was sick all the time, I didn't have the energy to be my real self."

After a moment, he slanted her a sideways look. "How about Christmas?"

She couldn't help laughing. "Do you ever give up?"

A wry smile curved his lips. "Never. I'm a lot like my baby sister that way."

"Noah, I'm serious. I keep thinking we're clear that I run my own life at last. And then you come at me again."

He did look contrite. "Sorry."

"Are you really?"

He nodded. "I get that you're feeling good, doing what you want to do and loving every minute of it. And that's great. I just… I still want to protect you. I can't turn that off overnight."

"Keep working on it, will you?"

"I am, Lucy. Honestly."

"Work faster, then." She said it gently. With all the love in her heart. "Please."

Lani Vasquez and Prince Maximilian whirled by them, eyes only for each other. And Lucy thought of Dami's surprise and disbelief when she'd said that there was something going on between them. Was it always like that in families? People got locked into roles—the sickly one, the grieving widower—and other family members just refused to see that the ones they love can change and grow.

But then Noah said, "Just remember that I'm proud of you. You were right to strike out on your own, not to let my fears for you hold you back. I wish you were coming home for the holidays, but if you insist on staying in New York, I'll get over it. Have a beautiful Christmas, Lucy."

So, then. Maybe her brother's view of her wasn't so locked in after all. She wished him the best Christmas ever and when that dance ended, he walked her over to the bar, where Dami and Alice were sipping champagne.

Alice set down her glass and held out her hand to Noah. He led her out on the floor. They gazed at each other the same way Prince Max had looked at Lani Vasquez.

Dami handed Lucy a crystal flute of champagne. They raised their glasses to the season. And when their glasses were empty, he asked her to dance again. It was an old standard that time, a slow holiday song: "What Are You Doing New Year's Eve?"

She felt a little sad to think that on New Year's Eve she would be in New York and Dami would be somewhere else. But not *that* sad.

Really, how could she be sad? She was getting exactly what she'd dreamed of: a fabulous Thanksgiving weekend and tender lessons in lovemaking from a man she trusted absolutely.

When that dance was over, she whispered, "It's long past midnight. I don't want to wait anymore, Dami."

He gave her a look that was totally hot. And then he took her hand and led her out of the crowded ballroom.

Chapter Eight

His sheets were gold that night. Gold satin.

They stood beside the beautiful carved bed with the finials shaped like crowns, the gold sheets turned back, lustrous and inviting in the soft low light. He kissed her for the longest time, an endless, tender, ever-deepening kiss.

As he kissed her, he touched her, caressing her bare shoulders, her back, the curve of her waist and lower. When he stroked his hands over her hips, she moaned a little, sharply aware of her nakedness beneath the long skirt of her dress.

Really, a woman's panties didn't cover all that much to make her feel so bare without them. But she did feel bare under her gown. Bare and revealed, somehow, though no one could see.

He lifted his mouth from hers. "Luce."

"Um?"

"Take off your dress."

"Yes." She turned around and showed him her back. He pulled her zipper down. The dress fell away. She caught it, stepped out of it, tossed it toward the nearest chair.

"No panties," he said approvingly.

She turned to face him. "I'm very obedient. When I want to be."

His eyes burned into hers. "The rest. Take it off."

So she did. Everything. There wasn't that much. Her strapless bra. Her peep-toe shoes. Her vintage earrings and antique bracelet.

He took the jewelry from her, set it on the table by the bed. And then, still fully clothed except for the jacket he'd taken off when they first entered the apartment, he started touching her again. He bent and kissed her breasts as his hands went roaming.

Time fell away and her knees went all wobbly. But Dami didn't let her fall. He scooped her up against his broad chest and then sat on the edge of the bed with her in his lap.

His skilled, knowing hands moved over her. She looked down at his long fingers against the pale flesh of her belly. Those fingers stroked lower.

And lower. He parted her. She didn't have to be told. She eased her thighs apart.

"Wider," he whispered, the word hot and a little bit rough. He scraped the side of her throat with his teeth.

She moaned. And she obeyed. It was only what she wanted after all. His fingers found her, delving in, moving in a rhythm her body already knew and welcomed.

"Dami," she cried. "Yes...more..." She tipped her head back and gave him her mouth for a slow, wet, hungry kiss.

He whispered things, naughty things. Each whisper took her higher, closer to the sky, to the darkness and the wonder.

To that moment when it all burst wide open into a midnight universe scattered with a million exploding stars.

It happened so quickly: her body contracting, pulsing, a fast, hard, beautiful climax. And then he was lifting her, laying her down across the gold sheets, pushing her thighs wide again as he knelt on the rug by the bed.

She felt his breath first, there, at the core of her. Then the skilled, tender stroking of his tongue.

And then, just like that, she was going over again, falling from one peak into the next one. Rising, rising and shattering again, stronger, deeper, better than the first time, as she clutched his dark head and moaned how she wanted him, how right it was, how perfect, exactly what she'd been dreaming of.

When he pulled away and stood over her, she didn't have the strength to hold him. She let out a little moan of satisfaction, a sigh of pleasured fulfillment. Still crosswise on the bed, her legs limp and dangling over the side, she closed her eyes and drifted on a sea of delicious afterglow.

Until he touched her again, the lightest brush of a touch, one finger tracking down from her hip bone to her thigh, to her knee, along her shin....

"Dami?" She opened her eyes to find him naked and so very fine, all broad, hard, muscled manliness, kneeling on the rug again. "Dami..." She reached for him.

He rose and leaned over her, bending close and kissing her, a quick, hard kiss. And then he lifted her, rearranging her so that she was full-length on the bed with her head on the pillows. He stretched out beside her.

She buried her face against his chest, breathed in his scent of sea foam and musk and man.

And the wonder began all over again. He kissed her—arousing, hungry, lingering kisses. First on her lips and then along her throat, across her chest, her breasts, her belly. He opened his mouth on her, using his tongue and, so carefully and deliberately, his strong white teeth.

By then she was wild for him, tossing her head on the pillows, begging him, "Please, Dami, please," as she clutched him with her hungry hands, pulling at him, yearning for the moment when she would have him within her.

He took his time about that. He drove her up to the brink again with his hands and his hot mouth—and then, just when she knew she was going over a third time that night without him inside her, he lifted up and eased his hard, hair-rough thigh between her two soft ones.

She opened her eyes and he was above her, gazing down at her, his eyes so dark, edged in deepest green.

He put one hand on either of her thighs and pushed them wide. She knew he could see everything. And that only made her hotter, made her want him more.

"Dami." She was breathless. So hungry. Needing. Wanting. Everything. All of him, now. "Please…"

"Now, Luce?"

She looked down between them and saw that he was more than ready for her. And also that somehow he had already put on the protection she'd totally forgotten they were going to need.

"Luce." He growled her name.

And she looked in his face again. "Um. I…"

"Now?" Softly that time. Patiently. Tenderly, too.

"Um, yes. Yes. Please. Now…."

He braced his forearms to either side of her, cradling her head between his two hands. "Look at me."

She nodded, eager. A little bit scared, too, thinking again of the size of him.

Would there be pain? How much?

"Stay with me." His eyes were on her. She met them, held them.

And then she felt him, nudging her where she was so wet and soft and sensitive now. The tip slid in. Wonderful. Perfect.

"More," she said on a low moan.

He gave her exactly what she asked for, sliding in by slow degrees.

It was good. It was heaven.

And then it was too much. And then it was hurting. She gasped, "Oh! I… Wait."

"Shh," he said. "It's all right." He lowered his head, pressed his forehead to hers. "We'll wait…."

They lay there half joined, still. Waiting. Her breath came swift and hungry; her body felt stretched, aching.

And then the ache was changing, easing into something electric and wonderful again.

She lifted her head and kissed his mouth, whispering, "Yes. Now," against his parted lips.

"More?" It came out on a low groan.

She nodded. "More…"

And he went deeper—until she gasped again.

Instantly, he went still for her. There was only the sound of their breathing, the burning down low that once again eased and changed to a thrilling fullness.

She said it again. "More…"

He bent his head, captured her breast, drew on it in slow, deep pulls.

That did it. She moaned and clutched him close to her, lifting to meet him that time as he went deeper.

And deeper.

And then, with a low, hard groan, he was in all the way, filling her completely.

Finally. At last.

She laughed a little, then stopped on a moan. "Oh, Dami. Yes."

He was still again, waiting for her untried body to accept his invasion.

"Yes," she said, pushing against him.

"Sure?" It came out a rough, painful growl.

"Yes. Yes, yes, yes…"

And then, at last, he started to move.

He did it carefully at first, gently, with slow deliberation. Bracing up his hands to give himself better control, he kept his thrusts steady, even.

But she was more than ready by then, more than eager. She lifted her hands and clasped his big shoulders and held on good and tight as she moved in rhythm with him.

She tried to keep her eyes open to see his face above her, to imprint every burning, beautiful second of this wonder into her memory, to seal it in her heart.

But the pleasure was too overwhelming. It was raising her up, making her dizzy with the flood of sensation. There was nothing to do in the end but surrender to it.

She closed her eyes. And once again she was whirling up and up—and over the edge of the world into an explosion of light and sensation as she felt her body pulsing around him, felt him surge into her deeper, fuller, harder even than before.

And by then she could only hold on and keep sighing,

"Yes, yes, yes," as the pulsing faded down to a lovely glow of happy satisfaction.

At seven o'clock on Sunday morning, Dami gave her a robe to wear and led her to the kitchen, where he made her coffee and served her croissants from Justine's café. She ate two. They were so good and she was hungry.

Then she returned to his bedroom and put on her clothes from the night before as he stood in the doorway, big arms across his broad chest, watching her, his expression unreadable.

Yeah, it was a little sad. A little strange. To be leaving him so soon after the complete fabulousness of last night.

But she remembered what she'd promised herself at his studio. Not to cling. Not to linger. She scooped up her evening clutch and went to him with a bright smile.

At the door to the outer hall, she kissed him. His mouth touched hers, tasting of coffee, making her long to lift her arms and pull him closer. It was early yet. They had time.

To share more kisses. To make love again in the morning light.

But no. That would only hurt more in the end. She was on her way now. Better to keep moving, go back to her room, get her things packed, call a cab....

She kept her arms at her sides and when he lifted his head, she said, "It was perfect, Dami."

He framed her face between his hands and there was such an ache within her. The end had come way too soon. Already she missed the beauty and rightness of all they had shared. "Travel safe, Luce."

She pressed her lips to his once more. "Have the best Christmas ever."

"You, too." His hands fell away.

She turned from him.

He reached around her and pushed open the door for her. She went out into the wide, beautiful hallway and started walking.

She didn't glance back to find out if he watched her leaving him. She didn't need the temptation of seeing him there staring after her—or worse, *not* seeing him.

Better not to look. Better not to know.

Chapter Nine

"Lucy, wait up!"

Her arms full of groceries, Lucy backed against the entry door, holding it open as Brandon Delaney jogged up the building steps toward her, wearing heavy running pants, a winter-weight hoodie and cross-trainers, his cap on backward.

Once he cleared the door, she let it swing shut. He was panting pretty hard, his handsome face red, his blond hair sweaty where it stuck out from under the cap.

"When did you get back?" he asked between breaths.

"Sunday."

"Good trip?"

"It was terrific, thanks." She flashed him a smile, wondering how he knew she'd been gone. She hadn't told him she was going away for Thanksgiving. Maybe Ed, the super, had mentioned her trip, or Viviana Nichols, who lived in the larger apartment on her floor, might have said something to him.

Flashing her a broad smile that showed off a dental hygienist's dream of straight, brilliantly white teeth, Brandon reached for her groceries. "Here. Let me carry those for you."

Okay. Weird. Brandon had been avoiding her for a couple of weeks, ever since she'd put that pitiful excuse for a move on him. Why was he suddenly so friendly now?

Then again, what did it matter why he was being nice? If he wanted to carry her stuff, wonderful.

The elevator had stopped up on five. Rather than wait for it, they took the stairs. Lucy's apartment was on the third floor. As they trudged up the two flights, he said, "I had no idea that you knew the prince."

He knew she knew Dami? She was certain she'd never told him that.

On second thought, it probably wasn't such a stretch that he would know. Pictures of her and Dami were not only all over the internet but they had made a few of the tabloids, too. Brandon could have seen them. "Yes. We're good friends."

"Wow." He shook his head. "Amazing. Thanksgiving at the Prince's Palace. That must have been something."

"How did you know I was in Montedoro?"

"Marie. She had a copy of the *National Enquirer*. She showed me the pictures of you and the prince. You know how she is...."

Marie Dobronsky, the super's wife, was a sweet woman. She did like to gossip, however. Lucy made a mental note not to be so chatty with Marie in the future.

They reached the second floor and started up to the third. Brandon said, "I don't think I've ever seen him here— I mean, I heard that he does own the building. Is that right?"

"Yes, he does," she said, and left it at that. They reached her floor. Brandon fell in behind her as she approached her door. "Thanks. You can just set the bags down. I'll take it from here."

"Oh, come on. Let me carry them in for you."

She started to refuse—but wait a minute. A week ago she would have been walking on air to have Brandon carrying her groceries for her. "Hey, if you insist..." She unlocked the door and ushered him in first, pointing down the short hall that opened into her small living room and the kitchen beyond. "That way."

He carried the bags in and set them on the retro chrome-and-red laminate table she'd found on eBay. "This is nice." He took off his cap and looked around her tiny narrow kitchen, which had a small skinny window with a view of a brick wall. Her cat, Boris, sat in that window, watching them with a bored expression on his broad face. Brandon turned his blinding white smile her way again. "We should catch up. Let's go get coffee or something."

Coffee. He wanted to get a coffee with her....

Last Wednesday she would have traded her Juki serger sewing machine for a chance to get a coffee with Brandon. But after Dami, well, Brandon somehow wasn't giving her the familiar thrill.

And that totally annoyed her.

The whole point of convincing Dami to teach her about sex had been to become more experienced, more sophisticated—not to lose all interest in Brandon, who was a good part of the reason she'd asked for Dami's help in the first place.

Uh-uh. No way was she turning down a coffee with

Brandon. Even if she didn't want to go. "How about the diner on the corner? But I need to put this food away first."

"I'll grab a shower, be back for you in twenty."

Lucy loved the Paradise Diner. It was owned by a Greek family, the Mustos, and served the usual diner fare, burgers and fries, meat loaf and mashed potatoes, coffee and pie—plus a few Greek specialties. The cook, Nestor, was a little scary. Sometimes he shouted through the service window in Greek. The waitresses treated Lucy like one of the family. There was just something so homey and comfortable about the Paradise. Lucy ate there every chance she got.

While she'd been out of town, they'd decorated for the holidays, painting the windows with Christmas greetings, hanging fat gold garland everywhere, putting up an artificial tree by the cash register and an almost-life-size crèche in the corner by the door.

She and Brandon took a booth and ordered coffee and pie. Brandon talked about the auditions he'd been on and the part he thought he was sure to get in an upcoming off-Broadway show. And his agent was pushing him to fly out to L.A. and audition for a major role in a new sitcom. Yeah, it was just television. But a guy had to eat.

And then he leaned closer. "Come on, Lucy. Are you sure you and Prince Damien aren't having a *thing?*"

She laughed at that. "Like I said, we're just friends." It caused a distinct ache in her heart to say those words. Maybe more of an ache than she'd bargained for. "He's always been good to me, that's all."

"'Good to you.'" Brandon arched a golden eyebrow. "I could take that any number of ways."

What was that supposed to mean? She didn't even want to know. "Why should you take it *any* way? Sheesh, Brandon. Are you writing a book or something?"

He gave her that blinding white smile again, the one that just a couple of weeks ago could rock her world. "I'm an actor. It's my job to understand what makes people tick—and 'always'? You said he's 'always' been good to you. Does that mean you've known him since childhood?"

Pushy. There was no other word for the way Brandon was behaving. And in any case, she just didn't feel comfortable discussing Dami with a casual acquaintance. Privacy mattered to Dami, to all the Bravo-Calabrettis. She doubted Brandon would go running to the tabloids with something she said. But still.

She said, "He's a friend of the family."

Brandon wouldn't quit. "I saw somewhere, I think, that your brother is marrying his sister Princess Alice."

"Yes," she answered with zero inflection. "They're very happy together."

He gave her a sly look from those golden-brown eyes she used to drool over. "Lucy, you are turning out to be a very big surprise."

And that had her feeling defensive somehow. "I'm the same person I was before."

"Well, yeah. But I just didn't know…" He was looking at her so intently, his gaze tracking from her eyes to her mouth and back to her eyes again. "God. Was I blind or what?"

Flirting. Omigod. Brandon Delaney was flirting with her. He was flirting with her and she didn't even care. In fact, it was kind of depressing that he was interested now and she felt nothing but vaguely annoyed with him. "Brandon, eat your pie."

He went on looking at her in that teasingly intimate way. "I want to spend more time with you."

She couldn't resist reminding him, "But I'm so innocent, remember? And you've got no time for me, because acting is your life."

He leaned his chin on his fist and gave her the long, lingering, melting, butterscotch stare. "I've changed my mind."

Yeah, well. So had she. She opened her mouth to tell him so—and his phone, which he'd set on the table beside him, started playing "Gangnam Style."

He snatched it up and looked at the screen. "I need to take this." And he did. Right then and there. "Maureen... Yes...They do?...Yes!" He flashed Lucy a thumbs-up. She had no idea why. "Tomorrow? Impossible...." He scowled. She could hear the person named Maureen talking fast. And Brandon started nodding. "Yeah, I do. I know...You're right, okay, tomorrow." There was more. He kept on agreeing with the person named Maureen and said that yes, he would, absolutely. He was on it. Lucy finished her excellent pie and sipped her coffee.

When he finally hung up, she guessed, "Big news?"

"Oh, yeah. That was my agent. That sitcom I told you about? They want me. They *really* want me. I'm flying out to L.A. tonight. It's big, Lucy. It's huge—and listen, I've got to get moving...."

"Absolutely." She wished him good luck in theater speak. "Break a leg."

He was already on his feet. "Thanks, Lucy."

"Break them both."

He chuckled. Then he bent close and kissed her on the cheek. "We'll talk...soon."

"'Bye, Brandon."

He straightened, turned and headed for the door.

Lucy watched him go. He hadn't touched his pie.

The waitress, Tabitha, who was the owner's daughter and around Lucy's age, appeared beside the booth, coffeepot in hand. She refilled Lucy's cup. "Not your type, huh?"

Lucy reached across the table and snagged Brandon's abandoned pie. "Was I that obvious?"

"Not to him, apparently—and look. He left you something." She waved the check.

Laughing, Lucy took it. "Not a problem. After all, I get to eat his pie."

It snowed the next day, Thursday. Not a lot. But enough that Lucy could look out her bedroom windows and see it drifting down onto the sidewalk outside, a frail bit of it collecting in the dip of the brown awning over the door of the Italian restaurant across the street. She wished Dami was there to see it with her.

And then she felt gloomy. Because he wasn't there, because it was only a little snow and she still wanted to share it with him.

She couldn't stop thinking about him. And she tried to excuse that by telling herself it was natural to miss him after all that had happened between them. It wasn't that bad to have maybe fallen for him just a little bit— not too much, oh, no. Only a thoroughly appropriate amount given that he'd seen her naked more than once and she'd done things with him she'd never done in her life before.

Good things. Wonderful things. Things she couldn't let herself think too much about or she'd only get gloomier.

Keeping busy. That was the key. No way was she

going to end up sitting in a chair staring out the window, thinking of Thanksgiving and wanting to cry.

As soon as the snow stopped, she went out and prowled her favorite fabric and notions stores, snatching up things that inspired her. She intended to work for several hours every day on clothing and accessory designs and on making a few of the ideas she came up with.

Lots of work should keep her from longing for Dami.

And, hey, it was Christmastime. There were so many organizations looking for volunteers.

On Friday morning she looked around online and chose two worthy causes. She called and signed up to wrap presents for disadvantaged kids and to put in five four-hour sessions making costumes for a children's theater organization called Make-Believe and Magic. She worked for a while sketching a few new accessory designs and then she went down the street to the Paradise for a late breakfast.

By then the regular breakfast crowd had cleared out and the diner was quiet for that hour or two before they all started piling in for lunch.

Tabby gave her coffee, took her order, stuck it on the rack in the pass-through for Nestor and then slid into the seat across from her. "Wow, Lucy. You always look so great."

"Thanks." Lucy fluffed the cowl neck of the white sweater she wore under her cutaway purple jacket. "Clothes are my undying passion, it's true."

"Didn't you say once that you make everything you wear?"

"Most of them, I do." She picked up her coffee cup.

Tabby was looking at her kind of strangely. "Okay." She sipped. "Something's on your mind. What?"

"God. I don't even know how to ask you...."

"Oh, come on. I'm totally harmless. Ask me."

Tabby puffed out her cheeks with a hard breath. "There's this guy. I've had my eye on him. He finally asked me out for Saturday, a week from tomorrow night. It's a cocktail-dress thing—and I mean, I know it's really short notice, but then I was thinking how you have such amazing taste and all and maybe you could give me a few tips on what to buy, that you could—"

"You want me to make something for you? I could so do that."

Tabby blinked. "Just like that. You would—you *could?*"

"Yeah. It would be fun."

"I would pay you. I mean, not a lot, but—"

Lucy waved a hand. "Not a problem. I'm just getting started in my career, anyway. I need cool projects."

"But I *would* pay you."

"Sure. Of course. We can work that out."

"But...I mean, something for *me*, right? For my body and coloring? Your style is killer, but it's not me." Tabby had streaky blond hair and amazing cheekbones. She stood five-eleven or so and rocked one of those realwoman bodies with serious curves.

"Oh, yeah. For you, only you. I'm thinking something that flows and clings and shows off a little of that gorgeous olive skin."

Tabitha asked in a breathless tone, "Can it be red?"

"Oh, yes, it can."

All at once Tabby looked like a kid having the best Christmas ever. "Lucy, I'm liking this. I seriously am...."

* * *

Tabby came right over to Lucy's after her shift was through.

Lucy ushered her into the bedroom, which was big enough that she not only had her bed and dresser in there but she'd also set up a cutting table, her two sewing machines and a couple of dress forms. Lucy took Tabby's measurements and they discussed fabric and detail. Lucy was thinking the red dress should be chiffon, with a flowing short skirt, a ruched strapless bodice and a sweetheart neckline. And there should be bling— maybe crystal beading or rhinestones to accent the bodice. She did some quick sketches and Tabby was sold. She wrote a check right then and there for the amount Lucy quoted her.

Then they started talking. Tabby talked about the guy who'd asked her out for Saturday night. His name was Henry O'Mara and he owned a shoe-repair shop in Chelsea. She said her parents were driving her crazy. She'd been engaged to a nice Greek man, but she'd called it off and they couldn't understand what could be the matter with her. Lucy shared her issues with Noah and her adoration of Alice. She even talked about Dami a little.

Tabby said, "Leave it to you to find yourself a prince."

And Lucy said the usual, "It's not like that. We're just friends."

At which Tabby made a snorting sound. "Yeah. Right. Like I believe that."

They ended up going across the street to the Italian place, where they each ordered the sausage ravioli. When they got back to Lucy's, Viviana Nichols opened her door. She had a plate of cookies fresh from the oven and she grinned at them, the lines around her eyes deepening, her brown face full of fun and mischief. So they joined her in her warm, cookie-scented kitchen for coffee and snicker doodles.

Later that night, alone in her apartment, Lucy felt pretty good about everything. She loved New York, she couldn't wait for her first semester at FIT NY and she had a feeling Tabby was going to be a real friend.

Okay, yes, she did miss Dami a lot. It had been nearly a week since she'd left him. She wanted to call him. But that somehow felt wrong. She'd been the one who'd initiated their weekend together, and she'd done it with the clear understanding that they would both walk away in the end. She'd promised herself she wouldn't pester him, which meant she needed to leave him alone for a while, till after the holidays, at least. And she absolutely would *not* be disappointed that he hadn't gotten in touch.

In the early half of the following week, Brandon called to tell her that he now had "several potential projects" lined up and would be staying in Los Angeles until after the New Year.

"And, Lucy…" His voice trailed off. He let out a long sigh. "I really like you, but I've met someone. Someone special. I may end up subletting my apartment and staying on here indefinitely. But in any case, it looks like it won't be happening for you and me after all."

Lucy told him she was happy for him and wished him well. She hung up with a feeling of relief that Brandon Delaney had found love in L.A. and that private "talk" he'd said he wanted to have with her would never be happening.

The next day, her brother called to see if maybe she'd changed her mind about coming home for Christmas. She told him—again—that she hadn't. He put Alice on and they discussed *the* dress. A little while later Hannah called just to chat.

Every time her phone rang, she couldn't quell a little thrill of hope that it might be Dami.

But it never was.

She bought gifts for her family, got them wrapped and packed and sent them off. She put in some hours making costumes for the Make-Believe and Magic Children's Theatre Company. And she made Tabby's red cocktail dress. Tabby came over Thursday for a final fitting. "Wow," she said, twirling in front of Lucy's full-length mirror. "Is that really me?"

"It's you and you are spectacular. Now stand up straight. That's it." Lucy marked the hem. "It'll be ready tomorrow. You can pick it up after your shift at the diner."

They went over to the Italian place to grab a bite to eat and Tabby insisted on paying the check. "You made me look fabulous. I can at least buy dinner."

Friday morning Lucy hemmed Tabby's dress and gave it a finishing press. She had lunch with Viviana, who made them turkey-pesto paninis and black-eyed-pea soup and then hardly touched either.

"Missin' my Joseph today," Viv said softly in that husky voice of hers, her beautiful dark eyes full of shadows. Her husband had died eighteen years ago in December. She and Joseph had owned two dry-cleaning stores, long since sold. "Missin' my babies, too." She had two daughters and six grandchildren. Two of the grandchildren were older than Lucy. Her eyes brightened a little. "I'll be going to Shoshona's for Christmas...." Shoshona was the older daughter. She lived in Chicago. Marleah lived in Denver. "You should go home for the holiday, sweet girl. Be with your family. We all need family at Christmas."

Lucy could not deny she felt a little ache in her heart right then to go home to the big house in Carpinteria that Hannah would have all done up for the holidays, to be with them—Alice and Hannah and even her bossy big brother. She longed suddenly to ride Dammerlicht, a steady-natured, smart Hanoverian, her favorite in her brother's fine stable of beautiful horses. She yearned to watch the sun set over the Pacific.

But no. She'd made her decision and she was sticking with it. "I'm spending my holiday right here in Manhattan, Viv. It's my first year on my own."

Viviana waved a heavily veined, beautifully manicured hand. "Pah. I've been on my own for almost twenty years now. My girls keep after me to move near one of them. They think I'm too old to be taking care of myself. But this is home. I love New York and I'm an independent soul. I keep busy and I'm happy with my life. But for Christmas, being alone sucks."

An hour later, Viv gave her a plateful of sugar cookies and she returned to her apartment.

She got out one of her sketchbooks and sat in the corner chair in her bedroom. With the plate of cookies in reach, she got to work on some ideas she had for Alice's wedding dress, which was to be totally Alice: dramatic and daring, with a very low back framed in lace, snugly fitted past the hips, flaring out to an ocean of lace and tulle.

An hour flew by. She sketched and munched cookies and the dress took shape. And then the buzzer downstairs rang. It was Tabby, running over on her break to pick up her dress. Lucy gave it to her, along with a couple of cookies. They chatted for a few minutes. Tabby grabbed her in a hug and was gone.

Lucy went back to work. About a half an hour later she glanced up and saw the moving haze of white out the window.

Snow.

Real snow this time, the flakes so thick and white, like a moving veil softly obscuring the buildings across the street. Perfect. Beautiful. Her first snowy Christmastime in all of her life.

If only Dami...

She cut off the thought. He wasn't there. He wouldn't *be* there. And she was going to be absolutely fine with that. She had a good life, damn it. A life that she'd fought for, a life in an exciting city where she was already making friends. A life that was just right for her. She didn't need the Player Prince at her side to make it all complete.

Someone knocked at the door.

Lucy tossed her sketchbook on the bed. It had to be someone in the building—Ed, the super, or maybe Ed's wife, Marie, or Viv. Anyone else would have to ring the buzzer downstairs first. To be on the safe side, she checked the peephole before pulling the door wide.

And her heart stopped dead in her chest at what she saw.

Dami.

Dami in New York. At her door.

Dami, looking like every woman's dream man, tall and dark and so very sexy in that smooth and smoldering way he had—and not only that. So much more than that.

Dami, her friend, who always stepped up when she needed him. The person she most wanted to talk to, to laugh with, to share the snow out the window with, to hold hands with....

Dami.

Oh, God. Dami. For real.

Lucy whipped off the chain, yanked back the security bolt and flung the door wide.

Chapter Ten

The door swung back and Lucy flew at him, calling his name. "Dami!"

He opened his arms and she threw herself at him, jumping up, landing against him with a happy laugh, wrapping her arms and legs around him. She smelled of vanilla and apples and something else, something he'd missed way too much, something that was simply her. "Luce." Her name escaped him in a strange rumble, surprising him with its rawness, sounding like hunger. Like not-so-carefully controlled desire.

Lucy was Lucy, all gushing, gleeful chatter. "Dami, Dami, Dami. I can't believe you're here. I wished and wished you might come. And poof, like a dream. Here you are. It's snowing and it's Christmas. And you came."

"Luce." Heat coiled in his belly, flared across his skin. He was all too aware of the press of her soft breasts to his chest, of those slim legs gripping around him....

And not only that. So much more. He drank in the sight of her, that glowing smile, the sparkle in her soft brown eyes.

Alive, that was it. Lucy was fully engaged, completely alive. Full of light, like her name. She pushed back every shadow, wiped out all cynicism. She made it impossible to be disinterested or disillusioned. She made everything fresh and new.

He should be ashamed, and he knew it, to have agreed to relieve her of her innocence in the first place. And then to have gone ahead and done just that.

And now to be showing up on her doorstep in the burning hope that maybe she would allow him to do it again.

And again.

She tipped her mouth up to him. "Dami…" Breathless. Hopeful. So damned sweet.

He couldn't resist—and who was he fooling? No one. He had no intention of resisting.

He cradled the back of her head, his fingers sliding into her shining silky hair. "Luce." He took her mouth.

She made a soft, yearning little sound as his tongue invaded the warmth and wetness beyond her lips. And then she tightened her arms and legs around him and kissed him back, with no coyness and no hesitation, with complete abandon.

He kissed her harder, deeper, needing the taste of her, needing to fill himself up with the sweetness of her.

And they couldn't go on like this here on the landing. Anyone might wander by.

The door was open behind her. He continued to plunder her mouth as he crossed the threshold with her all wrapped around him, her hands sifting in his hair, her thighs pressing him tight, her kiss as open and eager as her sweet face, her willing heart.

He swung the door shut with his heel. Laughing a little against his mouth, she instructed, "Wait. Back up." He did, and she reached out behind him and engaged the lock. "That way." She kissed the words onto his mouth and pointed over her shoulder down a windowless hallway.

He took her to the bedroom at the front of the apartment. Outside the arched windows that faced the street, snow was falling, thick and steady, reflecting light, filling the room with a silvery glow. The space was crowded with furniture—sewing machines, a wide table, adjustable dressmaker forms. Weaving his way to the bed took some doing, and she didn't help a lot—she was kissing him so hard and deep, moving against him, arousing him, making soft hungry sounds that thoroughly distracted him.

A good thing he was determined. He skirted the second dressmaker form and he was at the bed at last. Easing his fingers under her thighs, he peeled her away from him and gently laid her down.

She stared up at him, softly smiling, eyes wide and so bright, as he undressed her with the ease and swiftness born of years of undressing women. She wore black leggings, a big green sweater that went halfway down her slim thighs and thick socks. He had all that off of her in no time. Underneath, her bra was red lace and her little satin panties were pink. He rolled her over and unhooked the bra and whipped it away.

"Dami..." She rolled onto her back again, laughing a little. Incomparable. Everything about her—the complete lack of pretense or artifice, the small slanted white scars on her rib cage and the longer one, pale as milk, that ran straight down between her breasts. She had no shyness about those scars, no embarrassment. She made them beautiful by her complete acceptance of them.

He bent close, kissed the long one that bisected her above her heart. "You are like no one else I've ever known."

She wrapped her arms around his head, pulled him closer. The scent of her claimed him. "I hope that's good," she whispered.

"It is very good," he replied against her skin.

"Dami." She held him closer. "I have missed you so...."

He clasped her arms and gently peeled them away so that he could straighten and get out of his own clothes. That took even less time than getting rid of hers.

She reached for him again. "Please. Come down to me. Let me hold you."

He grabbed the condoms he'd stuck in a pocket and set them on the nightstand. Then he joined her on the bed.

She wrapped herself around him again. It felt so good, her flesh to his, the scent of her gone musky now, sweeter even than before.

He kissed her some more—starting with her mouth and then moving on, tracing the shape of her jaw with his tongue, trailing his lips down her throat into the warm dip where her collarbones met.

And lower.

He lavished attention on her breasts and her belly, then settled in between her thighs, easing her legs over his shoulders, guiding her knees wider to claim better access. She clutched his head and moaned broken encouragements as he kissed her long and slow and deep. He caressed her with his fingers at the same time, enjoying the feel of her as well as the taste, his mind a hot whirl of excitement and lust for her. At the same time, he remembered to be careful with her, to gauge her readiness. Her body was still new to this, inexperienced, in need of gentle handling.

New but so eager. She was a natural to loving.

It didn't take her long to reach the peak. He felt the quick, hot flutter of her climax against his tongue and she held him tightly to her, crying out, then whispering his name. Her body lifted, bowing up. He stayed with her, kept on kissing her, pressing his tongue at her core, his hands beneath her, cradling her, lifting her closer to his eager mouth.

She shuddered, cried out again and then, with a sigh, went loose. For a little while, he rested his head on her belly and she gently stroked his hair.

In time he rose above her again. Gathering her close to him, he settled her head against his shoulder.

She sighed and whispered, "I want you, Dami…."

"Shh." He kissed her temple.

But she pushed up on an elbow and met his eyes. "I want all of you." Her upper lip was damp with sweat.

He took her face between his hands, pulled her closer and kissed her. "Soon," he said against her mouth. "Shh…" He stroked the short wisps of chestnut hair back from her damp forehead.

"Now," she argued, catching his lower lip between her pretty teeth, biting down a little so that the fine ache of wanting her intensified and he groaned. And then, more firmly, she commanded, "Now."

Who was he to refuse her? Whatever she wanted, he would make sure that she had.

She watched him, her hair a wild tousle of short curls, her eyes low and lazy, looking equally satisfied and determined, as he took one of the condoms from the table by the bed. He had it out of its wrapper and on him in a quick well-practiced series of actions—and carefully, too, so as not to rupture or tear it.

She put her hand to his cheek then, urging him down to her until his mouth settled on hers and they shared another long, sweet kiss.

And what a kiss. She did learn fast. Kissing her now, it was hard to remember how very innocent she had been such a short time ago. This kiss was a woman's kiss, a kiss she took, a kiss she owned. And while she kissed him, she was moving under him, her hands all over him, urging him to cover her.

He gave her what she wanted, burning to have her, impatient as any green kid by then. She made him so hot and needy. She stole his jaded, world-weary nature, gave him back all this urgency, this greed, this heated, hungry tenderness.

He settled above her and she opened to accept him. He tried to go slow, to be careful, be mindful.

But there was no mindfulness for him with her. There was only the welcoming wet heat of her, only her soft hands all over him, pulling him down to her.

Into her.

She took him, she owned him, she moved beneath him and he was the one following, giving back what she gave to him, taking her cues and answering in kind without conscious thought, without calculation. His mind was a whirl of impressions and images. And all of them were of her.

Lucy, too thin, too pale the first time he saw her, running down the steps at her brother's house, her smile blooming in greeting for him, a stranger. Lucy in his arms for a dance that same night, the tip of the scar between her breasts fresher, deep pink. Lucy in her work-room at the house in California, her head bent over a sewing machine, feeding bright fabric under the hum-ming, swift needle....

And Lucy now, beneath him, flushed, sure, powerful.

He gave himself up to her. She took him and she opened him and she turned him inside out.

A little while later he made a quick trip to the loo to dispose of the condom. He returned to her and gath-ered her close and they lay on the bed in the silvery light from the big window, naked, together, watching the snow come down. Her fat orange cat jumped up in the window and watched the snow with them.

He felt content in a way he hadn't for a single day since she left him alone in Montedoro. She was so easy to be with. It had always been that way between them: comfortable. Right. He'd feared that having sex with her would ruin the easiness.

So far it hadn't. Maybe he'd get lucky after all. This new hunger they had for each other would run its course and they would still have their friendship.

God. He hoped so.

He stroked her hair and ran a finger up and down her arm.

She sighed. "That was so good. Oh, Dami, about sex? Seriously, I had no idea what I was missing. And I'm so glad I decided to learn from the best."

He squeezed her shoulder. "No regrets, then?"

"None. And it's not only the sex, Dami. It's...this. You and me, alone, just being together. *This* is so good."

He pressed a kiss against her hair, breathing in the womanly scent of her. "Better than good."

She lifted up enough to look down at him and meet

his eyes. "So tell me. I have to know. How long are you here for? Are you staying upstairs? You weren't wearing a coat, which I'm guessing means you went up to your apartment first.... And what *are* you here for? Business? Where's your bodyguard? When did you get here? Oh, Dami, how I have missed you."

He chuckled. "I missed you, too." *Far too much.* "And do you really expect me to remember all those questions?"

She kissed his shoulder. "Try."

That made him smile. "Fair enough, then. I'll be here through the first part of next week, at least. Yes, I'm staying upstairs. I have some meetings, a project in the works."

"What—?"

He stopped her next question with a finger to her mouth. "Wait until I answer the ones you already asked." She pressed her lips together and nodded in a promise of silence—one he knew she couldn't keep. He said, "Quentin, my bodyguard, is now in his room off my apartment. He's not happy that I refused to let him come down here with me so he could check your rooms for threats."

"Oh, right. I could be planning to kidnap you and hold you for ransom."

"Exactly. You could be a very dangerous woman."

"I could chain you to my bed and never let you go."

He lifted his head long enough to kiss the tip of her nose. "It's an intriguing idea, one we should discuss in depth later."

She put on a shocked expression. "Oh, now I get it. *You're* the one who's dangerous."

"Didn't I warn you about that?"

"You did. I didn't listen—and I'm so glad I didn't."

He caught her chin. "Kiss me." She lowered those soft, warm lips to his in a brushing kiss that ended too soon. He stared up at her and stroked her velvety cheek. "You *are* dangerous," he whispered.

And she giggled. "I guess you needed Quentin here after all."

"No, I didn't. He'd have gone around opening your cabinets and peering in your closets. I didn't want that for our reunion."

She kissed his shoulder. "Our reunion. I like it."

Damien did, too. Far too much. "Where was I? Ah. I arrived here only a little while before I knocked on your door. I went to my apartment, had my driver drop my bags in the foyer and took off my coat while Quentin went up and down the stairs checking for potential threats. Then I sent him to his room and came to find you. Next question?"

"What is the project you're here about?"

"Prepare to be fascinated," he said wryly. "Mass-transit apps."

"Like HopStop? GPS for a subway or bus system, showing you where to get on and get off and change buses to get where you're going?"

"Exactly. We want that for Montedoro. Rule was dealing with it and he had meetings set up here in New York for Monday and Tuesday of next week. But he had a scheduling conflict. I stepped up and volunteered to fill in for him." It sounded perfectly reasonable. But it wasn't the whole truth. He'd wanted to see her again, couldn't stop thinking about her. The transit-app project? Just an excuse.

She kissed him, her hand at his cheek, caressing. "How long will you be here?"

"Until the middle of next week, Wednesday or Thursday...."

"Will you have meetings every day?" She actually blushed. "And yes, I am working you totally, trying to find out how much of your time I can expect to monopolize."

Good. She wanted what he wanted. More of this, the two of them. More time together. More sex. More... everything.

He answered her easily, in a casual tone. "The meetings are scheduled for Monday and Tuesday. I'm hoping to keep them to the mornings both days, but they could go longer...."

"You're free for the weekend, then, and in the evenings?"

"Yes, I am."

"Yay!" She kissed him again, a brush of her lips along his jaw. "Four or five days, you and me. Together." But then she grew tentative. "I mean, if that's good for you. If it's, you know, what you had in mind?"

He clasped her bare shoulder. "It's exactly what I had in mind."

"Oh!" Her smile lit up her face again. "Wonderful."

"What about you? Will you be busy?"

"Well, I did volunteer to make costumes for a children's Christmas show and wrap presents for kids in need. But I can put most of that off until after you leave, so while you're here, I can spend every spare minute with you."

"Excellent." He pulled her closer and never wanted to let go—which of course was ridiculous. He *always* let go in the end. The heat and hunger never lasted, and when it went, his interest went with it. Some men weren't made for forever and he accepted that he was one of those. "We have a plan, then."

"Oh, yeah, we do. A Christmas love affair, the two of us. To go with our Thanksgiving love affair. I could really get used to having love affairs with you."

He stroked her hair and heard himself asking in a casual tone that belied the extent of his interest, "What about that Brandon fellow? Still hoping to make something happen with him?"

"Brandon." She groaned. "Oh, I don't think so. He's not all that after all— Plus, he's in L.A. and likely to stay there. And he's met someone special, he said."

Good. The guy with the butterscotch eyes was out of the picture. Dami smiled against her hair and baldly lied, "Too bad."

"It's okay. Believe me. It's not meant to be with Brandon and I'm totally good with that."

He tipped up her chin, rubbed his mouth across hers, savored her tiny sigh. "About our Christmas love affair?"

She grinned against his lips. "Now you're talkin'."

"Five days is too short." He spoke the bald truth without stopping to think if the bald truth was wise.

She made a happy little sound and tucked her head down on his chest again. "Maybe you'll stay longer, like until New Year's. After all, a Christmas love affair would logically last until New Year's Day, wouldn't it?"

The idea of staying longer held far too much appeal. "Love affairs and logic. I'm not so sure the two go together."

Her lips brushed the side of his throat and her breath flowed across his skin. "I suppose they don't. And I'm sure you have important things you need to be doing in Montedoro, so I'm going to be happy with what I can get. The rest of today and four more days. Maybe five. Too short, but so very sweet."

A little while later they made love again.

And then she cuddled in close to him and chattered away about all she'd been doing since she left him in Montedoro. She talked about her new friend, Tabby, whose family owned the diner across the street. And about the widow in the three-bedroom across the landing. She said that Viviana Nichols made the best cookies in the world.

"I love Viv," she told him. "Her door's always open and she's easy to talk to. It's already beginning to feel like I have a family here, you know? People I really like, good people I want to spend time with."

He wasn't surprised that she made friends so easily. She looked for the good in others and almost always seemed to find it.

Eventually, they shared a quick shower. He would have lingered to make love with her again, but he wanted to take her up to his place. So they put on their clothes and went up to the sixth floor.

"Wow," Lucy said when he ushered her in the door. "I'd forgotten how big it is." He'd brought her up to the apartment briefly when he'd first moved her to New York in October. "All these great windows. An open living space. A real, true New York loft apartment."

"I'm so pleased you approve."

She made a face. "It's just too white, though."

He said what the designer had told him. "Adds to the open effect."

She shook her head, her green sweater drooping off one shoulder, making him want to reach out and slide it down even more—or better yet, to take it off her again. "It needs color. But I do like the art." Large canvases, mostly modern abstracts in the vivid hues she so admired, covered the half walls that marked off the spaces: living, dining, kitchen, all large areas, each one flowing into the next. There were two bedroom suites on that floor—the master suite and a slightly smaller suite. Above, there was another bath, an office and a studio, along with two smaller bedrooms, one for his man, Edgar, when Edgar accompanied him, and one for his bodyguard.

Damien was about to take her up the wide steel staircase and show her the other floor when someone tapped on the door. He checked the peephole. "It's Quentin and the food." He let in the bodyguard and the man with the grocery cart full of meat, staples and produce from a nearby gourmet-food store.

Lucy smiled at the bodyguard, who gave her a respectful nod and then stood to the side so the deliveryman could carry the bags in from the cart and line them up on the kitchen peninsula. Once that was done, Dami signed the bill.

Quentin said, "I'll show you out." He ushered the deliveryman through the door and Dami shut it behind him.

Lucy began pulling things out of the bags. "Yum. Looks good. Is the chef coming soon?"

He came up behind her, drawn as though magnetized to her flesh, to her bright, joyous spirit. Just being near her made him feel electric with energy and heat. He clasped her hips and drew her back against him, lowering his mouth to the sweet-scented curve where her neck met her shoulder. "I *am* the chef."

She turned in his arms and put her hands on his chest. "You can cook, too? I knew it."

"Edgar cooks when I want him to, and brilliantly. But I left him in Montedoro this trip, so I'm on my own."

She stepped out of his hold, scooped up a carton of milk and carried it to the refrigerator. "Come on, Your Highness. Let's put the perishables away."

He watched her move, so light and quick. Desire, stirred by simply touching her, flared higher. He thought what he *shouldn't* be thinking: ways to keep her with him, to keep her close. Ways to have her for as long as he wanted her. Because he'd always been a junkie for sensation and she gave that to him—sensation. Pleasure. Excitement. The burning, false promise of continued delight. In recent years, there hadn't been all that much that gave him the thrill he craved.

But Lucy did. Lucy, of all people. She gave it to him. She made him burn again, made him *care*. Made the world brim with color and happy laughter, with hunger and fire.

He kept reminding himself that she was his friend and he owed it to her to help her get whatever she needed—and what she needed wasn't him. She had shining dreams and ambitious goals. He would only make her forget her dreams, distract her from her goals and leave her wiser in a bad way, hurt and disappointed.

"Dami. The groceries?" She sent him a glowing smile over her shoulder—and he was captured. Enchanted. Completely ensnared.

It was wonderful to feel this way.

His negative thoughts blew away. He decided to stop giving himself a hard time for taking her innocence, for not letting her go when she left him in Montedoro.

She wanted to be with him and he wanted to be right here with her. For now. He was making way too much of this, acting like Alex, his grim, thoughtful twin. He needed to stop that. Introspection, after all, had never been his strong suit.

There was no reason not to take this fine thing between them and go with it. At the moment, it was working for both of them. And who said it had to end badly? Of course he wouldn't hurt her. He would never hurt her.

He reached into the nearest bag and pulled out a crusty loaf of bread and a tub of unsalted butter. As he put them away, he reminded himself that she understood the situation. She had no illusions about him. He'd made it clear that this was no more than a mutually satisfying holiday interlude, that this visit would be a short one.

He only wanted to be with her a little longer. Only four days. Maybe five....

Lucy went down to her apartment later to feed Boris. And then she went back up to Dami's and spent the night in his bed. They made love for hours and it was beautiful. Making love with Dami was about as good as it got. She was so glad she'd chosen him to teach her about sex.

In the morning, she stopped in to check on Boris again and then took Dami over to the diner for breakfast. She introduced him to Tabby, who fanned herself and pretended she might faint when his back was turned. Quentin, the bodyguard, who was lean and sandy haired and mostly expressionless, came with them. He stood near the door, in front of the almost-life-size Virgin Mary and Jesus in the manger, where he could see the entire restaurant and keep Dami in view.

When they left, Lucy hugged Tabby and whispered, "Have a great time with that special guy tonight."

Tabby whispered back, "I will. You, too...."

It was cold outside but clear, with piles of snow left

against the curbs from yesterday. Dami suggested they do the usual Christmas-in-New-York things.

And they did. They went window-shopping on Fifth Avenue and ice-skated at the Rockefeller Center rink. Then his driver took them to Central Park, where they rode on the carousel and strolled the snow-covered paths. It was lovely. And nobody bothered them the whole day. Apparently, the paparazzi didn't know yet that he was in New York. They even stood on the most romantic bridge ever, the cast-iron Bow Bridge over the lake, as the snow started falling again.

Dami kissed her right there on the bridge. His lips were cold at first. But they quickly grew warm. When he lifted his head, the snow caught on his thick black eyelashes.

"Merry Christmas, Dami."

He gave her a slow smile. "Merry Christmas, Luce."

She thought that right then she was as perfectly happy as she'd ever been. She knew it couldn't last and she didn't expect it to. Life wasn't that way. Now and then there was great sweetness and if you were smart, you cherished the sweetness. You held it close and tasted it fully.

But nothing could stay sweet forever. The struggles came. They made you stronger. Even if they never were a whole lot of fun. You cherished the happy times, held them close to your heart to warm you and keep you focused on finding the joy again when things got tough.

That night he took her to a private party at a West Village hotel. They danced and they sat together on a white sofa and drank expensive champagne. He introduced her to the host and to a few other people he did business with in New York. It was all very glamorous and upscale and trendy. A great party, really.

But she had only a few days with Dami. She would have preferred to have been somewhere they could talk without shouting at each other. And then she spotted the photographer taking pictures of them.

Dami saw him, too. He leaned close. "Let's go."

"Great idea."

Quentin appeared with her coat and bag. They were working their way through the crush toward the elevators when she heard a woman's voice behind them. "Damien!"

The woman, tall and gorgeous with platinum hair, emerged from the crowd. She threw her arms around Dami and planted a big one right on his lips.

Dami laughed, a slightly weary sound. "Hello, Susie."

Susie wrapped an arm around his neck. "How long are you in town?"

"A few days. And we were just—"

She shook a French-nailed finger at him. "You know it's been much too long. Let's go somewhere private and talk—or not talk. I can think of any number of interesting ways to pass the time."

"As I was saying, we were just leaving." Dami was no longer smiling. "Let me go."

Susie gripped him tighter. She went further, reaching out her other arm and hooking it around Lucy so she had hold of both of them. "Who's this?"

He repeated flatly, "Let go."

Susie batted her eyelashes Lucy's way. She smelled of expensive perfume and too many drinks. "Aren't you a sweet little thing?"

Lucy gazed back at her patiently. She'd met a few women like Susie. Noah used to date women like her in the years before he found Alice. Beautiful, sexy women who liked to party. A lot.

"Oh, you are just too cute!" Susie hauled Lucy closer and cooed in her ear, "We could have a lot of fun, all three of us."

At which point Dami had had enough.

He reached around Susie and snared Lucy's hand as Quentin moved in behind the blonde, took her shoulders and lifted her neatly out of the way. Dami herded Lucy toward the elevators and Quentin took up the rear, leaving Susie behind.

Dami didn't say a word during the ride back to the apartment building. Lucy kept quiet, too. He seemed pretty upset about the encounter with Susie and she wanted to give him a little time to cool down before trying to talk to him about it.

The driver let them off in front of the building. Dami took her arm then. Her heart lifted a little just to feel his touch. Quentin led the way up the steps and opened the door.

On the elevator, Dami pushed the button for the third floor. Apparently, they were staying at her place tonight. That surprised her a little. His was larger and not chockablock with sewing equipment. But then again, it didn't matter to her where they stayed.

As long as they stayed together.

The elevator stopped. The doors slid wide.

"Hold it," Dami said curtly to Quentin. His brusque tone surprised her. He was never curt, especially not with servants and the people who watched over him. Lucy sent him a questioning glance, but he stared straight ahead as he led her out of the elevator and over to her door.

He turned her to face him then, there in front of her door. His eyes were distant, not really connecting with hers. He brushed a cool hand along the side of her cheek.

Behind him the elevator doors stood open. Quentin waited within, shoulders back, legs wide, expression carefully blank.

"Dami, what—?"

He didn't let her finish. "Good night, Luce."

And then he turned and walked away from her, leaving her standing there staring after him in disbelief.

Chapter Eleven

Damien stepped onto the elevator and turned to find Lucy right behind him.

"Oh, no you don't." She got on beside him.

He gave her his weariest glance. "It's late."

"Oh, stop. It's barely midnight." She reached over and pushed the button for his floor. The doors closed.

He longed to punch the button to open them again. But then what? Scoop her up and carry her bodily back to her door?

And what if she still refused to stay put?

And all right, yes. He was being a jerk. He knew it. He just didn't want to talk about Susie. Leaving Lucy at her door had seemed a way to avoid an uncomfortable conversation.

So much for that.

He maintained absolute silence for the short ride up. Lucy did, too, just as she had during the drive from the party. He found her silence both annoying and un-nerving. After all, Lucy was *never* quiet. He'd always thought her incapable of keeping her mouth shut for long.

Apparently, he'd got that wrong.

When the elevator stopped, Quentin exited first. He and Lucy followed, side by side but not touching. Quentin dealt with the alarm, opened the door and went in ahead.

"Thank you, Quentin. That's all for the night."

The bodyguard mounted the stairs for his room above. Damien shut and locked the door.

Lucy set her bag on the entry table and unbuttoned her coat. He took it and hung it, along with his, in the closet by the door. Her dress that night was snug and black, with a lace top that dipped low in back to a V shape. She looked unbearably sweet in it, good enough to eat.

He wanted to kiss her, to run his finger down her back, tracing that V. He wanted to take her straight to bed. However, her level gaze and set expression told him clearly that lovemaking wasn't happening anytime soon.

Then again, maybe he'd get lucky and she'd let him change her mind.

He did what he wanted to do, stepping in close, touching his finger to the nape of her neck, trailing it out along her shoulder to the outer edge of the V. Her skin seemed to beckon him. He needed his mouth on her.

So he took what he needed, kissing the tempting spot where the lace started at the curve of her shoulder while continuing the slow caress with the tip of his finger down to the middle of her smooth back.

She sighed. For a moment, he thought she would melt into his arms.

But then she drew herself up and turned to face him. Her eyes challenged him. "Make me some cocoa, please, Dami."

"Cocoa." He arched a brow, made his expression one of boredom and complete disinterest.

She wasn't buying. "That's what I said. Cocoa, please."

With a curt nod and no expression, he signaled her ahead of him into the kitchen area. She took one of the tall chairs at the peninsula and leaned her chin on her fist as he went through the process of heating the milk and chopping the chocolate.

He thought how he should send her back to her apartment now. He should end this foolishness tonight before it went any further. She was too good, too sweet, too innocent for him. He should tell her he'd been wrong to come here, that he was leaving in the morning.

And then he should check into a hotel, go to those damned meetings Monday and Tuesday and then fly back to Montedoro where he belonged.

As he chopped and stirred, he kept expecting her to start asking him questions.

But again she surprised him. She held her peace until he put the steaming cup in front of her. Then she sipped and said, "So good. Thank you." She set the cup down. "Tell me about Susie."

"That's a bad idea."

"Tell me anyway."

He poured himself a cup and took the chair beside her. "You won't like it."

"Maybe not. But I want to know."

"What, exactly, do you want to know?"

She studied his face for several seconds. He endured

that scrutiny. And then she asked, "How do you know her?"

"You're serious? You actually want to hear about Susie?"

"Didn't I just say so?"

"Luce. I've had conversations like this one with women before. They never go well."

She tipped her head to the side, considering. Then she simply tried again. "I am not *blaming* you. I am not looking for some way to make you the bad guy. I'm only trying to understand who Susie is to you."

"Why do you need to understand that?"

"Because you were going to leave me at my door and walk away in order not to have to talk about it." Damn. Was he that obvious? Apparently, he was. To her. She said, "So I think we need to clear that crap up right now. Tell me about Susie."

"There's nothing to tell. I hardly know her."

"Then this won't take long at all, will it?"

He opened his mouth to give her more evasions— and somehow the simple truth fell out. "I met her at a party very much like the one tonight. It was about three years ago. Here in New York. I think it was in SoHo. She had a girlfriend with her...."

Lucy had her chin on her hand again. "So it was the three of you?"

"That's right. The girlfriend had a loft a few blocks from the party. I spent the night there with them. And the next time I came to New York, I called Susie. There was another girlfriend that time."

"Is that...something you enjoy, Dami? Being with two women at once?"

He felt pinned, grilled. He struck back. "Why? Would you like to try it?"

She picked up her cup again. "I don't think so." Very carefully, she sipped and with equal care set the cup down. And then her sweet mouth trembled. She pressed her lips together to make the trembling stop and asked him hesitantly, "Do I...have this all wrong?"

"What are you talking about?" He growled the words.

Her gaze roamed his face as though seeking a point of entry. A small pained sound escaped her. Finally, she asked, "I mean, should I have let you go, stayed downstairs when you tried to get rid of me?"

All he had to do was say yes—and she would leave him, stop pushing him for answers to uncomfortable questions. But the lie stuck in his throat. "Why didn't you?"

"I told you. It seemed like we really needed to talk this through, so I kept after you. But now... Oh, I don't know. Maybe it wasn't such a good idea to follow you up here. You seem so angry, so defensive. Maybe I'm just butting in where I'm not wanted. Do you want me to go?" She waited for him to speak. When he didn't, she said, "All right, then. I can take a hint." Shifting away, she started to slide down from the chair.

He couldn't bear it. He caught her shoulder. "No." It came out ragged sounding. Raw. "I don't want you to go."

She turned to him again, so many questions in her eyes. "Dami..." She said his name so softly. With tenderness.

He let go of her, knowing he didn't deserve her tenderness. "What?" he asked, low and gruff.

"I'm not judging you." She touched the back of his hand—and too quickly withdrew. He wanted to grab her wrist, to hold on. But he did no such thing. She said,

"I promise you, I am, truly, your friend first of all. I don't want you to be anyone but exactly who you are."

He didn't believe her. "You say that now."

"Because it's the truth. I'm not judging you, but I do want to...understand. I want to understand *you,* Dami."

He felt outclassed. Overmatched. By a homeschooled twenty-three-year-old who'd been a virgin until two weeks ago. He gritted his teeth and confessed, "I've tried a lot of things you might not approve of."

She didn't look the least surprised. "I only wanted to know about Susie because of what happened tonight. For the rest of it, well, Dami, it's your life. I'm happy for whatever you want to share with me, but I really don't need to hear about every single sexual encounter."

"Good."

But she wasn't done yet. "As long as they were with other consenting adults."

He nodded. "They were."

"And no one was injured."

He almost smiled. "No one."

"And, well, now we're on this subject, there's something I should have asked you before, in Montedoro at Thanksgiving, but I was too nervous and afraid I might scare you off and not really planning ahead..."

"Luce."

"Hmm?"

"Go ahead. Ask."

"Do you— Have you always practiced safe sex?"

"Always."

She looked into her cup and then back up at him. "Well. Okay, then." She started to speak—and then didn't.

He commanded, "Tell me. Just say it."

"I… Well, I do care that while you're with me, you're *only* with me. I'm just kind of old-fashioned that way."

The unreality of it—of Lucy as his lover—struck him anew. Never in his wildest dreams would he have imagined himself having this conversation with her. At the same time, after last night and the nights in Montedoro, he couldn't imagine ever wanting anyone *but* her. Which was pure insanity. It might feel stronger with her, *better* somehow. But it was simple sexual attraction and that never lasted. It ran its course and faded, like cut flowers in a crystal vase, like a stubborn head cold.

She spoke again. "If you can't do that, can't agree to be exclusively with me, well, that *is* a deal breaker for me."

He had zero need to think it over. "Of course I can do that." For as long as it lasted, she'd said—which as of now was only until Wednesday or Thursday. And that was yet another absurdity. He couldn't imagine leaving her so soon.

And who did he think he was fooling, anyway? He shouldn't even be here. It would have been better for both of them if he hadn't shown up on her doorstep yesterday, better if he'd never let this thing with them get started….

"Dami, are you *sure?*"

He didn't flinch, but he wanted to. The question itself was bad enough. Did she have to ask twice? He wanted to be insulted, to lay on the irony: *Well, I might have to grab a quickie with a stranger between meetings on Monday. A man has needs after all.*

But he looked in her eyes and all he saw was sincerity. She was an inexperienced, truehearted woman involved with a man who had no idea how many women he'd had in his bed. Of course she worried that he couldn't be faithful.

So he answered her honestly. "I am sure, yes. Absolutely." He wanted to touch her, to reach for her and draw her close. But that seemed wrong somehow and unfair. He reassured her further. "Until you, I hadn't been with anyone in a while." Not since the last time with V, in August, which had ended in another of her big scenes. "And while we're together, that'll be it. There won't be anyone but you. I promise you that."

She put her hand on his sleeve then. That simple touch hit him deep. It was better by far than any three-some. "I'm so glad."

"It's no hardship. None at all."

She squeezed his arm. "I know you think I'm innocent."

He caught her hand, brought it to his lips. "Because you *are*."

"No."

He kissed the tips of her fingers one by one. "Yes."

She shook her head. "No. Okay, it's true that I haven't had much experience with men. And I like to keep a positive attitude. But still, I'm not innocent, not really. I know what life is. I've been up close and way too personal with death. My dad was dead before I was even born. And my mom…she wasn't right. You know what you said about the powerful love your parents have? Well, my mom loved my dad that way. She never got over that he died. And we lived in this tiny, run-down place and I was always sick and there wasn't any money and Noah wasn't anything like he is today. He was out of control back then, drinking and fighting all the time. And then when I was nine, Mom got sick and *she* died…."

He reminded her gently, "Luce, I know all this."

"I know you do. But what I'm getting at is, when Mom died, I made up my mind that I would be happy no matter what, that whatever suffering or heartache I had to endure, I would focus on the good things. I wouldn't let the losses and the hurts drag me down. I promised myself that I would keep a good attitude. It was not a decision made in innocence. I might have been only nine at the time, but believe me, when my mom died, I hadn't been innocent for years."

He dared to touch her sweet face at last, to trace the graceful arch of each brow, to trail his fingers down her cheek. She made a small questioning sound. And he said, "All right. Not innocent. Good. You are good, good to the deepest part of you. I'm not."

She held his eyes. "Yes, you are." And she laughed a little. "You are very good, I promise you. You are also curious and adventurous and I know you've been wild. So what? I find you generous and helpful, brilliant and fun. Not to mention a truly epic lover."

That did make him smile. "Epic, am I?"

"Legendary. No doubt."

He went ahead and wrapped his fingers around the back of her neck and drew her close enough that he could breathe in the scent of her. "You're just saying that to get me to have sex with you."

She rubbed her soft cheek to his rough one. "Is it working?"

"Truth?"

"Please."

"You had me in the entry when you took off your coat."

A smile bloomed full at last. "Apparently, I'm good in more ways than one."

"And a quick learner, too." He claimed her mouth in a kiss that started out sweet but swiftly turned steamy.

When he let her go, she picked up her cup again and drank the rest. And then she said, "Also, don't forget, I lived in my brother's house for eleven years. And Noah was never a saint. I may not have *done* things until I did them with you, but I know what goes on."

"Noah would hate that you saw more than you should have. His whole life has been about protecting you."

"Dami, get real. Noah likes women. I'm sure you can relate to that."

"Too well, I'm afraid."

"Okay, then. I'm not blind. I saw what was happening. Until Alice, Noah would not give his heart. He didn't want anything permanent and neither did most of the women he hooked up with. And none of that has anything to do with whether or not he protected me. He did protect me. He took excellent care of me and he kept me alive against all odds. That's what matters—and why are you scowling at me?"

"Your brother doesn't want you with me."

She fiddled with her cup and sighed. "That's still bothering you?"

"Think about it. There were paparazzi there tonight. Someone will have gotten pictures of that little scene with Susie. Noah is going to be pissed off when he sees them."

"Too bad. He'll have to look at it as more practice at minding his own business." She got down from the chair and held out her hand to him.

He stood and snared her outstretched fingers, reeling her in and wrapping her in his arms. She tipped up her mouth to him in an offer he couldn't resist. They shared another kiss.

When he lifted his head, she gave him one of those smiles that could light up the darkest night. "So what if Susie made an embarrassing little scene? Too bad if there are pictures online or in the *Enquirer*. And if Noah doesn't like that you're here with me, that's his problem. I only want to know whether or not you're going to let all that ruin the three days we have left."

"You're sure you still want to be with me?" His breath lodged in his throat as he waited for her answer.

She gave it without any hesitation. "Yes, Dami. I'm sure."

Relief poured through him, cool and sweet. And then he frowned. "Wait a minute. *Three* days?"

"That's right."

"How do you get three?"

"Well, it's after midnight, so it's Sunday." She ticked the days off on her fingers. "We have Sunday, Monday and Tuesday. You're leaving Wednesday, so we really can't count Wednesday. That leaves the three days, from Sunday on."

He framed her face between his hands. "I think I should stay until Thursday, at least."

Her eyes were shining. "Four more days." She twined her arms around his neck. "I do like the sound of that."

He bent and scooped her high against his chest. She wrapped her arms around his neck. And he carried her out of the kitchen and straight to bed.

Lucy woke at dawn, snuggled up close in Dami's embrace and thought how right it felt to be there. She burrowed in closer, loving the warmth of him, the smoothness of his skin over all those lovely hard muscles, the absolute manliness of him—and then she remembered Boris.

She kissed Dami's stubbled chin and whispered, "Good morning."

He made a grumbling sound and cupped a hand around the back of her head in a possessive, tender gesture that stole her breath away. "Early. Ugh. Go back to sleep...."

She kissed his chin again. "Can't. I have to go down and feed the cat."

More grumbly noises. His big arms tightened around her. "Stay here. I'll send Quentin to do it."

That made her smile. "There will be scooping involved."

"Quentin can scoop."

"Oh, now. That's just wrong, to send a highly trained bodyguard to clean up after Boris."

"Quentin's a soldier. He's dealt with worse."

"No. *I* have to do it. Boris needs cuddles. He's been alone all night. Don't you even try to tell me that Quentin does cuddles."

Dami ran a hand down her back, tucking her into him even tighter than before. She wanted to stay right there for a lifetime or so. "Promise to make it quick?" he growled in her ear. "Remember, we only have four days left of our Christmas affair."

She laughed at that. "Cuddles take time—but I won't be that long."

Grudgingly, he released her, and then he sat back on the gray satin pillows, laced his fingers behind his head and watched her scurry around naked finding her underwear, her dress—and finally her shoes, one of which had managed to end up halfway down the hall.

"I like that dress," he said, as she wriggled back into it. "I like *all* of your dresses. But I like it even better when you're wearing nothing. I'm thinking I should keep you naked all the time."

"There are so many ways that is totally impractical."

"Allow a man to dream."

She went over and sat on the bed, showing him her back. "Zip me up."

He did, pausing to brush a light kiss below her shoulder blades in the V where the zipper stopped. "I'll walk you out." He breathed the words against her flesh and she wanted to take her dress off again and get back under the covers with him.

But Boris was waiting.

Dami put on his robe and followed her out to the door, where he helped her into her coat. She grabbed her evening bag as he disarmed the alarm.

He kissed her one last time, there on the threshold. "Half an hour, no more," he commanded. "I want you back here with me so we can spend the day in bed together the way we planned."

Downstairs, Boris was waiting for her just inside the door looking very grumpy. She cuddled him, changed his water, cleaned up after him and filled his food bowl with fresh kibble. With ten minutes to spare of the thirty Dami had granted her, she had a quick shower and changed into jeans and a comfy sweater. She was just switching purses when her phone rang.

It was Dami. "You're late."

"I'm on my way. Keep your pants on."

"I'm not wearing any pants."

She laughed, dropped the phone back into her sturdy cross-body bag, pulled open her door—and saw Viviana.

Viv hovered in the open door to her apartment, still in her robe and slippers. She had her hand pressed to her chest. Her face, scarily gray and shiny with sweat, was screwed up tight in a grimace of pain. "Lucy. Hurts…" she barely managed to whisper. Lucy went to her, fumbling in her purse for her phone again as she ran.

Chapter Twelve

Lucy got the 911 dispatcher on the first ring. "Heart attack," she said, almost positive she had it right—and even if she didn't, the two scary words always got the ball rolling.

The dispatcher took it from there, ready with the usual long list of questions. Lucy gave the address and the cross street as she guided Viv down the wall beside the door to her apartment. Viv clutched at her, panting, but Lucy managed to get her seated and supported by the wall with her knees drawn up. The dispatcher asked the questions and Lucy answered, calmly and clearly.

Once the ambulance was on the way—six minutes, tops, the dispatcher promised—the dispatcher had her ask Viv if she was on nitroglycerin.

Viv shook her head and whispered, "No…first time anything like this has happened…."

"She's not on nitroglycerin," Lucy said into the

phone. "She says this is the first time this has happened to her."

Next the dispatcher wanted to know if there was aspirin available. "Chewable, if possible."

Lucy had none. She bit back a groan. At that moment, she almost wished she'd had valve-replacement surgery rather than repair. With an artificial valve, she just might have been on an aspirin regimen and could have whipped a bottle right out of her purse. Then again, she probably would have been on warfarin or…

Dear Lord, what did it matter? The point was she had no aspirin to give Viviana.

She asked Viv, "Do you have any aspirin?"

Viv gestured weakly toward the open door to her apartment. "Master bathroom cabinet…"

Her phone to her ear, Lucy raced inside and down the hall. In the gorgeous retro pink-and-black-tiled bathroom, she found what she needed. "Got them," she told the dispatcher. She grabbed the bottle off the shelf and read the label. "They're the regular kind, not chewable, 325 milligrams."

"Are they timed release, the coated ones?"

"No, the chalky white ones."

"That's better than coated."

"Wonderful. Perfect." Lucy ran back down the hall and out the door to Viv's side again.

The dispatcher gave her more instructions.

Lucy put the phone on speaker, knelt by Viv to set it down on the floor and then shook out one aspirin. She put her arm around Viv. "You need to chew this for thirty seconds before you swallow it. Can you do that for me, Viv?"

Panting, softly moaning, alternately clutching her chest and rubbing her shoulder, Viv managed a nod.

Lucy gave her the pill and counted out the seconds as Viv chewed. It seemed the longest half minute of her life. "All right. Swallow."

Once Viv had the aspirin down, Lucy picked up the phone again. The dispatcher stayed on the line with her, asking questions that Lucy answered as best she could, all the while holding Viv's hand—the one that wasn't tightly clutched to her chest.

After what seemed like forever but was probably no more than the five or six minutes the dispatcher had said it would be, they heard a siren coming on fast, stopping at full volume downstairs in front of the building. Lucy spoke gently, reassuringly, to Viv, who reluctantly let go of her hand so she could step inside the open door to the apartment again and buzz in the paramedics. Endless moments later the elevator doors slid open and two EMTs wheeled their EMS stretcher straight to Viv.

They were just assessing her airway, breathing and circulation and hooking her up to oxygen when Dami came flying down the stairs wearing nothing but a pair of black jeans, with Quentin right behind him.

Dami's face was dead white. "Luce. My God. I heard the siren and I thought…"

She dropped her phone into her purse again, eased around the busy med techs and went to him. "It's not me. Oh, Dami, it's Viv…." He grabbed her against his broad bare chest and she thought how very glad she was to have his arms around her at a time like this.

"What happened?" he asked against her hair.

"She had a heart attack, I think." Lucy looked up at him, drew strength from the simple act of gazing at his dear worried face. "The signs are all there—and I doubt they'll let me ride along in the ambulance with her, but I need to go with her, be with her. Her family's not in New York."

"I'll call for a car."

"Miss." One of the EMTs signaled Lucy. "She's asking for you...."

Dami released her and she went to Viv, who panted out a series of instructions about looking after her place, about getting her little red address book from the drawer beneath the phone and calling her daughters. "And my purse... Insurance card..."

Lucy ran back into the apartment and snatched the large brown shoulder bag from the end of the kitchen counter. One of the EMTs took it from her. She bent close to Viv again and tried to reassure her. "I'm here. I'll take care of all of it, and I'll be following you straight to the hospital...."

"Sweet girl, God bless you...." Viv clutched for her hand again, but the EMTs were already wheeling her toward the open elevator doors.

Lucy called after them, "What hospital?"

One of them told her. They got on the elevator. The doors slid shut. Lucy stared at those doors, suddenly immobilized, images of all the times she'd been the one on the stretcher pounding in strobe-like flashes through her mind.

And then Dami was there, wrapping his big arms around her.

She clung to him. "We have to get going," she said, and then she just stood there, holding him tight, safe in the circle of his embrace.

He pressed his lips to the top of her head. "The car will be here in a few minutes."

"Oh, Dami..." The tears were pushing, trying to get out to turn into a flood that would surely drown her. She bit the inside of her cheek, drawing blood. That did it. The sharp pain brought her back to herself.

He kissed her temple. "Get your coat. Lock up both apartments. I'll run up and put the rest of my clothes on and be right down for you."

Once they were in the limousine and on the way, Lucy called Viv's daughters to break the frightening news.

Marleah burst into tears. Shoshona was calm and thoughtful and then at the end said, "Oh, my sweet Lord. Just let her make it through...."

Lucy told both daughters that Viv had been conscious and still able to talk when they took her away. She promised she would be there until they had her stabilized, all the while sending silent prayers to heaven to match Shoshona's spoken one: *Please, God, let her make it. Let her pull through.* She gave them her number and promised to call them the minute she knew anything more. They both said they would call the hospital right away and be there as soon as they could make arrangements.

When she hung up, Dami reached for her. She unhooked her seat belt, slid across the wide plush seat and settled next to him.

"We're almost there," he promised.

She rested her head on his shoulder and kept on praying that Viv would pull through.

Six hours later they were still sitting in the waiting area outside Cardiac Intensive Care, with Quentin standing guard a few feet away.

A doctor came out to talk to them.

They had Viv stabilized, he said, and the prognosis

was good. They'd put her through the usual endless battery of tests and performed an angioplasty with stent placement. The angioplasty opened the nearly blocked artery that had caused Viv's heart attack, and the stent, a small mesh tube inserted at the same time, would keep the artery open.

Even though she wasn't family, Lucy talked the doctor into letting her go in and visit Viv briefly. As expected, Viv was exhausted and barely conscious. They'd given her a mild sedative to get her through the angioplasty without too much pain. She moved her hand restlessly against the sheet until Lucy settled her own over it, slipping her thumb into the smooth, dry heart of the older woman's palm.

Viv closed her eyes tight. Still, a pair of tears leaked out at the corners and trailed down her temples into her short tightly curled hair.

Lucy bent close and whispered, "You are going to make it. And your daughters are on the way."

Viv let out a tired little sigh at that and managed to give Lucy's hand a weak squeeze. Lucy stayed with her just holding her hand, gently stroking her forehead, until the nurse came in and signaled it was time to go.

A woman came rushing into the waiting area about ten minutes later. She was tall, slim on top and generous through the hips, with honey-colored skin and blond-streaked dark hair. She carried a large shoulder bag and a small suitcase. Lucy liked her style. She wore knee-high black boots, dark tights, a short wool dress and a fabulous heavy coat that reached to midcalf. And especially around the mouth and eyes, she looked a lot like Viv.

Lucy stood up. She had Viv's purse, which they'd given her at the front desk.

The woman spotted her and came right for her. "You have to be Lucy. I'm Shoshona." She dropped the suitcase and they grabbed each other and held on tight.

Lucy tried not to cry, but a tear or two got away from her anyhow. "Your mom's resting now. I know she can't wait to see you...."

Shoshona sniffled a little, too. Then she took Lucy by the shoulders, looked in her eyes for a minute and gave her shoulders a squeeze. "I do believe you saved my mama's life."

"No. I just happened to be there."

"That's what I'm talking about. You were *there* and you did what needed doing and I am so glad. Thank you." She swiped the tears off her cheeks with the back of her hand, which was as slim and beautifully manicured as Viv's.

"I'm just so happy she's pulling through." Lucy held out the purse. "This is your mom's. Her keys are in here, her wallet and cell phone, too— Oh, and there's a small brown bag with her rings."

A nurse appeared. "Mrs. Caudell?"

Shoshona nodded, then asked Lucy, "My suitcase...?"

"We'll look after it," Lucy promised.

"And the purse, too, for now?"

"Of course."

The nurse led Viv's daughter to the long hallway that led into the business end of the CICU.

Lucy took the suitcase and purse back to her chair. She slid them both under the corner table topped with a small artificial Christmas tree. With a long sigh, she sank down beside Dami. He took her hand and folded her fingers over a fresh tissue.

"So much for spending the day in bed, huh?" She

sagged against him and he gathered her in, cradling her in the shelter of his arm, guiding her head down to rest on his shoulder. Again she felt thankful to have him beside her. The awful day would have been ten times worse without the constant comfort of his presence, of his strong arms to hold her when her energy flagged.

"There will be other days," he reminded her softly.

His words warmed her—for a minute. And then she couldn't help thinking that the other days they had together weren't nearly enough.

Tomorrow and the next day, he had meetings. Maybe on Wednesday, which was their last day, they could laze around in bed.

One day for lazing. Uh-uh. No way was it enough.

Yes, Viv was going to make it and she was so grateful.

But why did their Christmas love affair have to fly by so fast?

Two hours later Marleah arrived. Though she was smaller and slimmer than her older sister, anybody could tell the two were related.

Lucy and Dami stayed in their chairs as the sisters shared a private moment. And then Marleah dried her eyes and went in to be with their mom for a while.

When she came back out, Shoshona introduced her to Lucy and Dami.

Marleah recognized him. "Mama's had a heart attack and the Prince of Montedoro is hanging around the waiting room to make sure she's going to be all right."

They all laughed at that, tired laughter. It had been a hard day and it wasn't over yet.

Then Shoshona said to Lucy, "You two go on now. You've been here all day. It's way more than enough."

Dami called for the car and then Lucy asked if maybe one of the two sisters wanted to go back to Viv's place with them. The sisters agreed that Marleah would go. She could take their suitcases, rest for a while and then return to give Shoshona a break.

The drive was a quiet one overall. Marleah seemed deep in thought.

But then, as they approached the apartment building, Marleah shook her head. "This is it," she said with certainty. "Mama can't be living on her own anymore. Denver or Chicago. The day has come when she will have to decide."

Lucy reached over and took Marleah's hand. Marleah didn't object—in fact, she held on tight. "Don't worry about it now," Lucy said softly.

"You're right." Marleah swallowed hard. "But the time has come, oh, yes, it has."

They helped Marleah carry the suitcases up to Viv's place. Quentin put them inside for her.

Lucy hugged her at the door. "I'll be back at the hospital in the morning. Call me if there's anything I can do before then."

"I will," Marleah promised. "You get some rest. Tomorrow, then." She and Dami shared a nod and she went in. Lucy heard her engage the locks.

When she turned back to Dami, he said, "Tired?"

"A little." She went to him, wrapped her arms around his waist and rested her head against his chest. "Life's too scary sometimes."

He stroked her hair. "Your friend will be all right."

She looked up into his waiting eyes. "Yes. I believe that. I know she will."

He kissed her, a light, sweet kiss. "Pack whatever

you need for the night. And we're taking the cat up to my place."

"Good idea." She intended to spend every second she could with him, and the time was flying by way too fast. She didn't want to keep running downstairs to fill Boris's food bowl and give him a hug. The cat could use the company, anyway.

So they collected Boris and all the necessary cat-care equipment and Lucy packed an overnight bag.

They stayed in that night. Dami cooked chicken cacciatore and Lucy had a large glass of wine. He took her to bed early and they made slow, tender love. She woke in the morning to the sound of Boris purring softly from down at the foot of the bed.

Dami came out of the bathroom looking sigh worthy, wearing nothing but a big white Turkish towel. "I've got a breakfast meeting at nine. I'm hoping to be finished by noon, but it could go later. I'll call and let you know."

She wanted to whine at him, to remind him that they had so little time left and he should get those meetings over with and get back to her fast.

But she caught herself. She had him with her only because of those meetings and whining never did anyone any good. She threw back the covers and went to kiss him good-morning.

He and Quentin were gone by a little after eight. She went down to her place to shower and change, stopping to knock on Viv's door on the way out. No answer. The sisters were probably both at the hospital.

She ran into Marie, the super's wife, on the elevator.

"I'm so sorry to hear about Viviana Nichols," Marie said. "I talked to one of her daughters yesterday evening. They say she should pull through all right. I wonder if she'll be moving to be closer to her family. It seems likely, doesn't it, at her age? That's such a nice apartment...."

"I have no idea what Viv's plans are." Lucy gave her a bland smile.

"How's the prince? I didn't realize you two were so...close." The elevator reached the first floor. Lucy got off, Marie right behind.

"Fine," Lucy said. "His Highness is doing fine. And yes, we *are* close. He's a friend of the family."

"But is that *all?*" Marie wanted to know.

"He's been very kind to me." Lucy headed for the door and couldn't resist adding sweetly under her breath, "Last night, he took off all my clothes and was kind to every inch of me."

"What was that, dear?" called Marie.

Lucy gave her a wave and called back, "Merry Christmas, Marie," as she went out the door.

At the hospital, she sat with Marleah and Shoshona. The sisters reported that Viv was holding her own and would be in CICU for another few days at least. After that, if all went well, she would be out of intensive care and into a regular hospital room. If she continued to improve, they hoped that by the weekend she could go home.

The nurses let Lucy go in and visit with Viv briefly.

Viv was awake but still very weak. She whispered in a ragged little voice, "Hello, sweet girl."

Lucy's heart lifted at the words. She pulled up a chair and sat by the bed until the nurse came in and said she had to go.

Dami called her at a little after eleven. His meetings were going late. "It will be after four, I'm afraid, before I can get out of here."

Lucy, in a cab on the way back to the apartment building, tamped down her disappointment and told him that Viv was doing well. "So, um, call me when you're finished?"

"You know I will." And he was gone.

Lucy wanted to cry. Like some big spoiled baby, she wanted to burst into tears because they only had until Thursday and now most of today would be gone before she saw him again. Really, how silly and selfish was that?

She stared out the window at the people rushing by on the street, at the Christmas decorations and window displays, at the Salvation Army bell ringer on the corner and the strange raggedy bearded fellow wearing a dirty fringed rawhide jacket and a coonskin cap. He stopped to throw bills into the bell ringer's bucket.

It was the happiest time of the year. All the Christmas songs said so.

What was there to cry about?

Nothing, she told herself. Not one single thing. Viv was getting better and she would be with Dami that night.

She had the cabbie let her off in front of the Paradise Diner, where she had a bowl of clam chowder and told Tabby about Viv.

Tabby pulled her up out of her seat, hugged her and asked her why she seemed so down. "I mean, she's going to make it, right?"

"Oh, yeah. I'm sure she will. And I'm not down."

Tabby gave her two bags of oyster crackers. "Where's the prince?"

"Working," Lucy grumbled.

"Uh-oh. You've got it bad."

"Oh, I do not. It's not like that."

Tabby frowned. "Like what, exactly?"

"I mean, we're just, you know, having fun…."

"How long's he here for?" Tabby asked way too gently.

Lucy opened one of the little bags and poured the crackers onto her chowder. "Not long enough."

Nestor yelled something in Greek. Tabby turned around and yelled right back at him, also in Greek. Then she muttered, "Why do I put up with him?"

"He makes great clam chowder?" Lucy suggested.

About then, Nestor bellowed, "Order up!"

Tabby waved a dismissing hand in his direction and said to Lucy, "I'm off at two. And I do need to tell you all about Henry…."

"The Saturday-night guy?"

"Oh, yeah." She put her hand against her chest and mimed a fast-beating heart. "He's the one."

Lucy hesitated. She did want to hear about Henry. And she could talk to Tabby. In fact, she might be tempted to start admitting things she hadn't even admitted to herself yet. It would be wiser not to go there.

But who was she kidding? She needed to talk. "Come over to my place. I'll be home."

Lucy made them coffee. They sat in her living room. The view in there was of the wall of the building the next block over, but it was a cozy room, and you could see a little bit of the gray winter sky if you craned toward the window and looked up.

Tabby said she was falling for Henry O'Mara. "Saturday night, Sunday night. He's coming over tonight, too." Her parents weren't happy. They were still after her to patch things up with the nice Greek man she'd almost married. "But *I'm* happy," Tabby said with a giant grin. "Very, very happy in a big, big way." She looked around the room. "Where's the cat?"

"He's up at Dami's. We took him up there last night so I wouldn't have to keep running down here to feed him. We took his litter box, too, which means if I haul him back down here, I need to bring the box. I mean, just in case, right? Ugh. It's complicated."

Tabby laughed. "So get a second litter box."

"It's only for a few days."

"Ah, so that's what's going on with you. The prince is leaving soon and you're missing him already." Tabby sipped her coffee. "Ask him to stay."

"It's not like that. It's not...that kind of a thing between us."

"Do you want it to be *that* kind of a thing?"

Lucy put her hand on her chest. "My heart kind of does. A little." *Liar,* a chiding voice whispered inside her head. *Your heart wants it a lot.* "But he's not a 'staying' kind of guy—or if he was, probably he wouldn't be with me."

"Why not with you?"

"It's just that it's not that way with us."

"What way?"

"We're friends. With benefits, for now. That part—the two of us being lovers, was supposed to be just for Thanksgiving. And now it's only until Thursday. And I'm just starting out, anyway. I'm not ready for anything serious, no matter what my silly heart keeps telling me."

"Shut the front door. Just for *Thanksgiving?*"

"Please. Don't ask me to explain. It's…"

"Do not say 'complicated.'"

"But it *is* complicated."

Tabby set her cup down and leaned toward Lucy. "You need to talk to him about it, tell him how you feel."

"But that's just it. I don't *want* to talk to him about it."

"Yeah, you do."

"No, I want to enjoy the time I have with him and then when it's over, I want us to remain friends."

"But you're *not* enjoying it."

"Yes, I am. Mostly. Mostly, I'm enjoying it a *lot*."

"Lucy, sweetie, you should see your sad little face. Talk to him."

"I feel like such a *child* again. It's the one thing I hate, to feel like a child. I've felt like a child for most of my life, sick all the time, not getting to do any of the things other girls did, with other people hovering, worrying and having to take care of me. And the whole point in the first place with me and Dami being more than friends was for me *not* in any way to feel like a child."

Tabby kicked off her duty shoes and folded her legs up to the side. "Is he treating you bad?"

Lucy gasped. "Dami? Never. Not in any way. And this whole thing, it was my idea. I'm the one who started it, okay? I asked him to be my first lover and he wasn't into it, but as usual, he was a hero about it and tried to let me down easy. But then he discovered that maybe he *could* be into it with me."

"Oh, right. He *discovered* this, did he?"

"No, Tabby. I'm serious. He always thought of me as a kid before, you know?"

"Oh, spare me. I'm a busy woman with my parents' business to run, but even I read the *National Enquirer* now and then. The man is like some world-class lover, right? I'm sure he can tell if he's attracted or he's not."

"Uh-uh. He's not like that, not with me. He's not a player with me. He really has been my friend first and foremost. And we really, truly were just friends until

Thanksgiving. That's when I went after him. I went after him and I kept pushing and finally, well, it happened. We made love and it was beautiful. Exactly what I dreamed it might be. And it's been that way every time since the first time."

Tabby had her lips pursed up and her brow furrowed. "It was supposed to be over after Thanksgiving, you said...."

"That's right. But he had meetings here in New York and, well..."

"What you're saying is *he* started it this time."

"Well, he was here and all, and he lives in the building whenever he's in New York, so of course we—"

"Oh, stop it. He's a prince with buckets of money, right?"

"I don't think I like the way you say that."

"Too bad. The point is, if he didn't want to be with you, he could have stayed at the Four Seasons. You'd have had no idea he was in town. He *wanted* to be with you. *You* want to be with him. It's what I said at the first. You need to talk to him."

"But I told you, this whole thing with him and me was always with the understanding that it was only for a little while."

"And maybe that was your mistake right there."

"What do you mean, my mistake? He's my friend and I trust him and I asked him to do me this very special favor. That's all it was supposed to be."

"So? Now it's more."

"No. You're not listening. I'm honestly not looking for forever right now."

"Oh, honey. Maybe *you're* not. But your heart? That's a whole other story."

* * *

Dami called at four-thirty.

The minute she heard his voice saying he was on the way, Lucy realized what an idiot she'd been. No matter what Tabby thought, she did *not* need to talk to Dami about how she wanted more from this thing between them.

She didn't want more. She was happy with things as they were. Yes, all right, she would be sad when he left. But that was the way it went. That was life. You needed to revel in every moment. You needed to get through the heartache.

And move on.

He took her out to dinner at a great steak house on the Upper East Side and they shared a bottle of very expensive cabernet sauvignon. Lucy ate almost all of her filet mignon—not to mention a prosciutto-and-melon appetizer, cold asparagus salad and a baked potato the size of Long Island. They split a slice of New York cheesecake for dessert.

The restaurant was exclusive enough that no paparazzi popped up to take their picture while they plowed through the huge, delicious meal. They laughed together and toasted Viv's recovery and Tabby's new man and the holiday season in general.

Then he took her back to his place and straight to bed. He made love to her slowly, looking in her eyes. And when he whispered her name at the end, well, she could almost have wished she *did* want forever right now.

Tuesday, like Monday, went by too fast. Lucy went to the hospital in the morning while Dami worked. Again his meetings went on and on. Lucy had time to buy an extra litter box for Boris. Then she went up to Dami's, got the cat and took him back to her place. He kept her company while she worked some more on the detailed sketch of Alice's wedding dress.

They stayed in that night. And in the morning when she woke up, he wasn't in the bed. But she could smell coffee brewing and something delicious cooking.

Breakfast in bed? Did it get any better? They were going to have a perfect day, lazing around without any clothes on, maybe getting up later and doing something festive.

How about a tree for her place? She grinned at the thought. They could get decorations, too. And then they could put up the tree together.

Her grin faded.

And then when he's gone, won't I love that? whined the sad little voice in her head. Every time she looked at the tree she would have to remember this last perfect day, the beautiful time they'd had choosing it and decorating it together.

Uh-uh. Forget the tree. Bad idea. Better just to stay in bed late, make love a lot and go somewhere nice for dinner. And then make love for half the night. That would be a perfect goodbye.

Goodbye. The word seemed to bounce around, echoing, inside her head. Her heart was racing. Her cheeks felt too warm.

She dragged herself up against the pillows and made herself take slow, deep breaths.

She was being an idiot and she was stopping that right now.

Big mistake to start planning out the day. They didn't need a plan. It would be lovely whatever they did.

Her breathing evened out and her pulse stopped galloping. There. She was fine. She wasn't going to break

down in front of Dami just because she was beginning
to realize she wanted more from him than she'd told
him she wanted.

A whole lot more.

You need to talk to him, Tabby had said.

But she wasn't going to talk to him. It wasn't *fair* to
put all this emotional crap on him. He hadn't bargained
for anything like this.

And neither had she, damn it. Neither had she.

Breathe. Slowly. Deeply.

It worked. Her tight throat loosened. The pressure
behind her eyes eased. The heat in her cheeks cooled.
It was fine. *She* was fine.

There would be no big scene. She was under control.

And then she looked over and there he was in the
doorway, his eyes low and lazy, his mouth made for
kissing, wearing a black silk robe exactly like the
one he'd worn on Thanksgiving morning when she'd
knocked on his door to ask him to teach her about sex.
He carried a footed tray with a carafe of steaming coffee, a covered dish of something wonderful and a crystal bud vase with a sprig of mistletoe sticking out of it.

All her deep breathing came to nothing. "Oh,
Dami..." She burst into tears.

Chapter Thirteen

Should he have known this would happen?

Of course he damn well should have.

In fact, to be brutally honest, he *had* known it would come to this. Exactly this. And he'd gone ahead and done what he wanted to do anyway.

Damien stood in the doorway, holding the tray with the breakfast she would probably never eat, and cursed himself for being a heartless, lust-driven dog. He shouldn't have come here. He never should have let this thing with them get started in the first place.

She was his friend, dear to him. She deserved so much—everything.

Instead he'd had to go and become her lover when he knew himself and knew how it would end: just like this. With her suffering and him hating himself.

He set down the tray and went to her. "Luce, my darling…"

She had her head in her hands. Her slim shoulders were shaking. He reached for her and she sagged against him with a lost little sob.

He gathered her closer, stroked her soft hair. "Shh…" He knew the words to say, the gentle reassurances. "It's all right. Don't cry. Everything will work out…."

"Oh, no." A gasp, another sob. "I don't think so." He felt the warmth of her tears against his throat.

He cradled her face, tipped it up to him, wiped at her tears with his thumbs. Her eyes glittered, wet. Yearning. Her mouth trembled and he wanted to kiss her, to taste the salt and the wet, to pull the covers away and make love to her again.

One more time. Before he left.

He didn't do what he wanted. For once.

Her eyes sought something in his face. He doubted she found it. She said, "Dami, I've been lying. Lying to you. Lying to *me*. I thought I could do it. Could just keep on lying until after you'd gone."

He did kiss her then. But he kept the kiss chaste, though her mouth trembled, willing, beneath his.

When he lifted his head, he saw she was on to him. "Kisses can't keep me from saying it," she whispered.

"Luce…" It was a warning. And a plea.

She said it anyway. "I love you, Dami. I'm *in* love with you."

There. She'd gone and done it. Said the three words that couldn't be unsaid. The ones that always made him feel restless, eager to be gone.

And she wasn't finished. "I think I've been in love with you since that first night I met you, when you danced with me and treated me with such complete consideration. You talked to me, *really* talked to me, and you listened, like you really were interested in me and what I had to say, as though I was more than some sickly, scarred-up, skinny girl. Like I was a grown woman, beautiful and whole and strong and well."

"That was exactly how I saw you."

Through her tears, she gave him a certain look. Knowing. Patient. "As a grown woman? Hardly. You saw me as a child, Dami. You might even have loved me, too—as a friend, I mean. Or at least felt affection for me right from the first. I knew that you did. I felt that you liked me. I knew you *noticed* me. And you were kind to treat me as a grown woman when you knew how I longed to be thought of as a fully functioning adult. But you didn't *see* me as a woman. Not then. Don't try to tell me that you did."

He gave it up. "All right. As a child. I thought of you as childlike. And I adored you from the first."

"Okay," she said halfheartedly. "I'll buy that." She swiped at her eyes with the back of her hand. He grabbed the box of tissues from the nightstand and offered it. She took it, pulled one out, dropped the box on the bed. "You liked me and I *loved* you. I just didn't realize the *way* that I loved you."

"Luce. It doesn't matter."

"But I've been dishonest, in my heart."

He shook his head. "I don't care."

She gasped. "But I...I used our friendship to get you to make love with me."

"Yes, you did. I knew that from the first. You did nothing wrong."

Her soft mouth twisted. "Why don't you get it?"

"But, Luce, I do get it."

"Uh-uh. No. All along I've been telling myself that it was just for Thanksgiving, just for these past few days, just for a little while, for *experience* so I could get some guy like Brandon to look twice at me. I've been telling myself that I didn't want anything permanent, that I only wanted a few lessons in love and then we would go back to being like we were before. That was a lie. A lie, do you hear me? All along, deep down where it matters, in the heart of me where the truth is, I've been hoping, praying, longing for you to fall in love with me. I've been wanting a chance at forever with you."

He took her hand. She allowed that, which surprised him a little. Her fingers felt cool and smooth in his. He kissed them. "I lied to you, too."

"No." She looked as though she might cry again, those big eyes filling. With the tissue in her free hand, she dashed the tears away.

He confessed. "I came here on Friday because I wanted to see you again, to be with you again. When Rule couldn't make it for the transit-app meetings, I jumped at the chance to fill in for him."

Hope lit her wonderful face from within. "You...you wanted to be with me, too?"

"Of course I did. I *do,* but..."

She saw the truth in his eyes and pulled her hand free of his. Bleakly, she said the rest for him. "Not in a forever way."

"That's right."

Dipping her head, she stared at the tissue between her hands. "So if not in a forever way, what kind of way, exactly?"

He'd thought he'd hated it when she cried. This was worse. But she was Luce and even if he was incapable of giving her the love she deserved, he still adored her, and she wanted the truth now. What else was there to do but lay it out there for her? "You excite me, Luce. From the minute I started to see you as a woman, from that first kiss by the harbor on Thanksgiving Day, I've wanted you. I seem to have developed a real obsession with you. It keeps getting stronger. I know I should leave you alone, but I, well, I know you want me, too. I couldn't stop thinking about you, wanting you. So I came here to you. For more."

She looked at him sideways and licked her lips, sending a bolt of lust straight to his groin. God, he was hopeless. She asked, "But it's just sex with you, that's what you're saying?"

He nodded. "And I do like you."

"Like. You *like* me." She seemed to be testing the words, turning them over in her mind.

He'd never in his life felt so completely inadequate. "Is that so bad? That I like you?"

"Not...love? Not the forever kind of man-and-woman love?"

"No. Not that."

"But...could it grow into love? Is that possible?"

"God, Luce. What do you want from me? You know how I am. I told you. I've seen the kind of love you're talking about. My parents have it. Most of my brothers and sisters have it. I understand myself well enough to accept that I don't have the attention span for that kind of love."

She tipped her head to the other side and she looked him up and down in a measuring way that made him want to grab her and pull her under him and bury himself in the welcoming wet heat of her. "But you want me? You *still* want me, even after what I said about loving you, about lying to myself about loving you. You want me right now. You want to grab me and kiss me and do all those things to me that make both of us happy, that make both of us burn."

He readjusted his robe, though he knew she'd already spotted the evidence that she had it right. "What are you getting at?"

She canted marginally closer. The scent of her drifted to him, unbearably womanly, so damn sweet. "You want me."

He gritted his teeth. "You keep saying that."

"But only because *you* keep saying it. Because I can see it in your face every time you look at me." She licked her lips again. Why did she keep doing that?

"What the hell?" He jumped to his feet and glared down at her. "What are you doing? What's going on here?"

She stared up at him. Proud now. Defiant somehow. "I'm not sure I can have children, Dami. I'm not sure it would be safe. Pregnancy puts a big burden on the heart and the circulatory system. I would have to consult with my doctors, assess the risks."

"Risks?" Now she was scaring him. "Children?" He backed away from her, from the bed. "What do children have to do with anything?"

"Nothing." Her eyes filled again. She blinked those tears away. "I just, well, I wanted you to know. I want you to know everything. All the truths that are so hard to say."

"Why?"

She closed her eyes, looked away. But then she straightened her shoulders and faced him again. "Because you are my hero, Dami. You're the one who danced with me and treated me like a woman when no one else could. You're the one who encouraged me to follow my dream. And then when Noah wouldn't let me go, you're the one who came and got me, the one who freed me, the one who brought me here to New York where I needed to be. You're the one who sat with me all day Sunday in the hospital, making the fear and the worry bearable for me, because I had to be there for Viv. You're the one who taught me the magic that can be between a woman and a man. You showed me... everything. And everything that you showed me has been so very beautiful. That's why I want, why I *need,* to tell you the truth. That's why I love you, am *in* love with you. How in the world could it be any other way for me?"

He felt shame then, a twisting, sour sensation deep in his gut. "I'm not. Not all that."

"Oh, Dami. You are. And I hope, I pray, that some-day you will see that you are." She pushed back the covers. Naked, glorious, she swung her slim legs over the edge of the bed and stood.

He feared she would come to him, touch him, lift her mouth to him. If she did, he would take her, make love to her now. And that would be another wrong to add to all the rest of it. "What are you after?" He growled the words at her.

She faced him, so beautiful in the gray light of that December morning. Naked and self-contained, her eyes dry now. "I'm going to get my things together and go back to my place."

"Right now. Just like that?"

"Just like that."

He wanted to argue with her, to shout at her that they weren't finished here. But why tell more lies? He might not be ready to let her go yet. But that didn't mean it was any less over. He couldn't give her what she needed, what a woman like her deserved.

The least he could do was to let her walk away now that she was ready to leave him.

"Suit yourself." He went over and poured himself some coffee from the carafe on the tray. Then he dropped into the chair there and sipped slowly as she put on her clothes and gathered up the few things she'd left around the apartment.

In no time, she stood before him, her overnight bag and purse on her shoulder, the fat orange cat under one arm. "Can you just send Quentin down with the litter box and food and water bowls and anything else I've forgotten to take?"

He set down the empty coffee cup and considered maybe begging her not to go.

A hero, she'd called him. She had it all wrong.

He said, "Of course I'll send Quentin down."

"Merry Christmas, Dami." And that was it. The end.

He watched her until she went through the door and disappeared from his sight down the hall.

Chapter Fourteen

Montedoro was beautiful at Christmas. This year, the beautification committee put up a forest of brightly lit trees in a rainbow of colors around the casino and the Triangle d'Or. As always, all the staterooms of the palace were decorated, each with its own Christmas tree, with swags and lights on every banister and mantel.

There were parades and special Christmas markets, and an endless round of gala celebrations. Damien went to the market as was expected. He attended the parties. At the Christmas Ball, he danced with his mother and sisters and sisters-in-law.

He went through the motions required of him. He smiled. He chatted. He held up his end. If anyone noticed his heart wasn't in it, they had the good sense to keep their observations to themselves.

Noah surprised him with a call on Christmas Eve.

"Merry Christmas, Dami. I saw the pictures of you and Lucy and that hot blonde. Didn't like seeing those."

What could he say? "It was embarrassing. I should have handled it better, seen Susie coming."

"Her name is Susie, huh?"

"We all have regrets, Noah," he answered flatly. "Things we should have done better. Things we probably shouldn't have done at all."

"Hey. I hear you there." And then Noah actually laughed. "I talked to Lucy about those pictures. She told me—again—to stay out of her business. I'm trying to do that. She says I'm getting better. Alice says so, too. I'm telling myself that's progress." A pause, then, "Lucy says you're not seeing each other anymore."

He felt a definite twinge somewhere deep in his chest. "That's right."

"That's too bad. I was kind of getting used to the idea of the two of you together."

He really didn't want to talk about it. He said nothing. Maybe Noah would take a hint.

No such luck. "Alice says..." Noah let his voice trail off, leading him on.

And Dami took the bait, demanding bleakly, "Alice says what?"

"That you're in love with my sister and that Lucy loves you back. That the two of you have been in love almost since you met—it just took you both a couple of years to figure it out."

Dami had no idea what to say to that.

Noah spoke again. "I make it a point to listen to Alice. She's usually right."

"Noah." It came out loud and very aggressive. He lowered his voice with effort. "It's over." He was not, under any circumstances, going to ask about her. But then, of course, he did. "How's she doing?"

"Okay, as far as I can tell. Celebrating Christmas with her new friends. That would be Tabby from Lucy's favorite diner and Tabby's new boyfriend, whose name is Henry, and the older woman on Lucy's floor in your building, the one recovering from a heart attack."

He'd been wondering about Mrs. Nichols even though he'd never actually met the woman face-to-face. "Viviana's her name. She's getting better, you said?"

"She's doing well. And she's at home now. One of her daughters is staying with her. After New Year's she's moving to Chicago, I think Lucy said. Lucy said her neighbor is very independent, but she also understands that the time has come when she needs to live near her family."

"Luce will miss her."

"I think she's already making plans for a visit to Chicago."

Damien made a low sound that could have meant anything and then kept his mouth shut. Better to leave it alone, stop talking about her.

When the silence stretched out, Noah said, "Well, I only called to wish you happy holidays. Alice sends her love."

"Take good care of my sister."

"I will— And, Dami?"

"What?"

"You're an idiot, you know that?"

He didn't even bother to get angry. There was nothing to be angry about. It was only the truth on a whole lot of levels. "Happy holidays, Noah." And that was that.

Christmas morning he had breakfast in his parents'

private apartments. Five of his siblings were there, along with their spouses and children. It was a happy time. They ate and opened the gifts piled high under the fifteen-foot Christmas tree, set up as always in the curve of the stairway by the door.

Around noon, on his own, he took several small brightly wrapped packages and walked to the café in La Cacheron where he'd taken Lucy at Thanksgiving. The café was always open on Christmas Day from nine to two. Regular customers appreciated being able to get their croissants and beignets fresh even on the holiday. The walk was a pleasant one and he didn't spot a single paparazzo. Apparently, even the tabloid vultures took a little time off for Christmas.

The café was quiet when he got there, with only two customers, one at the counter and another at a table by himself in the center of the room. Dami took a corner seat and put the presents on the table. Justine served him his usual coffee and pastry. She chose a gift and smiled a thank-you. One by one the others came by. Each took a gift and thanked him. They all knew what was inside. He gave them all the same Christmas tip every year, each one tucked in a small box and wrapped in bright paper tied with a shiny bow.

He was sipping the last of his coffee when the door opened and in strode Vesuvia. Before he had time to do anything but wish himself elsewhere, she spotted him and stalked over like a lioness on the hunt.

"There you are." She posed with her nose in the air, one hand on the back of the bentwood chair across from him. "I knew you would be here."

"Come on, V. Let's not do this again. I'm through, you're through. It's over, long over. And we both know it."

She yanked back the chair and flung herself into it.

"This is ridiculous." At least she was whispering. And the café remained nearly empty. It was just possible he could get rid of her without too much of a scene. She added, "I know that you and the tacky little wannabe fashion designer are through."

Fury blasted through him. "Do not speak of her," he said, very softly. And how did she know that he and Lucy were through? Better not to ask.

V sneered, "She doesn't matter, anyway."

He smacked his fist on the table. His cup, spoon and plate jumped.

Vesuvia's sculpted nostrils flared. But when she spoke again, still whispering, she had the sense to leave Lucy out of it. "You must stop being so stubborn. I want to get moving on our wedding plans. It's going to be the wedding of the decade, Dami. And as of now, we have only a year to put it together."

"There isn't going to be any wedding," he said.

For all the good that did. "Have you forgotten that you'll be thirty-two in exactly a month? Next year will fly by. And then what? You'll be thirty-three. Have you suddenly forgotten the Marriage Law?"

"I don't care about the Marriage Law."

"Of course you do." She swore softly in Italian. "If you don't marry soon, you'll lose your inheritance and your titles, too. You'll no longer be a prince of Monte-doro."

"How many ways can I say it? I'm not marrying you, V. It's long over with us. When are you going to accept that and move on?"

She rolled her eyes and asked in a smug whisper, "Why should I accept it? You need me. You need to marry and I want to marry you. It's all going to work out. You only have to stop denying the inevitable."

He shook his head. "No."

She stuck out her chin at him. "Don't tell me no. I understand you. I know how you are. Yes, I have a temper. Yes, I am sometimes unreasonable. But in the end, I'm willing to forgive you, whatever you do. I will forgive you and we can move on. We both know how you are, Dami—born to stray." He felt more than a little insulted. All right, he was no model of virtue, but he'd been faithful to V. It had mattered to him to be true to the woman he intended to marry. Even when they'd been on the outs, she'd been the only one in his bed until after it was undeniably over. Until Thanksgiving. Until Lucy. V sneered, "With you, Dami, there will always be someone new, and you will require a forgiving wife."

And by then he'd had enough. "You have no idea what I require."

"Yes, I do, I—"

"No. No, you don't. I require love," he said, and it was true. "I want forever, with the right woman."

Vesuvia sighed heavily and tossed her hair. "Oh, please."

"I want forever with Lucy Cordell."

There was a moment. Huge. Endless. Vesuvia gaped at him. He stared back at her. He hadn't planned to say it, hadn't even known he *would* say it until the words were on their way out his mouth.

But now he'd done it, now he'd let himself say it, the stark, simple truth in it stunned him.

V whispered dazedly, "You can't be serious."

"I am completely serious," he replied. "I'm in love with Lucy Cordell and I have been for a long time now. There's no one else for me. Lucy's the one."

* * *

On Christmas night, Lucy gave a little party at her place. Tabby came with Henry after taking him to her parents' house for an early dinner first.

"It could have been worse," she told Lucy. "At least they didn't yell. No heavy objects were thrown. I think we're making progress."

Shoshona and her husband, Tony, were staying with Viv until January, when they would take Viv back to Chicago to live. All three came to the party. Viv even brought frosted Christmas cookies that she and Shoshona had made together.

A couple who lived on the fifth floor, Bob and Andrew, came, too. Lucy also invited two new friends in their mid-twenties. Sandra and Jim were actors Lucy had met while making Christmas-show costumes for the Make-Believe and Magic Children's Theatre Company.

It went well, Lucy thought. She served drinks and snacks and they played a game called Cranium that Bob and Andrew brought along. Everyone seemed to have a good time. They all stayed until well after midnight.

Sandra was the last to go. She offered to stay and help clean up. But Lucy hugged her and shooed her out the door. She would deal with the mess in the morning.

She took Boris and went to bed. As usual, since Dami had left her, sleep didn't come easy. She missed making love with him, but she missed his big body wrapped around her in sleep even more.

That didn't make a lot of sense, and she knew it. They'd been lovers for such a short time. Two nights in November, five in December. It was nothing. A blink of an eye, really.

And yet for her it didn't seem to matter how few the

nights had been. Her bed felt too big and too empty without him.

In the morning, the sun was shining, making the snow on the windowsills glitter like sequins on a white party dress. She plugged in her tree lights, made herself breakfast and counted her blessings. After a second cup of coffee, she started gathering up the dirty glassware and dishes from the night before.

When the doorbell rang, she assumed it had to be Bob or Andrew. They'd left the Cranium game behind last night. She grabbed the game from the coffee table and carried it to the door, disengaging the locks and pulling it open without even stopping to check the peephole.

Dami stood on the other side.

A strange, incoherent little sound escaped her at the sight of him. She gaped at him, not believing, certain she had to be seeing things, that she'd missed him so much she'd gone delusional.

Dear Lord, he looked good. It wasn't fair that he looked so good. He wore a fabulous camel coat over one of those perfectly tailored designer suits of his. His dark eyes locked on hers and something inside of her went all wimpy and quivering. "Hello, Luce."

She almost dropped the Cranium game. But then by some miracle, she managed to hold on to it. She backed up without speaking, clearing the doorway.

He came in, bringing with him the wonderful, subtle scent of his cologne and a bracing coolness in the air. He must have come up straight from outside.

She gulped as he shut the door. "Uh. Where's your bodyguard?"

"I sent him on to the apartment."

"Oh. Well." Her mind seemed filled with cotton, her

thoughts not connecting properly. At the same time, her whole body ached. She wanted to launch herself at him, grab on tight and never let go. But no way was she doing that.

Okay, he might really be standing in front of her after all. But his presence didn't mean he'd come for her. He could be in New York for any number of reasons.

"Have a seat." She set the game on a side table and gestured in the general direction of a chair.

He stayed where he was. "God. Luce." He said it low. Soft and rough at the same time. As if he really had missed her. As if his arms ached to reach for her.

Or maybe that was only wishful thinking on her part. "What are you doing here?"

He stuck his hands in the pockets of his beautiful coat. He looked down at his Italian shoes, then lifted his head again and locked those amazing dark eyes on her. There was pain in those eyes. And hope, too. And longing. Wasn't there?

She didn't dare to believe.

But then he spoke. "I was wrong. So wrong. I didn't know, not really. I didn't let myself see. I'd convinced myself it wasn't going to happen for me, that somewhere along the line, between one barely remembered liaison and the next, I'd lost whatever it takes, that willingness of the heart. I'd lost whatever chance I had of finding a woman to love, a woman I could love with everything in me, the way my father loves my mother. But then I met you."

She put up a hand, palm out. "I don't understand. You said you couldn't love me…."

"Luce. I was wrong. You're the one. The only one for me. I'm here because I had to come, to take a chance that maybe you might forgive me for being such a complete ass, for turning you down, for not seeing the truth sooner, for not letting you show me what you've been trying to show me. I'm hoping, I'm praying that just maybe it's not too late."

Tears scalded the back of her throat. She gulped them down. "But how? When…?" Her throat clutched and she couldn't finish.

"Yesterday," he said. "Christmas Day. I was at my favorite café in La Cacheron. You remember the one?"

"I remember, yes."

His eyes went bleak. "Vesuvia cornered me there. She started in on me about how I was going to have to marry her."

"Because of the Marriage Law, you mean?"

"That's right. She started laying out all the reasons why she was the right wife for me. She said she understood me, she knew what I required in a wife. And then, out of nowhere, shocking the hell out of both of us, I just said it. I said it out loud without even stopping to think about it."

"Said what?"

"That what I require is love and forever. That I'm in love with *you.* That you're the only one I would ever marry, the only woman for me."

The chains of hurt around her heart loosened. The sunny day seemed brighter still. Could this really be happening? Could all of her dreams, every last shining one of them, miraculously come true? "I don't… Dami, what are you saying? Are you asking me to marry you?"

He raked a hand back through that thick midnight hair. "I know you're young. I know it's probably too soon to be talking about marriage. I was just telling you what I said to Vesuvia, which was only the simple, absolute truth. I love you, Lucy Cordell. I want only you. I want us to have a life together. I've been thinking about how we might make that happen. I know your dream is to go to school here. So if you would have me, if you would give me another chance to show you all you mean to me, I would make New York my home base. I would move in upstairs. *We* would move in upstairs. You could keep this place, if you want it, for your work. Or whatever.…"

Her silly mouth kept trembling and the happy tears wouldn't stay down. "Oh, Dami. I can't… I don't…" She had a million questions. She asked the first one that popped into her head. "But what about the Marriage Law? Don't you *have* to marry someone soon?"

He smiled then, at last, that wonderful, unforgettable killer smile of his. "Yes, if I don't marry within a year of my next birthday, I lose my titles and all I've inherited as a prince of Montedoro. But I do have three brothers ahead of me in line for the throne. And all three of them have children. And after me there are five sisters. The Bravo-Calabrettis will have no problem holding the throne whether I remain a prince or not. And my inheritance aside, I've done well for myself. I don't *have* to marry anyone to continue living in the style to which I've always been accustomed."

"So that's what you meant at Thanksgiving when you said you were going to leave it alone, not worry about the Marriage Law anymore."

"Exactly."

"And so…you *don't* want to marry me?"

He laughed. "Of course I want to marry you." He grew serious again. "I just think you need more time to deal with that. And I'm willing to give you as long as you need."

"Oh, Dami…"

"Whenever you're ready, say the word. We'll get married tomorrow if that's what you want."

"You mean that?"

"I do. With all of my heart."

"Is this…a dream? Am I still asleep?"

"No dream, Luce. Real. You and me forever. That's what I want. I found you—and then I lost you through my own blind pigheadedness. If you'll only take me back, I will always be here for you, always love you. *Always,* Luce. I swear it."

She didn't want to break the spell of all this wonderfulness with her deepest fear. But she knew that she had to. "I only… What about the children? What if I can't have your children?"

His gaze never wavered. "You're the one for me. That's what matters. We'll deal with the challenges as they come. If we never have children or if we adopt or find a surrogate… Whatever happens, as long as you're with me, as long as we can face it together, we can get through it. We'll be all right."

"You sound so certain."

"I *am* certain. I was an idiot. Your brother even told me so. But not anymore. Never again."

"Noah said you were an idiot?"

"Yes. He called me on Christmas Eve. He said I was an idiot to leave you. He was right. Luce, I know what I want now. I get it at last. I am absolutely sure that you are the one for me. The question is, what do *you* want?"

"Oh, Dami…"

He watched her, waiting for her answer. His eyes were so bright, full of hope. Full of yearning.

She saw the truth in him then, and she believed. His heart was hers to take.

"Yes," she answered with total conviction. "You're

the one for me, too. Oh, Dami, there's no one else, there never could be. I love you so much."

"Luce." He opened his arms to her.

She ran to him. He grabbed her close.

The kiss they shared made her head spin and her knees go weak. He was her friend, her prince, her hero, her hot and tender holiday lover. And now, at last, on the day after Christmas, he was giving her the gift she wanted most of all. That gift was his love.

She had his heart and he had hers. Forever belonged to the two of them now. They would claim it hand in hand, together.

* * * * *

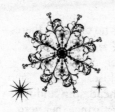

Merry Christmas

& A Happy New Year!

Thank you for a wonderful
2013...

A sneaky peek at next month…

Cherish™

ROMANCE TO MELT THE HEART EVERY TIME

My wish list for next month's titles…

In stores from 20th December 2013:

☐ The Final Falcon Says I Do — Lucy Gordon

& The Greek's Tiny Miracle — Rebecca Winters

☐ Happy New Year, Baby Fortune! — Leanne Banks

& Bound by a Baby — Kate Hardy

In stores from 3rd January 2014:

☐ The Man Behind the Mask — Barbara Wallace

& The Sheriff's Second Chance — Michelle Celmer

☐ English Girl in New York — Scarlet Wilson

& That Summer at the Shore — Callie Endicott

Available at WHSmith, Tesco, Asda, Eason, Amazon and Apple

Just can't wait?

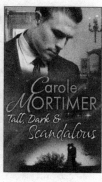

Come in from the cold this Christmas with two of our favourite authors. Whether you're jetting off to Vermont with Sarah Morgan or settling down for Christmas dinner with Fiona Harper, the smiles won't stop this festive season.

Visit:
www.millsandboon.co.uk

MB452

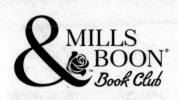

Join the Mills & Boon Book Club

Want to read more **Cherish**™ books?
We're offering you **2 more** absolutely **FREE!**

We'll also treat you to these fabulous extras:

- 🌹 Exclusive offers and much more!

- 🌹 FREE home delivery

- 🌹 FREE books and gifts with our special rewards scheme

Get your free books now!

visit www.millsandboon.co.uk/bookclub
or call Customer Relations on 020 8288 2888

The World of Mills & Boon®

There's a Mills & Boon® series that's perfec
for you. We publish ten series and, with ne
titles every month, you never have to wait
long for your favourite to come along.

Blaze®

Scorching hot, sexy reads
4 new stories every month

By Request

*Relive the romance with
the best of the best*
9 new stories every month

Cherish™

*Romance to melt the
heart every time*
12 new stories every month

Desire™

*Passionate and dramatic
love stories*
8 new stories every month

What will you treat yourself to next?

*Ignite your imagination,
step into the past...*
6 new stories every month

INTRIGUE...

Breathtaking romantic suspense
Up to 8 new stories every month

*Captivating medical drama –
with heart*
6 new stories every month

MODERN™

*International affairs,
seduction & passion guaranteed*
9 new stories every month

n o c t u r n e™

*Deliciously wicked
paranormal romance*
Up to 4 new stories every month

*Fresh, contemporary
romances to tempt all
lovers of great stories*
4 new stories every month